JOSEPH AND HIS BRETHREN

Joseph and His Brethren is a study of a single family and their environment, a small farm in eastern England, remote from towns and from modern life—'once you're away, twenty mile is as good as two thousand'. All that matters for Benjamin Geaiter and his five sons is the land which they work so intently and lovingly; no other life seems possible, and they care little for the rest of the village and the world beyond, so long as they are left in peace. Yet their life does not brutalise them; instead, they make the land almost human, 'humanising' its difficulties until it yields crops for them that it will for no-one else. H. W. Freeman conveys the tenor of their life, and (gradually, for such men do not reveal themselves quickly) their varying characters in a memorable novel which was widely acclaimed when it first appeared in 1928.

JOSEPH AND HIS BRETHREN

H. W. Freeman

THE BOYDELL PRESS

© H. W. Freeman 1928, 1983

First published 1928

First published in BOOKMASTERS 1983
by The Boydell Press
an imprint of Boydell and Brewer Ltd
PO Box 9, Woodbridge, Suffolk, IP12 3DF

ISBN 0 85115 217 1

Printed in Great Britain by
St Edmundsbury Press, Bury St Edmunds, Suffolk

British Library Cataloguing in Publication Data

Freeman, H. W.
Joseph and his brethren.
I. Title
823'.912[F]   PR4705.F/

ISBN 0-85115-217-1

BOOKMASTER is a registered trademark of
Bowaters United Kingdom Paper Corporation Ltd and is
used with their permission

PREFACE

My father was a headmaster under the old L.C.C. He was very good with handicapped children; he taught them singing, carpentry and bookbinding. His school was a show place for visiting foreign educationalists; and after a distinguished but ill-rewarded career he retired to a small poultry-farm in Suffolk that he managed with considerable success. This was the beginning of my connection with Suffolk, which has continued ever since. I worked for my father on his land, I helped our neighbours in harvest and I was also learning to plough with a team of horses. I wanted to be a farmer then, and my father was troubled that he could not afford to buy me a farm. The background to all this, however, was something different. I had been brought up as a classical scholar— it was the fashion then; with the classics behind you, there was no limit to the heights you might reach, they said. I was not at all ambitious. I should have been quite contented as an archaeologist digging up old Greek stones; but nobody seemed to want me and soon after my efforts with the plough I found myself in temporary charge of a sixth form in the Midlands. This was not at all to my taste. I had no intention of becoming a schoolmaster for good and I was already plotting my escape. With the money I should earn from my term's work I was going to Paris, I was going to live in the Latin Quarter, I was going to write a novel.

There was nothing to stop me, I already had my passport; but one morning, when I glanced at the appointments columns of *The Times*, I hesitated. A university in the North wanted a lecturer in classics at £300 a year and perhaps—perhaps I ought to make one more attempt at respectable employment; so I sent in my application. The university's answer was full of academic courtesy. I was invited to present myself for interview on a day in June and I was offered hospitality for the night that followed. At least I could go to Paris in the vacations, I told myself.

Two or three days later, to my puzzlement, I felt ill, but I soon knew why. A quarter of the school was down with chicken-pox and I had to join them in the school sanatorium, where I suffered more and stayed longer because I was now twenty-five. All that mattered little. What did matter was that, when I came out of the sanatorium, I was still infectious. I could not go to the interview.

I had been spared the necessity of a perhaps agonizing decision and at the end of term I left the school with a light heart. I stopped on the way home at a farm in Berkshire, to help an old friend with his harvest, and after three weeks I was thinking of moving on, when a letter arrived for me. It was a much-travelled letter. It had been originally addressed to the school in the Midlands, it had been forwarded to Suffolk and forwarded again to Berkshire; it was from the university in the North. Since my application, they said, one of their classical lecturers had died and they needed someone to take his place. If I cared to apply again, they would be pleased to interview me on such and such a day and to offer me the usual hospitality. There were now only three days to go to the interview, but I could easily send a telegram, and it almost looked as if they wanted me. It looked too as if I was not to be spared that agonizing decision after all. It was by no means as agonizing as I had expected. I had enjoyed myself in the cornfields and pubs of Berkshire and now I wanted to go to Paris. At the same time I was seized with a sudden disgust for the whole scholastic-academic rigmarole of the classics; they had let me down, I felt. Nothing would stop me from going to Paris now. I waited for the three days to pass and then made my excuses to the university. As anyone might have said, I had burnt my boats.

Three years later I was sitting in a modest upper room in one of the less desirable streets of Florence. I had lived in the Latin Quarter and had written a bad novel that had been very properly rejected; I had written two more novels that had suffered the same treatment and here I was in Florence, the traditional author in a garret, perhaps not starving, but setting out to write a fourth novel, quite probably for rejection. The trouble was I could think of nothing to write about. There was nothing in my head but old stuff, stuff like that short story—a literary agent had sent it back with the comment that it read, not like a short story, but like the synopsis of a novel. Was I to be reduced to that? And yet eighteen months ago, when I had written it, the subject had been much on my mind. A neighbour had told me about a farm in our parish where there were father, mother and five sons, all grown up and all unmarried, working on the farm for their father. That was all I could ever find out about them, except their surname, which I still remember. But the thought of this family stayed with me and I worried at it until I had found some sort of explanation; and so came the story. It was an indifferent story, with some episodes related in full detail and others, equally important, dismissed in a few curt sentences—whence perhaps the agent's impression of a synopsis. And the truth was I did not relish the task of working it all out and filling up the gaps. I did not relish it, but that is what, in the end, I came to. I could think of nothing else.

The first few chapters certainly bore out my reluctance. Each was like a leap in the dark, in a landscape I did not know because it hardly yet existed. But once the five brothers were on the scene, my reluctance dwindled. I do not reckon to know much about what goes on in my head when I am writing. But I knew now that for their sakes I must go on with the book and finish it. I was more than attached, I felt a duty to them, and I can remember saying aloud to myself: 'You must not spare them the consequences of their actions, but you must never, never laugh at them.' It was also as if I was learning from them, learning how to grow up, learning where my own roots were. I hardly thought so then, but already those years in Suffolk had not been for nothing, I suppose.

I began writing in the last week of October. I had my good times and bad times, including an almost blank month in January, when the brothers could not help me. Finally, in the last week of March, having rewritten the last chapter and copied out the last hundred pages, I packed the manuscript and sent it off to England to be typed and delivered to a publisher. Spring that year had come in cold and wet to Florence, but on the first fine day I started out to walk to Assisi and back through Urbino to Florence. This was the Italy of fifty years ago, with few tarred roads in the countryside and hardly any motorcars. I sat by wood fires in humble inns and told them what farming was like in England. For many years after I used to describe this 230-mile walk as the time of my life. Later I went on to Rome, where I caught a 'Roman fever', and after that to Naples, where I was bitten by bugs. But to Naples came the telegram to tell me that Chatto had accepted *Joseph*.

English publishers of the period were prepared to back their fancy, but they still remained wary. There was no advance on royalties for me, not even a dust-jacket with a picture. The book came out in October 1928 and after a couple of weeks the reviews began slowly to trickle in. I was amazed at the indulgence, even the sympathy, of the critics; it was the first time in my life that I had been taken seriously. Then on November 15th a telegram came with the news that *Joseph* had been chosen by the Book of the Month Club of America. At the time I hardly knew what that was, but when I did, I was even more amazed; for what had *Joseph* to do with that sophisticated American civilization? Nowadays if a book is chosen by the Book of the Month Club, its author's fortune is virtually made. It was not so then, for me at least; but the copies sold in America helped to keep the wolf from my door for a long time. Another sequel to that telegram was my first advance of £50 from Chatto and above all an artist's picture on my dust-jacket. Ben Geaiter in a battered bowler sitting a Suffolk Punch sideways, with Joey in front of him astride its withers—how that delighted me!

When I look back to those early years, it seems to me that the response accorded to *Joseph* was something that came from the country at large and not localized or regional. I myself was hardly conscious of it in Suffolk, and though I may be treading on uncertain ground here, that was my experience. In the last ten years, however, things have changed and I find the position reversed. The country at large has forgotten *Joseph* and it is people in Suffolk, borrowing copies from their friends or from library cellars and complaining that it is out of print, who are bringing it back to life. I will call some witnesses.

One day in the early seventies a library lady from Ipswich Hospital told me that *Joseph* was a favourite book for patients to ask for. A little later, when I was a patient there myself, I was talking to an elderly countryman who had worked on the land. We were discussing the vegetables in our respective gardens, but he suddenly changed the subject.

'Do you know a book called *Joseph and His Brothers?*' he said. 'That's a book about Suffolk, that's wholly worth reading.' He did not mention the author's name.

A few years later I was in the neighbourhood of Bruisyard, reviving memories. I wanted to look again at that old farmhouse with the crow-stepped gable where the brothers had lived and, being unsure of myself, I stopped a lad on the road; he was about seventeen.

'Where shall I find ——' I said, and gave him the real name, the one on the map.

'Oh, you mean Crakenhill Hall,' he said. 'The book says so.' He did not mention the author's name either. I could hardly believe my ears; for my fiction, the name in the book, had become his reality.

'My father told me to read it,' he added, 'and now I want one for myself. But you can't get it.'

This is a response that I can understand. It seems to come from people who, more than half a century since its publication, know that the book is about their own roots and who still hanker after them. Except as a sort of scribe, I hardly come into it; and that is how I like it. It is, as it were, their private myth.

H. W. FREEMAN

THE black soil of the hillside field glistened coldly in the meagre rays of the westering sun which were all that it caught of warmth and light during the day, surrounded as it was on three sides by dense pine copses. That was one of Benjamin Geaiter's grievances against the landlord of the farm that he had just rented to work along with his own : and such crops as did struggle up there would be devoured by the rabbits that the copses harboured. He thought greedily of the day when he would be able to buy the land outright and cut those copses down. Overhead a band of thieving rooks wheeled restlessly to and fro, every now and then alighting on the fresh-turned earth and soaring away with angry cries because they could find nothing there to eat. But five minutes later they were back again ; they could not believe that Benjamin Geaiter with two teams of horses and seven human beings at work on one field was not sowing his spring wheat, not realising that a man does not sow his wheat with two gangs of harrows. In those early days of spring the rook is a hungry bird, with a wary eye for the first man to put his corn in. But Benjamin Geaiter had other schemes on hand to-day. This piece of land had caused him serious misgivings although it was dirt cheap, for besides the copses and rabbits it was infested with twitch—a net of sinister, snaky white roots that choked the coulter of the plough and the tines of the harrow till they were forced to stop. It was a field that had been let go by the previous tenant, who was always in arrears with his work : it had missed a winter's ploughing which had never been caught up and so it had gone down to grass—self-sown, twitch-sown, no good either for tillage or pasture. Benjamin cursed these lazy, thoughtless farmers : they would have

done better to spend at the inn the money they had paid
in rent. A harrow would tear out a good deal of the
twitch ; but the tangle was so thick that what was left
behind would be enough to choke the crop and next year
grow as stubbornly again. He had his own ideas about
dealing with it. The task that the harrow had begun,
human hands could finish, so it seemed to him, and accordingly he had summoned out his whole family, not omitting
his wife and his youngest boy of twelve, to pick the field
clear with their fingers. That was why the rooks were
deceived.

Benjamin and his eldest son Ben, a full-grown man,
went on ahead with the harrows and piled up the twitch
they gathered in great heaps at the end of the field. What
the harrows missed the others grubbed up with their
fingers, advancing in a long, slow, straggling line behind
them : Hiram, Bob, Ernest, Harry, none of them more
than boys, and last of all Mrs. Geaiter, a bowed figure in
rusty black, working more slowly than the rest.

Emily Geaiter paused for a moment to straighten her
back and knock the caked earth from her fingers, to let
the breeze play in her wispy grizzled hair and cool her
cheeks. Her breath came rather short nowadays and she
was panting a little : it had been a hard day and she was
feeling it, although she could hardly remember a day in
her life which had not been hard—even at the age when
she and Benjamin were courting and she was in service,
with long hours and little wages ; but she was a lusty girl
in those days and there was something to look forward to
in the evenings. Then the struggles when she became
Benjamin's wife : while he was still a labourer, she went
out to wash, she plucked chickens, she sewed early and
late to make extra money ; when Benjamin first became
his own master on a small holding of seventy acres, she
had milked the cows so that he might give all his time to
the land : she had helped with the hoeing, the haysel and
harvest. And now that she was growing old she still made
the butter and cooked and cleaned and mended and

washed for her husband and her five boys. Life was work, beginning early and ending late. Each day would be like the next and she never thought of hoping that it would be better nor even of complaining, since she was hardly conscious that her lot was hard : she had a roof to her head and clothes to wear and she never went hungry. But for some months now she had begun to feel tired and to-day much more than usual : it was long now since she had last worked in the fields and there was a burning pain in her loins, her head was dizzy and her breath came harder than ever. But at that moment she thought less of these things than of the makeshift dinner she had had to serve up to her family, odds and ends of cold bacon and cheese and treacle. They always fed well in her house as a rule : it was her one pride. In her mind there was no room for thoughts of anything but housewifery. Still, the others were getting ahead of her ; the field must be cleared of twitch to grow a crop of corn, corn meant flour, and flour meant bread, and of course to-morrow was bake-day and now she would be all behind on account of to-day's neglect. Always back to housewifery.

She stretched her shoulders for the last time and bending to her task once more, picked up a clod. It was riddled with sinuous, flapping strands of the evil weed, almost human in the thoroughness with which they clutched and enveloped the soil in their grip. She twisted the clod in both hands, but it would not yield: the twitch roots flapped insolently on her wrist and she twisted harder, but still it would not yield. Suddenly her wrists went weak and the clod dropped from her hands, a feeling of sickness came over her and clouded her brain. What could be the matter with her ? She had never been like this before, and there was young Harry getting further and further ahead of her. She had to prop herself on her two hands to prevent herself from falling and her loins burnt more than ever. This would never do. She stiffened herself and seized the clod again. It should break at all costs. She screwed and ground it in her palms. It was giving, it was giving . . . it broke and she fell forward on her face among the fragments.

She lay there some minutes before anyone noticed her. Then young Harry, pausing to turn round and shy a stone at some rooks which had just settled, caught sight of the huddled black heap behind him. He stared for a moment and then ran over to her, almost tripping among the loose earth.

' Mother,' he cried, ' what's the matter ? '

She did not move and her eyes were closed. Harry felt frightened and began to whimper ; but he had enough voice to shout to the others. The other boys, Hiram, Bob and Ernest, hearing him, came running up and stood round the prostrate woman helplessly, not knowing what to do.

' Mother! ' said Hiram. ' What are you doing there ? '

She did not speak. Harry went on crying and the other three stood silent. Bob was the first to recover his senses.

' I'll go and fetch Ben,' he said hastily. ' He'll be sure to know what that is.'

' Ah, that he will,' said Hiram. ' We'll stay here and see after her.'

Two minutes later Ben and his father came running up, leaving their teams by the hedgerow. They knelt down beside her, loosened the neck of her blouse and spoke to her ; but she gave no sign.

' I never knowed her like this afore,' said Benjamin. ' She've sorterly fainted : fare to me, Ben, you'd better run to Frannigan for a doctor while we get her indoors.'

Ben rose to his feet with a nod and ran off with Ernest at his heels to the hedge where the teams were standing. Between them they unhitched the lightest of the cart-horses and threw off all its gear except the bridle. Ben tossed a sack over its back and jumping up, lumbered off with a clatter in the direction of the road at such speed as he could get out of his astonished mount with the aid of kicks and shouts and switchings.

As he rode off, the rest of the family, lifting Mrs. Geaiter in their arms as carefully as they could, carried her slowly across the fields to the farmhouse and laid her on the kitchen sofa. Benjamin was amazed. His wife had never known a day's illness in her life before and he could not understand this sudden collapse.

' I expect she've just fainted or something,' he said, shaking his head slowly. ' Do you go and get some water, young Harry.'

They moistened her wrinkled forehead and Hiram fetched a lump of ammonia which he held beneath her nose.

' Emily! ' said Benjamin, but she made no response. He looked blankly around him.

' I know,' he said at last. ' Put the kettle on, Hiram. Maybe she'll like a cup of tea when she come round.'

An hour later the doctor arrived from Framlingham in his trap with Ben at his side. His examination was of the briefest.

' She's dead,' he said curtly. ' Heart failure.'

' Dead? ' Benjamin echoed, staring with wide-open mouth.

' Yes, dead,' the doctor repeated. ' She shouldn't have been out there, working in the fields. There'll have to be an inquest. I'll come back later on and give you instructions. I've got another case now.'

He hurried out.

The boys began to cry. Ben, too old for tears, looked at his father with bewildered eyes, waiting for a lead. Benjamin was still dazed at the doctor's pronouncement. It had seemed so natural that she should go on for ever. At last, however, the truth seemed to penetrate his understanding.

' Well, well,' he said slowly. ' Wore up. I'd never have believed it. But I say, Ben, it's lucky young Harry's old enough now to do without her to look after him.'

II

CRAKENHILL HALL had always been one of the most talked-of farms in the parish of Bruisyard. It was not beautiful, at least not in the accepted sense, but only with the beauty of quaintness, because so many hands had been to work upon it at one time and another and had left their mark. The original architect had set out to build a plain long-fronted farmhouse of no great depth, with the rooms stretching from the front wall to the back, but at the last moment the whim had seized him to erect a pretentious Tudor chimney at one end. This part of the house was of brick like the rest, but at some unknown date it had become customary to cover the walls with a wash of pale cream colour in the Suffolk fashion. A later builder, starting from the Tudor chimney, had thrown out a wing at right angles to the first part as if he intended to make a courtyard of the little flower-garden which stretched right up to the front door ; but the other sides were never added. This portion was for some strange reason never painted and in consequence the whole building presented a somewhat pied appearance. A third hand, at a still later date, added to the second wing a curious crow-stepped gable of dark-coloured stone which was the most striking feature about the gaunt old house, and in the evening light when it stood out strongly against the darkening sky, added a touch of the grotesque to it. It was the sort of gable that, catching the eye of some seeker after the picturesque with romantic tendencies, might have inspired him with the fancy to stay and settle there ; but seekers after the picturesque are rare in that part of East Suffolk and the house, in remembered times at least, had the most unromantic history.

It was not for the ghosts seen there, the crimes or amorous adventures enacted there, that it became such a favourite subject of conversation in the neighbourhood, but simply for the long succession of bankruptcies connected with its name throughout the nineteenth century. As a farm it was insignificant enough—a hundred acres of the usual Suffolk heavy land perhaps a little heavier than most, half arable, half pasture. Yet no one seemed to have the knack of farming it. Now and again a persevering man would succeed in bringing it into condition : but to such a man it was only the stepping stone to something more profitable and easier to work : so many of the fields of Crakenhill lay on a steep hillside. But the failures, numerous and almost regular, provided an unending topic for discussion and the village was grateful for them. There were so many avenues of approach to the subject according to the prevailing temperament of the critic. The fatalistic attitude maintained that no good had ever come out of that farm nor ever would. The contemptuous held that it had never been farmed properly and was only waiting for the right man. But evidently none of them had ever regarded himself as the chosen saviour of Crakenhill, although they all knew well enough what ought to be done in each several circumstance, because within living memory no one from the village had ever dared to come forward and undertake the task even when the rent was almost a gift. There were others, too, who saw in the continual and inevitable failures a judgment upon some moral turpitude in the tenants and always regarded them with hostility and mistrust just because their evil destiny had led them to it. Accordingly, when there were no floods or storms, births, deaths, marriages, quoit matches, wars or earthquakes to talk about, the inhabitants of Bruisyard discussed Crakenhill Hall and its inmates : and naturally Benjamin Geaiter and his family, like all the rest, came in for their share of discussion, but with a difference, as will be after related. He came to the village with the reputation of a murderer, which promised well in conversational circles, but actually the incident which gave rise to that slander was in itself of minor importance compared with the less spectacular events which it set in train.

The career of Benjamin Geaiter was typical among small farmers. The son of labourers, he began life as a labourer at what would now be considered a very tender age. But those were the days when bread was baked once a week and eaten stale to prevent the children from being too hearty with it, when wages were a shilling a day and meat seldom or never seen in a labourer's cottage. As soon as he was old enough to hold a scythe, his father spent evening after evening teaching him how to whet his blade and making him practise his stroke on the nettles which bordered their cottage garden : and when he was fourteen years old he did his first harvest with the other mowers at his father's side as the quarter of a man. Of his many accomplishments his mowing was perhaps the most perfect and it was as a mower that most people seemed to remember him. ' A strong arm and a thick hid. That's what you want when you go a-mowing,' he used to say to his sons, and he certainly had them. The sight of his great bent back and long flat arms, knotted and rugged like elm branches, and the steady, measured swish of his scythe were things not easy to forget.

During his early youth he was of a restless disposition and seldom stayed long in one place, turning his hand to any trade that offered. He had already been ploughman, stockman, miller's man and maltster when he took service as potman at an inn on the outskirts of Woodbridge, and there it was that he killed his man. It was quite true that he drank and gambled a good deal, but he was not a quarrelsome man and did not deserve all the blame for what happened. One evening Emily, the maid at the inn, was taking his place in the bar for a few minutes so that he could tap a couple of fresh casks, when a drunken party came in and began making an uproar. One of them, more drunk than the rest, tried to kiss Emily over the counter and Benjamin, entering the bar at that moment, peremptorily ordered him out of the house. The man laughed and still clung to Emily's hand.

' If you don't git out and quick,' said Benjamin,

savagely biting his straggly moustache, ' I'll throw you out.'

' You go to hell,' replied the other.

Then Benjamin, jumping over the counter, seized the man by his belt and lifting him up bodily like a sack of potatoes, threw him out of the open window. It was, for a ground floor, rather a high window, the man broke his neck and Benjamin went to prison for manslaughter. After serving a year he came out, sobered rather than repentant, and so determined to settle down that in a few months he had married Emily, the maid at the inn, and taken a place as chief horseman on a large farm between Woodbridge and Orford. The change in his habits was real and permanent and he had married a good wife. Between them by dint of unremitting labour and grinding economy they saved enough in a few years to take a holding of seventy acres at Hasketon on the other side of Wood-bridge where, although the work was hard for only two pairs of hands with a little occasional help, everything went as they could have wished and Emily, to Benjamin's satisfaction, was beginning to bear him sons. But he was not wholly content : the holding was not his own and he wanted to reap the full benefit of his labour. It pained him to pay out money for which he got no apparent return. In this frame of mind he found himself one day at Bruisyard where he had gone to buy a horse, and heard that Crakenhill was for sale at a ridiculously low price. The house and buildings were now in such a woeful state of dilapidation and the land so neglected that the owner was determined to be rid of such an unremunerative pos-session and announced himself ready to close with any reasonable offer—which in the circumstances could not be anything but low. Even so, no one in Bruisyard or the neighbouring parishes cared to take the risk ; so that Benjamin, finding himself without competitors and unable to resist the opportunity, named a price and bought the place for a song.

It was some time since the farm had changed hands,

although there had been countless tenants, and there was
quite a flutter in the village, especially when it was discovered that the new owner was a little man and was
going to farm it for himself. It was years since such a
thing had been done and the air was thick with prognostications of failure. Moreover, some of the facts of Geaiter's
early life had trickled through to the village. The miller's
man had been to Woodbridge to fetch some middlings
when the local stock was running low, and had met a man
who knew Emily Geaiter before she was married. The
whole story came back to the mill and the miller's wife,
arch-contriver of all the scandals in the parish, duly gave
it out to her cronies that Benjamin Geaiter was a vagabond, a drunkard and above all a murderer. To her it was
indeed a judgment on him that he had been tempted to
Crakenhill, a dispensation from above for which she was
devoutly and maliciously thankful. It was, however,
somewhat disquieting to be at such close quarters with a
murderer and she declared herself uneasy. Her neighbours
awaited the issue with expectant interest : one year, two
years at most would be enough for him.

It was rash of them to make such prophecies with so
little to go on. Benjamin Geaiter was no fool and he had
bought the place with his eyes open. He had no illusions
about the quantity of work that would be required of him
—in all his long experience he had never seen a farm in so
shocking a condition—but, most important of all, he had
made an estimate of his own capabilities and had decided
that it was in his power to bring the farm round. The issue
showed that his decision had been correct.

Crakenhill itself was a mile from the village and most of
the hundred acres which belonged to it lay at a distance
from the road so that few of the neighbours ever knew
how hard he worked. All they could do was to judge by
his results and as they saw the ruined buildings slowly
repaired and the sour, weed-ridden fields gradually transformed into a fertile tilth bearing heavy crops of corn and
roots and even at times taking a pen or two of sheep, they

changed their tune without admitting that they had ever been wrong and talked of Benjamin Geaiter as a good farmer and a hard man to make a bargain. Crakenhill as a subject of conversation languished : some, the miller's wife among them, were frankly disappointed that their presages had not come true. There was not much to talk about in Bruisyard at the best of times : and now their most fruitful source of conversation had become quite barren. Crakenhill was merely prosperous. As for the murderer, he had not lived up to the reputation which the miller's wife had given him. The great, broad-chested, lumbering man with his bushy black beard and sluggish blue eyes was hardly ever seen in the village : he never drank at the inn, he never quarrelled with his neighbours. The only fault to find with him was that he prospered and kept himself to himself.

Some of the gossip and some of the scandal about himself must indirectly have reached Benjamin's ears, but he pursued his own course utterly regardless of them, having learnt in his rough life a certain contempt for the greater part of his fellow-beings—he had more respect for a piece of good land, well-tilled—and it did not trouble him a jot if they called him murderer so long as they left him alone : and when that flutter had died down and he was resignedly accepted in the parish, he did not become any the more sociable. There was something solidly constant in his way of living that remained unaffected by any of the human currents around him : he cared neither for the approval nor the blame of his neighbours. He only asked to be left alone. Other men would have been grateful for the chance to confide in some sympathetic ear all the anxiety and weariness of his first four years at Crakenhill. His estimate of his own powers had been true enough, but it left only the narrowest margin and he worked like a slave to bring his land into good heart. At that period there was little agricultural machinery in general use and most farmers still cut their corn with the scythe. In haysel and harvest-time Benjamin with his eldest boy, Ben, who was just

sixteen years old when they took over the farm, would
mow steadily from six o'clock in the morning if the dew
permitted, until six in the evening, and then, having sent
his son home, the father would go on mowing until sun-
down and even later if the moon was bright. His father
had taught him to good purpose. Often at these seasons
when he rose from the table after his midday dinner, he
left a pool of sweat behind him on the chair where he had
been sitting. There were wet springs when he might have
been seen among his swedes and mangolds long after nine
o'clock had struck, hoeing up the mat of weeds that the
rain had brought to birth. Of his sons Ben alone shared
with him the full burden of those four years, because the
others were too young for such strenuous and unflagging
labour : but there were times when he had his whole
family out to work if some pressing task demanded it.

The farm flourished : every acre was in prime condition
and no other land in the parish looked better. Ben was
now fully grown, Hiram and Bob, the twin brothers, were
just sixteen and their labour was beginning to be worth
taking into account. Ernest was fifteen. The estate
adjoining Crakenhill Hall was in process of being broken
up and another hundred acres was going—too good a
chance for Benjamin Geaiter to lose. Unable to buy outright, he had to be content with a five years' lease : but he
would buy some day. Meanwhile he now had two hundred
acres to scheme with. The new piece of land, though not
so bad as Crakenhill had been, was in poor condition ;
but that did not deter Benjamin, who could have re-
claimed a swamp if necessary. He set to work with his old
dogged and systematic energy. The first-fruits of that was
the death of Mrs. Geaiter.

III

MRS. PEARMAN, the miller's wife, lowered herself slowly into one of the two horsehair armchairs in her parlour with the utmost precaution so as not to disturb the elaborate white lace antimacassar which festooned it. She had attended morning service at Bruisyard church and had cooked a substantial Sunday dinner besides, the effects of which her husband was already sleeping off in front of the kitchen fire, where she had just left him snoring loudly. There were still two hours to go before tea-time and Mrs. Pearman, having done her duty by God and man, felt that she deserved her Sunday afternoon nap. She took off her spectacles, folded her hands upon her lap and gazed placidly at the white china dogs that presided over her green-tasselled manteldrape. The peace of a contented mind and a full stomach gradually descended upon her : the hard, shiny eyelids drooped and closed : her chin fell to her breast. Five minutes later she raised her head with a start at the sound of steps on the gravel path. A caller at this hour of the day when all decent folks should be asleep in their kitchens or their parlours according to their several estates : she was a little annoyed. But as the footsteps drew nearer and she saw from behind the curtain who her visitor was, all her annoyance faded and she opened the door wide to welcome her. It was Maria Cragg, who had gone up to Crakenhill to keep house for Benjamin Geaiter and his five sons after the death of Mrs. Geaiter. This was her first visit since she had left the village and Mrs. Pearman had been anxiously awaiting it. Maria Cragg was a tall, spare woman of sixty, brown-skinned and wizened, contrasting sharply with the pink and white rotundities of Mrs. Pearman. She was a poor woman who, even at her age, had to work for her living, and Rose Pearman was comfortable, well-to-do: but on the common ground of small talk they were at one.

'Well, Mrs. Cragg,' said Mrs. Pearman, drawing her in

by the arm and pressing her into a chair, ' I'm that glad to see you I can't say. I thought we should never set eyes on you again.'

'Well, I must say,' replied Maria, 'I'm glad to exchange a word with someone again, someone as I know.'

' Well, Mrs. Cragg,' said Mrs. Pearman, settling down in her chair for a good heart-to-heart talk, ' and how do you like it ? '

Maria shrugged her shoulders and showed the whites of her eyes.

' Ah, I told you so,' said Mrs. Pearman, ' now didn't I ? That man—and you mustn't forget, Mrs. Cragg, that he was a murderer—he drove his wife into the grave : he used to thrash her terrible, so they say, and throw cups of hot tea over her. You know she never dared to show her face in the village. You can't expect to be happy in a house like that, it stand to reason.'

' And they offer so little for the work they want done,' Maria chimed in.

' What can you expect ? ' said Mrs. Pearman, nodding vigorously. ' A real stingy man. He've never sent a sheaf to the harvest festival.'

' But when you're poor, Mrs. Pearman,' Maria continued, ' and old and a widow, with no one to look after you and not much to live on—you must do something, Mrs. Pearman. Beggars can't be choosers, you know.'

Mrs. Pearman tossed her head.

' All the same, Mrs. Cragg,' she replied, ' I think you're very unwise. A man that beat his wife like that and worked her like a slave. I expect he treat those children cruel, don't he ? '

' Well,' said Maria, reluctantly, ' I can't say as I've seen him lay a hand on 'em yet : but that may come later on. What get over me is the quiet of the place. When I first went there, I thought perhaps it was because Mrs. Geaiter had just gone like : but now I've been there a month and it's still the same. All those boys, too, and Ben and the old man, and hardly ever a word except "Oh, it look to me like rain to-night," or, " Ern, do you remember to shet the gate when you fetch them cows," or something like that. And there they set and set as quiet as mice and munch and munch : and the old man and Ben, they set and smoke. It fair give me the hump.'

' And I reckon,' added Mrs. Pearman, ' them boys don't get half enough to eat. They allus look half-starved.'

' Well, I can't say as I've noticed that yet,' said Maria, pensively, ' though I doubt it may come. That was a nice bit of bacon I boiled for 'em last night '—she licked her lips involuntarily at the thought of it—' but, I tell you, Mrs. Pearman, it's a cold, cheerless house, with no orna-mints anywhere like them lovely white dogs of yours on the mantelshelf and not a single text on the walls. I do like to see a line or two of holy writ about a house. They needn't think I'm going to bring any of my stuff up to decorate their old tumbledown house. I left all my ornamints with my married daughter before I went up there.'

' And I expect it's as dirty as a hogyard,' said Mrs. Pearman, in a disgusted tone.

' Well, not over-clean like,' Maria admitted. ' But it's hard work to keep all that house clean and do for all them boys—they're more like men already. Work, you never see such boys to work in your life. They'll all die young, I reckon. And in the evening time, you know, the old man never think of going down to The Garland to have a glass —he never did afore his wife died—nor Ben neither : and when the boys have done work, they potter round looking for some odd job to do. One grind up barley for the pigs in that little mill of theirs, another chop wood for the kitchen fire, while the old man, he set and smoke. Always working, it don't seem natural like. It drive me mad to see 'em. If only they'd go abroad and frolic a bit. They're not such bad boys after all.'

Maria had let herself go more than she intended and was waxing too enthusiastic for Mrs. Pearman's liking.

' When are you going to give notice, Mrs. Cragg ? ' she said solemnly.

' Well, I have thought about it,' replied Maria deliberately, considering the idea for the first time, ' but I think I'll wait a little while first and see how they turn out. Mr. Geaiter may sober up a bit now he have managed to worry his wife into the churchyard.'

' Well, if I was you, Mrs. Cragg,' Mrs. Pearman declared sententiously, ' I shouldn't wait, not one minute. It isn't safe with a man like that in the house. And the strain will pull you down terrible even if nothing don't happen.'

' Still, I can take care of myself,' Maria demurred. She had not the least intention of abandoning her post, knowing well enough already that she could do more as she liked at Crakenhill than at any other farm in the parish.

' Maybe,' said Mrs. Pearman severely, ' but, Mrs. Cragg, it's the last straw that break the camel's back. I don't like to think of you there, I really don't.'

' Well, we'll see,' said Maria, who was becoming a little uneasy at the line Mrs. Pearman was so persistent in taking. ' I've still only got 'em on trial. It depend how they behave.'

Mrs. Pearman shook her head dubiously : but before she had time to frame a reply, the garden gate clicked and someone walked heavily up the garden path. Both women looked up sharply.

' Who can that be ? ' said Mrs. Pearman.

' I wonder,' Mrs. Cragg whispered.

Mrs. Pearman peered from behind the curtain into the garden.

' Why, it's Mr. Geaiter ! ' she gasped.

' Talk of the devil,' Maria croaked cynically.

' What shall we do ? ' said Mrs. Pearman with desperation in her voice. ' I can't have a man like that in the house.'

She looked from side to side like a frightened animal ; but Benjamin Geaiter was already at the door and rapping on it with his knuckles. Mrs. Pearman opened to him at once, shrinking back as she did so, but her face was all smiles.

'Good afternoon, Mr. Geaiter,' she said ingratiatingly. 'Do come in.'

'I'm sorry, lady,' said Benjamin, as he stepped over the threshold with his hat in his hand, still wearing his workaday corduroys, 'to trouble you on a Sunday arternoon like this: but we've run out of pig food and that's the truth: and it fare as if our old sow's going to pig down to-morrow. Is your husband in?'

'Why, yes, Mr. Geaiter,' she replied, 'and it's no trouble at all. I'll fetch him at once. Please sit down, Mr. Geaiter.'

While she slipped into the kitchen to wake the miller, Benjamin with a nod to Maria sat down on a lace-covered sofa. The miller came in rubbing his eyes.

'Arternoon, Mr. Pearman,' said Benjamin from the sofa. 'I want a quarter-ton of barley meal early to-morrow. Can you do it?'

The miller thought for a moment.

'Yes, Mr. Geaiter, I think so,' he said. 'Leastways, we'd have to somehow for you. How early do you want it?'

'Before breakfast,' said Benjamin curtly, with a keen sideways look at the miller.

'Yes, I think so,' said the miller thoughtfully, as if making calculations. 'Yes, Mr. Geaiter, you shall have it before breakfast.'

'Much obliged, I'm sure,' replied Benjamin, getting up from the indescribably crumpled lace on the sofa. 'Arternoon all. Maria, are you coming up to get our tea?'

Maria meekly followed him out.

'There, Jim,' said Mrs. Pearman, as she closed the door on them, 'to think I've had a wife-beater and a murderer a-setting in my parlour—as cool as a cucumber too. I am that sorry for poor Mrs. Cragg. Look at that sofa!'

IV

BENJAMIN GEAITER drained his teacup, pushed back his chair, and having lighted his pipe, looked down the kitchen table at his sons as they in their turn drained their cups and lit their pipes. They were all men now, or nearly so, for Harry, the youngest, was eighteen and almost as tall as the others. They were all of middle height and stockily built, but none of them quite so deep-chested or strong in the arm as their father, though they all bore the stamp of his heavy, expressionless features and ruddy complexion except Harry who was pale and thin-faced like his mother. But Benjamin was not thinking of his sons. It was the sixth anniversary of Mrs. Geaiter's death, but he was not thinking of that. His thoughts were busy with the sheep, calculating whether there would be enough feed to last them till the turnips came on. Maria Cragg, hollow-cheeked and more wizened than ever, sat at the foot of the table pouring out another cup of tea for Harry who had a great appetite for tea and always drank one more cup than the rest. Maria no longer talked to Mrs. Pearman of giving notice : indeed she had long ceased to talk to Mrs. Pearman at all and counted the years since she last went down into the village instead ; she was only to leave the farm once more. All except Harry had finished and were quietly smoking. It was time to wash up and she was about to begin gathering the dirty cups and saucers together when the kitchen door rattled. She looked up.

'Who is it ?' she said, as she rose to go to the door.

'Fare to me it's a gentleman,' said Ben, who was facing the window. 'I wonder what he want here.'

'Shall I ask him into the parlour ?' said Maria, looking at Benjamin.

'No,' growled Benjamin. 'Ask him his business first.'

Maria shuffled to the door and opening it as narrowly as possible, peered through the crack at the stranger. At once a hearty voice, with a slight foreign twang in it, came ringing through the crack into the kitchen.

' Can I see Mr. Geaiter ? '

Everyone stared at the door.

' Let him in,' said Benjamin in a surly tone.

Maria opened the door, and the stranger, a tall, strongly built man, well-shaven and neatly dressed in town clothes, strode into the room. No one moved from the table.

' I hope you won't think me rude,' he said, stepping forward and addressing himself to Benjamin in the same cheerful voice, ' but the fact is I once had this farm myself twenty years ago, and jolly glad I was to get out of it, though I was bankrupt when I went. I happened to be passing this way to-day and when I saw how well the fields looked, I said to myself, " It's a real man who's got this farm now. I should like to ask him how he does it." So here I am.'

' Oh,' said Benjamin. ' I see.'

' My name's Wilburn,' said the stranger ' I hope I'm not intruding.'

' We don't mind,' growled Benjamin, still staring at the man as if he were some exotic animal.

As no one offered him a chair, he sat down of his own accord in Maria's empty place at the foot of the table.

' Well, Mr. Geaiter,' he said genially, ' how do you do it ? '

' Do what ? ' said Benjamin obtusely.

' Why, make a do of Crakenhill,' he replied. ' When I was here, it was the dirtiest, sourest, hardest, damnedest bit of land I ever came across.'

' So it was when I came,' said Benjamin.

Ben nodded in sympathy.

' But I never saw such a piece of wheat on it,' Wilburn went on, ' as you've got down there by the road. How do you do it ? '

Benjamin had never been asked such a question before : he could farm a piece of land well enough, but to theorise on farming was not in his line. He looked steadily at

Wilburn and pulling up his shirt sleeve, scratched his great brown arm.

' Ah,' said the stranger, ' now I see.'

' See what ? ' said Benjamin in surprise.

' Those arms of yours,' said the stranger. ' Now I know how it's done.'

Benjamin was not used to compliments and only stared harder at him : perhaps the man wanted to get something out of him : he distrusted him.

' Let me see,' continued the stranger, ' a hundred acres, isn't it ? '

' Two,' Benjamin corrected.

' What, do you rent another hundred ? ' said Wilburn.

' No, bought it last year,' said Benjamin.

Wilburn whistled.

' Well,' he said, ' I don't know how you do it. When I came here, I had quite a bit of cash behind me and I swore I'd bring the place round or bust : but I bust. Do you remember that field down by the gull, all sodden and under water sometimes in the winter, full of the foulest rubbish, dodder and twitch and bellbind and paigle ? '

The company became a little less hostile ; they knew that field too.

' Yes,' said Benjamin, ' that took us a tidy time to clean. We drained it first. It cost a lot, but it have paid for itself since.'

' Maybe,' said Wilburn, ' but it broke my heart. But if you have draining to do, you need a lot of labour.'

' I've got my five sons,' replied Benjamin.

He had never said such a thing before, and he experienced a rudimentary feeling of pride as he uttered the words. Maria went on clearing the tea things away : but no one offered the stranger a cup of tea.

' Yes,' said Ben, speaking for the first time, ' me and Hiram and Bob here, we go to plough.'

' Suffolk punches ? ' queried the stranger.

' Ay,' answered Ben. ' We like 'em best on this heavy

land: they keep their fetlocks clean. And Ern and young Harry look after the stock and milk the cows.'

' Now that is the way to farm,' said Wilburn. ' If only I had had five sons like that when I was here. Your sons work twice as well for you as a hired man because they know they're working for themselves.'

Hiram suddenly looked hard at him.

' And what might you be doing now ? ' said Benjamin, who was growing tired of all this eulogy. ' You don't fare to have a bankrupt look about you.'

' Me ? ' replied the stranger. ' Why, when I cleared out of here without a penny, I went to Canada. I worked my passage in a cattle boat and fell into a job on a farm as soon as I landed. Work's wonderful easy to get over there, you know. Then, when I'd saved a bit, I went up country and set up on my own. You don't have to pay for the land out there. They'll give you all you can farm. That's the style, I can tell you. I went in for wheat. We don't grow it by the acre out there, but by the square mile, and when the old country wanted wheat, we couldn't grow enough of it. That's the way to farm, I can tell you: no hacking away at this soggy old heavy land when you have to wait half the winter before you can get on it ; no messing about in cow-yards and pig-styes up to your ankles in muck and spreading it over those damned old fields.' The stranger's eyes glowed with all the resentment he must have felt in the days when he had farmed Craken-hill and failed. ' No,' he went on, ' over there, when a piece of land is played out, you just move on to another and don't bother about dunging. That's the way to farm, believe me.'

Ben and his father looked sceptical: they could not believe in such easy victories over the stubborn earth. Hiram alone seemed interested.

' But why have you come back, sir ? ' he asked.

It was difficult to avoid sirring a man who wore a collar on weekdays, even if he had lived on the same farm.

' Oh, I've just come across on a six months' holiday,' said Wilburn lightheartedly.

' A six months' holiday! ' Hiram gasped.

' Yes,' said Wilburn. ' And I think I deserve it after nearly twenty years out there.'

Benjamin grunted. He had never taken a holiday in his life.

' I wanted to see the old country once more,' Wilburn continued. ' My wife and kids didn't care about it, so I left 'em over there.'

Hiram gaped. This man could afford a six months' holiday, not only for himself but for his whole family as well.

' Are you going back ? ' said Bob, who was also becoming interested.

' You bet,' replied Wilburn warmly. ' Do you think I'd leave a good thing like that once I'd got hold of it ? '

' Are they still giving land away over there ? ' Hiram asked.

' Yes,' said Wilburn, ' just as much as you like to ask for if you can show that you can farm it. My advice to any young fellow over here who wants to better himself is, try Canada.'

He looked round at the company one by one to observe the effect of his words : but all their faces remained stolid and unresponsive. Benjamin blew a large cloud of tobacco smoke across the table and snorted.

' Yes,' he growled, ' and you're the chaps who sent the price of wheat down and half-ruined all the farmers at home. I've heard about you and your cheap corn before. There's quite enough of you already without any more of 'em going out.'

' That's all nonsense,' said Wilburn sharply. ' You're not ruined nor half-ruined neither.'

' Well,' said Benjamin, thumping the table with his fist, ' that's not your fault if I'm not.'

Wilburn laughed.

' Then why don't you cross over yourself,' he said, ' and get a bit of your own back. It's just men like you we want.'

' What, leave this farm ? ' cried Benjamin angrily.

' After all these years! What d'ye take me for?' He glared reproachfully at the stranger who was beginning to feel uncomfortable. ' I wonder you've got the cheek to come and talk to us like that. I don't know nothing of politics and that sort of stuff, but if you chaps can't find something better to do than undersell us poor folk—well, you and your bloody Canada can go to hell.'

He thumped the table again with his fist. A hot answer rose to Wilburn's lips, but he checked it at the sight of Benjamin's hairy, russet-coloured arm, stretched across the corner of the table. Maria had cleared all the tea-things away now and the last chance of a cup of tea had disappeared.

' Well, I was going to ask you,' Wilburn began, ' to let me see the old bedroom where I used to sleep, but——'

' There ain't nothing to see there,' interrupted Benjamin.

' But I won't trouble you now,' Wilburn concluded.

He got up from his chair.

' I think I'll go,' he said. No one pressed him to stay. ' Thank you for telling me so much, Mr. Geaiter.'

Benjamin did not answer, but continued to stare at him.

' You're welcome, I'm sure,' said Hiram at last, feeling that something was required of the family.

Wilburn walked across the room to the door and with some difficulty unlatched it. Maria who was washing up at the sink beside him, made no move to help him.

' Same jattery old door,' he said, with an embarrassed laugh, turning round to face the six men staring at him from the table. ' Good afternoon.'

' Good arternoon,' said Hiram, stepping into the breach once more.

The door closed behind him.

' Good riddance,' grunted Benjamin, rising heavily from his chair. ' I must go and look at that sick heifer.' He took a dark bottle of drench from off the dresser and went out, stuffing it into his trousers pocket.

' Well, that sound all right, and no mistake,' said Hiram, after he had gone.

' Ay, that do,' said Bob.

' What sound all right ? ' said Ben, turning round.

' Why, all that about Canada,' Hiram replied. ' Something like farming, I call it.'

' Don't you fill your head with all that nonsense,' said Ben, contemptuously. ' I don't believe a word on it. A fellow who go bankrupt on Crakenhill don't make his fortune in Canada or anywhere else. He was telling you the tale. I know the sort.'

' I don't know,' said Bob. ' I've heard something of them Canadian farms before.'

' Don't you worry your hid about that,' Ben growled. ' You've got a good thing here and don't forget it.'

' Yes, I suppose so,' said Bob, rather dubiously. ' Maybe you're right.'

Ben, having worked through the hard early years of the farm, was looked up to by all his brothers, and his word carried weight. The conversation languished and getting up from the table, they scattered to their various tasks. Hiram and Bob with their pipes in their mouths went off to the barn to grind up some linseed cake for their horses' bait in the morning. Hiram was unusually talkative tonight. The stranger's words had made a deep impression on him and he was by no means satisfied with his father's or Ben's denunciations of Canada.

' Do you mind, Bob,' he said, knocking out the ashes of his pipe on a tawny slab of cake, ' what that bloke said about us working for ourselves on this farm ? '

' Yes,' said Bob in his high-pitched voice, resting for a moment on the wheel of the cake-grinder.

' Well, I wonder if that's true,' said Hiram. ' Father don't pay us no more wages than any other hired man in East Suffolk get. And what do he do with all the money he make? Think of last harvest and all them quarters of wheat. And he's good to live a long time yet.'

' That's the truth, that is,' said Bob, wiping the sweat off his brow with the back of his hand.

' I call it hard,' said Hiram, savagely breaking the slab

of cake in two on the edge of an iron bin. ' If he can't treat us better than that, he might as well have hired men work for him.'

Ay,' said Bob, standing clear of the wheel to light his pipe. ' Fare to me, if we hev a chance to better ourselves, we might as well take it.'

' So you think so too ? ' said Hiram, looking at him sharply out of the corner of his eye. ' Well, Bob, will you stand by me ? '

' Stand by you, how ? ' Bob piped.

Hiram rubbed his little fair moustache and cleared his throat.

' Why, come along o' me to Canada,' he said.

' It's a terrible long way, Hiram,' said Bob, shaking his head.

' That don't fare to matter to me,' replied Hiram, disdainfully. ' Once you're away, twenty mile is as good as two thousand. But think of all them acres, Bob, and no manure to spread.'

' Ay, that sound wonderful good,' said Bob between puffs, as he lit his pipe.

' And when you've worked out the heart of one piece of land,' Hiram continued, warming to his subject, ' you just move on to another.'

' Ah, that's the way to farm,' said Bob, who was just beginning to feel worked up.

' And they'll give you as much land as you want,' said Hiram, 'and if you want six months' holiday you can have it and take your wife and kids too.'

Hiram had never taken a holiday yet and if he had, he would not have known what to do with it. He handed Bob a piece of cake to put into the machine, but Bob cast it down on the floor of the barn.

' I've had enough of this,' he cried at the top of his voice. ' Let's go to Canada, Hiram.'

' I wonder,' said Hiram, looking him hard in the eyes.

' That'd larn the old man,' said Bob excitedly, ' that'd

larn him to treat his own flesh and blood like the beasts of the field, wouldn't it ? '

' Ay,' said Hiram, ' and that might be doing the others a good turn.'

' Why, that's the truth,' cried Bob. ' Let's go to Canada and try our luck. I'm not going to set on this damned owd farm all my days.'

' Do you mean that, Bob ? ' said Hiram, holding out his hand.

' Bible oath I do,' said Bob.

They shook hands on it.

BENJAMIN GEAITER was suspicious of all men alike, farmers, shopkeepers, landlords, lawyers, parsons : he felt that they were all ready to cheat him if he only gave them the opportunity. That was a thing to be expected in the rough and tumble of farming business and he bore them no particular ill-will for it. But there was one class of the rural community that he suspected above all others and detested from the bottom of his heart—the one definite hatred shining through the general misanthropy which was taking firmer possession of him the older he grew—the butchers. As Crakenhill actually produced far more corn than beasts, Benjamin probably lost far more money to the miller than he ever did to the butcher and was well aware of it : he had been in the milling business himself, he knew all the tricks and he had a certain respect for the clever miller who knew just how far to go in his knavery. But there was something in the callous and deliberate extortion of the butcher which infuriated him. He could remember beast after beast of his, carefully and patiently fattened, sold as meat in the shop, even to him, at double the price he had got for it. No man, thought Benjamin, has the right to a hundred per cent. profit : and equally exasperating was the insolent manner in which they secured it : they knew the strength of their position and had no respect either for farmer or customer. The one was bound to sell to them, the other to buy their meat. ' Take it or leave it,' was their answer to all pro-tests from either side. They made no attempt to conceal their gross prosperity, but flaunted it before the whole world: they closed their shops whenever they felt inclined, they grew corpulent and bloated like the meat on which they prospered, they bought smart turn-outs, their wives gave themselves airs and tried to dress like ladies. It all seemed outrageous to Benjamin: he had always borne them a grudge, and he longed to pay them out. But while

he was still a little man, he had never dared to do so: it
was well to keep on the right side of the butchers; and
when he ceased to be a little man and became a warm
man, the occasion for getting his own back never seemed
to present itself, perhaps because the butchers now treated
him on a rather different footing.

During the spring, however, his chance came at last.
Benjamin had some exceptionally good lambs which he
kept late and fattened well in the hope of getting a good
price for them and he eventually sent them into the market
at Saxmundham. But none of the butchers would bid
within five shillings of the reserve he had put on them.
Benjamin, properly enraged, had them driven back and
swore that no butcher in the neighbourhood should touch
them. The next day three of the butchers who had refused
to bid his price in the market, came out specially in their
traps to Crakenhill and offered him even more: lambs
were becoming scarce. But Benjamin sent them off with
very little ceremony. ' If you'd wanted my tegs,' he said
to them, one after another, ' you could have bought 'em
yesterday. They're going to Ipswich: so much the worse
for you, you fool.' What with the carriage by rail and
the higher auctioneer's fees in the bigger market, he
would probably have done better to close with their offers,
but he was now in a position to indulge his pride and his
resentments and he had the satisfaction of knowing that
he robbed the butchers of quite a considerable profit, for
tegs became scarcer than ever.

Benjamin had said that his tegs should go to Ipswich
and to Ipswich they had to go. He seldom left the farm
now himself and Ben who did not care for the task, proposed it to Bob and Hiram who were generally to be
found together where the farmwork was concerned, although Hiram also acted as second-in-command to Ben.
Ben had half expected them to protest: it was no easy
matter getting those thirty tegs to the station at Saxmundham in good condition. To his relief they accepted
the charge with a willingness that startled him: he had

never known them so ready to go to Ipswich before. But Bob and Hiram had their own reasons for wanting to go and they could have hardly desired a better opportunity for furthering their own projects. Ever since the day of Wilburn's visit to Crakenhill they had been talking of Canada and rehearsing their grievances until life on the farm had become almost unbearable for them and they were firmly resolved upon emigration. It was not so easy to carry their resolve into action. Both Ben and more particularly their father would be bitterly hostile to any such idea. They had not forgotten Benjamin's outburst in front of Wilburn and they shrank from facing his anger themselves, never having crossed his wishes in their lives before. Moreover, if they announced their intention beforehand, they would be almost bound to wait until he could find men to fill their places: the prospect of living at close quarters with him in such circumstances, even for the space of a week, did not bear contemplation. The only possible course was to conceal the whole scheme from him and run away from the farm without warning at the first opportunity. At first they thought of waiting till after harvest when they would have some extra money in their pockets and labour would be easier to find in the district: they could not entirely forget their father's interests in spite of their own grievances. But this opportunity seemed too good to be lost. They could get away quite unobserved without any difficulty and at least their fares to Ipswich would be paid for them. Of ways and means after that they had only the vaguest notions, not having dared to make enquiries in the neighbourhood for fear of exciting suspicion, but they trusted to luck and their own enthusiasm to carry them through.

It was five o'clock on a fine, crisp May morning when they set out to drive the tegs to the station, outwardly as calm and stolid as ever, but pulsing with an inward excitement that was quite new to them. They were both wearing their best corduroys and buskins and carried their savings and a few of the barest necessities, wrapped up in their spotted blue handkerchiefs, stowed away in their capacious coat-pockets. Their toilet was a simple affair and one suit of clothes was enough for them. Bob was so nervous that he clumsily drove two of the tegs into a muddy pond three miles along the road and the poor animals were so exhausted by the effort to clear themselves that they kept the whole flock back for the rest of the journey, so that they almost missed the train. Further on, a fast-driving trap threw them into a panic on the turnpike road and they rushed headlong into a field of turnips from which it took ten minutes to collect them again. Things of minor importance perhaps, but wearing to the nerves. At last, however, they reached the market where the flock passed out of their hands. A more desperate pair of runaways might have forsaken their charges on the spot, but neither of them thought of doing such a thing. The day's work must be finished first. By twelve o'clock they had seen the tegs sold at a very fair price and strolled away to a small inn near the market with quite a considerable cheque in Hiram's pocket.

' It'd sarve him right,' said Bob, as they munched their bread and cheese in the taproom, ' if we got the money for that there cheque and took it with us. It fare to me, it wouldn't be as much as father owe us over and above our wages.'

Bob had grown very bitter and resentful in the past two months.

' Now, lookye here, Bob,' said Hiram, ' we don't want nothing of that. Even if father haven't treated us proper, we're not going to leave this place as thieves, so don't you make no mistake.'

' Well, he wouldn't miss it,' Bob grumbled. ' And anyhow, what are we going to do with the money ? '

'Wouldn't he miss it,' said Hiram sarcastically, 'and what are we going to do but send it off by post afore we leave? Don't you make no mistake, Bob. 'Twouldn't be fair else.'

' No, I suppose it wouldn't,' said Bob slowly. ' Well, drink up, Hiram, and let's get a move on us.'

They emptied their glasses and after paying the score, walked briskly up to the post office. An envelope was laboriously addressed for the cheque, assiduously licked and the stamp affixed. The operation took a long time because neither of them was used to writing. It was an accomplishment they could have dispensed with altogether on the farm and Benjamin had only sent them to school because he could not help himself : he did not hold with education. At length it was done and Hiram slipped the envelope into the post-box, peering nervously into the opening to make sure it was there.

' I say, Bob,' he said, ' don't you think now we're here, we might ask 'em how to get to Canada ? '

' That's a good plan,' said Bob. ' Do you go in and ask.'

Hiram went in again and approached the girl behind the counter from whom he had bought the stamp.

' Excuse me, miss,' he said, 'can you tell me how to get to Canada ? '

The girl stared amazedly at him.

' Canada ? ' she stammered. ' I'm sure I don't know. I've never been there. Have you tried the station ? '

' Ah, thanks, miss,' said Hiram. ' That's a real good idea and no mistake.'

The girl burst out laughing as he closed the door and rejoined his brother outside.

' She told me to try the station,' said Hiram, ' and fare to me we'd better hurry up if we're to get started to-day.'

' You're right, Hiram,' said Bob.

Ten minutes later found them in the booking-hall of the station.

' Do you ask, Bob, this time,' said Hiram. ' I did it last time.'

' No, do you do it,' said Bob. ' You'd put it better'n I should.'

' All right,' said Hiram, poking his head through the trap door of the booking-office. ' Can you tell me how to get to Canada, mister ? '

The booking-clerk looked rather puzzled for a moment ; then, his practical sense asserting itself, he frowned and said :

' You'll have to go to Liverpool first to get a boat.'

Hiram turned to Bob.

' We've got to go to Liverpool first,' he repeated.

' Well,' answered Bob, ' let's go to Liverpool, Hiram.'

' How do you get to Liverpool, mister ? ' said Hiram, turning to the booking clerk again.

' Take the next train to Peterborough and change,' he replied irritably.

' Well, let's have two tickets to Liverpool, mister,' said Hiram. ' Two single third class.'

The clerk slapped two tickets down in front of him.

' It do fare an awful lot of money, mister,' said Hiram, carefully untying the string of the little leather bag that held his savings and taking out some sovereigns.

' Do you want the tickets or don't you ? ' snapped the clerk. ' You don't expect to get there for nothing, do you?'

' All right, mister,' said Hiram apologetically. ' Here you are.'

Half an hour later they were seated in opposite corners of a railway carriage, jogging slowly towards Peterborough through the placid landscapes of West Suffolk and staring out of the window with all the interest of schoolboys on holiday, and to men like them, unused to travelling, a train journey was as good as a holiday. But they could not long forget what was for them the principal business of life as farm after farm unfolded itself before them : a farmer is perennially curious of the way other people farm.

' There's a rum 'un for you,' cried Bob excitedly, pointing to a piece of ploughland at the side of the line. ' The chap as did that was a jim and no mistake. Look at his hidland : he couldn't plough straight even when he had the hedge to go by.'

' No, that he couldn't,' said Hiram. ' That's a nice piece of winter wheat over there : that look well.'

' Not as well as ours though,' said Bob proudly. ' My!

Hiram, there's lambs for you. Did you ever see such poor little owd things?'

'He don't know how to feed 'em, he don't,' said Hiram, shaking his head ruefully. 'He's a bad farmer. Look at the rubbish in that field there; his turnips 'on't live long. Nice beans those.'

'Almost as good as ourn,' replied Bob grudgingly. 'But come to think of it, Hiram, hev you seen any land that look as forrard and well-kept as ourn?'

'No,' said Hiram reflectively, 'I hev not; and what's more, I've not seen no horses that look as if they had a real good bait every morning like we give ours: you can tell by the way their coats look. And the cows too and the lambs. Fare to me they don't know how to feed their beasts in these parts.'

'No,' said Bob in a more subdued voice, 'Crakenhill is a tidy little farm and no mistake.'

They both abruptly stopped talking and the silence was not broken until after they had left Bury St. Edmunds behind them. The train was unusually empty and they still had the carriage to themselves, which was important, because they could speak their thoughts without restraint.

'I say,' said Bob at length, 'how far is it to Liverpool, Hiram? Would you say it's further than from Saxmundham to Ipswich?'

'I couldn't tell you,' said Hiram, 'but I doubt it is.'

'Then it must be a terrible long way to Canada,' said Bob.

'Ay,' said Hiram, with a stoical grin. 'I wonder where we shall sleep to-night?'

'I wonder,' said Bob, thoughtfully filling his pipe.

They had never spent a night away from home in their lives.

'I say,' said Hiram suddenly, 'I wonder what'll become of those two teams of ourn. Best horses in the parish those.'

'They'll have to get two hired men,' replied Bob, 'unless Harry and Ern give up the stock: but they aren't much good with the plough.'

'No, that they aren't,' said Hiram gloomily. 'I hope whoever get 'em 'll look after 'em proper. They're rare fine horses, they are, to plough.'

'That's the truth,' said Bob. 'But you know, Hiram, hired men 'on't work like we used to. There's a lot in using a plough, isn't there Hiram?'

'Yes,' said Hiram stolidly, 'there is.'

'You've got to know how to set your hake,' Bob continued earnestly, as if he were giving Hiram a lesson, 'and your share and your coulter, and how to keep your furrow straight. I wonder if they'll be able to do all that.'

Hiram sighed.

'Yes,' he said, ' that summerland of ourn look a treat, don't it, so neat and reg'lar all over; and those clover ricks you and me built last summer—as trim as beehives, aren't they, Bob?'

'Yes, it's a tidy little farm and no mistake,' said Bob once more.

'It'd be a pity if that went down like after we'd gone,' said Hiram with another sigh.

'That it would,' said Bob, ' and I don't know as there's a man in the parish fit to work on that farm.'

'No, nor do I,' replied Hiram.

They sat and smoked in silence for a while. All their interest in the fields that flew past them had faded: they were both thinking of Crakenhill. Suddenly Bob looked up.

'I say,' he said impulsively, ' let's go back, Hiram.'

Hiram nodded.

'P'r'aps it'd be better,' he replied.

.   .   .

They were conscious of an intense feeling of relief when they set foot in Ipswich again that evening, as if they had just escaped from prison in a foreign land. The last train for Saxmundham had gone and they set out to walk the twenty-five miles to Bruisyard there and then. If they waited to go home with the empty milk-cans in the early morning, it would be too late. They had formed no definite plan to explain themselves ; only one thing was clear to them : they must see Ben first at all costs.

It was a cruel journey, even to men inured by months and years of labour to be always ready to bear an extra strain. They were already tired and hungry, but they could not afford to dawdle for food or rest and they were almost dropping with fatigue when at three o'clock the next morning they trudged up to the familiar homestead.

' I say, Hiram,' said Bob in a parched, husky whisper, ' it's good to be back again.'

' It is and no mistake,' rejoined Hiram in a similar whisper.

Everything was quiet, the doors were barred and all the lights were out ; evidently no one had taken the trouble to sit up for them. They prowled about a little aimlessly at first, looking for a way into the house and barking their shins on the tools, tubs and blocks of wood that littered the yard.

' I know,' said Hiram all at once. ' The dairy window.'

' What dairy window ? ' said Bob stupidly.

' Do you follow me,' Hiram hissed into his ear. ' I know.'

' All right,' Bob answered wearily, glad to resign himself into more capable hands.

Hiram led the way to the back of the house and found a place in the dairy window where the wire gauze was weak. It gave under the pressure of his fingers so that he could slip his hand in and undo the latch. They were inside the house in a minute, took off their boots in the kitchen and crept upstairs to the room where Ben slept alone. Hiram tapped softly on the door.

' Who's that ? ' said Ben gruffly, at once, as if he had not been asleep at all.

' It's us,' said Hiram.

' Wait a minute,' Ben replied. He lit a candle, opened the door and let them in.

' Well, you're a nice pair,' he said, sitting down on the

bed in his nightshirt and looking them up and down.
' How did you get in ? '

' Through the dairy window,' said Hiram.

' Funny I didn't hear you,' said Ben. ' I've been awake
all night, waiting to let you in.'

' Just like you, Ben,' said Hiram, seizing his hand fer-
vently. He was so tired that it would have taken very
little kindness to make him cry.

' Well, what's it all about ? ' said Ben.

Bob and Hiram looked at each other ; then they hung
their heads and looked at the floor.

' Well ? ' said Ben.

' It's like this,' Hiram faltered. ' We wanted to go to
Canada.'

' You damnation bloody fools,' Ben growled. ' You
don't know a good thing when you've got it.'

' We do now,' said Hiram in a hoarse voice, still looking
on the floor. ' That's why we came back.'

' Anyhow,' said Ben, ' you'd better not let father know
about it. He'd be that mad, he'd half kill you both.'

' That's—that's why we came to find you, Ben,' Hiram
stammered.

' H'm,' said Ben. ' He think you had a drop too much
and lost the last train. Fare to me he'd better go on
thinking.'

' Oh ! ' exclaimed Bob and Hiram together. They had
never been drunk in their lives : it was a serious imputa-
tion to admit.

There was a sound of shuffling feet in the passage.
Hiram paled.

' Who's that ? ' he whispered.

For answer the door opened, showing Benjamin Geaiter
on the threshold, candle in hand, looking rather like some
early patriarch in his white nightshirt and great black
beard.

' So you've come back ? ' he said grimly.

' Yes, father.' Hiram hardly dared to look at him.

' You young swine ! ' Benjamin took in a breath between his teeth. ' If I was a bit younger, I'd give you a basting, I would. Going on the spree as if you was gentleman farmers. I don't pay your fares into Ipswich for that. We've got to work for our living on this here farm, I can tell you. Where's the money for them lambs ? '

' We—we sent it off to you by post,' said Hiram haltingly.

' By post ? ' Benjamin's voice almost cracked as he echoed the words. ' Well, by God, you must have been drunk.'

' We paid for the stamp out of our own money, father,' said Hiram. ' I doubt it'll come in the morning.'

' So it had better,' snarled Benjamin, ' or you'll both hear of it—you young swine! '

He shuffled out with a vengeful look at them over his shoulder. He might have moralised further ; but to Benjamin it was not a moral question. As they heard his latch click, Bob and Hiram heaved a sigh of relief.

' Reckon we'll go and have a lie-down,' said Hiram.

' Yes,' said Ben, ' and you can thank your lucky stars.'

VI

THE wheezy old clock in the kitchen of Crakenhill Hall struck four with a rattle of chains and weights that could be heard all over the farmyard. The darkness became suffused with a faint pallor and a belated barn-owl sailed noiselessly into his home in the loft. A starling on the Tudor chimney chattered softly to himself; a thrush in the orchard tried a few of his notes half-heartedly; then a pair of robins began a fervent antiphony on the stable thatch, a cock crew and was answered from half a mile away. A red glow swelled up in the east; dawn was breaking. The old bob-tailed sheep dog stirred uneasily in his barrel as Ernest stumped across the yard to the pig-styes with a hurricane lantern swinging in one hand and something clutched tightly beneath his coat. He entered one of the styes and after carefully closing the door, dropped down on his knees among the straw where the big black sow lay inert upon her side with eight newly-farrowed piglings at her dugs. Undoing his coat, Ernest pulled out a small round bundle swathed in white flannel and began to unroll it—the ninth pigling as its high-pitched squeals very soon announced. He found a dug and put it to its nose; the squeals ceased suddenly and in less than half a minute to his great relief it was sucking greedily. He had sat up all night with the sow who was a clumsy mother, to make sure that she overlay none of her farrow, but for all that the last-born had managed to elude his notice and creep round behind its mother's back where, though it escaped being crushed, Ernest found it half an hour later half dead with cold. He took it indoors where he wrapped it in flannel and held it over the embers of the kitchen fire, but it was only when he tucked it under his coat against his own warm body, that it began to show signs of life. He looked contentedly at the litter; they all seemed safe now, all fine healthy little pigs, nine of them and he would bring them all up. Ernest

was good with pigs. He put out his lantern and dragging
wearily to the door, looked out over the farmyard. Daylight had come, the sun was rising and the birds' voices
were now swelling to a chorus. He could hear Harry getting up in his room over the kitchen door ; it was time to
go and fetch the cows. He opened the yard gate and
brushed through the dew-blanched grass bents until he
disappeared into the mists which hung over the pastures
down by the gull. Ten minutes later the cows began to
trickle into the yard and nose the door of the milking
shed. As Ernest closed the yard gate on them, Harry
opened the kitchen door and came out to join him.

'Hullo, Ern !' he said. 'What news ? '

'Nine of 'em,' said Ernest, ' and all fine little devils,
though I nearly lost the last one. He laid out and got cold.'

'Well done,' said Harry. 'You look uncommon tired,
Ern.'

'Yes, fit to drop,' replied his brother. 'Haven't had
a wink all night. That sow's a reg'lar old bitch, she is ;
she 'on't keep still. I had to watch her every minute.
Time to milk now.'

They let the cows into the shed, emptied several skeps
of sliced roots into the manger and set to work with the
milking. The milk was still plashing musically into their
pails when the other three brothers came down to get
their horses in to bait. Each of them stopped to put his
head into the sweet-smelling cloud behind the cow-shed
door and ask after the pigs and then passed on with a
satisfied grunt. The milking came to an end ; the cows were
driven out to grass again and the last of the milk carried
into the dairy to cool.

'I'm right sorry, Ern,' said Harry, as they paused to
clean their boots on the scraper outside the kitchen door,
'I can't take that milk in for you. But there's a real
maggoty ewe over there in the pen and I must get
straight away to her directly after breakfast.'

'No matter, Harry,' said Ernest with a yawn. 'I
expect I'll get there somehow or the pony will.'

They entered the kitchen and sat down to breakfast with the others. Maria Cragg was seated at one end behind the big blue enamel teapot though she continually rose and shuffled over to the fireplace to serve out bacon from the frying-pan. Benjamin sat at the other end talking over the day's work with Ben. The others silently drank and munched, looking straight before them ; there was nothing to say.

' All right ? ' said Benjamin to Ernest as he sat down.

' First rate,' replied Ern, stifling a yawn. ' A real good litter.'

Benjamin nodded and said no more ; no word of praise or thanks or even pity for Ern. He was the first to get up and go out. Ben soon followed him and, a minute after, Bob and Hiram went off to the ploughing of their beloved summerland of which they were always so proud. Harry was in a great hurry to get to his maggoty ewe and very soon Ern was left at the table eating his breakfast alone. His night's work had told heavily on him. His eyes were shadowed and he could not stop yawning. All those rashers of bacon ; it was an intolerable labour to eat them. His jaws moved more and more slowly, he could not hold his chin up any longer, his eyes would close. A moment later his head dropped down on to his arm beside his plate and after one fruitless attempt to raise it, he fell fast asleep. Maria, feeling sorry for him, cleared the table without removing the cloth and let him sleep on.

An hour later he was awakened by a heavy slap on the shoulder. He opened his eyes and saw his father standing over him. Benjamin's eyes were alight with rage.

' D'you want to lose that there train,' he cried, ' you son of a bitch ? If that milk get left behind, it'll spoil in this weather. A nice time to go to sleep ! '

' Well, father, I've been up all night,' protested Ern.

' No reason for going to sleep now,' roared his father.

' I doubt you 'on't pay me extra wages,' said Ern sarcastically, ' for sitting up all night with the owd sow.'

Benjamin, who was not used to being answered back, grew more infuriated ; he seized Ern's shoulder and shook him.

' You darn young pup ! ' he shouted. ' Not fit to wear shoe leather, you aren't. Any more of your lip and I'll give you a hiding, double-quick. D'ye hear ? '

Ern looked at him blankly. Benjamin had never been a man to mince his words, but this hectoring, unreasonable fury was a new thing—although undoubtedly his temper had grown worse since Bob and Hiram's supposed escapade in Ipswich.

' All right, father,' he said, in a weary voice. ' I'll get along now. There's still plenty of time to catch the train.'

' You lazy young swab, you,' muttered Benjamin as he watched him get up and go out. ' No son of mine, you aren't. I'll larn you to fall asleep, I will.'

Ern was still too sleepy to make any further retort, but his father's words sank deep into his consciousness and came to the surface a little later on while he was driving the milk into Saxmundham and the rumble of the wheels on the road and the swaying of the milk-float scattered the drowsiness from his senses. All the old man's threats and abuse came back to him and he thought of all the withering answers he might have given and would give another time. After a long sleepless night to be treated in this fashion! Not his father's son! He knew more about pigs than his father ever had, and although he was only twenty-one, he was accounted one of the best judges of a pig in the parish. With rising indignation he chewed and chewed his grievances over and over again until he arrived at the station in a thoroughly enraged and rebellious mood. At any rate he was old enough to be his own master ; his father should see.

After seeing his milk churns on to the station platform well in time for the train and loading the returned empties into his float, he did not drive away immediately, but left the float in the station yard and went off for a stroll round the town with his hands in his pockets, an unheard of thing for Ern to do in the middle of his day's work. He looked into all the shop windows and read all the advertisements and sale notices: he even bought a newspaper and read the local news columns, not very interesting perhaps, but at least better than work. He would show his father that he could take a holiday when he liked. However, he soon exhausted the sights of Saxmundham and the morning only half gone, he found himself standing in the market-place with his newspaper under his arm, wondering what to do next. He caught his breath: someone had gripped him by the arm so firmly and suddenly that he almost slipped off the kerb. He turned round: it was a soldier in full uniform with three stripes on his arm and a red, white and blue cockade in his cap. Ern had never seen anyone so magnificent.

' Hullo, my lad,' said the sergeant breezily. ' You look as if you was at a loose end. Come and have a drink.'

How different from Benjamin! Here was a man who took such an interest in his neighbour that he knew instinctively when he was at a loose end and promptly offered him a drink. Ern warmed to the man.

' Well, I 'on't say no,' he replied. ' That is getting a bit slow here and no mistake.'

' Well, come on, my boy,' said the sergeant, leading the way to a little public-house on the opposite side of the market place.

' What's yours ? ' he said, when they were inside the tap-room.

' A glass of porter 'll do me,' said Ern modestly.

' Come on, my lad,' the sergeant drawled, slapping him on the back. ' Have something with a bit more kick in it than that. I don't meet a chap like you every day of the week. Make it a whisky. That's a man's drink.'

Ern was awestruck by his grand manner.

' I'll hev a whisky then,' he said, ' since you are so good.'

' Don't you talk about goodness,' returned the sergeant, loftily waving the suggestion aside. ' I'm only too glad to have the chance of a drink with such as you.' He turned and winked at the barmaid, who smiled back at him. 'Two whiskys, miss,' he said, 'and don't be unkind with it.'

' I couldn't be unkind to you,' giggled the barmaid, ' could I ? '

' No, Dolly,' he replied, ' and what's more, you can't complain that I'm unkind to you either, can you ? '

' No, dear,' she replied, smiling and squeezing his hand as she pushed the glasses across the counter.

' Well, see you to-night, Dolly,' said the sergeant, carrying them over to a table in the corner. ' Business to do now.'

' Good-bye,' said the girl, blowing him a kiss as she retired. Another maid who was passing along the passage put her head in and waved to him. He drew himself up and saluted gallantly.

' See you to-night,' he called after her as she hurried on.

Ern watched him with open-mouthed admiration. What a wonderful way the man had with him. The girls smiled at him and squeezed his hand in public ; he already had two appointments for the evening. He was a dashing figure to be sure and carried himself with an air. He was handsome, too, with shining bronzed cheeks and carefully trimmed moustache. Besides, a man could not help looking handsome in such a uniform, be-ribboned tunic and striped trousers, clanking sword and spurs. No wonder the girls ran after him.

' Nice girls those,' he said to Ern with a knowing wink. ' Here's your good health.'

He tossed his whisky down in two gulps almost before Ern could say ' Good health.' Ern emptied his glass more slowly and licked his lips after it.

' Ah,' he said, ' I wanted that.' He was not used to whisky.

' Have another,' said the sergeant.

' Not for me,' said Ern.

' Come along, man,' said the sergeant. ' Don't be afraid of it. It'll make a man of you.'

'Well, I 'on't say no,' replied Ern reluctantly. 'But I'll pay.'

The sergeant would not hear of it. He rapped on the counter for two more whiskys, which the barmaid brought.

'Well, my lad,' said the sergeant, as they sipped them, 'how's farming?'

Ern made a grimace: he was certainly out of humour with farming to-day.

'Yes, I know,' said the sergeant sympathetically. 'It's a poor trade, I think.'

'Ah, that depend so much on your master,' said Ern. 'I know a bit about that myself.'

'Ah, do you now?' said the sergeant, more sympathetically than before. 'Between me and you, I thought you looked as if somethink was on your mind out there in the market place.'

'Well, you see,' said Ern, 'it's like this.'

He was only too glad of a chance to air his grievance and poured out his story in all its details, not omitting the pigling and the flannel and how he had brought it to life again by the warmth of his own body. The whisky was going to his head and his indignation grew keener than ever.

'Do you think it fair,' he cried, 'for your own father to treat you like that when you work yourself to the bone for him?'

'Fair?' cried the sergeant fiercely, striking the floor with the butt of his scabbard. 'I should damn well think not: partic'larly to a fine young feller like you. If you ask me, I think you're being wasted on a slow old place like that. You're worth something better nor that. I can tell that by just looking at you and I know at a glance. I've had to do with men, you see.' He drew his chair closer to Ern's and assumed a confidential tone. 'Look here, my lad, I want to do you a good turn. I like you, liked the looks of you the first minute I see you out there, all angry and out of sperrits like—as you might well be after all that there shameful treatment. Now have you ever thought of the Army?'

' The Army ? ' said Ernest slowly. ' I can't say I hev.'
He drained his glass.

' Now that's a career for a man,' said the sergeant, drawing his chair still closer and putting his elbows on the table. ' Not for any man, mind you, but for a chap what's worth his salt and got some ambition, like you. No old fathers there to boss you about and stop you from enjoying yourself. No, you get a chance there to live like a free man and have a good time. Well, look at me. Do I look as if it disagrees with me ? ' He sat up straight and expanded his chest.

' No, that you don't,' declared Ern emphatically. After two whiskys the sergeant seemed a finer fellow than ever.

' Now listen here, my lad,' the sergeant went on, looking him hard in the eyes and tapping him on the shoulder. ' You're just the sort of chap we want in the cavalry. You've been used to horses, I guess, and we make it worth your while. Listen. We give you thirteen pence a day and feed you like a fighting cock all for nothing. You get all your work over early in the day and the rest of the time's your own to enjoy yourself in how you like. Pretty good, ain't it ? '

' Ay, that sound all right,' said Ern, who was now listening with all his ears and hanging on the sergeant's words.

' It's a grand life,' said the sergeant, still keeping his eyes fixed on him. ' Your work's a man's work and you may get the chance to go to foreign parts and become a real man of the world ; and a fine uniform like this to wear and spurs on your boots.' He squared his shoulders and clanked his sword on the floor ' What more can a man want ? '

' Well, I couldn't think,' said Ern in admiration.

' And I can tell you,' the sergeant dropped his voice to a whisper, ' you get more girls than you know what to do with. They know as a man in our uniform's a man and they go straight for him. You've only got to take your choice. Look how sweet that filly across the counter is on me and I haven't been in the town a week yet. That's the life for you, young feller. You're made for a soldier, I can see, not a stay-at-home.'

'That do sound all right,' said Ern pensively. 'But what happen if there's a war, mister?'

'Well, my man,' said the sergeant, proudly throwing his chin in the air, 'you have to go and fight. That's a great game, I can tell you. Charging down hell for leather with your sabres all flashing in the sun and the enemy so as you can't see his arse for dust, trying to get away from you. Then, when you've won the battle, you come home with the flags flying and the band playing and all the girls kiss you in the streets. And a man like you—I can see you're a brave feller by the fire in your eyes'—Ern blinked involuntarily—'a feller like you wouldn't have no trouble in picking up a few medals. The ribbons look nice on a tunic. Why, look at me: I'm only an ornery bloke, I am.' He pointed modestly to the row of ribbons on his chest.

'Ah, that fare to me a fine life,' said Ern. 'And now I think of it, I do know a bit about horses: though pigs are more in my line.'

'No, no, a chap like you could turn his hand to anything,' said the sergeant, brushing away the imaginary objection with a sweep of his hand. 'Of course, you may get killed, but tell me, I arst you, what is nobler than to die on the field of battle, fighting heroically for your queen and country with all your beaten enemies around you?' He slapped his chest and stared fiercely at a stuffed squirrel on the mantelpiece. 'Can you think of a better death?'

'Now I come to think of it,' said Ern, 'I can't. That's a real grand life, that is. I'd like to die for my country and no mistake.'

'Well, why have you been wasting all this time?' said the sergeant, seizing him by the shoulder and peering intently into his face.

Ern felt embarrassed by his stare, but at the same time he was so fascinated that he dared not drop his eyes.

' I don't know,' he mumbled. ' Fare to me I've been a fool.'

' Well, young feller, it ain't too late even now,' said the sergeant, still gripping his shoulder.

' No ? ' said Ern. ' Well, I must say that's the life I've always wanted.'

The sergeant let go his shoulder and pounded the table deliberately with his fist.

' If that's the case, my lad,' he said, ' you ought to be there. You're a bit late in the day, but still I think I could get you in with a bit of graft.'

' That's uncommon kind of you,' said Ern.

' Don't speak of it.' The sergeant waved his hand in the air. ' I'm only too glad to help a chap what's got the right stuff in him. It ain't hard for me : I know all the officers, you see.'

' Thank you, thank you, I'm sure,' said Ern. ' The soldier's life for me! ' He pounded his fist on the table in his turn.

' That's the sperrit, my boy,' said the sergeant, ' that's the sperrit. Now look here. I've got several more young chaps from hereabouts who want to 'list. All fine young fellers—though I must say you're the likeliest I've found yet—and I'm going to take 'em along to Ipswich to-morrow to the recruiting office. You can come along of us. I'll pay your fare. I know times is hard.'

The money did not come out of his pocket : but it did not matter if Ern thought so.

' You're wholly kind,' said Ern. ' Come ? Becourse I will. I've only been waiting for a chance like this.'

' Shake on it,' said the sergeant, seizing his hand.

' God! what a hand,' he exclaimed, as he heard his bones crack in Ern's enthusiastic grip. ' You're the chap for us. We'll make you break all our colts. Have another drink.'

' No, I must be going,' said Ern. ' I've got a horse up at the station.'

' Well, a quick one,' said the sergeant, who wanted to clinch Ern's resolve.

He called for two more whiskys: they clinked glasses and drained them.

' Now look here, my lad,' said the sergeant. ' You come along to-morrow at ten o'clock. I shall be outside here with the other boys.'

' Trust me,' said Ern. ' Good-bye to farming! '

' That's the ticket,' said the sergeant. ' So long.'

They shook hands once again, the sergeant more cautiously this time for the sake of his fingers, and Ern walked away with a jaunty but unsteady step to the station yard where the patient cob still stood quietly waiting for him. He drove back in the highest spirits, nodding cheerfully to everyone who passed and regaling his imagination with pictures of the life in store for him—honour and glory, women and fine clothes and junketing, and thirteen pence a day for it as well. It was within half an hour of dinner-time when he reached the farmyard again. Harry came out of the pig-styes to open the gate for him.

' Where hev you been, Ern ? ' he said.

' Oh, just taking a look at Sax,' replied Ern vaguely, stepping down from the float to unhitch the traces.

' Oh,' said his brother. ' I thought p'r'aps you'd gone to the fair at Frannigan.'

' Fair?' said Ern scornfully. ' What d'ye take me for ? Besides, 'tisn't till to-morrow. Where's father ? '

' Lucky for you he've been all the morning in the beet with the horse-hoe,' said Harry.

' Lord! what if he hev?' his brother sneered. ' I don't care for him.'

' Ern,' said Harry solemnly, ' you smell of drink.'

' I don't wonder I do,' Ern snorted, ' after the way father nagged me this morning.'

' I fed the pigs for you after I'd done the ewes,' said Harry, ' and cleared up round the yard. Father 'on't notice you've been away.'

' I don't care if he do,' said Ern recklessly. ' But you're a decent little chap, Harry, and I 'on't forget it.'

' Well,' said Harry as casually as he could, seeing that Ern was not in the mood to be mollified, ' I hope you 'on't stir him up : he've been laying down the law to all on us this morning. We shall suffer for it as well as you.'

' P'r'aps you're right,' replied Ern. ' So long as he don't set me off.'

He was not anxious for another quarrel just now : moreover, the effects of the whisky were beginning to wear off.

' Oh, Ern,' shouted Harry, as Ern led the cob off into the little paddock by the yard, ' that little owd pig is dead after all.'

' I hope the rest follow it,' was all the answer he got.

VII

ERN'S resolve had been taken under the influence of alcohol, but notwithstanding that it persisted. At first he thought of announcing his intention at breakfast and calmly walking out of the house ; but when it came to the point, he shrank from provoking the old man unnecessarily. Like the others, he was at heart afraid of him and in any case it would hardly further his plan to leave in an uproar. He quietly finished his day's work in the usual way as if nothing had happened : but that night as they went upstairs to bed, he asked Harry if he would care to take the milk in next day. Harry, who was only eighteen and still possessed some youthful enthusiasms, snatched at the chance : he had always been ambitious to do the task, but it had fallen to Ern by right of age. All was well.

The next morning Ern milked, fed the pigs and had breakfast with the others. No one would have suspected him on account of his morose silence : he was always silent at meals like the rest. After breakfast he pottered about waiting until Harry had left with the milk-float and then, taking care to avoid the others, he slipped down the cart-way to the Saxmundham road and set out with a joyous, swinging stride ; he was embarking upon adventure at last. Like Bob and Hiram he carried his savings with him, tucked away in a pocket, but he was not wearing his best clothes : the army would provide him with a far better suit than he had ever had. By carefully choosing his road later on, he managed to avoid meeting Harry on his way back from Saxmundham with the empty churns and he had ten minutes to spare when he entered the market place : he had timed himself well. There was a small group of men standing outside the door of the inn, conspicuous among them the sergeant in uniform and tricolour cockade. Ern approached them.

' Ah, here he is !' cried the sergeant. ' We were waiting for you, my beauty. Good for you. I was afraid yo' wasn't coming after all. Well, boys, if you're all ready, we'll be off to the station.'

They moved noisily off up the street with the sergeant at their head, joking and swearing among themselves. Ern brought up the rear by himself, a little diffidently. He was not used to crowds and this certainly was a mixed crew. He recognised none of them, but they all seemed to belong to a lower level of rural society than his own. That, however, did not matter: they would all be equal as servants of the queen and they were all in lively spirits as was fitting for men setting out on so great an enterprise.

While the sergeant paid for their tickets at the booking-office, they all trooped on to the platform and cracked jokes with the porters, whom most of them seemed to know. Ern felt a strange reluctance to be seen with them there lest any of the porters should recognise him : it was an unreasonable feeling, but he could not suppress it. Five minutes later the train steamed in and all twelve of them bundled into one third class compartment. One corner next to the platform was kept for the sergeant. The rest went to those who scrambled in first and Ern found himself squeezed on to the edge of the seat in the middle.

' Good-bye, Saxmundham! ' shouted the man in the corner opposite the sergeant, as they moved out of the station. ' Good-bye for ever! ' He pulled out a big black bottle from his pocket and handed it to the sergeant. ' Rum, sergeant,' he said. ' Have a drink.'

' Just the thing,' replied the sergeant, taking a swig at the bottle. ' Here's to the regiment.'

The bottle passed round and Ern had his pull at it with the rest : but he did not like it and drank little. With twelve men in the same small space, smoking, spitting and chattering, the atmosphere soon became thick and oppressive. The sergeant seemed to lose some of his glamour in such surroundings. Ern was a little disappointed ; he had expected him to go on being kind and talking about honour and glory. But he smoked and swore and spat and told bawdy stories : he was like other men after all. He caught sight of Ern sitting silent with his arms folded and slapped him on the thigh.

'Cheer up, old cock!' he cried. 'You've finished with mud and dung for good now. No more cows to milk, no more pigs to cuddle.'

They all laughed at him.

'All right,' said Ern with a sickly smile. 'I was listening to the rest of you.'

The bottle passed round again and they forgot him.

The sergeant's remark had been actually rather unfortunate : but he could not be expected to know the workings of Ern's mind. No more pigs to cuddle, no more cows to milk, no more mangold to slice : he had not thought of that. Of course, there were no such things to be done in the army : but he had been doing them for so long that he could hardly imagine life without them and he began to wonder whether he really disliked them. The din in the carriage grew louder : another bottle was passing round and the liquor was going to their heads. Ern had never heard such swearing in his life. They were not mealy-mouthed at Crakenhill and they swore hard and loudly enough when occasion demanded it. But this was another matter : every other word seemed to be an oath or an obscenity. It was all such a contrast to the calm silence of Crakenhill. He turned to his neighbour.

'You on the land?' he asked for the sake of saying something.

'Too true,' replied the man, 'but I've finished with it now, thank God. Too dam hard for me. I was a cowman on a farm near Middleton. Them cows! I hope I never milk another—dirty brutes!'

Ern thought of his own sleek animals and of the dark beam under the manger in the cowshed, rough-hewn and worm-eaten, at which he gazed each morning when he began milking, with his head pressed tightly into the first cow's flank. He knew every hole, every gloss on that beam : strange that he should think of that now. He was beginning to feel that he did not like these men. He was a rough fellow himself, but these were the dregs of the neighbourhood, ruined dealers and fish-hawkers, knacker's men, stone-breakers, tinkers, men who were joining the army because nothing could be worse than their present estate. He thought of his brothers : they were better men than these, and as he thought of them, he realised that he was fond of them : he had lived so long with them that they were almost part of him. It was good of young Harry to do his work for him and say nothing to anyone else about it : a pity if he never saw him again : and Ben, too, although he was so much the elder brother. He missed them already among this sordid crowd. Still, a uniform and spurs would make a great deal of difference to them all and he was going to see life : it was no use being sentimental.

' We shall all be gentlemen in the army, shan't we, sergeant ? ' shouted the man who had originally produced the bottle of rum.

' The glorious defenders of our dear country,' guffawed a Friston chimney-sweep at his side.

' Our dear owd East Suffolk, you mean,' put in a man from the other end of the carriage.

East Suffolk, East Suffolk, the words echoed in Ern's head. He had never been out of it. Why should they sneer at it ? Crakenhill was in East Suffolk. Why was he leaving it ? Honour and glory ?

' Don't you talk so much about glory,' the sergeant was saying. He had drunk a good deal from one bottle and another and was growing rather incautious. ' You've got to learn your trade first. You wait till I put you through it on parade and you've done a few fatigues. You won't talk so much about glory then.' He spat viciously between his knees. ' You won't either when you get shot,' he added with a grin.

The others, quite unalarmed at the prospect, laughed loudly : they had no illusions about the life that awaited them. But the sergeant sank still more in Ern's estimation.

' Look at old Spuds! ' he cried, as if he divined Ern's
thoughts. ' He's still thinking of his blasted old cows and
pigs : still wishes he had a cold little pig under his arm,
I'll take my oath.'

' What you want, Spuds,' shouted the man in the
corner, ' is a nice, plump, warm young filly under your
arm. That'd cheer you up.'

' I'm all right,' said Ernest, thinking of his cows and
pigs more than ever. ' Don't you bother about me.'

' Well, leave him alone,' said the sergeant. ' He'll cheer
up later on, I expect.'

' Yes, I'm looking forward to that uniform of yours,'
said the chimney-sweep hoarsely. ' I want to try my luck
with the girls. Ah, yes, and the spurs, too. They love a
pair of spurs, don't they ? '

' Haw! what will your mother say ? ' mocked his neighbour, a fishmonger.

' Hark at him,' retorted the sweep. ' He smell too
strong of fish for 'em to run after him.'

' Well, you'd better not talk till you've had a wash, old
sooty-face,' replied the fishmonger, and had the laugh.

The conversation had worked itself out for the moment
and they all sat back, looking furtively at one another, as
people in a train will. The sergeant's eye fell upon Ern
again.

' Look at old Spuds,' he said in a thick voice, pointing
at him. ' He's still hankering after his damned old cows.
Blast me if I ever see such a one.'

Ern was sitting with his head on his hands, looking
intently out of the window, and he was hankering after
his cows. He had just caught a glimpse of a farmyard
with cattle chewing tranquilly in the byre, just as they did
at Crakenhill : he wondered why they were not out at
grass at that time of year : perhaps the man was short of
feed. They were all redpolls, too, like his at Crakenhill.
In a neighbouring field five big black sows were routing in
the turf with their litters tumbling happily around them :
they looked up with a grunt, snout in air, to watch the

train roar past. One of those sows was the image of the mother whose pangs he had watched over the night before last. All the longing which had been struggling within him for the last two hours, suddenly burst out and took possession of him—the longing for his cows and pigs, for Crakenhill with its sagging roof and crow-stepped gable, for his brothers, even his father, because they belonged there. All these men in the carriage were nothing to him. Gentlemen and servants of the queen? They denied and mocked all the things he valued: he despised and hated them. Honour and glory? They thought nothing of it. He came to himself with a start, realising that they were laughing at him. He smiled weakly at them, but he felt like a hunted animal. Then the train drew into the suburbs of Ipswich and they forgot him again.

As the train slowed up, they all tumbled out with a clatter on to the platform. The sergeant ran his eye over them to see if all were there. A sorry crowd they looked, but he would make them sit up, knock them into shape. Still, they were not yet properly enlisted and he must keep them in a good humour for a little while longer. He pointed to the station refreshment room.

'What about one more drink, boys?' he said.

'Let's go and drink the sergeant's health, boys!' shouted the sweep, leading the way to the door.

The rest followed him with a shout and the sergeant made a note of the sweep for rigid discipline in the near future—too spry by half. They invaded the bar in a mass, clamouring for drinks and chaffing the barmaids. Three of them offered the sergeant a drink: the position was changing now and he was a person to be propitiated.

Ern, pretending to laugh with them, drank a glass of porter, but it nearly made him sick. His thoughts were running wildly. He had never known how happy he was at Crakenhill till now: Crakenhill, the milking shed, the beam under the manger—he could not do without them. And now he had ruined himself, was going to swear his life away.

' Now, boys, come along,' said the sergeant, as the last glass was emptied. ' Pull yourselves together and march up to the recruiting office like the smart lot you are.'

They trailed after him out of the station, still grinning and talking in subdued tones, and so across the river and past the empty market place. People in the street looked strangely at them as if they were condemned criminals. A few jeered as they passed, but when they tried to answer back, the sergeant sternly checked them. The only way of showing their resentment was to spit and this they did freely. Ern, walking in their midst, felt that honest folk had a right to look down on him : his heart ached with shame and misery. The sergeant stopped in front of a drab, bare house in a side street with curtainless windows, on which was painted in large white letters, Recruiting Office.

' Here we are, boys,' he said. ' This is where you take the shilling. In you go, up the stairs.'

He pushed open the door and they filed past him, slowly and clumsily, grown more serious now that the moment for cutting themselves off from their former lives drew near. At the end of the line came Ern, lagging a few paces behind.

' Come on, my lad, hurry up,' said the sergeant impatiently.

Ern put his hand in his pocket and took out half-a-crown.

' I'm not coming, mister,' he said. ' There's your railway fare. You can keep the change.'

The sergeant's cheeks went red with anger.

' Here, none of that, you young swine,' he shouted. ' You've got to come. You belong to the queen now.'

He shot out an arm and seized him by the shoulder. Ern clenched his fist.

' Let me go,' he hissed.

The sergeant laughed.

' No good trying that on,' he said. ' Hi, you chaps, give a hand ! ' he shouted up the stairs.

Ern ducked and catching him by his striped trouser-leg, gave a heave with all the weight and force of his thickset frame. The sergeant, taken by surprise, lost his hold of Ern's shoulder, his foot slipped and he fell backwards into the gutter. Ern hurled the half-crown after him and bolted. The others came tumbling down the stairs into the street and at the sight of the sergeant sitting bedraggled in the gutter, rubbing the back of his head, they set after Ern with a hue and a cry. But it did not last long, for the road was steep and he soon outdistanced them. The townsfolk turned in astonishment to stare at the burly young countryman as he went clattering past in his hobnails, sweaty-faced and panting, with fear in his eyes. He did not pause to breathe or look around him until he had left the town well behind him and felt the smooth, wiry turf of Rushmere Common beneath his feet. There was not a soul in sight : over on his left stood the square tower of Rushmere church, solid and peaceful as the church tower in his own village. He sank down behind a furze bush and buried his throbbing head in the grass for very relief.

.   .   .   .

It was a little past milking-time when he reached the farm again, helped on his way by a fast dealer's cart that was going to Yoxford. He cast about for a few minutes before he summoned himself to enter the farmyard and then, having made sure that his father was not in the offing, he sidled through the gate and up to the door of the milking shed. The air smelt sweet : he could hear the cows stolidly champing inside and the milk spirting into the frothing pails, blessed sound! Back in the dim interior Harry was hard at work milking and Ben behind him with slower, clumsier hands—Ben was a horseman. Ern tiptoed through the door and knelt down on the floor at Ben's side.

' Here, let me have that,' he said almost in a whisper, taking the teats from his hands.

Ben's jaw dropped.

' What, Ern ? ' he gasped.

He started up from his stool in amazement and as he did so, Ern slipped on to it himself and began milking as if his life depended on it. Harry, leaving his pail, came up and stood by Ben.

' Where hev you been, Ern ? ' he said.

They both stood and stared at him, but Ern paid no heed to them : he did not raise his head or utter a word until he had drained each teat and milked the udder dry. Then, rising from his stool and lifting the pail clear, he looked up into Ben and Harry's bewildered faces : a moment after he turned his eyes away again, blushing scarlet.

' What's the matter, Ern ? ' said Ben slowly ' What hev you been a-doing ? '

' I reckon you'd better hide me away, Ben,' replied Ern huskily.

' What for ? ' said Ben, opening his eyes wider than ever.

' I doubt they'll soon be after me,' said Ern, rubbing his hands nervously. ' They shoot deserters, don't they ? '

' What, were you going off for a soldier ? ' said Ben.

Ern nodded.

' You blasted young fool! ' said Ben with an angry snort. ' What made you do it ? '

' Well, father went on at me so bad,' Ern faltered, ' I thought the army'd be better : but that wasn't.'

His tongue loosened and the whole story came out with a rush. Ben and Harry listened in silence, both with their hands on their hips and straws in their mouths.

' Did you take the shilling ? ' said Ben, when he had finished, savagely spitting out his straw.

' No,' replied Ern. ' I gave him half-a-crown.'

' Well, that's all right.' Ben heaved a sigh of relief. ' They can't get you.'

' Can't they ? ' said Ern eagerly.

' No,' replied Ben. ' Don't you be afraid of 'em. You're not a deserter 'cause you never were a soldier : not cut out for it, you aren't. But look here, young feller, what about father?'

'Ah!' A frightened look came into Ern's eyes.

'Well, you've fair messed our work up to-day,' Ben scolded. ''Struth, you have, and you'll have to pick a bone or two with father. You're a proper young fool to take all he say to heart : he don't mean it all. Now listen here. When you went off, I told him, "P'r'aps Ern have gone off to the fair at Frannigan," I said. I didn't know, becourse. You'll have to stick it out with father somehow : still, better not let him know you tried to 'list : he might take it hard. So—well—if you like, me and young Harry 'on't know nothing about it.'

'Ay, that's it,' said Harry with a nod.

'Ben,' said Ern, seizing his hand, ' you're a real good 'un.'

'I thought you'd come back somehow,' said Ben, slouching off to the door. ' Fare to me you'd better finish that milking now.'

'And that's the truth,' answered Ern.

It was exactly what he wanted to do.

VIII

HARRY stood back from the handle of the root-slicer and having wiped his damp forehead on a bare arm rolled his sleeves up a little higher. Another spring had come to Crakenhill and though the lambing was all over, there was still more than enough work to keep a pair of hands busy in the sheep-pens. He folded his arms and leant up against the machine to rest for a while. Overhead the sun, still a shy and wayward neighbour, played hide and seek behind a chain of wispy, white clouds in streams of golden light which filtered down between the greening larch boughs, to glance back in dazzling reflection off the sluggish runnels of water and bare flinty pebbles on the cartway running down from Crakenhill to the road, Crakenhill Drift as they called it in the village. It was little more than a track, rutted and grass-grown, and so seldom repaired that in winter-time it was often ankle-deep in mud. Even now at the beginning of May it had hardly recovered from the winter rains, as the runnels on its surface still showed; but in the sun it glistened like a live thing. The whole air, the whole earth seemed alive with light and sound and growth. Chaffinches chased one another along the hedgerow with their sprightly bouncing note: a nightingale's trill could be heard from time to time above the medley of song which filled the spinney; and over all brooded the rarefied music of a distant lark, sprinkling ceaselessly down like a shower of fine rain. There were countless buds in the hedge swelling rapidly for bloom, hawthorn and crab-apple and even wild rose: the leaves were greener than they would ever be again, and already so thick that it was no longer possible to see between them. Harry had seen many springs like this before, but never as now had he felt it so good to be alive. He looked down at the ewes beside him fumbling the hay in the wooden racks with their noses or chewing placidly while they watched the lambs scampering gaily among the

bins and troughs. A little puff of air with a rustling eddy
of scattered elm-flowers came and played against his
cheek, flickered over his bare arms and was gone; it
seemed neither hot nor cold, only infinitely soft, infinitely
caressing. He watched the long, shapely muscles in his
forearm stir as he clenched and unclenched his fingers:
there was life in him too. He took in a deep breath to
taste the sweet air again: it savoured of so many good
things, of earth and wood, young leaves and grass, cowslips and pear-blossom.

' A lovely day!' he exclaimed, almost involuntarily,
with half-closed eyes. Then the sun went in for a moment
and all at once he felt sad. Spring was always like this: it
always promised something—what, he did not know—it
promised and never fulfilled its promise. One day was like
another with work, eating and sleeping, and he would not
have had it otherwise, but there ought to be something
else besides, something that was constantly on the point
of coming but never came: it was not the summer he was
thinking of. He had never been conscious of this lack
before, and yet, when he thought of it, it seemed to have
been always there. Still wondering obscurely what it could
be, he opened his eyes. The sun was out again and everything as beautiful as ever; but still there was an emptiness. Then, unused to so much abstract reflection and
quickly tiring of it, he pulled himself up and began to toss
mangold into the trough of the slicer: the ewes must be
fed and there was no time to waste in wondering. The
wheel sped round with a grinding swish as he bent his back
to it and the slices of mangold poured out into the basket
in a faster and faster stream. He stopped to rest again:
the basket was only half-full; what a quantity of roots
those ewes got through in a day: anyhow, it would soon
be dinner time.

He tossed some more roots into the trough and was
about to start at the wheel again, but something made
him pause. Someone was coming up the drift. Still
gripping the handle, he raised his head to look. It was

only Jessie Eves after all, the postmaster's daughter, who helped her father to deliver the letters—Crakenhill, lying at a distance from the village, generally had to wait until the middle of the morning for its post. As she came level with the pens which were about twenty yards from the drift, Harry gave her his usual curt nod which she answered in like manner: she never expected more from that family. Harry bent to the wheel again, but after a few strokes a strong, sudden impulse made him stop and turn his head to watch her up the hill. For the first time he noticed how different her gait was from a man's, how supple and slender her body, by comparison fragile, but in a print frock how alluring. As she reached the meadow gate, she too, prompted by a like impulse, turned round to look at him. Their eyes met unexpectedly and both, caught in the act, turned away in confusion, trying to appear as if they had never looked. A moment after Jessie was over the gate and out of sight.

Harry, quite red in the face although she could no longer see him, went furiously to work at his machine and the mangold came out in such a rapid stream that the basket filled and overflowed in large heaps on every side before he saw what was happening. He shifted the basket and nervously gathered up the fallen slices. There was one more meadow to the farmyard and she would be back in less than five minutes: he was longing to see her again, but frightened at the prospect, not knowing what would happen. The rattle of the chain on the gatepost suddenly made his heart thump wildly: she was clambering over. He took up his stand behind the machine and fussed about with the basket, trying to seem so intent on his work as not to notice her at all, though all the time watching her out of the corner of his eye. Jessie did the same herself, walking demurely with eyes apparently fixed straight in front of her. At last, however, when she came level with the pens again, she could hold out no longer and turned her head. Harry, too, could hold out no longer: something must be done. In desperation he waved his arm. She stopped.

' Here! ' he shouted.

She hesitated a moment, then turned and began to pick her way across the trampled grass to him. Harry's brain had never worked so violently as it did in the short minute she took to reach him, but it did not fail him. He dived into his basket and pulled out a clean white finger of mangold, streaked faintly with pink.

' I thought you might like a bit of beet,' he said, holding it out to her and blushing to the roots of his hair. ' It's wonderful sweet.'

Jessie, a little taken aback by this strange gift, stared for a moment—it was perfectly clean—and then blushing herself, she took it from him and began nibbling it like a sugar-stick. Harry pulled out another slice from the basket and began to eat too. The sight was too much for Jessie's susceptibilities and she burst out laughing. Harry, glad of a chance to break the tension, followed her example.

' Why, we look like a couple of sheep and no mistake,' she said, still giggling, when they had partially recovered.

' Why, so we do,' said Harry, looking her squarely in the face for the first time. The laugh had been an immense relief and had given him courage. ' But that's good, isn't it ? '

' I don't know,' she said, critically, putting her head on one side, but continuing to munch.

' Them ewes do, anyway,' said Harry. ' They keep me hard at it, cutting up for 'em. That was a lovely field of beet that was. I can't remember how many load to the acre we got—something enormous. But the ground was so wet, we could hardly shift it. It was down by the gull, that field with the tall elm trees. I expect you know.'

' No, I don't,' said Jessie, poking the last inch of beet into her mouth. She was not interested in such details, but Harry knew of nothing else to say.

' Have another bit,' said Harry. ' That's as good as a drink.'

No, thank you,' said Jessie, shaking her head. ' I've got several more letters to take round yet. I'm now gooing. Farewell.'

' Farewell,' said Harry with a grin.

They both blushed again quite suddenly and Jessie, promptly turning round, ran as hard as she could for the bottom of the hill, her mail-bag flapping on her back. Harry watched her the whole way without any attempt to conceal himself and was rewarded by seeing her turn and wave to him as she climbed over the gate. He went back to work with greater fury than ever, partly to make up for lost time and partly to work off his nervous excitement : it was a new feeling, but by no means unpleasant —as if the emptiness of which he had just become aware were on the point of being really filled up. More than ever he felt that it was good to be alive.

The impression of Jessie that he carried away was vague enough—curly golden hair, a freckled face and round pale blue eyes with white curving lids : but it was constantly before his mind and he fed upon it for the rest of the day and a good part of the night. The next morning he took especial care to be down at the sheep pens early in case Jessie came before her usual time : once more he was palpitating with excitement, but he was no longer afraid of her. Every five minutes he was peeping over the top of the machine to see if the print frock was in sight at the bottom of the hill and some of the sheep that morning had to wait a long while for their breakfast. But she did not come and he went disconsolately back to dinner, realising, as of course he should have realised before, that the arrival of a letter was such a rare occurrence at Crakenhill—and even then as a rule nothing more than a bill—that he need not expect to see Jessie on the drift again for another month.

Once more the whole complexion of life seemed to have changed for him and the void in it became greater than ever now that he knew what might have filled it. Never before had he seen anything so entrancing as Jessie : he longed to see her again, to hear her voice, to be near her, to touch her, to have her for his own : it was a delightful dream. He rehearsed over and over again to himself their brief conversation by the sheep-fold and tried to recapture something more of her voice, her smile, her features, as they really were. But it was useless : she was just the same dim, indefinite, adorable figure that she had been to his bewildered gaze on that first morning and perhaps it was just as well, for a clearer picture might have tormented him more. Harry was indeed very much in love.

For some days he carefully arranged his work so that he spent the whole morning among the sheep, hoping for a miracle to happen. If she did come he could not miss her : but the miracle never happened. He had hardly been able to hope that it would and now he became really dejected. Although at the farm, of course, no one noticed it, at the end of a week Maria remarked that his appetite was poor and he saw that the time had come to take action. The most obvious course would have been to go down into the village and seek Jessie out : but for Harry that was out of the question. Down there he would be exposed to every prying eye, he might even be laughed at and Jessie perhaps had other gallants : but worst of all, from there the matter would come to the ears of his father and brothers and that, quite apart from its material consequences, was more than he could face: he wanted his precious secret all for his own and the only thing that would content him was to be alone with Jessie. Nevertheless, on two separate occasions he set out to go to the post office and once he even reached as far as the road; but each time his shyness turned him back. Meanwhile he grew more and more miserable.

Even his own brothers admitted that Harry was a quick-witted fellow. He did not possess Ben's knowledge of cultivation, Hiram's way with a horse, or Ern's quickness at milking : but in any difficulty he was always the man to produce the obvious solution when it had occurred to no one else. It was he who had proposed that the milk should be sent to London when the price of butter fell : he had gone down into the village for a bottle-jack when the barn wall collapsed, and he had proposed that Tom Betts, the thatcher, should be given his dinner every day for a week on condition that he taught Hiram to thatch : Tom Betts was never employed at Crakenhill again. It would have been hard if this faculty of Harry's had not served him in his own need. The idea came to him one night when he saw his father, pen in hand, laboriously composing a protest against his assessment for tithe. He managed to secure a piece of paper and a pen and without attracting attention retired to his room for half an hour. The same evening he slipped across to the neighbouring village of Dennington and posted a letter with a high heart. His only regret was that he had wasted a week before thinking of it.

IX

THE next morning Harry went down earlier than ever to the sheep-pens, but though all the time he kept one eye on the gate and still inwardly contemplated what he could remember of Jessie, his work had never gone better. The root-slicer creaked and groaned under his strokes and the beet showered into the basket. He was full of strength and courage, sure that she would come this morning. He was not deceived.

Jessie's print frock appeared at the bottom of the hill at her usual time, almost to the minute, and as soon as Harry caught sight of her, he made haste to fill the basket and then in a more leisurely fashion began to tip the beet into the troughs, with every now and then a glance over his shoulder to see how far away she was. There was no need to stare at her ; they would soon be face to face. She trudged laboriously up to the machine, stamping the mud off her boots.

' That is a wholly long way up here,' she gasped, a little out of breath. ' Why do you live so far away ? ' She opened her bag. ' I've got a letter for you here.'

' Ah, good! ' said Harry, with a broad, satisfied smile. ' I was expecting that.'

' Ah, were you ? ' she said, looking at the address again. ' Yes, Mr. Harry Geaiter, Crakenhill Hall, Bruisyard, Suff.'

' What I wanted to say,' said Harry, putting it into his pocket unopened, ' was, I shall be down here again with the sheep to-night to set out a fold.'

He reddened, and his voice shook a little : it was not so easy as he had thought after all, when it came to the point.

' Well, what about it ? ' said Jessie, pouting.

' Well, I thought p'r'aps you'd care to come along,' he faltered, ' if you've got nothing else to do.'

It was Jessie's turn to blush ; she dropped her eyes and pecked at the turf with her toe.

' What will your girl say to that ? ' she murmured in a strange weak voice.

' What girl ? ' Harry gasped.

' Why, the one who sent you that letter,' said Jessie, a little ruefully.

Harry laughed ; he felt himself a bold fellow to-day.

' Why, Jessie,' he said, ' I wrote that letter myself. Do you open it and see.'

He handed her the letter. Jessie tore open the envelope and drew out from it a blank sheet of paper. She turned it over twice carefully, and then looked up wonderingly at Harry's face.

' What did you do that for ? ' she said.

' Well, you see, Jessie,' he said, ' that was the only way I could get you to come up here again.'

He watched her face anxiously, wondering how she would take it. As comprehension dawned upon her, the corners of her mouth quivered, her fresh pink lips parted slowly, revealing the whiteness of her teeth, two dimples deepened in her cheeks, a bright liquid gleam crept into her eyes, and her whole face broke into a smile as a bud might have burst into flower. Harry was enchanted at the sight of it. A faint tremor ran through her, but he did not notice that.

' D'ye mind ? ' he whispered : his voice seemed to have gone.

' Mind what ? ' she said.

' Bringing you all this way up here,' he replied.

' Of course not,' she said in a low voice. ' I wanted to come, Harry.'

' Will you come to-night,' he said, ' about an hour after tea-time ? '

' Yes, I'll come,' she said, suddenly pressing his hand which was resting on the wheel of the machine. ' Farewell, Harry.'

She scampered away down the hill as she had done the time before, pausing again at the gate to wave to him. Harry gazed after her longingly.

'I hope she 'on't always run away like that,' he muttered: and then he smiled.

.   .   .   .

Dusk was falling as Harry drove in the last hurdle of the new fold which was to take the flock next morning. He hid the folding iron under a trough, wiped his forehead with the back of his hand and straightened his neckerchief; it would not do to look untidy to-night. Then, taking his coat off the hurdle on which it had been hanging, he picked the ends of straw off it one by one and banged the dust out of it with a switch; he put it on with great care, pulling the skirts down hard to remove the creases. There was nothing more now to do but sit down on a hurdle and wait. He picked up his switch and taking out his knife, began to peel off the bark in strips, leaving every other inch for ornament's sake—a useless occupation such as none of his brothers would have dreamed of indulging in, nor indeed Harry himself before to-day. But things were different now, he had felt another man all day, full of all the delicious impatience and joyous anticipation of his first assignation. For the first time he had been conscious of the expressionless stolidity of his brothers' faces as they sat at the kitchen table, and had chafed at their surly lethargic silence: but, poor fellows, not knowing his secret, they were not to be blamed. There were new things to think of, too, now that he had seen Jessie again: her lips, her dimpled cheeks, her eyes, so moist and alive, he knew her whole smile off by heart. But his mind was not quite easy yet: she would have to be properly entertained and he must think of something pleasant to talk about. He scratched his head: it was no light matter. He was still racking his brains when a light rustle in the grass at his side made him look up suddenly and slide off the hurdle. Jessie, wearing a light coat over her print frock, but hatless, strolled up to him with her hands in her coat pockets.

'You made me jump, that you did,' he said. 'I didn't hear you come nor see you neither.'

' Didn't you ? ' Jessie giggled. ' Well, you fared to me so wholly thoughtful, I didn't want to disturb you, so I slipped up along the hedge.'

' Oh,' said Harry, ' I see. What d'you think of our lambs ? '

' They're very nice,' replied Jessie, leaning against the hurdle at his side. ' They keep you busy, don't they ? '

' Yes, that's the truth,' said Harry. ' They do.'

' It fare a pity to have to work after tea,' said Jessie, with wry little smile, ' when there are so many other nice things to do.'

' Yes,' answered Harry regretfully. ' I might have met you an hour earlier else. Look at that little chap over there. I thought I should lose him, but he pulled round and now he's as fat as butter, isn't he ? '

' I can't see properly,' said Jessie, nonchalantly. ' It's getting dark, isn't it ? '

' That is,' replied Harry. ' Let's go and have a look at the winter wheat down by the gull.'

They turned and sauntered slowly down the hill side by side. Harry remained silent for a few minutes, waiting for Jessie to speak, but she said nothing. He must set the conversation going again.

' Our Topsy calved last night,' he ventured.

' Oh ? ' said Jessie.

' She's all white,' he went on, ' but for a black star on her forehead and, what d'you think, her calf is wholly red.'

' Is it ? ' she replied.

' A heifer calf, too,' he said. ' We wanted one badly. I don't like bull calves.'

' No ? ' she replied, without turning her head.

She did not give him much encouragement, he thought.

They walked on in silence again till they came to the wheat field. Harry rather awkwardly helped her over the stile and then relinquished her hand : it was very warm and he wished there were more stiles.

' There ! ' he said proudly. ' Look at that wheat : have you seen a better piece anywhere ? '

' I really don't know,' said Jessie a little crossly. ' I never notice things like that.'

' Oh!' said Harry, in a disappointed tone. ' Still, just look at it. That's wholly forrard.' He bent down and ran his fingers through the bushy green stalks. ' Thick as your hair, Jessie,' he said, looking up.

' Is it ? ' she said, with a greater show of interest. Her hair was thick : if only he would talk more like that.

' Let's go down to the bottom,' said Harry, stepping out of the wheat. ' There's a fine little moorhen's nest down in the pond : seven eggs in it. I've watched her setting a long while now.'

Jessie clutched his arm.

' No, don't let's go there, Harry,' she said in a querulous voice. ' It's too dark to see anything and I don't want to look at the moorhen's nest.'

' Well, where shall we go ? ' said Harry, who had come to an end of all his resources, but did not mind what they did so long as she went on holding his arm.

' I should like to set down,' said Jessie very decidedly. ' I'm tired.'

' All right,' he said. ' Where shall we go ? '

' There's a nice haystack just across the gull there,' she replied, ' and a fine heap of straw beside it. I was along there this morning-time.' Jessie knew her way about.

' I know,' said Harry, only too glad to resign the lead to her.

She did not let go his arm as they walked on, but drew closer to him so that he could feel all the warmth and yieldingness of her body : her plan certainly seemed better. They crossed the gull by a little plank bridge and the haystack loomed above them in the twilight.

' There!' said Jessie. ' Isn't that a nice heap of straw ? '

' That is,' said Harry, leaping on to it and stretching out his hand to swing her up.

She scooped a hole in the straw large enough for the two of them and made a pile for their heads.

' There, that'll do,' she said, and dropped down abruptly into the rustling, springy mass.

Harry sat down with great care and deliberation at her side and diffidently slipped his arm through hers again. It was then that Jessie took him in hand. Gently disengaging his arm, she passed it round her waist and nestled close to him.

' Harry dear,' she murmured.

His arm came to life and tightened round her : she nestled closer. Harry had never believed he could be so happy ; the soft, living warmth of her side against his own was a strange and wonderful thing to him. They looked straight in front of them for a few minutes, watching the moon rise above the elm trees and saying nothing : there was nothing profitable to be said. Jessie turned her head ever so slightly and after a glance at Harry's rigid profile, she let her head fall back on his shoulder so that her fair curls brushed his ear. He drew her closer, but did not move.

' Harry dear,' she whispered a moment later.

He turned his head and found her looking up into his eyes with her lips parted in a provoking smile. Then, closing his eyes, he kissed her, trembling. She taught him many things that evening. An hour and a half later when they parted by the stile at the cross-roads, it was Jessie who had to free herself from his embrace.

' I must now be gooing,' she whispered. ' Let me goo, Harry, and don't you tell anybody.'

' No, sweetheart,' he said, still holding her to him and kissing her once more.

She gently unlocked his arms and slipped away from him up the road.

' To-morrow night, Harry dear,' she whispered over her shoulder. ' Farewell.'

' Farewell '

SIX weeks passed and haysel came. Ben, Bob and Hiram were lolling in the stable after dinner, smoking a pipe before they harnessed up to take the waggons back to the hayfield. The kitchen door slammed and the chorus of 'Cherry Ripe' came floating into the stable as Harry strode out across the yard, bellowing at the top of his voice. His three brothers looked at one another. Harry stepped briskly up through the stable door.

'Where's that bridle?' he said, peering up at the wall. 'I must go and catch the cob now.'

'Here you are,' said Ben, reaching it down from a peg above his head.

Harry took it from him and nodded his thanks.

'I'll have that field beyond the spinney raked up for you before tea,' he said, laughing. 'You see if I don't'

'Don't you be so sure, young man,' said Bob, knocking out the ashes from his pipe.

Harry went out jingling the bridle and still humming the chorus of 'Cherry Ripe.'

'That's a rum 'un if you like,' said Hiram, as he watched him up the yard. 'I can't make young Harry out. He fare to have gone all queer like. He's allus singing at his work.'

'Yes,' said Ben, scratching his chin, 'and at meal-times he chatter and chatter. Fare to me as if he's never going to grow up.'

'He allus was a bit childlike,' piped Bob in his rapid, high-pitched voice, so difficult for any but his brothers to follow, 'and he's always going off into the fields at nights with that gun of his and he never bring anything back.'

'No,' said Hiram. 'Come to think of it, he don't.'

He took down a horse-collar and carried it over to the manger. 'Steady, girl!' he cried, as a mare stamped violently on the brick floor and caught him on the cheek with a flick of her long chestnut tail. ' Those flies are sharp to-day and no mistake. Steady, girl! ' He killed a horsefly on her flank with the palm of his hand and stroked her neck. ' She look well,' he said. ' You wouldn't think she'd been pulling all them loads the last week. And yet he work well, don't he, Ben ? '

' What, young Harry ? ' said Ben. ' He do that. I reckon he'll steady down soon enough. What is he ? Only nineteen, isn't he ? They do get a bit wild like at that age, don't they ? '

' Yes, that's the truth,' said Hiram heavily. He was only twenty-three himself.

' Time to move, Bob,' said Ben, looking at his watch and taking down another collar.

They put the gear on the horses and lumbered noisily out of the stable one by one, leading their animals, just in time to see Harry vault lightly on to the back of the cob and go trotting off through the open gate of the paddock, still singing at the top of his voice.

' There's a caution for you,' said Bob, pausing to look after him over his mare's back. ' He sing like a lark, he do. Well, come on, Flower.'

Harry trotted on quite oblivious of the disapproving eyes that were watching him ; his thoughts were else-where. He was always singing now—mostly old songs that he had learnt at school, for he had never heard any others, except one or two popular airs that Jessie had picked up in Framlingham and taught him. He had good reason to sing too. Life had become a new thing, all its former emptiness filled and forgotten. The brilliant June sun, the sweet, juicy odours of the fresh-cut hay, the strong air, the honeysuckles hanging in the hedge, all the world seemed made for him and his enjoyment : he felt that he was a man at last and living as he ought to live, with something of a bravado, now that he had his girl. He was different from his brothers, too, even out of harmony with them ; but they and their doings mattered little to him now. The day was full of familiar lusty tasks that stretched his young sinews and gave his food a relish ; and when evening came, there was always Jessie. They were never at a loss now what to say or do together.

Harry had been at work alone all the morning in a meadow on the lower part of the farm, raking the hay up in readiness for the rest of the family who were still carting from a field higher up. Already the hay lay in long regular lines across half the field ; it would be hard work to finish before milking time, but there was no need to spare himself if the cob could stand it. He had him hitched to the horse-rake and was away down the field at once : there might even be time to get some of it cocked before he left ; he would show those fellows how to work. The little cob, who was of the sort that pull themselves to death, stepped out valiantly with the rake lurching noisily behind and bouncing Harry high in the air on the spring seat whenever it crossed a water-furrow. The sun beat down hard, mercilessly hot and dazzling, but Harry did not stop to rest and the heaped rows of hay gradually lengthened out across the field. He was turning for the twelfth time now and was beginning to calculate how many more bouts would complete the work.

' Harr-y ! Harr-y ! ' A faint high voice reached his ears from the far end of the field. Shading his eyes with his hand, he descried a girl in a blue sunbonnet and a blue print frock, waving to him in the distance ; it was Jessie. Waving his hand in answer, he shouted to the cob and came rattling over the hay at a greater speed than ever to the spot where she was standing. He drew the rake into the hedge and jumped down beside her.

' Why, Jess ! ' he exclaimed, ' how did you get here ? '

It was their rule never to meet till evening and then always on some fairly distant part of the farm : they had kept their secret well.

' I've been all over the place looking for you, Harry,' she said breathlessly. ' I wondered where you could be, and then I heard the jatter of the rake and peeped through the hedge and it was you.'

' Well, what made you come afternoon-time ? ' said Harry, wiping his dripping face on his shirt-sleeve.

' I met Jim Rivers, the oilman from Peasenhall, in his cart,' she replied. ' You know him, don't you, Harry ? ' Harry nodded. ' He was just coming back from Frannigan and he say a circus have pulled in there, and that's going to stay for one night and they've got two real lions and an elephant.'

' Lord! ' said Harry, opening his mouth. ' Have they ? That sound grand and no mistake.'

' I wondered if you'd like to go,' Jessie suggested shyly, looking hard at the horse-rake.

' Oh! ' said Harry, staring at the horse-rake too. ' Let me see.'

Jessie seized his hand in her own and swung it playfully from side to side ; she looked up into his face and smiled. Harry smiled too.

' How'd we get there ? ' he said.

' Well, Jim Rivers say,' she replied, ' that he's going to drive in from Peasenhall to-night and he'll pick me up and anybody I like to bring.'

' Oh,' said Harry, ' but that depend on father. It's haysel time, you know.'

Jessie stopped swinging his arm and her face fell. Harry thought hard.

' I know,' he said. ' I think I can manage it. I'll say the sheep want a fresh lot of feed and get away down there right after tea. We can slip away from there and I'll get the work done when I come back. That's the thing of it.'

' Oh, Harry! ' Jessie danced with joy. ' 'On't that be lovely ? '

' Do you meet me down by the sheep after tea, Jess,' said Harry. ' You know where they are.'

' I know,' said Jessie, stroking his hand. ' I'll be there; you're a dear, Harry.' She dropped his hand. ' I must goo,' she said a little reluctantly. ' Farewell, Harry.'

' Stop,' he said. ' You don't need to go yet, do you, Jess ? '

'Well, no, I don't,' she faltered, looking at him sideways, ' but I thought you fared hard at work.'

Her lips curled into a smile as she spoke and Harry laughed.

'Do stay, Jess,' he coaxed, putting his arm round her waist and leading her to the nearest heap of hay. 'Let's sit down here for a bit. Work? That can wait.'

'Well, I'll stay just a few minutes,' she said, drawing his arm closer round her and sinking down in the hay. ' How sweet it smell.'

'Not so sweet as your cheek, sweetheart,' Harry whispered. He had learnt some pretty speeches in the last few weeks.

'Do you really mean that?' she queried, looking coyly at him.

'Yes, sweetheart,' he said, kissing her cheek for proof.

'Do you think, Harry,' she said, suddenly turning to him, ' that your father'll stop you going to the circus when we're married?'

'He'd better not,' said Harry fiercely, ' or he'll have to find someone else to mind his sheep for him.'

Jessie gazed at him admiringly: he was rather a handsome boy with his thick dark hair and pale skin, unbrowned by the sun: his eyes shone with anger and the muscles stood out on his powerful neck: a puff of wind blew his shirt aside and revealed the smooth white flesh on his shoulder.

'He'll soon see if he can drive me about,' continued Harry warmly. ' I'd soon leave his durn old farm. The others don't stand up to him like men. You never saw such a lot of fools to sit down to tea with. They never speak a word: they've got no spirit and they desarve to be driv about.'

He was quite indignant, and Jessie thought he had never been so handsome before. She gently smoothed his warm neck with her own cool palm. Harry looked down at the little blue veins in her arm and kissed them; her white flesh, delicate, breathing and flower-like, was a perpetual wonder to him. He stroked her side with his great hard hand as she loved him to do, and the flimsy stuff of her print dress clung to his coarse, roughened skin.

' But we shan't bother about them, shall we ? ' she murmured. ' Harry darling, do you love me ? '

She held up her mouth to be kissed. A yellow-hammer chanted monotonously above the nodding meadowsweet in the hedge. They lost count of time.

The cracking of a stick an hour later brought Harry to his senses. He sat up and listened.

' Ah, that must have been the cob,' he said, taking out his watch. ' Why, it's half an hour off milking time,' he cried. ' I must do another bout.'

He leaped to his feet, mounted the rake and swinging the cob round, set off down the field with a wave of his hand to Jessie who picked herself up and strolled out of the field, brushing the hay off her dress.

An hour and a half later he sat down to tea with the rest of his brothers, Benjamin having already finished and gone off to the rickyard. He and Ern were generally a few minutes late on account of the milking, but this afternoon Harry had lingered in the hayfield and was later than usual. He was conscious of a strange atmosphere as soon as he entered : they all looked up at him with an air of expectancy and though they said nothing, they stared at him from time to time as he devoured his bread and jam and gulped his tea. Used as he was to their silence, to-day he found it oppressive. Bob was the first to speak.

' So you didn't finish that field after all, young Harry,' he sneered.

' How do you know ? ' said Harry, looking at him over the top of his cup.

' I came round to see how you were getting on,' replied Bob, ' so as to tell father, but I didn't bother to interrupt you.'

' Oh,' said Harry rather morosely. ' Still, there's more'n enough for you to go on with now. I'll finish it to-morrow morning. I must go down to the sheep to-night. They want a bit more feed and that owd ewe that went maggoty last year is bad again.'

' Oh,' said Bob and was silent.

The others had all finished, but they continued to watch Harry until he had emptied his last cup of tea. Maria had retired to the dairy to strain some milk. Suddenly Ben bent forward over the table on his elbows.

' See here, young Harry,' he said gruffly. ' If you've finished your tea we want a word or two with you. Come along to the barn if you're ready.'

Harry turned to him with a wondering look.

' All right,' he said impatiently. ' I'll come.'

They clattered out of the kitchen one by one and made their way to the barn in a straggling line. Ben, having seen them all inside and closed the door, sat down beside Bob and Ern and Hiram on a pile of sacks ; Harry alone remained standing. They looked like some primitive court of justice with a prisoner before them.

' Well, what's it all about ? ' said Harry rather testily.

' It's like this,' said Ben, taking out his pipe and rubbing the bowl on the palm of his hand. ' Bob seed you this afternoon fooling about with Jessie Eves in the hayfield.'

Harry reddened.

' Well, what of it ? ' he said hotly.

' It's got to stop,' said Ben firmly.

' Who are you to say so ? ' said Harry defiantly.

' We all think so,' said Ben quietly, ' don't we, Hiram ? '

' Ay,' said Hiram. Bob and Ern nodded.

' That's not the way to get your work done,' Ben continued, ' and we're not going to have any of that dam nonsense on this farm.'

' Well, d'you think I spend all my time like that ? ' said Harry, nervously rubbing his hands together.

' Well, you've wasted a good deal of time these last weeks with your gun of an evening,' Ben replied, evading the question. ' I don't know what you've been doing ; but it's got to stop.'

' But I'm in love,' said Harry.

They all stared at him.

' I want to get married,' he added

They stared harder ; Bob caught his breath.   Ben clutched the stem of his pipe and pulled himself together. First Bob and Hiram, then Ern, now Harry : this was the third time that the safety of the family had been imperilled and it was high time to clear the air : he was glad of the opportunity.

' Now, look here, Harry,' he said, gesticulating with his pipe-stem, ' I want you to look at it reasonable like. There ain't no room for a woman on a farm like this.'

' What about Maria ? ' said Harry, quickly picking him up.

' Ah, Maria's different,' Ben replied. ' She fare almost like a man. But we can't have a young woman in the house. That'd wholly mess us up. She'd cost too much for one thing and she'd be in the way and always want to be frolicking.'

' Well then, I'll go somewhere else,' muttered Harry sulkily.

' Do you think father'll let you ? ' said Ben, with a scornful laugh. ' And how'd you like to work for a new master ? You've never been away from the farm in your life, have you ? '

Bob and Hiram nodded significantly. Harry heaved a sigh and impatiently scraped his feet on the floor.

' You know that when father die,' Ben went on doggedly —he was determined that they should all hear this—' the farm'll come to us five chaps and the better we make it, the better for us, eh ? Well, you know, there's not a bloke in the parish'll work as we do or the hours we do. So you see it's our advantage to stick all together here and put all our labour into the farm and there ain't no room for a woman on the place ; and if young Harry go away and live in a cotterage and have a wife and kids, stand to reason he 'on't work like he did before.'

' Oh,' sneered Harry, ' wouldn't I ? And why should

I stay here just to save you paying a hired man and put money in your pockets?'

'It isn't for us,' said Ben, 'so much as for the farm. It's the best farm in the parish, now, ain't it?'

'Ay,' said Bob and Hiram both together.

'Well now,' Ben went on, 'we was all brought up here and made it what it is, and it fare to me it's our duty to carry it on.'

'Well,' said Harry, 'there are four of you to do it: why shouldn't I go my own way?'

''Cause it needs five to farm this place,' replied Ben, 'that's why: and what's more, you sorterly belong to the place.'

'What do you think, Ern?' Harry appealed desperately, knowing that Ern at least had tried to break away from the farm himself and counting on his sympathy.

'Fare to me it's your job to stay here,' Ern replied inexorably. His own experience had frightened him too thoroughly to permit his entertaining such ridiculous notions any longer: he knew only too well now what in life was of real value: he was not going to encourage young Harry to be a fool.

'Becourse,' said Hiram emphatically, 'we don't want no young women here.' Bob nodded. They too had no sympathy with Harry: their own little adventure had taught them a lesson and they were firmly established at Crakenhill.

Ben rejoiced at the strength of his position: it was more than he had expected. Harry felt as if the ground were falling from under his feet: but he could still defy them.

'I shall do what I dam well like,' he cried. 'I'm going to be my own master. Who are you to tell me my business, I should like to know?'

Ben's forbearance was a marvel to his brothers: but Ben felt he could afford to be forbearing.

'Do as you like, young Harry,' he said, rising and patting him on the shoulder. 'But if you want to stay

here, you can't have a wife and you can't have a girl,
'cause that ain't proper. If you want to go off—well,
you must settle it with father. You go and see after the
sheep now and think it over, my lad.'

Harry turned away and walked slowly out of the barn
and down the drift. He was still trembling with indignation—as if his brothers should dictate to him!—and yet
every one of Ben's words had struck deep. He was not
frightened of his father as the others were; but he remembered what Benjamin had said last year when Ern
came back after his vain attempt to enlist: 'I've only got
two sons now who are worth their salt and one of them
only a boy.' Still, he had taken it as a great compliment.
He certainly pulled his weight on the farm now: the
sheep were almost entirely given over to him, and few men
became responsible shepherds at so early an age. The
others had all said that his place was on the farm, the best
farm in the parish, that he belonged there—he did not
know why, but he wondered if it was true. They did not
hanker after money or wives; they thought only of the
farm which their united labours had made what it was:
he had been brought up, learnt his trade on it: was it his
duty to stay there, to give up Jessie? Jessie—his whole
spirit rose in revolt at the idea: Jessie, her gentle, teasing
voice, her soft white skin, her round arms with their little
blue veins, her pouting lips, her kisses—he almost sobbed
at the thought of it. Jessie had done more for him in those
six weeks than the farm would do in half a life-time. He
steeled himself to brave it out. Any farm would be glad
to take him as cowman, perhaps even as shepherd: neither
father nor brothers should stop him from making Jessie
his wife before the year was out.

So engrossed was he in these reflections that, but for the
bleating of a restless ewe, he might have passed the sheep-
fold without noticing it, and then he would have met
Jessie down on the road. But the sound made him raise his
head and seeing where he was, he went over to the fold
and leant his elbows on a hurdle.

Once again the ground seemed to sink beneath his feet. The ewes he had fed and watched throughout the lambing, the lambs he had tended from birth, the hurdles he had penned out across acre after acre—they all seemed to cry out for him. Sheep and lambs, to be sure, would be much the same on one farm as another—but not Crakenhill sheep: the land they had fertilised would bring forth crops to feed them and be fertilised again, an endless process that he must for ever watch; for they were one with the soil of Crakenhill and so was he, his roots deep set in it: torn up, who knows, they might bleed to death.

Jessie came tripping up the hill, pink-cheeked and radiant: her eyes shone. Harry did not see her until she was at his side.

' Sweetheart,' she whispered in his ear.

His tongue cleaved to the roof of his mouth and he dared not look at her.

' Harry!' she cried in alarm. ' You look wholly pale. What's the matter?'

With great effort he found his voice.

' I can't take you to the circus, Jessie,' he said huskily, still gazing over the hurdles at the sheep. ' Do you let Jim Rivers take you.'

' Well, I don't mind not going, if you're not well, darling,' she said. ' I'll stay here.'

' You mustn't,' he said, looking at her dolefully.

' Why?' she gasped.

' 'Cause you mustn't,' he replied, ' and you can't come to-morrow night nor the night after neither.' His voice grew fainter and fainter.

' But tell me, Harry,' Jessie pleaded, putting her arm round his shoulders, ' darling, sweetheart.'

' Oh, don't ask me,' he cried desperately, breaking away from her and swinging his leg over the hurdle.

Jessie gazed at him for a moment incredulously and then walked away down the hill, her shoulders shaking with sobs. At the bottom of the hill she turned and looked behind her. Harry was hard at work with the folding iron setting out the hurdles for to-morrow's fold, as if it were all the world to him. Jessie leant upon the gate and buried her face in her hands.

If only the ewe had not bleated. . . .

XI

MRS. PEARMAN strolled slowly up to the gate of Bruisyard church and cast her eye round the churchyard. A few feet from the opposite wall a heap of fresh earth marked a newly-dug grave ; a tuneless bell chimed dismally in the little round tower, summoning the living to come and take leave of the dead. The mid-October sun struggled weakly between two masses of cloud and a rising wind shrilled viciously among the elm-tops, sweeping the speckled leaves away before it in angry gusts. Mrs. Pearman, shivering under it, walked up to the door of the church and peered inside ; George Grebe, the village carpenter, in his spare time sexton and parish clerk, was tolling the bell slowly and laboriously. Mrs. Pearman nodded curtly to him and sauntered back into the churchyard ; George Grebe did not belong to her circle and was no friend of hers ; secretly she was afraid of him, feeling that one day in the natural course of things he would have to dig her grave, being ten years her junior. She had a grudge against him, too, to-day, for starting to ring the bell so early and fetching her out on such a morning before anyone else had arrived ; a funeral, like a wedding or a christening, was a poor entertainment without someone to talk to. She pulled her coat tightly round her and, to keep warm, began to walk down the road towards the ford where the Alde stream, not yet a river, crosses the road. It was not worth while going back to the mill now, but she hoped the others would soon come.

A shabby little trap, drawn by a scraggy chestnut pony, came jogging round the corner and Mrs. Pearman, recognising the driver, heaved a sigh of relief. It was Betsy Barnes from Badingham, who made a precarious living by hawking tapes, buttons, stockings, mufflers and similar articles among the cottagers in the surrounding country. She was an ugly old woman, fat and red-faced, with

a large iron-grey moustache and she always wore men's
boots ; the children were all afraid of her and her deep
hoarse voice, yet she was welcome at almost every house she
visited, because she could often save a needy housewife a five
miles' journey into Framlingham and above all because,
being continuously on the road, she knew all the gossip
from Framlingham to Saxmundham. There was little news
that she missed and it was her best stock-in-trade. She
was an old friend of the miller's wife.

' Good morning, Mrs. Pearman,' she said, pulling the
pony up at the ford. ' What are you doing out on a cold
day like this ? '

' There's a funeral, Betsy,' replied Mrs. Pearman.
' Can't you hear the bell ? '

' Why so I can,' said Betsy, looking up at the church
tower. ' Who is it ? '

' Haven't you heard ? ' cried Mrs. Pearman in surprise. ' Why, it's Maria Cragg as went to keep house at
Crakenhill eight years ago.'

' Well I never ! ' exclaimed Betsy. ' And her only
two years older'n me and I'm sixty-six come November.
Still, she always fared wholly thin and poor. Her
sisters were all like her and they died young. Poor
Maria ! '

' Ah, Betsy,' said Mrs. Pearman, shaking her head,
' there's more in it than meet the eye. I warned her
about going up to that there bleak, damp place and
working for that owd villain, Benjamin Geaiter, and his
sons. " Maria," I say to her, " one day you'll be sorry
and that's the truth ".'

' Ah, that's right,' said Betsy. ' I've not been up there
since afore Mrs. Geaiter died and I could never sell 'em
a button or a pair of socks then. But how did Maria goo,
Mrs. Pearman ? '

' Very quick, very quick,' said Mrs. Pearman, shaking
her head again and clasping her hands on her breast.
' You remember how poor Mrs. Geaiter went, all sudden
like too, without any warning. The other night after she laid

the supper, she say, " I sorterly don't feel well. I think
I'll goo to bed." Next morning she couldn't get up and
there she lay and lay, getting paler and paler till at last
she went green and died. But a lovely corpse she made,
so Mrs. Dibber say, who laid her out. Skin as soft and
white as a baby's. You wouldn't have thought it to look
at her face. Something wrong with her inside, the doctor
say, but if you ask me, she was all wore up like poor Mrs.
Geaiter was. Who know what they did to her all alone
up there, poor body ? '

' Ah, who know ? ' echoed Betsy tragically.

' The first year she was up there,' continued Mrs. Pearman, ' she'd come down and have a chat with me of a
Sunday once in three months like. She didn't say much,
but you could tell, Betsy. But the last four years they
say she haven't left the house once. What can you expect,
Betsy, with a man who's—well, really a murderer, though
they tried to say he wasn't, and driv his wife into the
grave. I reckon he driv poor Maria there too. Poor
Maria ! ' Mrs. Pearman dabbed her eyes with her handkerchief.

' Ah, he's a wicked old man and no mistake,' said Betsy,
scratching her nose with a squat red finger. ' But how will
they make out now without her, Mrs. Pearman ? '

' Well,' replied Mrs. Pearman, ' Mr. Eves, who took
a letter up there yesterday, say that Hiram stay at home
to get the meals and make the beds, and a nice pickle the
house is in, I doubt.'

' Ah, that want a woman in the house,' said Betsy,
wiping her nose on the back of her hand. ' For real cleanli-
ness and comfort that do. But they 'on't allus go on like
that ? '

Mrs. Pearman pursed her lips in scorn.

' No, that they 'on't,' she snapped. ' I know for certain they're looking for a housekeeper. I had it from Mrs.
Spatchard, the blacksmith's wife ; and she said that
yesterday young Bob Geaiter came down with a pair
of horses to be shod and he asked her husband, Abe, if

he knew of a good widow woman, who'd go up and keep house for 'em, and Abe, he said the only body he knowed of was little Mrs. Thriddle and Bob said they'd ask her after the funeral. But I want to get hold of Mrs. Thriddle first and tell her a thing or two I heard from Maria. She's a nice little body, Mrs. Thriddle.'

'Ah, that she is,' said Betsy sympathetically. 'Such a nice-speaking woman too.' They had spent many hours together on Mrs. Thriddle's doorstep.

'Why, there she is,' cried Mrs. Pearman, looking over her shoulder towards the church. 'I must catch her afore the rest come. Are you coming to the funeral, Betsy ? ' she said, as she set off up the road.

'I can't leave the pony,' said Betsy with a sigh, ' though I do like to hear a funeral service well read. But I'll stop and see the hearse.'

She shook the reins and walked the pony through the ford and up the road behind Mrs. Pearman who, however, soon out-distanced her as she bore down upon Mrs. Thriddle. She stood by the church gate with a vaguely expectant air, a short, compact little woman, with a plump but narrow face and little brown slits of eyes surmounted by very high, thin eyebrows: her round wiry body, toughened by years of work, dairying, housewifery and child-bearing, looked capable of any endurance : her very skin looked tough—an admirable woman to be housekeeper on a farm : and yet she had a timid, wistful way with her as if she did not expect the world to be kind to her.

'Good morning, Mrs. Thriddle,' said Mrs. Pearman, a little patronisingly as befitted her superior station. 'So you've come to the funeral.'

'Yes,' replied Mrs. Thriddle. 'I allus like to see a funeral and I thought I might do a bit of business too.'

She broached the subject at once, being anxious to confide in Mrs. Pearman and ask her advice.

'Ah, yes, I heard something about that too,' said Mrs. Pearman. 'Abe Spatchard said old Geaiter was going to ask you to-day.'

' Yes, so he told me,' said Mrs. Thriddle a little nervously. ' What do you think about it, Mrs. Pearman ? '

' Well, I think you'd be most unwise, Mrs. Thriddle,' replied Mrs. Pearman very decidedly. ' You know how poor Mrs. Geaiter went, and now Maria after her. Do you want to be driv into the churchyard too ? '

' No, that I don't,' said Mrs. Thriddle, ' but you know, Mrs. Pearman, I'm a poor woman and it's not easy to make ends meet : and if only I could be sure of my food and a roof over my head—I know they're queer, but I've never heard nothing certain against them.'

The little woman had had a hard life since her husband died, taking in washing from Framlingham and going out to work by the day in any house that required her.

' Well, I know nothing certain,' said Mrs. Pearman, lowering her voice significantly, ' not what you might call certain ; but they do say he used to thrash poor Emily Geaiter and no one know what he did to Maria : she went off sudden, too.'

' Yes,' Mrs. Thriddle admitted, ' that may be, but they'd soon hear of it if they tried that on me. I know how to take care of myself, I do.' She fired up at the thought : she could be courageous enough when she liked. 'And I should be glad of the money too.'

Mrs. Pearman shook her head : she was sorry to see her so set on going to Crakenhill.

' Ah, Mrs. Thriddle,' she said, ' that isn't much money I know, 'cause poor Maria told me. All found and twelve pound a year. That isn't enough.'

' No, that don't fare much,' murmured Mrs. Thriddle thoughtfully.

' I should think not,' said Mrs. Pearman emphatically, moving a little further down the road to avoid the throng of villagers which was now beginning to gather round the gate. ' Not for all you'd have to put up with : and it isn't as if they can't afford it. I can't tell you how much my husband had to pay them for their wheat last year—sacks and sacks of it, Mrs. Thriddle. No, if I was you, I wouldn't take a penny less than twenty pounds. 'Tisn't worth your while else. And they'll have to give it you 'cause there's no one else in the parish to do for 'em.'

'No, that isn't much,' Mrs. Thriddle confessed.

'And for a woman that work like you, that's an insult,' added Mrs. Pearman.

'That is and no mistake,' said Mrs. Thriddle, firing up again. 'You're right, Mrs. Pearman. I'll have twenty pound out of them or they can look out for someone else. It's wholly good of you to put me up to it.'

'Ah, don't speak of it,' said the miller's wife. 'I'm glad to be able to help you : and I know a thing or two about that family. Why, here's the hearse. What a miserable little owd thing it is and not a flower on it—just like them, that.'

A little hand-bier with a large, bare coffin on it appeared below the ford, trundled by Ben and Bob and followed by Benjamin, Ern and Harry, Hiram having been left behind to look after the house, all of them clad in the ill-fitting and moth-eaten black that they had worn at Mrs. Geaiter's funeral. Harry was wearing Hiram's suit, but even that was far too small for him, for Hiram had only been sixteen when it was bought. Everyone stared at Benjamin, chiefly out of curiosity to see him for the second time in their lives without his corduroy trousers and sleeved corduroy waistcoat : and apart from that, Benjamin was always a striking figure whatever he wore. The big black beard was plentifully sprinkled with white now, but his chest, arms and shoulders were still as massive and tree-like as ever. But Benjamin walked on quite heedless of their stares. He showed no sign of grief because he felt none, but only annoyance at the loss of half a day's work and the trouble of finding a new housekeeper.

As the coffin turned into the churchyard, the villagers lined up behind it and followed it up to the door, where the four brothers took it on their shoulders to carry it into the church. All the women of the village, a good many children, and all the men who were not working for a master, were there, dressed in the customary rusty black which they kept for such occasions like a uniform. A funeral was not to be missed: it did not sadden them so much as fill them with unquiet awe, almost dread, of the unknown which they would sooner or later have to face themselves, whatever mask they assumed to cover their feelings, light-hearted cynicism, sentimental regret or moralising piety. Curiosity and a certain sense of loyalty impelled them to follow the dead as far as they could on its new journey, to see the last of it: one day the living would do the like for them.

'It do fare indecent,' whispered Mrs. Pearman to Mrs. Spatchard, the blacksmith's wife, as they left the church after the service and followed the coffin to the graveside. 'Not one of them answered the responses: they might have moved their lips for reverence' sake.'

'Ah, but what can you expect?' Mrs. Spatchard whispered back. 'This is the second time they've ever been in the church. Poor Mrs. Geaiter's funeral was the first. I know 'cause my daughter've been here every Sunday since they came to Crakenhill.'

'I wholly wonder the old man don't pull out his pipe,' added Mrs. Pearman sarcastically.

The ceremony over, the coffin lowered and the dust scattered, the throng began reluctantly to break up: no one came to cast flowers on the grave for all Maria's relatives had left the district. The vicar took Benjamin aside and expressed his regret that they should only meet on such distressing occasions. Maria, he hoped, was now at rest in a better place: it was the duty of those left behind to bear up and make the best of life. Benjamin ignored the implied rebuke.

'Thank you, mister,' he said shortly. 'We must get back to our stubbles. Good morning.'

His four sons made their way home at once, but Benjamin himself lingered among the crowd on the look-out for Mrs. Thriddle. He did not doubt to find her there: it was quite enough to mention the matter to the blacksmith's wife. No one spoke to him, but they all waited to watch him, knowing what he was waiting for too. At last he caught Mrs. Thriddle's eye and lumbered over to her.

' Want a word with you, Mrs. Thriddle,' he said.

' Yes, Mr. Geaiter ? ' she said, looking humbly up at him.

' Come you along here,' he said, leading her down the road to the little foot-bridge by the ford.

' I expect Mrs. Spatchard have told you,' he said. ' Would you come up to Crakenhill and keep house for us ? '

' Well, that depend, Mr. Geaiter,' she replied, a little hesitantly. ' What wages do you offer ? '

' Twelve pound a year and all found,' said Benjamin gruffly.

Mrs. Thriddle shook her head.

' I couldn't come under twenty pound,' she replied. Benjamin shook his head.

' Can't give you more'n twelve pound,' he said. 'A fair offer, that.'

' Couldn't do it for the money.' Mrs. Thriddle's voice was very firm. ' Mrs. Pearman say I oughtn't to do it for less.'

' Oh, do she ? ' said Benjamin. ' I see. Well, I can't offer you more. Good morning, Mrs. Thriddle.'

He turned and left her astonished on the bridge : she had been so sure of getting her twenty pounds, but now she wished she had been humbler, for she wanted to be housekeeper at Crakenhill. She walked slowly back to the now dwindling throng by the church gate and related to them what had happened.

' Quite right,' said Mrs. Pearman. ' That'll larn the old skinflint. He'll be back at your door soon enough and I reckon you can ask just what you like.'

' I admire your spirit, Mrs. Thriddle,' said Mrs. Spatchard.

For the moment Mrs. Thriddle felt her courage rise, but

when she was back in her cottage alone, her neighbours' praise seemed cold comfort and when she thought how bitter the winter there would be, she laid her head on the table and cried.

Benjamin meanwhile strode away up the hill to the farm, raging inwardly against Mrs. Pearman and every now and then swearing violently between his teeth. He remembered now how querulous Maria had been after her occasional visits to Mrs. Pearman during her first year at the farm and how later when she had settled down, she had dropped a sarcastic remark or two about Mrs. Pearman's tongue and the value of her words : he could see now which way the wind was blowing down at the mill. He did not care what she said about him, but it infuriated him to think that she should dare to meddle with his affairs. They badly needed a housekeeper at Crakenhill and he had counted on Mrs. Thriddle. For three days they had lived on cold bacon and jam and slept in beds as Hiram had made them : it could not go on much longer : there would soon be washing to do. For a moment he thought of meeting Mrs. Thriddle half-way, but that would be a victory for Mrs. Pearman and he spurned the idea at once. Crakenhill had survived worse than that : he would show them down in the village.

It was dinner time when he reached the farm and the brothers were all seated round the kitchen table. They looked up as he came in, but he sat down without saying anything. Hiram handed him a plate. Benjamin examined it critically.

' What's this ? ' he said, jabbing his fork into a piece of dark shrivelled-looking stuff.

' Bacon,' replied Hiram apologetically. ' I thought you'd like a hot dinner to-day for a change, but the fire was too fierce and burnt it. I boiled some 'taters too.'

' Oh, did you ? ' said Benjamin, holding up a pale green chunk on the end of his knife. ' They fare to me as if you'd just dug 'em up out of the garden. Where's the jam ? '

Bob pushed the jampot over to him and Benjamin

began to eat, clutching the arm of his elbow chair. He held up his hand and looked at it: it was black with dust.

' You ain't much of a housekeeper, Hiram.' he growled.

' No,' said Hiram, nervously scratching his fair moustache. ' Fare to me I'm better with a plough.'

' That's the truth,' said Benjamin.

' When's Mrs. Thriddle coming, father ? ' asked Ben.

' She ain't coming,' said Benjamin, looking up. ' She want too much. Oh, that remind me. We want some more pig food, don't we, Ern ? '

' Ay, we do,' said Ern.

' Well, Ben,' Benjamin went on, ' you'd better go into Badingham and get it this arternoon. We're not going to have any more from Pearman's. That woman's an interfering bitch.' He glared fiercely down the table.

' All right, father,' said Ben. ' But who's going to look after the house ? We can't go on like this.'

' No, we can't,' said Benjamin, knitting his brow. ' I don't know why Maria wanted to go off like that.'

' Nor do I,' said Bob in an aggrieved tone. ' She fared good for another ten year.'

' She was as strong as a man too,' added Ern, ' by the looks of her. A real good housekeeper she was. To go off like that! That wholly put you out.'

They all looked annoyed and resentful as if Maria by dying had played them a malicious trick.

' That do put you out,' said Benjamin, thoughtfully stroking his beard. ' Lookye here, Hiram, do you leave the house this arternoon and get on with that stubble o' yourn : it's no use wasting time, the weather may break any minute now. Young Harry, go you and catch the cob and put him in the trap. I'm going to Frannigan and I shan't come back till I've settled it.'

When the brothers came in again at five o'clock, they found Benjamin seated at the head of the table in his usual place, at the foot the new housekeeper, pouring out the tea, a girl of eighteen, tall and well-made, with dark brown hair and plump red cheeks. None of them had seen her arrive and they all stared at her as they sat down and she passed their cups along the table one by one. Benjamin sat steadily and contentedly munching with his eyes on his plate, but every now and then one of the brothers would turn his head and look wonderingly at the girl until their eyes met, and then look sheepishly away. Her cheeks were flushed with embarrassment and her hand trembled as she passed the cups to and fro, uncomfortably conscious of the surreptitious glances with which every movement that she made was being watched. The brothers too seemed equally embarrassed, afraid to look at her, yet unable to keep their eyes off her : the kettle on the hob sang aggressively in their ears and they shuffled in their seats. Benjamin alone seemed quite oblivious of any feeling of strain : the tea was hot and strong, the bread well buttered and the kitchen dusted: he felt that he had done his duty by the farm. Everyone else was relieved when the meal came to an end in the welcome clatter of knives and spoons and plates and the grinding of hobnails on the brick floor of the kitchen as the girl retired to the sink to wash up and the brothers walked out into the yard. Benjamin remained in his chair : he felt tired, the first time for many years : it was his sixty-fifth birthday.

While Harry and Ern went off to strew some fresh litter in the cowshed, Ben drew Bob and Hiram aside into the rickyard.

' Well, what d'ye think of it ? ' he said, leaning up against a brown clover rick and lighting his pipe.

' That's a rum 'un and no mistake,' said Bob, putting his hands in his pockets and staring vacantly over the paddock gate.

' I can't think what father have been doing,' Ben growled, ' to bring a young woman like that into the house. She's not our style, is she ? '

' No,' said Hiram, ' she ain't that. You want a full-grown woman to work proper like : there's a wonderful lot to do in that house.'

' Ah, yes,' said Bob, ' and you ought to know, Hiram.'

' And a young woman like that,' Hiram continued, ' she'll be always worrying about her looks and prinking herself. Now Maria, she was like a man, she knowed what to do in a farmhouse.'

' I wonder if she know how to do the milk ? ' said Ben.

' Or cook ? ' added Hiram. ' That's wonderful difficult too.'

' Ay,' said Bob, ' she must know that : and them milk pails are terrible heavy : she don't fare real strong : not like Maria, that is.'

' No,' said Ben, puffing hard at his pipe, ' she don't. Becourse we had to have someone, but still, I don't like it.'

' Nor I, neither,' said Bob.

Ben suddenly took his pipe out of his mouth and looked Hiram fixedly in the eyes.

' Now lookye here, Hiram,' he said slowly, ' I tell you what. We shall have to keep a sharp eye on young Harry with a girl like that in the house. It's only a year last June, you remember.'

' That we shall,' Bob agreed. Hiram bit his pipe stem hard and nodded sagely.

' I shan't forget seeing him through the hedge that time,' Bob went on, ' the silly young fool : and then I trod on a stick in the hedge and he start up and say, "Ah, that must have been the cob." I remember. We must watch him careful like.'

' That's true,' replied Ben, ' or with a young woman like that in the house, there'll be trouble, sure's this is a clover rick. A pity too : he fare to have settled down all right now, though he did take it hard at first. This may send him all wrong again.'

' Yes,' said Bob, ' he have an unsteady character : we must watch him.'

' That's right,' said Ben. ' We must, and hope for the

best. Well, come on now, boys, and let's have a look at that seed wheat for to-morrow.'

He turned away with a worried look ; the new house-keeper was still on his mind.

' I can't make father out,' he added, as they strolled over to the barn ' It fare to me he's getting old.'

XII

THE saddlery business which Josiah Hambling inherited from his father was reputed one of the oldest and most prosperous in Framlingham. Generation after generation of Hamblings had sat in his doorway, white-aproned and ample-bellied as saddlers should be, patching horse-collars and stitching saddles in the midst of a litter of cobbler's wax, saddle-soap, old harness and leather shavings : and there seemed no reason why Josiah, after himself reaching a ripe age like the other Hamblings, should not hand the business on to another generation. But it happened otherwise. His wife, an excellent, hale, cheerful woman, who had already borne him a daughter nine years before, died in giving birth to a son who did not survive her. Josiah was devoted to his wife and the blow struck him hard : he was already forty-five and he had no desire to marry again. Nancy, his little daughter, was sent away to be brought up in the family of his sister, a Mrs. Burbidge, who had married a baker in the town, since Josiah had resolved to live alone in his shop with nothing more than a day-woman to look after him. It was his intention that Nancy, when she was sixteen years old, should come back and keep house for him and he expressly asked his sister to do her best to make a good housewife of her and above all to teach her to cook : Josiah was fond of good living. He paid liberally for her keep and Mrs. Burbidge neglected nothing ; indeed, she fulfilled his request so zealously that almost from the beginning Nancy was little better than maid of all work to the baker's family. She cleaned the boots, she washed the linen, she scrubbed the floors, she learnt to cook. It was of little use to complain to her father : he merely laughed and told her it was all part of her training. All she could do was to hope for her sixteenth birthday, when she would gain her freedom and become mistress of her father's house.

One night, when only six months of her bondage re-

mained to go, Josiah slipped on the wet pavement as he
was leaving the inn where he generally spent his evenings,
and broke his thigh. It would not mend and before anyone
had realised how serious his condition was, pneumonia had
set in and he died. Even more surprising than his death
was the discovery that contrary to all expectation he had
nothing to leave behind him. Not only had he saved
nothing since his wife's death, but the considerable sums
that he must have inherited from his father had melted
away too. It emerged that he had been drinking more
than was good for him (some even ascribed his death to it)
and on the quiet had betted a good deal : but most of his
money had been frittered away in fraudulent investments
which a local solicitor had persuaded him to make. The
man was known to be a rogue, and after ruining several
other people, had absconded : but Josiah, for some reason
or other, had never made his loss public. From that time
onwards he had drunk harder and neglected his business
more and more—to such an extent that after his death
the moneys produced by the sale of his shop and goodwill
were more than swallowed up by outstanding debts and
Nancy, instead of being comfortably off as she might
reasonably have hoped, found herself penniless and an
orphan. As there was no other relative to take her in, she
remained with her aunt, the baker's wife, and became
maid of all work now in earnest. No drudge ever had to
work so hard for her keep and no matron ever had a
cheaper maid, for the baker's wife, feeling that it was an
act of charity to take her in at all, paid her no wages.
There was no doubt now of Nancy's becoming a good
housewife : she did everything there was to be done in the
house, from the dirtiest work in the yard to the cooking
of the Sunday dinner and the embroidering of the pillow-
cases. She got no thanks for all she did and more often
than not harsh words and scanty food. It was a hard life,
with little rest and no pleasure, and although Nancy grew
up into a strong, handsome girl, there was a suffering,
hunted look about her eyes. She often thought of running

away to service elsewhere: she would be valuable in any household: but in the hands of her uncle and aunt she was powerless: they were her guardians. She still dreamed of running away, however, although she had no idea where to run.

Such thoughts were passing in her mind one chill October afternoon some two years after her father's death as she squatted on her knees in front of the bakery door, scrubbing the steps that led down into the shop, with her sleeves rolled up above the elbow. The cold weather was just beginning and she had six months and more of icy water and red chapped hands to look forward to, cold nights on a hard bed and bleak frosty mornings laying fires with numbed fingers: how she would repay anyone who would give her a little comfort, be kind to her or only take her away from her uncle and aunt: how she hated them! She brought her hearthstone down on the steps with a crash that echoed across the street. A big, broad-shouldered man with a bushy, grizzled beard, who was passing on the other side, turned his head at the sound and stopped to gaze at her strong white arms. They slapped and pounded like flails with cloth and hearthstone, venting upon the steps all the ineffectual, rebellious hatred she cherished against her oppressors. He did not look at her face, her hair or her bosom as a younger man might have done, but only at her arms: they seemed to fascinate him, so much so that at last he walked across the street to the bakery steps and stood there for a moment, a yard away from her, still staring at her arms. Nancy looked up defiantly: yet another indignity, to be the gazing-stock of strangers while she worked. He was speaking to her now.

' Look here, young woman,' he said, ' I want a housekeeper on my farm.'

She struggled to her feet and wiped her hands on her sack apron. He took in her broad shoulders and sturdy white neck with an approving eye: she was almost as tall as he was.

' Six of us,' he went on, ' me and my five sons: we all

live together out Bruisyard way : we farm two hundred acres and we want someone to do for us. You fare as if you can work, young woman. Would you come ? Eleven pounds a year and all found.'

Nancy could hardly believe her ears : the blood raced through her veins all a-tingle with excitement and her head whirled. A chance of escape at last, a farm of two hundred acres and eleven pounds a year, real wages : six men, too, instead of a nagging woman. She could hardly find words to answer.

' I'd wholly like to,' she managed to blurt out at last, quite breathlessly.

' My name's Geaiter,' said the man, ' and I want you at once. I've got my horse and cart in the town and I'll drive you out this arternoon.'

Nancy puckered her brows in a troubled look.

' I don't know what my aunt will say,' she faltered. ' You see, I'm only eighteen. Why, here she is.'

' Oh,' said Benjamin.

The baker's wife, attracted by the sound of voices, had come into the shop to see why Nancy was wasting her time. The girl stood aside to let her pass.

' Good afternoon, sir,' she said, as soon as she perceived Benjamin in the doorway. ' What can I do for you ? '

' Arternoon, ma'am,' said Benjamin. ' I want this young woman to come along o' me and keep house for us at Bruisyard. Geaiter of Crakenhill : p'r'aps you know the name.'

' Ah, that I do,' said Mrs. Burbidge. Everyone in Framlingham did, and in Saxmundham too.

' Well, what about it ? ' said Benjamin bluntly.

Mrs. Burbidge put her finger to her lip and thought hard : it was awkward to be taken by surprise like this.

' We should be that sorry to lose her,' she said slowly, to gain time, ' but I must go and ask my husband about it first.'

She retired into the kitchen and held a hurried conversation with the baker, leaving Nancy alone with Benjamin in the shop. He ran his eye over all the loaves, the cakes and buns in their glass jars one by one and then over Nancy from head to toe, carefully taking in all her points after the way of a man used to judging stock. There was a little anxiety, too, in his glance : she was just the girl for him and he wanted her badly. Nancy, hardly noticing him in her own anxiety, nervously watched the kitchen door for her aunt to reappear, quivering with sudden, tumultuous hopes : the whole of life seemed to depend upon their fulfilment. She never knew all that went on behind the door during the ten minutes her uncle and aunt took to confer together : how they balanced the value of her services against the cost of her food and clothes, the money that her bedroom would bring in if let to a lodger, and the advantage of having her off their hands. The issue was close and in the end it was only the bad times on which the bakery trade had fallen that decided them : it seemed worth their while, after all, to save whatever money they could and a servant was not a necessity to them : it was best that she should go. They even hoped that she might some day be of use to them in the service of a warm man like Benjamin Geaiter, blind to her burning desire to cut herself loose from them and their house for good. Mrs. Burbidge came back into the shop at last, followed by her husband, both with very serious countenances.

' Well ? ' said Benjamin, looking up.

' We both of us think, Mr. Geaiter,' she replied, rather mournfully, ' that we oughtn't to stand in the girl's light if she have a chance of bettering herself. Of course, we shall miss her terrible, but we know she'll be in good hands.'

' Ay, we'll look after her all right,' said Benjamin gruffly.

Nancy could hardly keep her tears back for joy, marvelling at her own good fortune and still half-dreading that it might vanish like a dream.

' I'll bring the cart round in five minutes,' said Benjamin, ' and then we can get back afore tea-time. Good arternoon, ma'am.'

It did not take Nancy long to bundle her scanty belongings together and in less than half an hour she was bowling along the Bruisyard road at Benjamin's side.

Nancy had no clear notion what life with the Geaiters, or indeed life on any farm at all, would be like : but of one thing she was sure, that, whatever it was, it could not be worse than what she had had to put up with in her aunt's house : any change from that must be for the better. She soon recovered from her first nervousness, natural enough to a girl of her age, or anyone for that matter, in a strange house for the first time : but at the end of a week she began seriously to wonder if the change had been for the better after all. The house was certainly in a bad way when she arrived, four days after Maria's death, and it took her a whole week to make it clean and tidy again to her own satisfaction—almost another spring-cleaning : and apart from this, each day brought a round of tasks that kept her hands full from morning till night. There were seven beds to make, seven breakfasts, dinners, teas and suppers to get ready, the milk to cool and the milk-pans to scour, the chickens to feed, and a score of other things besides. But she was used to such work and ought to have found it simple enough. What really troubled her was the atmosphere of the place. She had been conscious of it the first day she entered the house. These six big, silent men who sat down with her four times a day to meals were beyond her comprehension. They seldom spoke to one another and hardly ever to her, taking whatever she passed to them without a please or a thank you : and yet they were continually looking at her strangely as if they suspected her and disapproved of her. Benjamin alone paid no attention to her : but he, too, said nothing to her. She herself was afraid to speak and yet sometimes she longed so much for someone to speak to her that she could have screamed. She was humble and willing and anxious to please : she could not fathom it. But it was not only at meals that she suffered. Even when she was alone in the house, and that was for the greater part of the day, she was still aware of the same atmosphere, the same sense of oppression. It seemed as if the whole place were full of hostile, critical eyes that jealously watched each thing she did and counted each minute she wasted : the bare silent rooms chilled and frightened her as if they were haunted, and each morning her work seemed such a burden that she would never be able to last through the day. Several times she caught herself longing for the bakery kitchen in spite of all the hardship and humiliation it had meant, and even for the rasping, censorious voice of her aunt, for whom nothing that she did could be right : but at least she had told her so. Nancy felt that she would soon go mad and each night she cried herself to sleep for sheer misery.

As her second week at Crakenhill drew to a close, the weather broke and for two days the rain poured down relentlessly. The farmyard and the drift became a quagmire and it was hard to keep the kitchen clean with six pairs of feet continually bringing in fresh mud from outside, however much Nancy scrubbed. Her depression deepened.

On Saturday evening Harry, who had been at work among the sheep, came blundering into the kitchen with the folding-iron on his shoulder. He dropped it with a clatter in a corner, sending flecks of mud and fresh earth all over the floor, and went over to the sink to wash his hands. When he had dried them, he leant up against the wall to take off his boots, and his shoulder, still sticky with mud from the folding-iron, left a long, dirty brown streak on the roller-towel he had just used. Without noticing what he had done, he picked up his boots and having left them in the fireplace to dry, sat down opposite Nancy, who was darning socks. She looked up, hoping he might speak to her : he was better-looking than his brothers and she felt he must be different. But Harry said nothing, knowing too well already that the others were watching his behaviour : moreover, Bob was seated by the fire between himself and Nancy; he had failed to find anything

to occupy his hands that wet evening, else he would not have
been there. As Harry settled down with his pipe and began
to stare into the fire, Nancy fetched a sigh and looked
slowly round the room, from the fireplace to the sink.
The mud stain on the towel caught her eye and offended
her at once. She kept on looking up at it for the next five
minutes while she darned her socks, and then, unable to
rest any longer, she went over to the linen drawers in the
old bureau at the end of the room, took out a clean towel
and put it up in place of the dirty one, which she tossed
into an empty clothes-basket. That done, she resumed
her place by the fire and went on with her darning. Five
minutes later Ben came in, shaking the rain off his clothes.
He, too, stopped by the sink to take off his boots. He
stared at the clean towel for a moment and then turned
round towards the fire.

' Oh, Nancy,' he said abruptly, ' Maria never used to
change that towel till Sunday morning.'

' Yes, I see,' said Nancy faintly, looking up at him.

She bent to her darning again more assiduously than
ever as Ben too came and sat down by the fire, but her
thoughts were busy. There was no anger in Ben's voice :
he had not told her not to change the towel on Saturday
night—and in truth it made no difference whether it was
changed then or on Sunday morning : he had merely
intimated that Maria had done otherwise and therefore it
was better. Nancy remembered how when she had asked
where various household utensils were to be found, or
when they wanted their meals, they had replied, ' Maria
kept it here,' or ' Maria laid the table at such a time.'
Maria this, Maria that—it was obvious to her now that in
everything she did they were comparing her with Maria
and judging her according to the resemblance : that was
the cause of their hostility. But yet, such traces as Maria
had left behind her gave no indication of a high standard
of housekeeping, certainly not so high as she herself had
been accustomed to in her aunt's house. If she could not
do as well as Maria—— Her course now became plain :

she set her teeth and took heart again ; they should see what she could do.

The next morning the whole house seemed different, its size no longer oppressed her ; she even felt proud to have so large a place to manage. Already it was as clean and tidy as she could make it, but she could see nevertheless that it would repay a little care and thought : it wanted brightening up. There was no reason why she should not devote herself to the house in the same way as the others were devoted to the land : even she had already noticed that. This devotion was now almost a tradition in the family, a tradition created by Benjamin Geaiter : he himself was its slave, Maria, his sons and now Nancy, had all succumbed to it. Nancy's spirits rose at the idea : it was something worth doing for its own sake.

When the family sat down to dinner that Sunday they found a vase of flowers, faded marigolds and chrysanthemums, on the middle of the table. They looked first at the vase and then at one another.

' Where did them things come from ? ' asked Benjamin.

' I found 'em in the garden,' replied Nancy a little timidly from the fireplace where she was busy with the oven.

Benjamin snorted contemptuously, but said no more. He could hardly complain at her taking liberties with the few flowers which still struggled in the grass-grown patch of ground against the house which had once been a garden : neither he nor any of his sons had ever done a hand's turn in it. Nancy's lip quivered, but she did not look up. A moment later she staggered to the table with an enormous pie and a dish of potato cakes. They all stared at her as she began to carve the pie with a shaking hand.

' What's in there ? ' growled Benjamin.

' The two rabbits,' Nancy replied, ' that Harry shot yesterday.'

' Oh,' said Benjamin, taking the plate she had passed up the table to him. ' And what's this other stuff ? '

' They're potato cakes,' said Nancy. ' They should be nice.'

' I've never seen potatoes as looked like that before,' grunted Benjamin, toying nervously with his fork.

Nancy wanted to cry, but she restrained herself and went on serving out the pie. The others all looked suspiciously at their plates and toyed with their forks as Benjamin had done until at last the smell of the gravy somehow found its way into their nostrils and they began to eat. Nancy, who had not much appetite herself, watched them out of the corner of her eye. Rabbit, pie-crust and potato cakes were disappearing faster and faster: they no longer had time or inclination to stare at her. It was not for nothing that she had learnt to make pastry in her uncle's bakehouse. Benjamin dropped his knife and fork on to his empty plate and held it out.

' I'd like some more,' he said.

Nancy flushed as she ladled him out another helping. As soon as it reached the end of the table, Hiram passed up his plate: in five minutes the pie-dish was empty. She followed it with a vast dish of apple dumplings, frail, white and sugary, the apples inside cooked to a creamy froth. No one asked any questions this time, but they went on eating steadily with an occasional wondering glance at Nancy until the dish was empty: such pastry had never been seen on the table at Crakenhill before. Replete and contented, they pushed their chairs back from the table and lighted their pipes.

' That must have cost a wonderful lot,' said Hiram at length, while Nancy was still finishing her second dumpling.

' Ay,' said Ben.

That was what they all felt. Benjamin looked up at Nancy, obviously expecting her to explain herself.

' Well,' she said in a hesitating voice, ' it all come off the place, and that's the truth. Harry shot the rabbits, I found the herbs for the stuffing in the garden under the window, and the apples were up in the stillroom.'

' Oh,' said Benjamin. He paused to press the tobacco

into the bowl of his pipe with his thumb. Nancy waited in suspense for him to finish with some word of praise or thanks. ' Maria never used to touch them apples till Christmas,' he said with a grunt.

' No,' said Ben, ' she didn't.'

Nancy looked round the table for a sympathetic face; but they all appeared equally stolid and hostile—except perhaps Harry, and he was staring vacantly at the bread-knife. Nancy got up wearily from her seat and began to gather the dirty plates together. All the heart had gone out of her and when she went to the sink to wash up, her tears overcame her altogether and she wept outright. But there was no one there to see her.

In spite of this initial discouragement, however, Nancy did not abandon her plan. For one thing, she was naturally fond of cooking, with something of an artist's pride in her handiwork, and it kept her from brooding over her own unhappiness. Moreover, the doggedness which had enabled her to survive and grow up strong and healthy in spite of all she had suffered in her aunt's household, began at last to reassert itself: and at bottom she had a good deal of faith in her own capabilities. For a week she continued to feed the Geaiter family as they had never been fed before. There had always been abundance of good coarse food in the house both in Maria's and in Mrs. Geaiter's time; but Nancy's cooking belonged to another order altogether: nothing so ambitious had ever been attempted in the kitchen before. Each morning she gave them something different for breakfast—baked eggs, potato cake, fried bread, toasted cheese: it was wonderful what she could turn out of a frying-pan with the help of an egg, a few breadcrumbs and odds and ends of meat and vegetables left over from yesterday's dinner. The joint which she cooked at the beginning of the week reappeared in four different forms before it was finished, as stew, as pasty, as shepherd's pie, and finally as meat-balls for breakfast: and only twice during the whole week were the potatoes cooked in the same way. Each day there was a different

pudding or fritters or jam tarts, and on Friday, which was
bake-day, she made them a huge batch of little yellow
cakes, delicately spiced and flavoured with candied peel;
she served them hot and crisp at tea-time and they were
all devoured without a word to the last one. No one less
taciturn than the Geaiters could have refrained from
saying that they melted in the mouth. For supper there
was a fresh cream cheese which she had made from half a
gallon of milk left behind one morning after Ern had
returned from the station a churn short the day before.
All the dainties which she had learnt to make for the
benefit of the portly saddler, her father, she lavished upon
them, and they were all solidly and silently consumed: but
the family made no sign of pleasure or of gratitude.

It was Saturday morning when she gave them meat-
balls for breakfast, juicy, tender and cunningly seasoned
with herbs. Benjamin was still out in the stable examining
a horse that was thought to have glanders. Ben at the end
of the table, next to his father's place, stuck his fork into
one of them and looked at it scornfully.

' What's this stuff ? ' he said.

' Meat-balls,' replied Nancy, a little curtly. She was
rather tired of his ponderous, authoritative air : he expected to be taken too seriously. ' Don't be afraid of 'em,
there's plenty more in the frying-pan.'

' H'm,' Ben grunted, ' Maria allus used to give us bacon
for breakfast every morning.'

Nancy's cheeks went white and she bit her lip ; she was
very near losing her temper.

' Well, bacon you shall have to-morrow morning,' she
replied tartly, walking away down the dairy steps in a huff.

The brothers looked up at her in surprise.

' My ! ' said Ben. ' What a tongue she've got on her ! '

' And no mistake,' said Ern, with his mouth full.

They proceeded to finish the meat-balls.

The next morning there was bacon for breakfast and
for six mornings after : on two of them it was cold. The
joint which she roasted on Sunday was served up each day

until the bone was bare—cold, twice with chilly, blue boiled potatoes, and twice with nothing but pickles : there followed boiled rice or suet-pudding made in quantity at the beginning of the week and warmed up each day ; no more dumplings, no cakes on Friday—Nancy herself was so cold and distant that even the brothers noticed it : she felt afraid of nobody now.

' I wonder what's come over Nancy,' said Bob on Friday night after a lifeless supper of bread and very stale cheese. ' She's all hard and haughty like.'

' I can't tell,' said Hiram. ' Fare to me she's not well.'

The thought of the good things they had tasted for one short week made them lick their lips, but they said nothing about it to each other. Then Saturday came and Hiram grew desperate. He took a gun with him when he went to plough that morning : he was glad Bob was not working with him to see how much time he wasted. He came back to dinner earlier than the others and slipped into the kitchen unobserved. Nancy was laying the table. He sidled up to her a little sheepishly.

' Oh, Nancy,' he said.

' Well ? ' she replied coldly.

' I've got something might do for to-morrow's dinner,' he said, holding up a hare by its hind legs.

Nancy took it from him and smiled—just a little triumphantly.

' That would do well to jug,' she said.

' P'r'aps, p'r'aps,' Hiram stammered—painfully, but it was worth it—' we could have some of them potatoes again.'

' H'm, well, we'll see,' said Nancy non-committally.

' And some of them dumplings too,' added Hiram timidly, scratching his little fair moustache that never seemed to grow any bigger.

' Well, that depend,' Nancy replied, her lips curling into a smile again. ' I'll have to see what I can do.'

Hiram sidled out again and Nancy carried the hare into the larder, laughing softly to herself.

Ten minutes later Hiram came in again with the rest and they all sat down to a bleak meal of pressed beef and mashed potatoes. Benjamin looked down a little wearily at his plate : he had eaten a good deal of pressed beef in his time and once more would not hurt him : it was good, wholesome food. He sighed and looked up at Nancy.

' Can't you let us have some more of that stuff you gave us for breakfast, Nance ? ' he said.

Nance : there was nothing affectionate about it, but the mere familiarity made something within her dance. She artfully passed her hand across her brow with a harassed look ; they must learn that she was not to be trifled with.

' Well, p'r'aps I can,' she said slowly. ' I'll see what can be done.'

' Yes, do,' said Benjamin. ' I don't know what it was called, but that was good, that was.'

' And that's the truth,' said Hiram. Bob nodded.

XIII

A MONTH passed and the November gloom deepened: the skies were greyer than ever, the bare elm trees on distant landscapes grew blacker and colder and the grass became colourless and sodden. Nancy, casting her eye around the farm kitchen one dismal afternoon, while she waited for her irons to heat, thought how dull and shabby it looked. Everything was spick and span, all the pots and pans in their places, the windows and the brick floor spotless. But there were limits to her powers : she could not make a dead room live, and the room was dead. She looked at the drab horse-hair sofa, the torn patchwork hearthrug and bare mantelpiece, the unrelieved white china, the ragged white lace curtains ; some new curtains would make a world of difference, but she did not know where to get the stuff. She had rummaged in all the drawers upstairs, but they seemed to contain nothing but moth-eaten corduroys and flannel shirts ; if she had had the opportunity of going into Framlingham or Saxmundham, she might almost have bought the stuff herself; but no one had paid her any wages yet. There was no remedy and yet it seemed a pity, for she had already done much to civilise the house. Her cooking had worked wonders. There was no doubt now of her being accepted by the family : they did not express their gratitude, but she knew that they were grateful because they were content to feed well and ask no questions. The old atmosphere of distrust to which at first she had been so sensitive seemed to have lifted and they even began to talk to her a little. She had to speak to someone : even at Framlingham she had always been able to exchange a word or two during the day with some passing errand-boy or tradesman or customer, and her aunt's voice was always in her ears. She would ask Harry about the sheep, Ern about the cows, Bob and Hiram about people in the village : they could not tell her much, but they did answer her questions and that led them to talk among themselves. Sometimes she managed to draw even Benjamin out to tell her something of the earlier history of the farm in his time : he was not eloquent, but he did not discourage her. Ben alone seemed to remain hostile : he never looked her squarely in the face as the others did now, but with the same furtive glances that he had cast at her the first day she arrived. Nancy felt that he still regretted Maria and she in her turn had not forgotten the meat-balls or the roller-towel. However, Ben's hostility was no longer any burden to her ; what sat upon her mind now was the untidy kitchen window. Nothing could make those tattered lace curtains look tidy and they were too far gone to mend; but it was no use worrying, she would have to forget them.

She went over to the fireplace and knelt down to see if her irons were hot. A knock at the door brought her to her feet at once: visitors were too scarce at Crakenhill to be neglected. Only chance people came there, like the postman (Jessie Eves had changed rounds with her father for obvious reasons), the tax-collector or a farmer on the look-out for a deal. Ern brought all the meat and groceries back from Saxmundham in the milk-float and there were no tradesmen to call. Nancy opened the door.

' Good arternoon, young woman.'

It was Betsy Barnes who had driven all the way up the drift, not so much in the hope of doing business at the farm as of finding out something about the new housekeeper. Mrs. Pearman had put the idea into her head, having heard from the postman that she was only ' a bit of a girl.' Betsy had seen Nancy in Framlingham many times and recognised her at once : she knew her whole history better than the girl herself. She, too, was a familiar figure to Nancy, but they had never spoken together before.

' Well, young woman,' Betsy croaked, ' and how are you getting on ? '

' Very nicely, thank you,' replied Nancy, a little awk-wardly : these few weeks at Crakenhill had already made her somewhat shy with strangers.

' Oh, I'm glad to hear that,' said Betsy incredulously, putting a foot on the doorstep and poking her face into the room. ' Do they drive you hard ? '

' Oh, not so bad,' said Nancy, shrugging her shoulders. ' That keep me busy.'

' So I see,' said Betsy, pointing to the ironing board on the table. She leant up against the doorpost and assumed a confidential air. ' They're a rough owd lot, aren't they ? '

Nancy's eyes opened wide. These were her men, they belonged to her house : she was not going to hear them run down.

' Not that I've noticed,' she replied, visibly bridling.

' Oh ? ' said Betsy in a tone of surprise. ' Why I thought they treated you dreadful bad.'

' Well, they don't,' snapped Nancy. ' They're a real good, steady family, and Mr. Geaiter's wholly kind to me.'

' Oh, is he now ? ' sneered Betsy. ' So he may be. But I could tell you a thing or two about him. Poor Mrs. Geaiter, poor Maria Cragg ! '

' Well, I don't want to hear it,' said Nancy emphatically, ' none of it. And what have you come here for, anyway ? '

' Now then, young woman,' said Betsy as soothingly as her hoarse voice would allow, ' that ain't the way to talk to an old woman fit to be your grandmother. I only wanted to give you a little advice.'

' Well, I don't want any,' said Nancy, preparing to shut the door in her face, ' if that's all you've come for.'

Betsy slung her basket round on to the threshold to prevent the door from closing.

' I suppose now you've set up as housekeeper,' she replied sarcastically, ' you're too proud to buy anything from a poor old body like me.'

Nancy was on the point of making an angry retort when something in the basket caught her eye and the words died on her lips.

' What's that ? ' she said, putting her finger on a roll of stuff.

' Cotton print, my gal,' replied Betsy, taking it out and

holding it up. ' Make a pretty frock, that would, or a nice pair of curtains.'

' That wholly would,' said Nancy, taking it from her and examining it. It was white with a border of large blue checks. ' How much ? '

' Ninepence a yard,' said Betsy, pursing her lips and putting her head on one side. ' That's right cheap : that's wholly wide.'

' That is,' said Nancy slowly, biting her lip.

She was thinking hard : four yards would do for both the kitchen windows ; it was a good chance, but she had no money.

' Well, my gal? ' said Betsy impatiently ; she was not going to wait for a young hoity-toity like that.

' Ah, I know! ' exclaimed Nancy, more to herself than Betsy. Ern had taken in a basket of eggs to the grocer's that morning with the milk and the money had been left in the old bureau at the end of the kitchen. There was more than enough to buy the stuff and it was for the house after all.

' What's that ? ' said Betsy.

' Nothing,' replied Nancy curtly. ' I'll take four yards. You can come in and measure it off on the table,' she added graciously, consumed all at once with a desire to show off her spotless kitchen.

Betsy's manner improved at once : it had been worth while coming up here after all. She stepped into the kitchen, laid the stuff on the table and cut off the length Nancy wanted.

' There,' she said, as Nancy put the money in her hand, ' I've given you an extra three inches. I allus like to be generous.' She could well afford to be, having put the price up especially for Nancy's benefit. ' How nice and clean your kitchen look : that's real smart, that is.'

Nancy beamed with pride : the old woman was not so bad perhaps—apart from her foibles.

' Do you think so ? ' she said.

' That I do,' said Betsy. ' It's wholly fine for a gal like you. Why, Maria could hardly have done it better.'

' Oh, couldn't she? ' said Nancy with a sniff. ' I see. Well, there's nothing more I want this afternoon, thank you. I've got some work to do.'

Betsy took her roll of stuff and hobbled out of the room, cackling to herself. Then having picked up her basket, she thrust her ugly red face back into the doorway and shook her finger.

' Do you look out, my gal,' she said, with a knowing laugh, ' them blokes don't go running after your skirts.'

Nancy slammed the door hard behind her in a pet, but the stuff on the table soon made her forget her annoyance : it was just what she wanted. She carefully carried it upstairs to her bedroom ; no one should see it until the curtains were made and hanging in the windows—a surprise for them. After tea she spent the greater part of the evening feverishly at work on them in her room, and only two hems remained to do when she came down to lay the supper. The next morning she had to make the time to finish them : the dairy could wait till the afternoon for its scrubbing. Half an hour before dinner they were done, and with trembling fingers she slipped them on to the rods in the window frames. She clapped her hands with delight : the kitchen looked another place altogether, bright, smart and dainty. She could not have wished for better ; but the old hearthrug now looked shabbier than ever.

She was as excited as a child giving its first present when the men came in to dinner, and though she was busy at the stove, she could not help looking over her shoulder to see what effect the new curtains had on them. They had already noticed them from outside and each of them in turn, as he came in, stopped and stared at the window. Harry nodded appreciatively to her and she rewarded him with a smile. She looked pretty when she smiled, Harry thought, almost like Jessie. Benjamin came in last and went over to the window to feel the stuff with his fingers.

' Where'd this come from ? ' he grunted.

' I bought it yesterday of Betsy Barnes,' said Nancy, getting up from the stove and turning round. ' We wholly needed 'em. Those others were all to rags and that stuff only cost three shillings.'

' Ah! ' said Benjamin. ' Where'd you get the money ? '

' I took it out of the egg money in the desk,' she said boldly. ' We wholly needed 'em.'

Benjamin put his hands on his hips and thrust out his chin.

' Now look here, my gal,' he said very gruffly, ' we can't have you spending the farm money on fal-lals like that : we can't afford 'em and we must do without 'em.'

' Ay, that's the truth,' put in Ben, looking up from the table. ' We can't afford that sort of thing.'

' Well, it's got to stop,' said Benjamin. ' D'ye hear, my gal ? '

' Yes, I do,' replied Nancy sulkily : she did not want to cry this time ' But I'll buy them curtains for you out of my own money,' she added defiantly, '—when you pay me my wages.'

Benjamin looked at her strangely for a moment, a little startled by her sharp answer, then walked to his chair and dropped heavily into it, while Nancy went on with her dishing up, already meditating a plan of revenge.

The next day being bake-day, there was a loaf of new bread on the table when they came in to tea and a large plate of stale bread and butter.

' Where's the jam ? ' said Bob, helping himself to a slice.

' Oh, I didn't put it out to-day,' said Nancy casually, from behind the teapot.

Bob said nothing in reply, but went on with his slice of stale bread and butter, not having the courage to get up and fetch the jam for himself. Hiram and Ben looked wonderingly at Nancy, but she paid no attention to them : there was a distinct tension in the air. Benjamin, after manfully eating three slices of the same bread and butter, peered round the table and then looked up at Nancy.

' Haven't you made any cakes to-day, Nance ? ' he said.
' It's bake-day, isn't it ? '

' No, I haven't,' replied Nancy haughtily. ' It fare to
me we can't afford it.'

' Ah ! ' exclaimed Benjamin. He scratched his head and
thought. ' Lookye here, Nance,' he said, a minute after,
' don't you bother whether we can afford it or not. You
know we like them cakes of yourn ; so you can go on
making 'em '

' Oh, can I ? ' said Nancy, still on her dignity.

' And,' continued Benjamin, ' you needn't worry your
head about paying for them curtains. They do look wholly
nice and smarten the place up.'

Nancy thrilled all over with pride and triumph.

' All right,' she said. ' I'll see what I can do before
supper The oven's still hot. Ah, I've forgotten the jam.'
Her eyes twinkled. ' We shall be wanting a new hearthrug
soon.'

.   .   .

Autumn wore into winter and the new year came in
with a heavy fall of snow. Nancy sat on the sofa in front
of a sparkling fire, watching the snowflakes sifting down
outside while she waited for the men to come in to tea.
She had never felt so contented in her life : every corner
of the kitchen, of the whole house for that matter, bore her
stamp. Upon the mantelpiece stood the new art calendar
she had bought with her own money at Christmas, adorned
with holly berries and a picture of a flock of sheep in the
snow. Under her feet lay the new hearthrug which Benjamin had let her go into Framlingham to choose. On the
dresser hung the gay blue tea pot with which she had re-
placed the old cracked brown thing she had had to make
shift with so long. Over on the window the bright check
print curtains—those curtains ! She smiled to herself as
she looked out over them on to the dirty white trampled
morass which the farmyard had become : it was ankle deep
in slushy snow. She instinctively thought of the clean

yellow bricks on her kitchen floor. She had scrubbed them twice already that day : after tea they would have to be done a third time. She got up suddenly and went to the door. The men had been carting faggots all day and were just bringing the horses back to the stable. She opened the door

'Hiram!' she shouted.

Hiram slung the halter rope on which he was leading his team into Bob's hand and came running over to her across the snow.

'Yes, Nancy?' he said breathlessly.

'Get me a couple of sacks, Hiram,' she said. 'There's a good chap.'

While he ran back across the yard, Nancy took a bass broom and stood it up against the wall by the door. When Hiram came back with the sacks, she spread them carefully over the doorstep.

'There,' she said. 'You know what that's for, don't you?'

Hiram grinned.

'I expect I do,' he said

'What's more,' she cried after him, as he went off to his horses again, 'they're going to stay there for the rest of the winter. I reckon I've scrubbed that floor enough.'

She retired into the kitchen and began to make the tea. Hiram was the first to come in : he carefully cleaned his boots with the broom and wiped them scrupulously on the sacks. Ben and Bob followed and then Ern and Harry : they all did the same. Nancy, who had been watching them with a smile of approval, sat down to pour out the tea. Five minutes later Benjamin, who had been trimming the paddock hedge, came in stamping the snow off his boots.

'Hi, father!' shouted Ben from the table, 'haven't you seen the broom?'

'What broom?' said Benjamin.

'Why the broom outside the door and the sacks what Nancy put for your feet,' Ben replied. 'Can't you see?'

'Ah, so I do,' said Benjamin. 'Don't you worry.'

He went outside again and began to clean his boots. For the first time since she had been at Crakenhill Nancy's heart warmed towards Ben, not, however, without a certain feeling of triumph: she was really mistress of the house at last.

XIV

SUNDAY at Crakenhill, like other days, had its routine in spite of the general spirit of relaxation that prevailed everywhere. In the morning, when the horses had been groomed and baited, the cows milked and the stock fed, the whole family continued to potter about the farm looking for odd jobs. There was nearly always something to be done : harness to mend, chaff to cut, implements to oil, a gate-post to sink : and it was the only day of the week that a spade was ever put into the vegetable garden. They were no respecters of the sabbath, the Geaiters : and on two occasions Benjamin had scandalized the village by carting wheat on a Sunday morning to save it from an impending thunderstorm. In the afternoon, however, like any other farmers in the parish, they followed the country tradition and made a perambulation of the whole farm, sometimes in a body, sometimes in twos and threes, to see how their crops grew and decide what would have to be done in the coming week, besides finding out how their neighbours' fields compared with their own. But since Nancy's installation as housekeeper, although they had made no change in their habits, there was a subtle difference in the Sunday atmosphere. In the morning, however busily they were occupied, the time seemed to drag on them with infinite slowness, as if the dinner hour would never come, and they were continually looking at their watches. The food was certainly nothing to grumble at during the week, but on Sunday Nancy laid herself out to give them a feast : dinner was always a mighty meal and even when the dishes were quite unpretending—which they seldom were—the quality of the cooking alone was always enough to make them look forward eagerly to it all the morning and linger long over it once they were seated at the table. Their afternoon walk began later and later and one day Benjamin, complaining of a sudden attack of rheumatism, had stayed behind when the others went out, to sleep off the effects of his dinner in front of the fire. For similar reasons the actual visitation of the farm tended to become more and more abridged as the winter advanced. The outlying fields could well be left to take care of themselves on those bleak, misty afternoons when the cold seemed to creep into the very bones: someone would be bound to go up there one day next week and he would see how they were getting on. Meanwhile down in the farm kitchen there was a bright, bustling fire awaiting them and a clean cloth on the table—Nancy always washed so white—and a tea that was no unworthy counterpart of the dinner, with enormous slabs of solid, spicy doughcake and a pile of fresh Suffolk rusks: it was well for them that a stern sense of duty made them take a walk between the two at all. Then, when the spring came, what had become a relief from the winter now became an added pleasure, and they still waited as impatiently as ever for their Sunday dinner.

On one such morning, at the end of April, Hiram, who was digging up a piece of potato ground in the vegetable garden, tossed his spade into the trench and pulled out his watch. He had left Nancy in the kitchen basting a brace of ducks, but it was only half-past ten and two hours yet to go before dinner. He yawned, sighed and stared with vacant eyes over the hedge, thoughtfully rubbing the back of his neck. Something more than the mere remoteness of his dinner was troubling him: for some time now he had felt unsettled, in a way he could not comprehend: he wanted to be alone and he had shunned Bob's company, there were even times like this morning when he felt a deliberate distaste for work, and yet he was not unhappy: it was difficult to be so among so much solid comfort and good living. Without stopping to consider why, he left his spade lying in the trench and, slipping through the little wicket gate, sauntered off across the paddock. The winking April sunshine streamed down over the valley below him, dappling with radiant colour all the fields he had ploughed in the last six months: how stubborn and cold they had seemed then : now they looked kind, like the sunshine itself which he felt warm upon his cheeks. It was spring once again and the sun was kind, Hiram thought : Nancy was kind, too, to give them all the good things to eat that she did, indeed, she was a most agreeable person to have about the house : he would like to do something to please her as much as she had pleased him, to be kind to her ; it must be a great pleasure, kindness : but what could he do? The pale green and soft yellow of a cowslip spray, nodding shyly at the foot of a sombre blackthorn hedge, drew his eye and held it while his mind travelled back to the day when Nancy had first put flowers on the kitchen table at Crakenhill, marigolds and chrysanthemums, all ragged and tarnished : there were none of them in the garden now and the table had been bare for months. Cowslips—a common weed—he wondered if she would like them : at least she would not be angry with him and there was the chance of pleasing her : it was worth the risk of disappointment. He picked the cowslip and began to look for another. They were scarcer than he thought, those that he wanted, for he had suddenly become intensely critical and only the lushest and most velvety blooms with long juicy stalks would content him. He learnt much about them in that short time, fingering their wrinkled sepals, looking deep into their orange-streaked hearts and filling his nostrils with their elusive, tender fragrance which strokes the senses like a fleeting kiss. The morning did not seem half long enough as he moved from field to field : he could not pick too many for her.

Nancy was still alone in the kitchen when he came down to the farm again.

'What have you got there, Hiram?' she said as he edged in awkwardly with the cowslips under his arm.

'Fare to me, you might like these,' he replied sheepishly, holding out the bunch and going rather red.

'Oh, how lovely, Hiram!' she cried, burying her face in the blooms. 'How sweet they do smell!'

A sudden sensation of vast well-being swept over Hiram : he had never consciously set out to please anyone before, and his pleasure at Nancy's pleasure was a new and heart-warming experience.

'Let's get a vase for them,' said Nancy. 'That was so nice of you, Hiram.'

'I'm wholly glad you like 'em,' he mumbled, smiling broadly in spite of his confusion : he could not think why he was smiling, but he was quite unable to prevent it.

Nancy filled a jar with water and he helped her to arrange the cowslips in it : delicious to be so near her and doing something in common with her : he made it last as long as he could. They were still bending over the vase when the door opened and the others trooped in, headed by Benjamin. Nancy stood up straight at once, holding out the vase in her hands.

'Look what Hiram's brought me,' she said. 'Aren't they beautiful ? Do you smell, Mr. Geaiter.'

Benjamin dug his nose into the golden mass with a searching sniff. He lifted his head and grunted.

'I can't smell nothing,' he said, going over to his chair and sitting down.

'No,' replied Nancy pertly, ' you smoke too much.'

She set the vase tenderly on the middle of the table, which was already laid for dinner, and stood back to look at it.

'There,' she said, ' don't that look wholly nice ? I do love to see flowers about a house and no mistake. Thank you, Hiram.'

Hiram felt rather uncomfortable, realising now that he did not want his brothers to know anything about his gift or to share it with Nancy : but now they knew everything. He went red again and grinned, but said nothing.

'Here, Nance,' growled Benjamin from the other end of the table, ' when'll dinner be ready ? I'm getting hungry.'

'All right,' said Nancy. ' I'm now going to dish up.'

Five minutes later the ducks were on the table in a

cloud of savoury steam. Nancy took up the carving knife:
then bending over the table, she brushed her cheek on the
cowslips and took a deep breath. Hiram looked hard at
her and Ben looked hard at Hiram: Benjamin shuffled his
feet impatiently. Nancy raised her head and attacked the
ducks. For the next half-hour their minds were wholly
on their plates, but when they looked up, they could not
help staring at the cowslips in the middle of the table.
Benjamin hardly looked up at all—the juicy duck and the
sugary, subtly-flavoured plum pudding which followed
it needed all his eyes. When he had finished, he leant back
in his chair with two or three satisfied grunts and lighted
his pipe: in less than five minutes it had dropped from his
mouth and he was snoring. To Nancy's surprise all the
others except Harry rose from the table as soon as they
had finished their second helpings of pudding: they had
not failed to do it ample justice, but they generally sat
and smoked for a while, at least until she had cleared
away; the fine weather was drawing them out, she
thought. They all scattered in different directions as soon
as they were outside the door: that seemed strange:
Hiram generally went with Bob or Ben, and Ern with
Harry. But they did not wait a moment, as if they were
anxious to avoid one another; almost at once the yard
was empty again. Harry, after a short smoke, got up in
his turn and slouched out into the yard with his hands in
his pockets, stretching himself as he walked: Benjamin,
still snoring hard, was left in possession of the table.
Nancy, who was at the sink washing up, tapped at the
kitchen window as Harry passed. He stopped and she
went out to him, wiping her hands on her apron.

' Oh, Harry,' she said, ' how are those lambs of yours?
They must be getting a nice size now.'

Harry's face lit up.

' They do look well,' he replied. Not a poor one in the
lot.'

' I wonder,' said Nancy a little shyly, casting her eyes
to the ground for a moment, ' if I could go down and see

them this afternoon. I do wholly want to before they grow up.'

Harry knitted his brows.

' I'm afraid that's not fit yet,' he said. ' It's terrible dirty still up by the fold. You'd never get there.'

' I don't mind a little mud though,' replied Nancy with a sidelong smile.

' Ah, that's too bad up there,' said Harry, shaking his head. ' I've got to go up there myself this afternoon to set out a bit more feed and I wish I hadn't. It's up to your ankles on and off all the way there. Them fields want draining agin.'

' Oh, I see,' said Nancy dully : she turned round and went back into the kitchen, shutting the door behind her.

The unconcealed disappointment in her voice was not lost on Harry as he walked away down the yard to the drift : she must have known that the mud could not have been so deep or the sheep would not have been there : and she had looked most inviting. Nancy was not exactly a pretty girl, but there was something satisfying about her upright carriage and her strong white arms ; to-day the colour on her lips was fresher than ever and there was a warm glint in her bright hazel eyes that illumined and softened the outlines of her firm round chin and her low white forehead. Harry could not help liking her and he had begun to perceive that she liked him, but he hesitated to respond so soon : his brothers were watching him, he knew, and after Jessie   . . there was nothing strong or firm about her, she was all yieldingness. With a sigh he swung himself over the hurdles among the lambs : he was glad to be with them again : no one minded how much he loved them.

Nancy retired to her bedroom after she had finished washing up and spent the afternoon on a bib-apron she was making for herself, from time to time looking out of the window over the glistening fields. She would have liked to be there herself—not alone, but with someone there to talk softly and kindly to her, to make her laugh, to show her things, to put himself out for her. She was not discontented with her life at Crakenhill ; no one was unkind to her, she enjoyed having her own way and much of her work was a veritable pleasure ; but she was tired of having to supply alone all the human needs of the house. She certainly managed to draw them all out at times, but no one ever attempted to draw her out ; they were friendly enough, she knew, but they never took any steps to show it. Hiram's bunch of cowslips was the first outward token of goodwill she had yet received : poor clumsy Hiram, she thought, he had a warm heart after all: but why not Harry ? His face was not cast in a dull, unemotional mould like the others : he could smile, too, in a way that went to a woman's heart ; she wondered if he had ever smiled on a woman before. He knew how to talk once he had started, but like the rest, he seldom spoke to her unless she spoke first and he had rejected the manifest opening she had given him this afternoon. She felt a sudden hunger for a little laughter, a little affection, for some more intimate human relationship than she had hitherto experienced. It was nothing to weep over, but it made her drop her sewing at length and lose herself in her reflections. A step in the yard brought her back and she picked up the unfinished apron with a little sigh of annoyance. She was already thinking of going down to the kitchen to see the time, when someone called her name up the stairs in a rough, bold voice that sounded like Ern's. She thrust her sewing into a work-basket and walked slowly downstairs, a little out of humour : they were surely not clamouring for tea yet awhile. Benjamin had gone out and Ern was alone waiting for her by the staircase door with a large bunch of cowslips in his hand.

' I thought p'r'aps you'd care for these,' he said rather hoarsely, ' seeing as you're that fond of flowers.'

' Why, thank you very much, Ern,' stammered Nancy, somewhat flustered by this sudden solicitude for her personal fancies.

' I must now be off to fetch the cows,' said Ern, backing

nervously out of the room and clearing his throat ; it was very tiresome and he was quite red in the face with it. ' I'm glad you wanted 'em.' He disappeared through the door.

Nancy looked at the bunch of cowslips before her, turning it from one hand to the other. Beautiful blooms all of them, and as sweet as those Hiram had brought her in the morning. She was glad enough to see them for their own sake ; but they also showed that some of the brothers at least were beginning to think of her. She filled all the vases she could find with them and set them in every available place, on the mantelpiece, in the window and on the table. The whole room was redolent of their fragrance ; it floated on the air, yet the slightest breath moved it, it could not cloy. Nancy, after one last delighted glance at the gay appearance of the kitchen, stepped briskly into the dairy and began to get the milk-pans ready for the milk that would soon be coming in. The kitchen door opened and she heard the sound of hobnails on the bricks : the feet advanced hesitatingly to the dairy door and a very red, square, clean-shaven face, with one eyebrow slightly raised above the other, peered round into the dairy : it was Bob.

' Oh, is that you, Nance ? ' he piped, rather short of breath. She was Nance to all of them now.

' Yes, it's me, Bob,' replied Nancy reassuringly, with her eyes still on her milk-pans. ' Who did you think it was ? '

' I've now got to go and see to my horses,' Bob gabbled at his fastest pace—he had been thinking this speech out all the afternoon—' but I thought I'd bring you these before I went.'

He took a large bunch of cowslips from behind his back and held them out to her.

' Want 'em ? ' he said.

' Thank you, Bob,' replied Nancy graciously. ' That's so kind of you.'

' Good,' said Bob, his voice soaring right up the scale for

sheer relief. ' I must now go off and give 'em their bait.'

He turned and walked away, looking furtively around him as if he wanted no one to know where he had been. In the doorway he met Ben with something bulky in his arms wrapped up in a sack. Bob looked sharply up at him.

' What you got there ? ' he asked.

' Never you mind,' snapped Ben, with a stern glance.

Bob quailed before him and hurried away into the yard. Ben carefully shut the door and tiptoed up to the dairy steps so quietly that it was only his quivering, laboured breathing that betrayed his presence to Nancy.

' Oh,' she cried, looking up at the doorway, ' you made me jump, Ben.'

He descended the steps, still clutching his parcel to him, and deposited it carefully on one of the shelves: then, snatching the sack away, he turned round and faced Nancy. For a moment he blinked quite painfully, unable to find his voice.

' Some cowslips for you, Nance,' he managed to stammer at last.

He retreated up the steps so fast that in his nervousness he tripped at the top and fell with a clatter on the kitchen bricks ; but he picked himself up and stumped out without a word. Nancy burst out laughing, not merely at the sight of Ben's burly frame flying head-foremost through the door, but also at the size of his bunch of cowslips. Ern's and Hiram's had been generous enough and she could hardly span Bob's with her two hands ; but Ben's eclipsed them all, it would almost have filled a half-bushel basket. She wondered what to do with such a mass of flowers : all the vases were full and she was short of jam-jars : a handful of violets would have smelt as sweet and taken up far less room ; it was nice of them to try to please her, but they were terribly unimaginative. She filled a pail with water and dropping the two great bunches in it, burst out laughing once more as she remembered how funny Ben had looked stretched out full length on the kitchen floor.

' Ho!' exclaimed Benjamin half an hour later, when he sat down to tea. ' More cowslips, eh?'

He looked up at Nancy, who could not help smiling: it was the first time she had ever seen his eye twinkle.

' Yes,' she replied. ' I don't know what I'm going to do with 'em all—four great bunches.'

The brothers glanced self-consciously at one another across the table: Nancy thought of Ben and bit her lip to keep herself from laughing. Then, as the latch lifted and Harry came in from the yard, she became suddenly serious again, her cheeks flushed and her ears drummed: perhaps he, too, had brought her something: cowslips, violets or any humble weed, it was all one to her so long as he had remembered her. But his hands were empty and he sat down in his place with a preoccupied air. He was speaking now, but not to her.

' One of them lambs is sick,' he was saying. Nancy hardly heard him.

' Oh?' said Benjamin. ' What's the matter?'

' Don't know,' replied Harry, shaking his head. ' That's all shivery like on its legs. I'm afraid that'll go.'

Benjamin grunted and went on with his tea.

The colour slowly burnt itself out of Nancy's cheek: she felt chilled and lonely. Her mind wandered back to practical problems.

' I know what we'll do with the cowslips,' she exclaimed all at once. ' We'll make 'em into wine.'

XV

THE next evening when Nancy had cleared the tea-
things away, she settled down in the dairy with a heap
of cowslips at her side and the big stone jar that they used
for preserving eggs in front of her knees. Each floweret
had to be plucked separately from its close-enfolding
sepals before it had lost its freshness and there was no
time to lose. She had already managed to steal two hours
from the afternoon and had just succeeded in covering
the bottom of the jar, it seemed. It was tiring work, as
trying to the eyes and wearing to the nerves as reading in
a faulty light. However much she tried to force the pace,
she could not pluck more than a quart of flowers in an
hour and they did not go far inside a five gallon jar. She
passed her hand across her warm forehead : her eyes
ached. The kitchen door opened and someone came in.
She could tell it was Harry by his short, brisk step. He
stopped by the kitchen table.

' Oh, Nance,' he called, ' here's half a dozen eggs I just
found in the orchard. Old Rocky want to set. I've left
'em on the table.'

' Thank you, Harry,' she replied, without getting up
from her chair. ' Oh, Harry,' she cried, as she heard his
footsteps move towards the door.

' Yes, Nance ? ' he said, coming back and standing at
the top of the dairy steps.

' Are you doing anything special, Harry ? ' she asked,
smiling up at him.

' No, nothing much,' he said. ' Why ? '

' Do come and give me a hand with these cowslips
then,' she coaxed. ' I'm so tired and you'll never get your
wine if we don't hurry up.'

Harry glanced stealthily out of the kitchen window :
none of his brothers was in sight. He could not resist her
this time.

' All right,' he said. ' I'll come in for a few minutes.'

He dragged one of the kitchen chairs into the dairy and sat down beside Nancy. She took up a big handful of cowslips and dropped them on his knees.

' There,' she said, laughing, ' there's something to get on with ; throw the stalks into this box.'

Harry picked up one of the sprays and began awkwardly tearing off the flowers, stalks, sepals and all. Nancy grabbed his wrist and took the spray from him.

' No, stupid,' she said, ' like this. You catch hold of the flower between your finger and thumb and pull it out of the green. You mustn't let any of that go into the wine : that spoil it. Now, hear it click as it comes out. You've got to pull hard with one hand and pinch hard with the other.'

' I see,' said Harry, picking up another spray and gingerly setting to work again.

' Ah, that's better,' said Nancy, watching him critically. ' We'll soon get done at that rate. Practice make perfect.'

' And no mistake,' added Harry.

They both laughed, which put them more at ease, and Harry realised all at once how pleasant it was to be sitting next to Nancy : there was a freshness hung about her, rather like the fragrance of cowslips, restful and soothing. All Nancy's tiredness vanished : Harry was so friendly and the sound of his voice was balm to her ears. They went on plucking steadily for a few minutes, each of them trying to think of something to say : it was not so easy, although the ice was broken between them.

' How nice they do smell,' said Harry at last. ' That do you good.'

' Ah, you smell these,' said Nancy, tipping the jar over against his knees. ' There's almost half a gallon in there— nothing but flowers.'

Harry put his head in the mouth of the jar and took in a deep breath. The scented cloud which smote his nostrils, delicate and distant in spite of its strength, almost intoxicated him with its sweetness and he still kept his head over the jar while he took another breath. Nancy bent her head down beside his to smell herself. Then both raised their heads again.

' That is wonderful sweet,' said Harry : yet what he caught now was the warm fragrance of Nancy's cheek.

' That is,' she replied : she was gazing deep into his dark grey eyes and thinking how soft they looked.

The grate of a boot on the dairy steps made them start up a little guiltily. Bob was standing in the doorway, looking very self-conscious. Harry and Nancy began to pluck furiously.

' Well, Bob ? ' said Nancy, having regained her presence of mind, ' what do you want ? '

' I thought p'r'aps you might like a bit of help,' said Bob diffidently, his left eyebrow twitching violently with embarrassment.

Nancy did not want him there, but she could hardly refuse without showing her hand and she was not quite ready for that : she was not yet sure of Harry.

' Glad of it,' she replied. ' The more we have, the sooner it'll be done and the better the wine. Do you fetch a chair and come along.'

Bob sat down on the opposite side of the jar and picked up some cowslips with a rather tremulous hand. Harry fidgeted uneasily on his chair ; he never felt comfortable with Bob now and here in front of Nancy it seemed as if Bob were taking note of all he said and did. He could not endure to remain there any longer.

' I must go and look at that lamb of mine,' he said, rising to his feet abruptly. ' I'd forgotten all about that. Sorry, Nance.'

' All right,' she replied as he went out, ' but come back here when you've finished.'

' I'll see,' he called back from the kitchen.

Bob, with an obvious air of relief, shifted his chair a little nearer Nancy's and put his nose in the jar. He raised his head and stared at her with his pale blue eyes wide open.

' Ah, that smell real good,' he said, gravely shaking his

head and picking up a cowslip in his fingers. ' I like a job of this sort in the evening.'

' Do you ? ' said Nancy. ' Well, so much the better for me.'

' It's nice to have a chat now and again,' said Bob.

' That is,' replied Nancy.

They remained silent for nearly ten minutes, plucking solemnly. Someone softly opened the kitchen door and crept up to the dairy steps. Bob looked up sharply just in time to see Hiram peering round the door at him. Seeing the pitch already occupied, he was about to creep away again, but Nancy caught sight of him and called him back.

' Come along, Hiram,' she said cheerfully, ' give us a hand. The more there are of us, the sooner you'll be able to drink it. Bring in a candle with you. We shall want it soon.'

Bob grudgingly made room for Hiram and managed to edge a little closer to Nancy.

Hiram looked into the mouth of the jar.

' My ! ' he exclaimed. ' What a lot you've done. But mind you don't work too hard, Nance. I'll do it all for you.'

' Don't you worry, Hiram,' she replied with a smile. ' I'll stop when I'm tired. It's so nice to have a little help.'

Hiram beamed back at her : he felt he had a superior claim to her goodwill, having been the first to think of the cowslips.

' Yes,' he said, quite boldly for him, ' and to have a little company of an evening, eh ? '

Nancy smiled without answering.

A few minutes later the clink of stones on a spade struck their ears through the dairy window. Nancy turned round.

' Why, it's Ben,' she said. ' I wonder what he's digging so close to the house for. P'r'aps he's looking for treasure.'

Bob and Hiram stared at each other with bewildered eyes.

' I don't know what he's up to,' said Hiram. ' Fare to me he's crazed.'

They went on plucking for half an hour mainly in silence; Nancy was beginning to feel tired again and did not want to talk. Bob and Hiram could not refresh her with their presence as Harry did. Darkness was falling and the candle alight when Ben came in. He walked up to the dairy door and having taken in the group around the jar with his eye, went back to the sink to wash his hands. He returned a minute or two after and stood by the dairy door, scratching his bristly black moustache with his thumb-nail. Bob and Hiram glanced suspiciously at him.

' Here, you two,' said Ben, ' there's no hay in the stable for to-morrow's bait. You'd better see about it sharp. I've been busy all the evening.'

' Oh, I see,' said Hiram. ' You'd better go and see after it, Bob. I cut it last time.'

' Yes, but I shan't be able to see where you put the knife,' Bob protested. It was a weak excuse. ' Do you go, Hiram.'

' Fare to me you'd both better go,' said Ben impatiently. ' That'll want two to carry it.'

Bob and Hiram rose unwillingly from their chairs and lumbered out. As soon as they were gone, Ben stepped down into the dairy and seated himself at Nancy's side.

' Let's give you a hand with that, Nance,' he said.

She looked up with a roguish smile.

' You too ? ' she said, picking up a handful of cowslips and throwing them on his lap. ' What were you doing outside there with the spade just now, Ben ? '

' I've been digging up the garden,' replied Ben in a solemn voice, feeling that it was a weighty announcement. ' Now that the house is that smart indoors, it fare to me the garden want trimming up a bit too : and you're fond of flowers, aren't you, Nance ? '

' That'd be wholly nice,' said Nancy. ' I've always wanted a garden : that do smarten things up and you can always have flowers on the table then.'

Ben smiled complacently to himself, feeling that he had

scored heavily: Hiram was not the only man in the family with ideas.

' You shall have a garden, Nance,' he said in as soft a voice as he could command, ' and anything else you want too.'

Nancy shot a keen sidelong glance at him and looked down into the jar to see how the level had risen. Ben, confused by his own audacity, stared hard at his knees and laboriously pulled a cowslip to pieces: it was a good thing Nancy could not see in the candlelight how red his face was, he thought. The kitchen door rattled and he turned round.

' Hullo, Ern ? ' he said. ' What do you want ? '

' I thought you might like some more cowslips, Nance,' said Ern rather huskily, ' to put in your wine.' He had another very large bunch in his hands.

' Well, Ern,' said Nancy, sitting up in her chair to straighten her back, ' we've really got enough now, but if you'd come and pull a few flowers for us, that'd be a great help and no mistake.'

' Are you sure ? ' said Ern, a little timidly, seeing Ben already in possession.

' Yes, come along,' replied Nancy. ' Here's a chair. Move up, Ben.'

Ben reluctantly shifted his chair with a contemptuous sniff: his face was as sour as vinegar. Nancy watched him out of the corner of her eye.

' Mind you do it proper, Ern,' he said severely. ' We don't want no green stuff in the wine.'

' All right,' replied Ern irritably. ' I can do it. You're not the only one who know.'

' Now then, you two,' Nancy scolded, ' don't you be cantankerous.' She put her arm in the jar. ' Here's a bit of stalk you dropped in just now, Ben. I saw you.'

Ben stared a moment and then his face fell.

' I'm that sorry, Nance,' he said humbly.

They went on plucking for another quarter of an hour: neither Ben nor Ern had anything to say and Nancy herself became moody and silent. She was really tired now and there was no sign of Harry : she wondered what he could be doing : he could hardly have spent all the time on his sick lamb and it was already dark. The kitchen clock struck eight : it was no use waiting any longer for him. Nancy got up from her chair.

' There, that's enough for to-night,' she said, stifling a yawn, ' but we mustn't leave all these cowslips in here all night. That might turn the milk.'

She bent down to pick up the jar, but Ben took it out of her hands.

' No, you mustn't do that,' he said. ' That's too heavy for you. Let me carry it.'

' All right,' she said, getting up again. ' Put it in the larder.'

Ern stretched out his arm to help with the jar, but Ben snatched it away from him.

' Don't you touch, Ern,' he growled. ' You'll have it over. I can manage.'

Nancy stood watching them with an amused smile playing round her lips : there was no doubt in her mind now that they were all making up to her—all except Harry.

XVI

THE sun was setting slowly in an intense carmine glow behind the chimney pots of Crakenhill, so that the old crow-stepped gable looked like some fragment of a picturesque Gothic ruin : the crooning twitter of tired birds in the copse or the raucous cry of some distant amorous pheasant only made the evening hush seem more profound, and the outlines of things, already blurred by the rankness of the mid-May growth, became yet softer and more indistinct. Harry leant up against a hurdle and watched his sheep settle down for the night. The fold was ready for to-morrow, there was water in the troughs and hay in the racks. It had all been done half an hour ago and yet he had still hung about the fold looking for something else to do ; he had examined all the hurdles and hay-racks and troughs, but none wanted mending: he had oiled the root-slicer and cleaned the folding-iron : he had pinched the backs of all his lambs to see how fat they were : the only thing that remained was to stand and watch the sheep, for he was loth to leave the fold. The only sound to be heard now was the placid chewing of his black-faced ewes—a soothing sound, most precious to him, and for some time now he had lingered on at night to listen to it : he needed soothing.

It was not difficult for him to guess what was happening up at the farm. The cowslips which he had helped Nancy to pull were now well on the way to becoming wine. Two days after they were gathered she had drowned all their fragrance in gallons of boiling water and sugar, and the next day had put the barm into the handsome golden liquor she strained off them. Each night his four brothers had hovered round her in the larder, vying with one another in their zeal to help and quite embarrassing her with their attentions. They would not allow her to lift the jar, to move a chair or fetch the kettle herself : and all the time they pressed closely round her, greedily devouring every movement she made with their eyes. The change wrought by the barm on the tempting liquor in the jar was astonishing. It turned green and thin, sinister, brown, frothy scum rose and floated on the surface, it hissed and bubbled and stank disgustingly. It was hardly credible that so much foulness could have come out of so much beauty and it seemed a sin to have spoilt it : but Nancy declared that the wine was working finely. Every night at eight o'clock it had to be stirred to help the working, but slowly and carefully so as not to cloud it. The four brothers, having acquired a taste for Nancy's company over the cowslips, did not abandon their interest in the wine. Each night they solemnly followed her into the larder and stood close round her while she stirred, craning their necks and gaping over the jar. Then one night Ern was seized with a new notion.

' Let me do that, Nance,' he said. ' You'll tire yourself.'

' All right,' she said, relinquishing the stick with a laugh, ' go ahead.'

' Now then, young feller, not so fast,' grumbled Ben, quite consumed with envy, ' or you'll spoil it.'

' Don't you talk so much,' snapped Ern savagely, as he went on with the stirring.

The following night Ben came in ten minutes early. He went into the larder and fetched the stick.

' Let's go and stir the wine, Nance,' he said.

' Better wait till eight,' said Nancy. ' It's best done at a reg'lar hour.' She knew the others would be in by then.

Next day Nancy hid the stick behind the plates on the dresser and when eight o'clock came, she gave it to Hiram to keep the peace between them and after that they took it in turns to stir the wine while Nancy watched them. Meanwhile, in his spare time Ben went on digging the flower garden : it was a perpetual monument to his devotion and his position seemed very strong. The others, however, were not at the end of their resources ; Hiram took the feeding of the chickens off her hands, Bob pumped the water and carried it into the kitchen; Ern went into the vegetable garden every morning before he drove the milk in to the station and pulled the greens for dinner. Nancy found her daily labours considerably lightened, but although she knew perfectly well what was happening, she affected to be serenely unconscious of it all.

The four brothers were undoubtedly jealous, but with a bad grace they accepted one another's rivalry, assured that Nancy would choose the best man among them and each one knew that he was the best man. But Harry they refused to admit to the competition, largely because they suspected that his chances were better than theirs; he knew more about women and might take an unfair advantage. The night Nancy had put the barm into the wine, Ben had found him in the larder, sniffing the liquor, and had curtly told him to go off and mend a gap in the hedge he had noticed down by the sheep: Ben had a remarkable memory for such omissions nowadays. Two other nights when he had come home earlier than usual and found them all standing round Nancy in the larder, their sharp, scowling glances had shown him plainly enough that he was not wanted there: even out in the fields they were surly with him as if there too he were an intruder.

Harry, with the lofty superiority of an old hand, could not help being secretly amused at their clumsy way of getting to work, but he too had his troubles. His experience told him well enough that if he wanted Nancy, he could have her for the asking, but with his brothers all against him, that would mean leaving the farm, and if he had to leave the farm, he would sooner have done it for Jessie because he knew in his heart that he liked her better. That issue had been settled long ago and the farm had won. It was far the best thing to stay down among the sheep where he liked to be; the others could have the whole house and all the stinking cowslip wine in it to themselves. That was how he reasoned it out and if the matter had ended there, all might have been well and Harry deemed fortunate for seeing the issue so clearly. But he still remembered that Nancy was a woman and liked him; he could well guess what she might be to a man she loved and having once been in the warm, he longed to come in out of the cold, a longing more bitter than any of the others had experienced. For these three weeks, however, Harry had kept himself aloof from her and his brothers and had spent his evenings among the sheep from whom he extracted a deeper, truer solace than most other rustics would have done, just because the memory of what he had given up for their sake had attached him more closely to them. But to-night he could not help thinking of the warm, fleshy sweetness of Nancy's cheek over the jar of cowslips and how pleasant it was even to be at her side: the mere desire for human companionship made him waver and curiosity decided him: he wanted to see what was going on; no one could complain if he just put his head in the door. He slung an empty sack over his shoulder and made slowly for the drift.

When he reached the farm, he found the kitchen in darkness, but there was a glimmer of light in the larder, and he could hear the hum of voices. He strolled slowly up to the door with the sack still over his shoulder: in that style no one could suspect his intentions.

' Hullo,' said Nancy cheerfully. ' Have you come to see me put it in the cask? I reckon you must have smelt it.'

The four men turned round and stared at Harry.

' A week ago I might have smelt it as far as the sheep,' laughed Harry. ' That was high and no mistake.'

' That's not now, though,' said Nancy. ' I've taken all the scum off and it's clear and sweet. You should see the hid it's got on it too.'

Ben coughed impatiently: Harry was monopolising the whole conversation.

' Come on, Nance,' he said, turning his back on Harry, ' let's get on with it.'

He and Hiram between them picked up the jar and tipped the pale green liquor through a funnel into the little four-and-a-half gallon cask which Bob and Ern were holding straight on the larder floor, down on their knees at either end of it : Nancy from behind steadied the funnel.

' Now then, Hiram,' said Ben, ' hold hard : we durstn't go too fast.'

' All right,' replied Hiram. ' Mind you hold that tight now, Bob.'

At that moment Ben's fingers slipped on the belly of the jar : it shot forward and before he could properly recover his grip, a pint of the bubbly liquor had slopped out of the funnel on to Ern's trousers.

' Look what you're doing, Ben,' he shouted, ' or we shall lose the lot. My trousers don't want washing.'

' Well, do you keep the cask still,' retorted Ben. ' How d'you expect me to pour straight when it's wobbling from one side to the other ? '

' That's as firm as a rock,' expostulated Ern. ' Isn't it, Bob ? Fare to me you talk too much, Ben.'

Harry suddenly caught Nancy's eye from the doorway and his face expanded into a broad grin.

' Who are you making faces at, young Harry ? ' said Bob, looking up from the floor. ' If that's all you can do, you might as well cut off.'

' You did look wholly funny then,' said Harry, suddenly overcome and almost choking with laughter, ' swimming in all that wine. Waste of good drink I call it.'

' Oh ! ' said Bob angrily. ' Well, look ye here. If you don't hurry up and git out, there'll be trouble.'

' Now then, you men,' scolded Nancy sharply, ' stop squabbling and get on with it. Do you be quiet now, Harry.'

Ben grunted and he and Hiram lifted the jar up once more, clinging to it grimly with set faces, while Bob and Ern gripped the cask so tightly that the staves creaked. This time the wine came out in a steady stream without any accidents and Ben and Hiram were on the point of up-ending the jar to pour off the dregs when Nancy laid a hand on Ben's arm and stopped them.

' No,' she said, reaching down a jug from the shelf, ' we'll keep the last half-pint to taste. Do you knock the bung in, Bob.'

When the last drops had drained off the edge of the jar into the jug, she took a tea-cup, poured a little into it and walked over to the larder door.

' Here you are, Harry,' she said, putting it into his hand. ' Do you try that and tell us if we've been wasting our time.'

Harry's lips quivered and the warm blood raced up to his cheeks. There he was, singled out among all the brothers for the privilege of the evening, and he had not raised a finger to help ; Nancy ought to have known better. The others were all glaring at him jealously ; it was not his fault, he had not asked for it and they knew that well enough : why should he worry about them ? What could they do to him ? His thoughts flew back to that scene in the barn nearly two years ago with his brothers sitting solemnly in judgment before him and he shuddered. All this passed in his mind while he raised the cup to his nose and sniffed it. Then his courage failed him : he handed the cup back to Nancy untasted.

' No thanks, Nance. I ain't used to that sort of thing,' he said lamely. ' Do you let somebody else try it. I must go and grind up some cake : that's what I brought this sack down for.'

He turned round awkwardly and walked to the kitchen door. Nancy's face clouded with annoyance.

' Oh, all right,' she called pettishly after him. ' You needn't drink it if you're afraid to : there isn't any poison in it.'

She was about to hand the cup to Ben when a loud rap on the larder window made them all turn sharply round. The window opened and Benjamin's head appeared.

' Well,' he rumbled, ' when's that wine going to be ready? '

' I've got some here in the cup,' said Nancy. ' Like a taste ? '

Benjamin stretched his hand through the window and took the cup from her. He drained it at a gulp.

' My! that's good,' he exclaimed, smacking his lips. ' Real good, I call it. Got any more ? '

' Just a little,' said Nancy, holding out the jug.

Benjamin took it and emptied it into the cup. He swallowed it slowly, appreciatively.

' That's not properly fit, yet,' he said slowly, ' but that's the best-flavoured cowslip I've ever tasted. Well done, Nance.'

He handed the empty cup and jug back to her through the window. Nancy took them and turned round nonchalantly to the others.

' You'll have to wait now,' she said, ' till someone put the tap in the cask. It's all bunged up.'

She no longer cared who tasted the wine or what they thought of it ; Harry had wounded her deeply and it was obvious that he did not want her. She walked out of the larder with her head in the air. The four brothers stared stupidly after her and then at one another.

' Well, if you like,' said Bob, turning to go out himself, ' that is a rum 'un.'

XVII

WHEN the ash came out into full bloom that spring before the oak had even burst its bud, Benjamin, wise in weather-signs, had predicted a wet summer, and he was not deceived. It began to rain in the beginning of June, it rained on St. Swithin's Day and all through harvest never seemed to cease. The corn was cut in snatches whenever some fitful burst of sunshine had made it tolerably dry : and when it was cut, the shocks stood for days on end in the drenching rain before they could be carried : shock after shock had to be overturned to dry out in the wind and in one field of oats every sheaf had to be untied and spread out to prevent the grain from sprouting where it lay. They managed at length to gather everything in at Crakenhill, but there was much damp corn in the ricks and Benjamin determined to thresh out early and cut his losses.

One evening, towards the end of September, Ben went into the barn to make the final preparations for the threshing : there was a tackle already at an adjoining farm and it was due to move on to Crakenhill in two days' time. Coal and water had been carted into the rickyard and the empty sacks were all handily piled by the barn door ; the only thing that remained to do was to shift the few sacks of last year's wheat that had been kept for seed, to a more convenient place, so as to make room for the newly-threshed grain. Eight sacks, each well over two hundredweight, to be trundled on the trolley from one side of the barn to the other and stacked against the wall in two rows, one on top of the other—it was really a job for two men : but Ben strained and sweated at it all by himself. Six months ago he would have fetched in one of his brothers to help and done the work in half the time ; but things had changed and he preferred to work by himself now ; so did Hiram and Bob and Ern. In the day-time they could not choose but go wherever their work called them and they were often perforce together : but in the evening they deliberately avoided one another's company. All four were still making up to Nancy as assiduously as ever, and each day found them more burningly jealous of one another. Half their time was spent in thinking out ways and means of earning her favour or snatching a brief hour of her company. They never actually quarrelled, but all the harmony with which they formerly worked together had vanished. An outsider might hardly have noticed it, because they had never been demonstrative at the best of times, although now and then when one of them by some lucky stroke had secured some temporary advantage, the rest would put on black looks and sulk furiously. Ben's garden had been dug and planted long ago with seeds he had bought in Saxmundham one market day : all through the summer there were flowers on the table, which constantly tormented the other three with envious misgiving : it was difficult to go one better than that. Nevertheless, Hiram managed to find out the date of her birthday and bought her a needle-case from the village shop, Bob whitewashed the dairy and Ern conceived the idea of getting up a quarter of an hour earlier than usual every morning to lay the fire for her.

Nancy still behaved as if she noticed nothing and accepted all their attentions graciously enough, showing no sign of preference for one or another, but equally pleasant in her manner to all—though latterly she had assumed a more cool and distant, almost queenly, demeanour towards them ; there were times when what had at first caused her much inward amusement, became distinctly annoying, and she did not want four clumsy great men hanging on to her skirts and pestering her with their services. As the summer drew on, she took more and more to spending her evenings in her bedroom, sewing, and anyone who could catch her alone in the kitchen for half an hour to help her wind wool or shell the peas was a lucky man. None of them had the courage to precipitate matters by attempting to make love to her ; they all felt that sooner or later she would have to decide between them and each one, seeing himself no less favoured than the rest, considered his chance at least as good as theirs and continued to hope. They bore her no ill-will for her apparent apathy towards them, but after being kept on tenterhooks in this way for five months, they began to suffer from the strain. They ate and drank and slept well enough—Nancy's housekeeping ensured that— but they grew reflective and solitary and there was at times a haggard look about their eyes that told of suspense and desire unsatisfied.

It was impossible for Benjamin and young Harry, living in the same house with the rest, to be unaware of what was going on around them ; but whatever they thought, they kept it to themselves. The four brothers worked as hard as ever and Nancy's cooking did not deteriorate ; for the rest, Benjamin regarded all their antics with seeming indifference. Harry, on the other hand, had long ago dropped voluntarily out of the running and spent the greater part of his time with the sheep ; it was best to keep out of the way. Nancy no longer took any notice of him and was always distinctly curt with him whenever she spoke, although Harry with a rather malicious satisfaction perceived quite clearly that she wanted none of the others ; but however inoffensive his behaviour, they still eyed him with suspicion ; they had not forgotten that cup of cowslip wine.

It was, then, no unusual thing for Ben to be doing two men's work by himself in the barn that September evening and he hoisted the last sack into position with a grunt of relief : his back was broad, but the wheat weighed heavy and he was breathing hard. He wiped his steaming forehead on his shirt-sleeve and putting on his coat, leant up with a weary sigh against the sacks he had just shifted, to light his pipe ; he was tired of being unhappy. The latch of the door clicked and Ben frowned : someone come to disturb him, they ought to know better. The door opened softly and Nancy came in with a wooden measure in her hand. Ben's frown disappeared and he got up from the sacks: she might have come on purpose to find him at last. His cheeks warmed and he felt strangely excited.

'Where's the maize, Ben?' she said. 'I want a little for that pair of chickens I'm fatting for Sunday's dinner.'

She was perfectly composed and did not even smile. Ben was disappointed.

'It's over there in that bin,' he said, pointing across the barn. 'Let me get it for you.'

'No, thanks,' she replied coldly. 'I know just how much I want.'

She went over to the bin and bending down, scooped out some grain in her measure, then shook a little back. Ben watched her from the other side. She straightened herself awkwardly as if she were not used to bending her back, and walked out of the barn with the laborious gait of one tired and stiff after a long journey. Ben, a little puzzled, went out behind her and, having shut the barn door, followed her into the kitchen.

'I must put my watch right,' he said, to give himself a pretext for being there.

'That reminds me,' said Nancy. 'I must wind up the clock.'

She stretched up to the mantelshelf, unhooked the key from the back of the clock and opened the face. The shelf was high and she paused to rest for a moment before she began to wind, with her hand on the edge. Turning her head suddenly, she caught sight of Ben gazing curiously from the table at her waist and her cheek flamed up. Ben hastily averted his eyes and walked out of the room. He strolled about aimlessly among the buildings for a little while with a pensive air, and at length wandered into the orchard where he found Hiram sitting on a fence he had just mended, moodily smoking his pipe. Hiram looked round suspiciously at him.

'Lookye here, Hiram,' said Ben, 'I want a word with you.'

' Yes ? ' said Hiram guardedly.

Ben put both his elbows on the fence.

' That girl, Nance,' he began slowly.

Hiram's heart beat fast and he coughed nervously. Ben was the eldest brother, after all, and had most right to her : he had dug the garden up too.

' That girl, Nance,' Ben repeated, ' is in the family way.'

Hiram dropped his pipe in astonishment.

' How d'ye know ? ' he said huskily.

' You've only got to look at her, Hiram,' Ben replied. ' She walk like a cow : and when she seed me look at her, she went all as red as fire.'

' What's to be done ? ' said Hiram blankly.

' We must find out who've done it,' said Ben firmly. ' She hardly ever go abroad at all : it stand to reason that must be somebody in the house, don't it ? '

' Yes,' admitted Hiram. ' But it's not me,' he added sharply.

' Now, I never said so, did I ? ' Ben replied in an injured tone. ' But who d'you think have most likely done it ? '

Hiram raised his eyebrows.

' Young Harry ? ' he muttered between his teeth.

' I shouldn't wonder,' said Ben, slowly nodding his head. ' It's him if it's anyone. We'd better ask him and find out, it fare to me.'

' Ay, that's the truth we had,' replied Hiram, picking up his pipe.

They walked over to the stables where they found Bob mending some harness : Ern was passing the door on his way to the rickyard to fetch a pitch of straw for the pigs. Ben called him over to the stable and briefly explained the situation.

' Ah, that's our man,' said Bob at once. ' I know his ways, I do. Remember how she wanted him to pull those cowslips with her and that wine she gave him to drink ? '

' Young swine ! ' growled Ern, clenching his fist. ' Wait till I get at him. Let's go and find him.'

They searched all the buildings, the rickyard, the vegetable garden, and walked down the drift as far as the sheep-pens, but there was no trace of him : it was already dusk when they came back to the house. Ben opened the kitchen door and put his head in. Nancy was sitting on the sofa with Harry's hand on her lap, sewing a piece of rag round his thumb. Harry was staring vacantly into the fire and Nancy's eyes were fixed intently on her needle : but the apparent intimacy, confirming all their suspicions, made Ben's temper rise.

' There, that'll do,' said Nancy a little crossly. ' And mind you don't go pulling it off.'

' Thanks, Nance,' said Harry, getting up from the sofa.

' Harry ! ' Ben called sharply.

' Yes ? ' he answered.

' Come you out here a minute. We want you.'

Harry, full of misgivings, went out into the yard and shut the door behind him.

' What's up ? ' he said, blinking in the dusk at the four shadowy forms, awkward but menacing, which confronted him.

' Do you come along of us,' said Bob. ' We want to talk to you.'

He followed them through the yard into the cartshed, which they chose this time for tribunal because the barn was too dark, and guessing from their hostile demeanour that they had something against him, he sat down on the tool-box of the sail-reaper and folded his arms defiantly. They stood round and glared at him.

' Well, what's it all about ? ' he asked, looking Ben squarely in the face.

' It's about Nance,' said Ben.

' What about her ? ' retorted Harry. ' Can't I ask her to tie up my thumb if I like ? I tore it on the root-cutter half an hour ago. What harm is there in that ? She sewed a button on your coat yesterday. Fare to me you've all got a down on me.'

Ben flushed angrily, but checked himself.

' It's not that, young Harry,' he said quite quietly.
' Nance is in the family way.'

' How d'you know ? ' said Harry hotly.

' You've only got to look,' replied Ben.

' But what's that got to do with me ? ' said Harry.

' Well, you ought to know,' put in Hiram, ' if you're
the father.'

' Ay,' murmured the other three together.

' Well, I'm not,' said Harry, biting his words and gazing
from one to another.

They angrily looked him up and down.

' Prove it,' said Hiram.

' That's your business to prove I'm to blame,' said
Harry. ' If she is in the family way—and I didn't know
she was—who's to know you or Bob or Ern or Ben didn't
do it ? '

' What's that ? ' came from the four mouths simultane-
ously.

' He want a leathering,' said Ern.

' And we'll give it him,' said Ben grimly.

The four closed on him. Harry leaped up, and snatching
a heavy curved spanner from the tool-box on which he
had been sitting, brandished it at their heads.

' Keep off, you bloody louts,' he cried at the top of his
voice, ' or I'll lay you out. God help me if I don't ! '

They drew back a little : there was a dangerous gleam
in his eyes. Suddenly a slow, calm, rather hoarse voice
broke upon their ears and made them start.

' What's all this dam noise about ? ' it said.

They all turned round : Benjamin was standing with
his arm round one of the posts which supported the cart-
shed roof, glowering at them.

' What the hell are you all quarrelling about in the shod
at this time of night ? ' he growled.

They turned their heads away for a moment, unable
to meet his eyes, and looked shamefacedly on the ground.
Ben, having recovered himself a little, stepped forward
as spokesman; there seemed no reason to conceal the truth.

'It's like this, father,' he said. 'That Nance of ourn is in the family way and it fare to us it was Harry got her into trouble.'

'Oh,' grunted the old man. 'Well, what have you got to say, young Harry?'

'I never did no such thing,' said Harry emphatically 'When have I been alone with her?'

'And that's the truth,' added his father. 'If you want to ask any questions about Nance, you'd better ask me.'

They all stared at him, dumbfounded.

'So it's you?' Ben gasped at last.

'Yes, it's me,' said Benjamin sardonically, putting his hands in his trousers pockets and sticking out his paunch. 'Is there anything else you'd like to know?'

'No, father,' Ben replied brokenly, 'nothing'

XVIII

THE next morning a cloud hung over the breakfast
table. Nancy kept her eyes fixed steadfastly on the
teapot, her cheeks flushing and paling alternately. She
could tell from the very constraint in the air and the triumphant way in which Benjamin from time to time
glanced round the table at his sons, that they all knew now
what had happened, and although she hardly dared to
raise her head, she seemed to feel their eyes upon her as
she poured out the tea, wondering, contemptuous and
reproachful : it was the atmosphere of her first week
at Crakenhill all over again, but infinitely worse. The
brothers too were conscious of it, still looking half-dazed
by the shock of what they had heard the night before ;
it was as if their eyes had been suddenly opened to the
wickedness of the world and the sight of it had saddened
and subdued them. Here was an act totally removed from
their circle of ideas, that made null all their five months of
hopes and striving : yet for the moment at least, they felt
no definite resentment against Nancy or even Benjamin,
who had always been a law to himself ; they did not even
regard the thing as wrongful at the moment : it was only
something alien and mysterious and their own little world
seemed to be falling in pieces around them. For once they
were not hearty with their breakfast and left food on their
plates untouched Even Benjamin, who was generally
far too busy with his own plate to notice theirs, stared
at them and read their behaviour as a sign of silent protest.
He noisily pushed back his chair from the table and cleared
his throat. They all looked up at him.

' See here,' he said. ' I'm going in to Sax to-day to have
a look at the market. I'll take the milk-float in this morning. D'you hear, Ern ? '

' Yes, father,' replied Ern absently.

Benjamin stumped off into the yard to look at the pigs :
he would be seeing some butchers to-day. The others, not

wanting to be left alone with Nancy, soon followed him out. Ten minutes later he put his head through the door of the stable where Ben, Hiram and Bob were harnessing up to go to plough. He was tugging at his beard with his fingers and his eyes blazed furiously ; there was trouble brewing for someone.

' Where's young Harry ? ' he cried in a loud voice.

' Over here, father,' called Harry, coming out to the barn door, with a slab of linseed cake under his arm that he was about to grind up for the sheep.

' Well, lookye here, you son of a bitch,' shouted Benjamin. ' If you don't clean that neathouse out properly to-day, I'll give you what for. That's wholly filthy.'

' Why, father,' stammered Harry, ' I only helped Ern to clean it out yesterday : that was as clean as the dairy.'

' Well, never you mind about that,' bawled Benjamin. ' Do you clean it out agin to-day and no back answers. D'you hear ? '

' Yes, father,' replied Harry, retiring into the barn.

' When's that float going to be ready ? ' shouted Benjamin to Ern who was laboriously trundling a full milk churn out of the kitchen door.

' Not for a bit, father,' Ern panted. ' I haven't caught the cob yet.'

' Why not ? ' returned Benjamin. ' You're all too dam slow in this house.'

' Well, I've been on ever since breakfast,' Ern retorted. ' I can't go any faster than I can.'

' Well, look sharp and hurry up,' shouted Benjamin. ' I don't want to be kept waiting round here all the morning.'

He turned round and walked into the stable : the other three were all staring at him over the backs of their horses.

' Now, you chaps,' he said, ' mind you get on with that ploughing while I'm away.'

' Well, don't we allus, father ? ' replied Ben, somewhat provoked by this unlooked-for distrust.

' I don't know so much,' grumbled Benjamin. ' You

fare to think 'cause that's heavy land, you can take as long as you please over it. And up there on top of the hill there's some wholly bad ploughing : the furrows go half-way to Bruisyard and back.'

' Well, none of us did it then,' said Ben, ' that's certain.'

He and his two twin brothers were known for the best ploughmen in the parish beyond all manner of doubt, however grudgingly it was admitted.

' Don't you go contradicting,' snarled Benjamin. ' I haven't been farming these fifty years without knowing what's what. D'you think I can't tell a piece of bad ploughing when I see it ? And see here, it's high time you jacked up and stopped this running after Nance. She don't want none of you and she's in a ticklish state now : so don't you get worrying her. See ? I'm going to have her treated proper. All this prancing around and the farm going to hell.'

' But that ain't, father,' Ben protested. ' The farm have never looked better.'

' Don't you say that is when I say that ain't,' shouted Benjamin. ' I've had my eye on you for some time. I know how you've wasted your evenings. I haven't forgot the time you two bloody young fools went on the spree at Ipswich, nor Ern neither, when he took a day off to go to the fair. Well, I'm master in this house. See ? '

He turned on his heel and strode out of the stable, still fuming. Harry, having heard his father abusing Ern from inside the barn, had slipped out and caught the cob to save him another rating. He had already harnessed it to the float and was now helping Ern to hoist the last churn in. Benjamin walked over to them and snatching up the reins, climbed in.

' I've waited long enough,' he growled. ' Do you get off to your work, young Harry. This ain't your job. You mind that ne'thouse is clean by then I come back or you'll hear of it.'

He gave the cob a cut on the flank with his whip and drove out on to the drift with a defiant air. The effect of his violent tirade had filled him with satisfaction : these sons of his might be indispensable, but they needed putting in their place. He had not realised before how much he hated them : but their manifest dejection this morning showed him how much they had taken to heart his forestalling and outwitting them : they were more serious rivals than he had imagined and all the old bitter fighting spirit within him was stirred. Benjamin had always had to struggle hard against a world that he was used to regard as his natural enemy : but for all that he was used to having his own way and he did not spare his enemies, even his own sons: he had shown them now who was master of the house.

The three brothers stared dumbly after the float as it disappeared down the drift, and then stared at each other.

' Well, I'm damned! ' exclaimed Hiram at last. ' There's a rum 'un for you! '

' That is the truth, that is,' said Bob. ' A real rum 'un.'

Ben propped himself up against the manger and gazed pensively at the brick floor.

' It fare to me,' he said slowly, ' that father's getting real old now, real old and pernickety.'

' Not so old either, though,' growled Ern who had just come into the stable and joined them. Harry had retired to the cowshed. ' What about Nance ? '

' No,' Ben admitted, ' not in that way, Ern : but his temper get worse and worse. I can't make out what he want to treat us that way for.'

' After all that, too, about Nance,' added Ern angrily. ' That's a real disgrace, that is.'

' Ay,' said Ben, nodding, ' that is. I wonder what they'll say down in the village when they get hold of it. I reckon they say enough about us as it is.'

' Ah, I doubt they'll talk,' said Bob. ' They've nothing else to do. All the same, that is a disgrace to the family.'

' I reckon that's hard,' said Ern, with whom the discomfiture of losing Nancy still rankled. ' The old man must have had the laugh of us these five months; we look like fools.'

' Yes, Ern,' replied Ben quietly, ' but father's getting old and he can't help some of the things he do. But what about Nance ? '

' I don't know,' said Hiram, sucking hard at his pipe. ' Fare to me she couldn't help it. No wonder she was that cold and haughty all these months. Poor Nance! She've been uncommon good to us.'

' Ay, that's the truth she have,' said Ben, ' but we'd better get off to plough, boys, or father'll have a tale to tell when he come back.'

He took his two horses by the bridle and led them out of the stable, followed by Hiram and Bob. Ern walked a little way with them and then went off to see to his bullocks ; but the other three talked long together that morning.

. . . . .

It was a miserable morning for Nancy. She had heard all Benjamin's bad-tempered abuse through the kitchen window and guessing that she herself was the prime cause of it, she wondered if it would all eventually recoil on her own head. She might be mistress of the house in one sense ; but they were five and she was one ; she was already beginning to feel the weight of her child and it was in their power to make life difficult for her. There was no one to champion her cause—except Benjamin, and she was hardly sure if she wanted that. Yet she had no serious regrets about her seduction : it was a thing that had just happened without her willing it. Benjamin had found her alone in the kitchen one day and almost before she knew, he had taken what the four elder brothers had not had the courage to ask for, what she might have given freely to Harry if he had wanted her : but he had repulsed her and she was angry with him. Benjamin had come again and—she was not unwilling. She did not love, but now she did not care ; it was a thing that happened and things had always happened to her in that fortuitous manner ; her mother's death had taken her to her aunt's and her father's death had left her there: a chance encounter with Benjamin had brought her to Crakenhill and now she was with child by him. In a dim, resigned way she was conscious of having always been the sport of circumstance and hitherto she had always somehow managed to make the best of it—a sort of fatalism tempered with shrewdness. So for the time she had not worried over her plight although she knew in her heart that sooner or later it would have to be disclosed and the consequences faced: but that could wait; in the meanwhile it amused her to watch the brothers paying court to her, to receive their attentions and laugh quietly at them behind their backs. But now that the truth was out, all her light-hearted indifference, her self-control, her mastery of the household, seemed to have vanished. Here she was, behaving like the diffident, self-conscious girl she had been when she first arrived at Crakenhill: she was frightened now of these five big men, or at least, the four of them she had disappointed; in their chagrin they might jeer at her, do violence to her, even turn her out of the house when her baby was born, and she had nowhere to go. All sorts of terrors assailed her that morning and she went about her work half-heartedly, with an anxious eye on the clock, dreading the approach of dinner-time and wondering how she could endure to face the brothers alone while Benjamin was away at market.

Half-past eleven had just struck when she heard the clatter of hoofs in the yard. She looked over the print curtains and saw Ben come in with his two horses, riding sideways on one of them, ploughman fashion. He slid down off his mount and took them both into the stable. Nancy looked round the kitchen in dismay; the dinner was not cooked yet, the table was not even laid: they surely could not be wanting their dinner yet: or were they just taking advantage of their father's absence to annoy her? It hardly seemed probable, but all the same she began feverishly to lay the table. Five minutes later Ben came out of the stable and opened the kitchen door.

Nancy looked round sharply at him from the dresser and went on taking down plates. Ben strode up to her side.

' Oh, Nance,' he said rather hoarsely.

' Yes, Ben ? ' she replied timidly, turning round.

' We've been talking things over this morning,' he said, a little hesitantly at first, ' and it fare to us that perhaps you wouldn't like it to be known in the village, leastways, not yet awhile. They do talk so.'

Nancy blushed and hung her head.

' No, I suppose that would be better,' she faltered, looking up at Ben. His face no longer seemed dull and expressionless, but full of strength and helpfulness : it gave her courage.

' Well,' continued Ben, gaining more confidence—he had not spoken to her with such ease for months now, ' there don't come many people here in the day ; the postman now and again and Betsy Barnes mayhap. So us chaps are going to see that Harry's down near the drift every morning when the postman come, so as he can take the letters ; and if Betsy or anybody else come up here, you can just shet the door and bolt the window and they'll think you're abroad. If you want anything, Ern'll get it for you in Sax when he go in with the milk.'

Nancy's eyes filled with tears.

' Why, Ben,' she said, ' that's wholly good of you. I was afraid about them down in the village and no mistake.'

' That's no trouble,' Ben replied, ' and that's worth it. I know what they're like down there.' He turned round to go and then paused. ' Oh, and Nance,' he added, hesitantly again, ' if you get tired later on and want anything done, you've only got to ask.'

' Thanks, Ben,' said Nancy, seizing his hand and pressing it. ' You're that kind, I don't know what to say.'

Ben, suddenly blushing with embarrassment, strode hastily out of the room, colliding noisily with the door on his way. Nancy sat down on a chair and wept.

Ben, after looking into the barn for a moment to have a word with Ern, strolled away down the drift in the direction of the sheep-pens. A hundred yards further on he caught sight of Harry with his coat over his shoulder, coming up the hill for his dinner. Ben stopped by a gate in the hedge and waited for him.

' Oh, Harry,' he said, stepping out as his brother came level, ' I've got something to say to you.'

' Well ? ' replied Harry, a little defiantly, as if suspecting some further charge against him.

He threw his coat across the gate and put his hands in his pockets. Ben shook his head.

' Don't you worry yourself, Harry,' he said rather hoarsely. ' All I wanted to tell you was, we're main sorry about this. We've treated you pretty bad and we hope you'll forget it.'

Harry, quite taken aback for the moment, cast his eyes down in confusion.

' That don't matter, Ben,' he muttered, raising his head at last. ' That ain't nothing.'

' That is,' replied Ben firmly. ' That's a durn lot. We treated you shameful and you behaved real handsome. If you'd forget it like——'

He held out his hand. Harry took it and gripped hard.

' And Ern say,' added Ben, his voice shaking a little, ' that you're the dam finest little feller as ever wore a pair of leathers : and so do I.'

Harry flung his coat over his shoulder again and they walked off up the hill together.

XIX

A MONTH passed over their heads at Crakenhill and life went on much as before, at least in all that was of importance : but there were changes. Ben continued to look after the garden, Hiram still fed the chickens, Bob fetched the water, Ern pulled the vegetables and laid the fire ; these things had become almost a habit to them : and as Nancy's burden grew, they found more and more duties to take off her hands until there was hardly any heavy work left for her to do. On washing day one of them always arranged to be about the farm to peg out and take in the clothes, they took it in turns to scrub down the kitchen floor and Harry and Ern would never let her touch a milk-pail—they could hardly have been more considerate. But there was a vast difference in their attitude to her. All their jealousy, their anxiety and constraint of manner had disappeared ; they were no longer rival suitors contending for her favour, but all that they did for her was done quite disinterestedly for her sake : it was as if she had become another being in their eyes, an inhabitant of a sphere different from their own, no longer to be aspired to with ordinary human desire—a feeling, however, not unmixed with a considerable portion of disillusionment, because her apparent choice had implied the rejection of them all. Many of their original habits gradually returned ; they did not talk any the more, but they sought one another's company again, the old, almost mechanical harmony was restored to their work in common, they looked for jobs in the evening ; and now that Harry had been admitted to their esteem and a place in their counsels, they had gained in solidarity. In many ways they seemed far happier than they had been for a long time.

It was well that they had become united again, because Benjamin now did much to try them. His ill-humour, which had formerly revealed itself in periodic outbursts alone, now became chronic and although his sons still worked for him as diligently as ever, he was continually finding fault and when he did so, as often as not he flew into a violent rage and cursed them up hill and down dale. But this was not all they had to put up with. He was still quite unrepentant about Nancy and he lost no opportunity of rubbing it in—as if his first impulse to hate them as rivals had been succeeded by a bitter contempt because he had defeated them : in every respect he felt himself a better man than they were. For some time now he had been doing less regular work on the farm himself and had lingered more by the kitchen fire, but for all that he was constantly turning up at unexpected moments in the fields to see how the work was going on, and find something to grumble at. One misty November morning soon after breakfast he suddenly appeared in the rickyard where Ern and Harry were earthing up a beet-clamp, straddling along with that heavy, deliberate gait of his which during the last few months had become more heavy and more deliberate.

' See here, you two,' he said, as they leant on their spades to look up at him, ' I'm expecting a letter this morning and I want one of you to fetch it up to me as soon as that comes. I'm going up to the wheat land to give Ben and Hiram a hand with the drilling. Mind you bring it up at once : important that is, the five bob change Jim Gilliver, the wheelwright, owe me from yesterday.'

' All right, father,' said Ern. ' You shall have it.'

Just then the kitchen door opened and Nancy walked out into the yard with a dish of scraps which she proceeded to scatter to the chickens. Benjamin watched her over the yard gate, moving clumsily, almost painfully, about.

' Ah,' he sneered maliciously, put in mind of his own triumph once more by the sight of her, ' you didn't think I'd cut you out at my age, did you ? '

Ern and Harry, still standing on the side of the clamp, said nothing : he seemed to be talking to himself rather than to them. He faced round to them once more.

' When I was a lad of fifteen,' he said, ' I was turned out

and had to shift for myself. I lived hard, I did, and look where I am now : you blokes haven't got no guts. Don't stand there gaping at me : get on with that there clamp, blast you.'

He swung round on his heel and stumped off : Ern and Harry looked curiously after him.

'I should like to know where the farm'd be,' said Ern grimly, ' without us chaps.'

' Fare to me, Ern,' said Harry, picking up his spade, ' father's going into his second childhood.'

' That's what Ben say,' Ern grunted, ' but I don't know so much. Look here, young Harry, you'd better soon cut off down to the sheep, afore the postman come. Do you go now. I'll soon finish this.'

' All right,' said Harry, plunging his spade in the side of the clamp. ' If that's all the same to you, I will. We'd best take no risks.'

So far their plan had worked well. Two letters had come during the month and Harry had intercepted them both on the hillside : the only other visitor had been a travelling tinker who had pushed his barrow up the hill one afternoon to find the doors all bolted and the curtains drawn ; he had trundled his barrow down again, swearing under his breath the whole way, and at the bottom of the hill he turned round to shake his fist at the house. Benjamin was told nothing of all this : he was not the man to care whether Nancy's condition was known in the village or not, and had he heard of their precautions, as likely as not he would have done his best to thwart them out of sheer perversity.

Harry was soon at work among his sheep, at the same time keeping a close watch on the drift ; it needed a sharp eye on such a misty morning in spite of all the sun's valiant efforts to break through. Benjamin was not to be disappointed. At half-past ten a figure emerged from the cloud at the bottom of the hill and began to climb the slope. Harry advanced to the drift to meet it, but after a few yards he stopped. It was Jessie Eves ; her father must be ill this morning and she was doing both the rounds herself. Harry hesitated a moment; it would be difficult to face her; on the other hand he must not fail Nancy: he moved forward again resolutely. Jessie, seeing him coming towards her, quickened her pace and darted past him. Harry waved his arm and shouted. But Jessie, instead of stopping, glanced nervously over her shoulder and took to her heels: she was even shyer of him than he was of her. Harry stood still and despairingly watched her disappear up the hillside; the harm was done now and it was no use chasing her up to the farmyard gate and taking the letter from her by force; she would see at once that something was wrong. He could only hope that Nancy would not be about the yard or in the kitchen when she arrived. He was not surprised after Jessie's behaviour that she did not come back past him again along the drift: she had found another way down to the road across the fields. Harry gloomily went on with his work: he had not the spirit to go up to the house and find out what had happened: in any case Ern would have been about the yard and got hold of the letter.

An hour later, when the mist had cleared away and the sun burst out in dazzling brightness, he descried a cart making its way slowly up the drift. It was almost a hundred yards past him, and had already reached a point in full view of the farmyard—Harry had not expected anyone else after Jessie and had been too busy to notice it. He shaded his eyes with his hand and saw that the driver was Betsy Barnes; she must be stopped at all costs. He ran wildly up the hill and overtook her just before the gate of the last field.

' Hi, Betsy!' he shouted. ' That's no use going up there. Nance is abroad.'

' Oh, is she? ' replied Betsy sarcastically. ' Young Jessie Eves told me only ten minutes ago she'd just now seen her.'

Harry looked confusedly from one side to the other.

' Well, anyhow, she's ill,' he said doggedly, ' and you can't see her.'

' Oh,' said Betsy, with a grim smile, ' that's just what Jessie say. "I think she don't look well," she say, "but I don't know what's the matter with her." So I came up to see what was wrong : I haven't seen her but once since she first came to Crakenhill.'

At that moment Nancy came out of the kitchen with a bowl of potato parings on her arm, limped across the yard and tossed them into the pig-styes : even at that distance her condition was plain to see. Harry wondered what could have possessed her to display herself in that reckless fashion so soon after Jessie had managed to penetrate to the farm.

Betsy kept her eyes fixed on her until she had disappeared into the house and then turned round on Harry with a cynical smile.

' I think I know what's the matter with her,' she said drily. ' I shan't bother to go up and see her now. Good morning, Harry.'

She wheeled her pony round and ambled down the hill, chuckling to herself, with now and then a malicious glance behind her at Harry who had walked slowly back to his sheep in the deepest dejection ; he had done his best, but everything was against him that morning. Betsy, having reached the road, drove straight on into Bruisyard and did not stop until she reached the mill house. She tied her pony to the gate-post and knocked at the door. Mrs. Pearman was making pastry and came out with her arms all floury.

' Why, Betsy,' she exclaimed, ' back again already this morning! I thought you were going on to Badingham.'

' Ah, so I was, Mrs. Pearman,' replied Betsy, ensconcing herself between the doorposts, ' but I've got something to tell you.'

' Oh, have you ? ' said Mrs. Pearman eagerly. It must be worth hearing if Betsy had turned back on purpose.

' After I left yours just now,' said Betsy, ' I met young Jessie Eves along the road. She'd just been up to old Geaiter's place with a letter and she say to me that that girl Nancy they've got up there was rather poorly like. Young Jessie only seed her through the door, but it fared to her she couldn't walk properly. But Nancy only laughed and said she had a sore back.'

' Ah,' said Mrs. Pearman tragically, ' she've had a thrashing, I can guess.'

' Do you wait,' replied Betsy, interposing a finger, ' and hear the rest. When I heard that, I took the trap and driv up Crakenhill drift to find out for myself : and what do you think, young Harry—he's the youngest, ain't he ? —he tried to stop me. He say to me, '' She's abroad.'' And when I told him Jess Eves had just seen her, he went all red in the face and looked silly and uncomfortable like. '' Well,'' he say, '' you can't see her : she ain't well.'' And then, the lying young wretch—what do you think happen ? Why, Nancy go lumbering across the yard right in front of us with a bowl on her arm, all slipperty slop like. I came away after that ; I didn't need to see no more.'

Betsy paused to heighten Mrs. Pearman's suspense.

' Well ? ' demanded Mrs. Pearman excitedly.

' Why, it's as plain as you're a-standing here with your arms all white,' replied Betsy tantalizingly.

' What is ? ' said Mrs. Pearman, quite breathless with excitement.

' Why,' said Betsy, ' that that girl's going to have a baby if anybody ever was.'

Mrs. Pearman stared amazedly at Betsy for a moment with her mouth wide open : she closed it with a snap.

' What did I tell you, Betsy ? ' she said, laying her finger on Betsy's shoulder. ' When you first told me who it was they'd got up there to do for 'em, I say to you, '' There'll be trouble there as sure as sure,'' I say.'

' And what did I say to her,' rejoined Betsy, cutting in before the last words were out of Mrs. Pearman's mouth, ' that day I sold her that piece of check cotton print ? '' You look out, my gal, some of them blokes don't go running after your skirts.'' That's what I say to her.

She's a saucy young baggage she is : look how she cheeked me that day when I tried to be kind to her. Fare to me she desarve it.'

' Well, what can you expect, Betsy,' pursued Mrs. Pearman, ' with those five great sons up there and that wicked old wretch of a father ? You know what it is. All the women who've been up at that there farm, something happen to them; first poor Mrs. Geaiter, then poor Maria, both wore up, and now Nancy Hambling—she's not wore up yet, but she soon will be. And, Betsy——'

She solemnly raised her hands and fixed her with a glassy eye.

' Yes, Mrs. Pearman ? ' replied Betsy meekly.

' Think what they may have done to poor Maria up there,' Mrs. Pearman went on. ' I can believe anything of 'em now.'

' Yes, so can I,' said Betsy in an awestruck voice : Mrs. Pearman was well in her stride now ; there was no room for her to talk now : she could only stand and listen admiringly.

' And which of 'em d'you think have got her into trouble, Betsy ? ' asked Mrs. Pearman, wrapping her floury arms in her apron.

' Lor! how should I know ? ' replied Betsy. ' I only stayed there long enough to get a sight of Nancy. To tell you the truth, I don't much like going up there. But Harry looked pretty foolish when she came out into the yard. I shouldn't wonder if he've got something to do with it.'

Mrs. Pearman pursed her lips and shook her head.

' No, Betsy,' she said, with a decided air. ' I don't think so. Why, he's the youngest of all. If you ask me, it was all of 'em. You can depend on it, Betsy ; that's what it was. They're a real wicked lot, that family, fit for anything, they are. My husband 'on't have no dealings with 'em ; he haven't for this past twelvemonth.'

She tossed her head indignantly.

' Yes, I can believe it all,' said Betsy mournfully, the

gloom settling deep upon her big red face. 'Those six great men. Poor Maria! Poor Maria!'

'Ah, there's Mrs. Spatchard,' cried Mrs. Pearman, looking out across her garden gate. 'It fare to me she ought to know about it : don't you think so, Betsy ? '

'Becourse,' replied Betsy, nodding emphatically.

'Mrs. Spatchard,' called Mrs. Pearman, 'here, I want you a minute.'

'Well, Mrs. Pearman,' said the blacksmith's wife, coming up the garden path, 'what is it ? '

'Why, Mrs. Spatchard,' replied Mrs. Pearman, 'you know the bit of a girl who went up to keep house for that old devil, Benjamin Geaiter, a twelvemonth ago ? '

'Yes,' said Mrs. Spatchard, 'but I never hear nothing about her ; she never come down here. I've not seen her above once.'

'I should think not,' said Mrs. Pearman acidly, 'I should think not. She's going to have a baby, she is.'

'Well, I never!' ejaculated Mrs. Spatchard. 'And who's the father ? '

'Who ? ' repeated Mrs. Pearman scornfully. 'Why, all six on 'em to be sure. What else d'you expect in such a house ? Poor little Mrs. Thriddle's right lucky to be out of it ; I'm that glad I kept her from going there. I knew she'd repent of it. You know my husband 'on't have any dealings with 'em now, Mrs. Spatchard.'

'And no wonder,' replied the blacksmith's wife. 'I don't blame him. That Benjamin Geaiter is a wholly wicked old man and no mistake.'

'A wife-beater,' said Mrs. Pearman, raising her chin high in the air and letting it drop on her breast to emphasise her words.

'Yes, a wife-beater,' echoed Mrs. Spatchard.

'And a murderer,' added Mrs. Pearman, with another nod.

'And a murderer,' repeated Mrs. Spatchard, quite fascinated.

'And now, now,' Mrs. Pearman faltered a little, 'I can't think of anything bad enough to call him.'

' No, nor can I,' agreed Mrs. Spatchard.

' Well, what shall we do ? ' asked Mrs. Pearman abruptly.

' Ah, that's it,' replied Betsy tragically. ' What can we do ? '

' I don't know,' said Mrs. Spatchard with a despairing shake of the head, ' I really don't.'

' But something must be done,' said Mrs. Pearman severely. ' That sort of thing can't be allowed to go on. First Mrs. Geaiter, then Maria, and now Nancy : a regular old Bluebeard, he is. It ain't proper, in a nice, quiet, respectable little parish like Bruisyard. Why should they make all this scandal among us and set up this wicked example for our young folks. Besides, that's ungodly, Mrs. Spatchard ; that's sin before the Lord and that old wretch'll go to hell, sure's I stand here. It's not nice to have a man condemned to the eternal flames so near. That make me feel all of a tremble.'

' Ah, that do,' said Betsy, herself shivering sympathetically.

' I wouldn't go up there by night for anything in the world,' added Mrs. Spatchard, clutching her skirts tightly round her.

' By night ? ' cried Mrs. Pearman. ' I wouldn't go there in broad daylight, no, not if you was to offer me a thousand pound. I don't know how you brought yourself to go there, Betsy.'

' Well, I didn't get right there to-day,' replied Betsy apologetically. ' And I shall never set foot there again.'

She could safely say it : there was no trade to be done there.

' But what shall we do ? ' repeated Mrs. Pearman. ' We must do something. Why, any night we may all be murdered in our beds or worse.'

The two other women shook their heads helplessly. Mrs. Pearman unrolled her arms from her apron and held up a finger. A scheme had been hatching in her brain the whole time : she had not forgotten how Benjamin had revenged himself on her a year ago and she was longing to be even with him.

'Look here, Betsy,' she said. ' When do you go into Frannigan next ? '

'I was going this arternoon,' replied Betsy.

'Well then,' continued Mrs. Pearman, ' do you go in and tell Ted Burbidge, the baker, what have happened to Nancy. He's her uncle, and it fare to me he ought to do something.'

'Ah, that's the thing of it,' whispered Mrs. Spatchard excitedly. ' Do you do that, Betsy.'

'That I will,' replied Betsy vigorously. ' You're quite right, Mrs. Pearman. He ought to do something. Besides, that bouncing young hussy need a strong hand.'

'And to-night,' Mrs. Pearman went on, dropping her voice to a whisper, ' I'll go and see the vicar and tell him all about it. He can remove the sin from our midst if anyone can, and warn 'em of the wrath to come. He'll have to do something, that's sure, and I shall tell him so. Would you like to come with me, Mrs. Spatchard ? '

'Well, I don't know,' faltered the blacksmith's wife. ' I'm not much good at that sort of thing, Mrs. Pearman.'

'Oh, you 'on't have to talk,' said Mrs. Pearman reassuringly. ' You needn't be afraid of that. Only it's wholly nice to have someone with you to back you up times like that. I should be much obliged, Mrs. Spatchard, if you would.'

'Well, all right, I will,' replied Mrs. Spatchard half-heartedly, still rather shy of the idea ; she preferred Mrs. Pearman to carry out her schemes by herself.

'That's wholly kind of you, I'm sure,' said Mrs. Pearman, looking relieved : she was a little frightened of facing the vicar all alone. ' I'll expect you round after tea and we'll go to the vicarage together. I must now go back to my cakes.'

'And I expect my husband 'll be wanting his dinner,' said Mrs. Spatchard, moving away from the door. ' Good morning, Mrs. Pearman.'

'Now don't you forget this arternoon, Betsy,' cried Mrs. Pearman, as they walked down the garden path together, 'when you get to Frannigan.'

'No, that I 'on't,' replied Betsy over her shoulder. 'Do you trust me.'

'Good,' said Mrs. Pearman. 'That'll larn the old sinner,' she called after them in a loud whisper.

'That will,' answered Mrs. Spatchard and shut the garden gate behind her.

XX

THE following afternoon when his sons had all gone out
to work, Benjamin settled down in front of the fire for
a nap in his big wooden elbow-chair. Nancy had already
washed up and retired to her bedroom ; she was continually going off by herself now, Benjamin thought, but
it did not worry him. Her meat pie had been particularly
luscious that day, he felt agreeably full and sleepy and he
soon began to nod. The sound of feet on the garden path
five minutes later made him raise his head with a jolt : he
muttered something inarticulate between his teeth and
closed his eyes again. A sharp rap on the front door
brought him properly to his senses ; it was years, positively
years, since anyone had knocked at that door. He started
up from his chair and peered out of the window. There was
a tall strange woman standing at the door, in a black
bonnet trimmed with silver, a long black coat of fine cloth
and shiny black button boots ; she carried an umbrella
and wore a massive gold brooch at her throat : undoubtedly a real lady, Benjamin perceived ; ordinary
folks would have come to the kitchen door. He walked
into the passage and opened the door just wide enough to
put his head out.

'Good afternoon,' said the lady in black. 'Are you
Mr. Geaiter ? '

'Yes, ma'am, I am,' replied Benjamin.

He looked a forbidding figure with his great grizzled
beard framed between the edge of the door and the door
post, still rubbing the sleep out of his eyes and curiously
scrutinising her pale blue eyes, her pale pouchy cheeks
and drooping mouth.

'I should like to speak to you for a moment, please,'
she said in a severe, authoritative tone ; she was evidently
used to having her own way.

'Yes, ma'am, what is it ? ' replied Benjamin, still
glaring at her through the crack of the door.

' Can I come in, please ? ' she said, tapping her foot impatiently on the doorstep.

' Yes, ma'am, you can,' said Benjamin, opening the door wide, ' and don't forget to wipe your feet on the mat. Our Nance is that partic'lar.'

He shut the door behind her and led the way along the passage into the parlour. Everything there was in perfect order ; not a fleck of dust to be seen, new muslin curtains in the windows and dazzling white antimacassars on all the chairs ; but the room was hardly ever used and smelt fusty. The lady stood still for a moment, waiting to be offered a chair, but when Benjamin, who was still under the influence of the meat pie he had eaten at dinner, dropped heavily into the arm-chair in front of her, she frowned critically and sat down without being asked.

' Well ? ' said Benjamin expectantly.

' I am Mrs. Nusthwaite,' she replied, ' and my husband is vicar of Bruisyard.'

' Oh,' said Benjamin.

' I don't think I've had the pleasure of meeting you before,' she continued.

' No, ma'am, you haven't,' Benjamin replied.

The vicar of Bruisyard was a knowing man. He had listened to all Mrs. Pearman's righteous invective the previous night with sympathetic approval, assuring her that he would look into the matter and see that justice was done, and Mrs. Pearman had gone away at Mrs. Spatchard's side feeling comforted that God had delivered her enemy into her hand. The first thing the vicar did was to seek out his wife. He had met Benjamin Geaiter only twice before, each time at a funeral—a morose, ill-spoken man who never came to church ; faint echoes of the gossip about him had reached his ears. Things could not be so bad as Mrs. Pearman alleged, he was sure, but he did not altogether relish the prospect of going up to Crakenhill and taking this man to task. After all, where a seduction was concerned, it was a woman who was wanted ; she could make discreet inquiries, she could offer consolation, she could persuade. He himself perhaps could step in afterwards when the time was ripe, to unite the guilty pair and, when appearances had been saved, to administer the pastoral blessing. It was fortunate for him that Mrs. Nusthwaite was a strong-minded woman who prided herself on being able to deal energetically with these farmers. She acquiesced without the least demur : a load off Mr. Nusthwaite's mind.

' If you came to church more often,' she added, unwilling to let slip the chance of a wholesome rebuke, ' we might be better friends.'

Benjamin grunted irritably : was this all the woman had come for ?

' I hear,' continued Mrs. Nusthwaite, overlooking the discourtesy, ' that there's a young woman in your house who is, who is—so.'

' If you mean,' said Benjamin, putting a hand on either knee and fixing her with a stolid gaze, ' that she's in the family way, there is.'

' Ah, I see,' said Mrs. Nusthwaite solemnly.

' Who told you ? ' asked Benjamin.

' Mrs. Pearm—— ' she began, and then checked herself. ' But that's really of no consequence, Mr. Geaiter.'

' Ah, I thought that was her,' said Benjamin. ' She's a real meddlesome baggage, ma'am, that woman.'

' She a good upright woman,' corrected Mrs. Nusthwaite, ' but that's neither here nor there, Mr. Geaiter. I didn't come to discuss that. You know it's really a very terrible thing about this young person.'

Benjamin snorted.

' It don't fare to me much to make a fuss about,' he said.

' Oh, doesn't it, Mr. Geaiter ? ' she replied. ' Well, I'm very glad I came, because I hope I can put you on the right path. It's a most wicked crime, Mr. Geaiter. Think of the poor girl's shame at her sin, and the wretched child's shame all through its life at being born in sin ; and everybody in the village pointing the finger of scorn.'

' That don't bother us what you do down there,' said

Benjamin, scratching his beard. ' We're far too busy on the farm.'

' Oh, I'm grieved, Mr. Geaiter,' she sighed, shaking her head, ' grieved and shocked, that you're so lost to all sense of shame ; and you ought to be ashamed, Mr. Geaiter, at such a disgrace to your house, because, Mr. Geaiter, it's real wickedness. The Bible forbids it and you'll be punished for it if you don't do something to set things right. You're master of the house.'

' That I am,' growled Benjamin.

Mrs. Nusthwaite felt that she was gaining ground and pushed on vigorously to make the most of her advantage. It was no use being shy with these farmers ; they needed a sharp tongue and a strong hand.

' Now tell me, Mr. Geaiter,' she said, ' which of your sons is the father ? '

' It ain't none of 'em,' replied Benjamin, still staring grimly at her.

' Look here, Mr. Geaiter,' she said severely, leaning forward on her umbrella handle, ' you don't expect me to believe that. Do you mean to say you haven't troubled to find out ? '

' I know,' said Benjamin emphatically.

' How do you know ? ' she demanded.

' Because it's me,' he replied deliberately, with his eyes still stolidly fixed upon her.

Mrs. Nusthwaite gasped. She could no longer face Benjamin's stare and dropped her eyes to the toes of her shiny black boots ; her lips went dry and she fidgeted nervously with the handle of her umbrella ; she felt most uncomfortable. Benjamin stared at her boots.

' Well, Mr. Geaiter,' she said at last in a faint voice, raising her head and moistening her lips, ' I'm astonished at you and grieved, most grieved. To think that in my husband's parish, a man of your age—I hope you realise the extent of your sin, Mr. Geaiter. Do you ? '

Benjamin said nothing, but continued staring at her feet. Mrs. Nusthwaite took his silence as a sign of contrition.

' Ah, I can see you do, Mr. Geaiter,' she went on, ' and I hope you will go on repenting all your life.'

Still Benjamin said nothing and did not raise his head.

' Ah, you are speechless with shame,' she cried triumphantly. ' I can tell you are, and well you may be. You must pray, Mr. Geaiter, night and day, and perhaps at the last God will forgive you. But there's one thing at least that you can do to make amends. I hope you'll marry the girl as soon as possible and make an honest woman of her so that the child can be born in Christian wedlock. You will, won't you ? '

Benjamin went on gazing at her feet with his head on his hands as if paralysed with remorse.

' Come, my man,' she said sharply, ' bestir yourself and answer me. A thing like that doesn't need any thinking over at all.'

' No, it don't,' replied Benjamin, looking up at last. ' What I've got to say to you, missus, is, mind your own business. I ain't a-going to have nobody interfering with my concerns. I know how to look after myself and I'm master in this house.'

Mrs. Nusthwaite opened her mouth wide and closed it with a snap, her pale blue eyes blinked and watered : she felt even more uncomfortable than before. Never before had a common farmer dared to address her thus. She stammered helplessly, quite unable to speak.

' I've got to go out and see how my sons are getting on with their drilling,' said Benjamin, getting up from his chair. ' I'll trouble you to go, ma'am.'

Mrs. Nusthwaite rose slowly from her chair and with a dignified air swept out of the room to the front door, which she opened herself as Benjamin did not bother to do it for her. She paused on the threshold and turned round.

' I shall never set foot in this house again,' she said haughtily.

' Nobody axed you, missus, I'm sure,' replied Benjamin as he shut the door on her. ' You bitch! ' he muttered to himself.

Mrs. Nusthwaite walked slowly away from the house, amazed and distressed at her humiliation; never, never in her life had such a thing happened before, and worst of all, she saw no way of getting her own back on Benjamin. He did not go to church, he owned his house and all his land, he employed no outside labour; there was no quarter from which he could be attacked.

Benjamin strode back into the kitchen and out into the yard, still muttering angrily between his teeth. Ern, who had been screwing a new latch on to the cowshed door, came over as soon as he saw him.

'There's a bloke from Frannigan want to see you, father,' he said. 'Come up here on a bicycle. He wouldn't go indoors, so I put him in the stable.'

'Oh, did you?' grunted Benjamin. 'All right.'

He stalked over to the stable with his hands in his pockets and put his head in at the door.

'Who's there?' he called.

A tall, thin, rat-faced man came forward out of the shadow.

'It's only me, Mr. Geaiter,' he said rather nervously— 'Ted Burbidge, Nancy's uncle.'

'Oh,' said Benjamin gruffly, stepping inside. 'What do you want?'

'Well, you see, Mr. Geaiter,' replied the baker hurriedly, 'they told me that niece of mine was in the family way and I came up to find out about it.'

'Oh, you did, did you?' rejoined Benjamin.

'Yes,' said the baker, who was beginning to regain courage. Benjamin was nothing to be afraid of after all— he only came up to his shoulder. 'It fare to me something ought to be done about it.'

'What?' said Benjamin.

'Well, you know,' said Burbidge, 'she's all we've got. We've never had any children of our own and we're that fond of her.'

'Well, why did you let her go?' demanded Benjamin.

'We didn't want to stand in her light, Mr. Geaiter,'

replied Burbidge. ' But we never thought she'd bring this disgrace on us. Which on 'em have done it, Mr. Geaiter ? '

' I ain't a-going to tell you,' said Benjamin. ' That ain't your business.'

' But that is my business,' protested Burbidge, putting his hands on his hips and trying to look Benjamin squarely in the face. ' She's my niece.'

' Maybe,' returned Benjamin, ' but she belong to us now ; she live in our house. If you'd treated her proper, she wouldn't have come away.'

' Becourse, if you talk like that, Mr. Geaiter,' said Burbidge, shrugging his shoulders, ' we can't let her stay with you any longer.'

The threat had not the least effect on Benjamin ; he laughed in the baker's face.

' All right,' he said, ' do you go over to the kitchen and tell her. If she'll go off with you, you're welcome to have her. But she 'on't. Fare to me Nance know where she's well off.'

He was quite right and the baker changed his tune : Nancy on his hands again, with a baby at her breast, was the last thing he wanted.

' Well, I 'on't go so far as that, Mr. Geaiter,' he said condescendingly, ' but it fare to me it's your duty to see that he marry her, whoever he is. I'd like to see our Nance married and nicely settled down. I look to you to do it, Mr. Geaiter.'

He rubbed his hands together and peered craftily at Benjamin with his head on one side.

' Oh, do you ? ' snapped Benjamin. ' Well, see here, Ted Burbidge, I tell you I ain't a-going to do nothing of the sort. I can manage my own affairs well enough without people like you poking their dam noses in. This is my house and Nance belong to it.'

A threatening light crept into the baker's eye.

' I don't want to have to bring the law on you, Mr. Geaiter,' he said, raising his eyebrows significantly, ' but if you will be obstinate, becourse there's nothing left to do. We must stand up for our own.'

Benjamin laughed out loud at him.

' Ay, that's the truth,' he said. ' That's just what I'm a-doing. When Nance begin to complain, then'll be the time for you to knock at the lawyer's door, and I reckon that'll cost you several shillings.'

Crakenhill was Nancy's only home and Benjamin was shrewd enough to realise it. The baker realised it too and decided to play his last card.

' Well, Mr. Geaiter,' he said cringingly, ' I 'on't say another word about it in Frannigan or anywhere, I promise you I 'on't, if you'll make it worth my while. The baking trade's that low, I can't tell you, and that's a real hard time for us now. I should be wholly glad of a five pun' note just now, I'm sure.'

He looked appealingly at Benjamin who stared at him for a moment with a sinister frown, his lips twitching. All at once he dived to the floor and snatched up a heavy plaited leather horse-whip.

' By God! ' he roared, brandishing it over his head, ' if you don't git out of this bloody stable double quick, I'll lay this about your blasted back till you can't stand, you ——'

The baker did not wait for him to finish. He dashed out of the stable, jumped on his bicycle and pedalled away down the drift as hard as he could go. Half-way down his front wheel caught in a deep rut and, slipping sideways, tipped him full length in the mud.

' Huh! ' sniffed Benjamin, who was watching him from the farmyard gate. ' That'll larn 'em, that will.'

XXI

AT midnight on the last day of January, with the help of a midwife from Cransford—Benjamin would no longer have any truck with Bruisyard—Nancy bore her child, a boy as strong and healthy as any other babies born in the parish. The midwife had never brought a finer into the world, she averred, when in the early hours of the morning she came down to announce the birth to the five brothers who had sat up all night round the kitchen fire, anxiously waiting : Benjamin was in bed long ago, fast asleep and snoring. He never showed the least sign of solicitude or affection for Nancy : and yet he was far from unkind. He never grumbled at her and he was always grateful for her cooking ; when her time began to approach, he had in a charwoman—also from Cransford—to help with the house-work and kept her on until a full month after the confine-ment had passed ; but the baby itself hardly interested him at all.

' H'm,' he grunted, when the charwoman told him the news at breakfast. ' A boy, eh ? Well, we'll call him Joseph.'

He said no more about it.

Nancy, however, was far too engrossed with her own concerns to be troubled by what Benjamin thought or did not think of the baby ; indeed, she had almost entirely lost sight of his fatherhood now : it was her child and hers alone, and it had possessed her with a new feeling of immense contentment, at once vital and soothing, which irradiated her whole being. In part it was what almost every mother feels ; the blessed relief of freedom after months of pregnancy, the pride and tenderness inspired by the sight of her child, a new life, fragment of herself, sucking at her breast—a mighty, primæval, earthy, life-giving emotion, bringing unconscious harmony with all space and all time. But for Nancy there was something more besides. Her child had suddenly provided her hitherto vague existence with a point of attachment which it sorely needed. It was not that her existence had been purposeless—good housewifery is a worthy enough end in itself—but it had always lacked human interest, it was emotionally empty ; and during the last months, for all that she was mistress of the house, she had taken up a passive, almost quiescent attitude to things and had let herself drift with the stream. There was indeed nothing else to do ; it followed inevitably from the circumstances of her seduction and it was useless for her to assert herself in any direction. To go back to her uncle and aunt, even if they had been willing to take her in, was impossible, and without a friend in the rest of the world, she was completely at the mercy of the Geaiters. What they would do with her she could not tell and she did not trouble to think. They might turn her out of the house along with her baby, and if they did, she could not stop them ; but so far she had had a warm enough place by their hearth and she could not complain of her treatment ; Crakenhill, if anywhere, was her home. The stream might engulf her, it might bring her safely to land ; meanwhile she had drifted on unreflecting and let her baby be born. Even after, she went on drifting, still uncertain of her course and quite unable to determine it ; but she now had a more active interest in survival. The mere bringing to birth of this new creature put her under an obligation to preserve it ; here was something to live for, to fight for, to tend, to love, and at moments when the world bore too hardly on her, something to turn to for solace and companionship.

The five brothers like their father did not show much interest in the baby once it was born : it was a long time since they had themselves been children, and to them the child was more of a curiosity than anything else. But towards Nancy they still maintained the same attitude of almost paternal consideration as before, and when the charwoman went back to Cransford and Nancy was left alone in the house, they redoubled their efforts to lighten her work. Each day now, instead of sitting over the table after meals to smoke, they took it in turns to wash up the dirty things ; they never allowed her to scrub a floor or carry a scuttleful of coal and they even cleaned the windows themselves. Altogether between them they must have been responsible for nearly half the housework and Nancy was grateful to them. It was no light burden to keep the household going single-handed and attend to her child properly as well ; even with their help there were times when she seemed only just able to keep her head above water.

Benjamin watched all these kindnesses with jealous suspicion ; at the back of his mind he could not help feeling that in spite of their apparent disinterestedness his sons wanted to get Nancy away from him again. At present she was obviously too much wrapped up in her baby to pay much heed to anyone ; but later on, when the first enthusiasm of her motherhood had worn off and her baby had become less exacting, she might easily begin to make comparisons at his expense. He never did anything for her, he seldom talked to her, he never smiled at her : it was natural that when she found time to be gracious, it was his sons and not himself who benefited by her graciousness ; it was to them that she talked, on them that she smiled ; they were infinitely closer to her than he was, they possessed more of her than he did ; and every day he was growing older. On the other hand, he was well aware that but for the services which his sons performed for Nancy, he would have had to employ a day-woman to help with the housework which was obviously beyond Nancy's unaided powers—even Benjamin saw that—and his thrifty soul revolted at the idea : he dared not say anything to discourage them. Thus torn between jealousy and self-interest, he chafed bitterly, no longer feeling himself master in his own house, and outside in the yard and fields his temper grew more evil from day to day ; nothing his sons could do was right and he hardly ever seemed to open his mouth except to rage at them ; that at least he could do without fear of the consequences ; but, nevertheless, the longing for some more effective way of asserting his mastery preyed upon his mind continually. In this fashion three months slipped by.

One fine morning at the end of April, Benjamin dropped his knife with a clatter on the breakfast table and cleared his throat. He looked up at his sons.

'I've got some business at Frannigan this morning,' he said, 'and I shall want you, Ben, and you, young Harry, to come and help me. You might come along too, Nance,' he added. 'I expect there'll be one or two things you'll be wanting. Do you go and get the trap ready, young Harry.'

'But what about dinner for the rest?' asked Nancy.

'Well, if we aren't back in time,' replied Benjamin, 'they can get some bread and cheese out of the cupboard theirselves.'

'Oh, well, if it's like that,' said Nancy, 'I don't want to come.'

'Well, you are coming, my gal,' replied Benjamin stubbornly. 'So don't make no fuss about it.'

Nancy said no more : it was no use trying to cross Benjamin once he had made up his mind.

'I wonder what he have taken into his head now,' said Bob, as he helped Harry to put one of the lighter cart-horses into the trap. 'I can't make father out nowadays.'

'No more can I,' replied Harry. 'Why, he only went into Frannigan yesterday. P'r'aps it's some lawyer business.'

'P'r'aps that is,' assented Bob, 'but all the same that'll properly mess up our summerland, we shan't finish to-day even if Ben do get home by dinner time. Fare to me Ben was right, and father's getting old.'

'Now then, Bob,' shouted Benjamin, coming out of the kitchen in the faded black suit he had worn at Maria Cragg's funeral and a battered old bowler hat, 'get you off to your horses. It don't need two to put a horse into that there trap.'

He hoisted himself into the seat and took up the reins.

A moment after Nancy came out of the kitchen with the baby on her arm, followed by Ben, who helped her up into the seat beside Benjamin and then climbed up behind. Harry, letting go the horse's head, jumped up next to his brother and with a crack of Benjamin's whip the trap went lurching down the drift.

' In his best clothes, too,' said Hiram, peering warily round the stable door, ' and his hard hat. That's a rum 'un, if you like.'

' That is,' said Bob.

.   .   ◦

It was high noon when they reached the farm again. They were all silent. Nancy seemed shut up in her own thoughts and almost unconscious of the world around her ; Ben and Harry had a cowed and hang-dog look about them ; but there was a triumphant gleam in Benjamin's eye. Nancy went off indoors at once to get some sort of a meal ready and Benjamin followed her. Ben and Harry, having unharnessed the horse and put the trap away in gloomy silence, strolled down into the rickyard to meet Bob and Hiram who were just bringing their horses back from plough. Ern, catching sight of them from the pig-styes, ran over and joined them.

' Back late ? ' said Ben, as Bob and Hiram pulled their horses up by a straw stack.

' Ay,' replied Hiram, ' we tried to finish all but the hidland before dinner, but that was too much.'

' Oh,' said Ben nonchalantly, ' I see.'

He hardly seemed to care if they had finished or not.

' Well ? ' said Bob.

' Well what ? ' growled Ben.

' What have you been a-doing of all the morning ? ' said Bob.

Ben groaned and looked down, fidgeting in the straw with the toe of his boot.

' What's up, Ben ? ' said Ern, alarmed.

' He've been and done it,' replied Ben in a tragic voice.

' Done what ? ' said Hiram, opening his eyes wide.

' Why, gone and married our Nance,' said Ben savagely.

The three brothers gaped stupidly at him. Hiram pulled a straw out of his horse's mane and bit the end off.

' 'Struth ! ' he exclaimed. ' Did he tell you he was a-going to do it ? '

' Not a word,' answered Harry. ' He take us straight into the register office and say, " Me and Nance are going to get married. You two are the witnesses." That was the first we heard of it. You could have knocked me down with a feather.'

' And what's more,' added Ben, ' he didn't tell her neither.'

' What did she do ? ' said Ern.

' Why, she go white as death,' replied Ben, ' and just say, " Oh, are we ? " That's all.'

' And what did she do then ? ' said Bob, his left eyebrow twitching violently.

' She just followed father in without a word,' said Ben. ' The bloke there was expecting him. He'd been in the day before and fixed it all up.'

' Ah,' said Bob, ' I wondered what he was after, a-going into Frannigan yesterday morning.'

' Yes,' said Harry, ' and when the bloke asked Nance how old she was, father up and say "Twenty-two:" and we had to sign the book as witnesses.'

' The old liar ! ' exclaimed Ern. ' And what then ? '

' Why, then,' replied Harry, ' he take us into The Feathers and call for three half-pints of beer and make us drink his health : and he laugh and say, " I never seed two fellers enjoy a glass of beer less." That's what he say ; and then he get Nance a slice of cake and a glass of lemonade and driv us home.'

' There's a caution for you,' said Ben grimly, shrugging his shoulders.

They stared vacantly at one another.

' Well,' said Hiram at last, ' I doubt that make Nance respectable like now.'

' So that may,' replied Ben sarcastically. ' But what else d'you think that'll do ? '

' I couldn't tell,' said Hiram, shaking his head.

' Why, don't you see,' Ben went on, ' now father have married her and got a boy, he'll leave all he've got to 'em 'cause they can't support theirselves. Nance is only a slip of a girl. You see if he 'on't.'

' Lord ! I never thought of that,' said Hiram, scratching his moustache.

' Nor me neither,' added Bob. ' But that's what he'll do, right enough.'

' I call it hard, real hard,' said Ben bitterly. ' Father have taken all our young life and used it up : we might have been hired men for all he've ever done for us. We stayed on here for the sake of the farm when we might have went away and bettered ourselves : and now that'll go to somebody else. That's cruel hard and no mistake.'

' Yes,' said Harry, ' and he curse and swear and rave at us from morning to night ; but I should like to see what he'd do without us.'

' Ah, so should I,' said Bob.

' That wouldn't make no difference,' pursued Ben, taking off his hat and scratching his close-cropped head, ' if we knowed we should have the farm for ourselves. Becourse, we don't know what he'll do, but we can't say nothing to him : that might put the idea into his head.'

' That's the truth we can't,' said Hiram.

They stood silent for a moment, eyeing one another helplessly.

' I say,' burst out Ern impetuously, ' let's clear out. We're not too old for that.'

' Yes, let's clear out,' echoed Harry. ' It have got a bit too much. First he get Nance into trouble and then he marry her. It's no place for us.'

Bob and Hiram nodded approval. Ben wearily shook his head.

' Yes, that's all right, Ern,' he said, ' but what about the farm ? It's us have made it what that is. If we go, that'll go to hell, sure as I stand here. Father's getting real old now and you know yourselves what hired men are like.'

The other four turned their heads and looked away, shuffling their feet uneasily in the straw which littered the ground. Each of them was feeling what he had felt when he had tried to leave the farm before, and thinking of what would have to be sacrificed: sheep, cows and horses, friendly roofs and a familiar hillside.

' Yes,' said Ern at last, rather shakily, ' you're right, Ben. We can't let the farm go to pieces after all these years, can we, boys? '

' No,' said Hiram and Harry together, ' we can't.' Bob shook his head.

' No,' said Ben in a low voice, ' I thought you couldn't. Time for dinner now, boys.'

He put on his hat with a sigh of relief and walked off towards the house. Bob and Hiram seized the bridles of their horses and with Ern and Harry beside them trudged slowly after him.

XXII

BETSY BARNES drew slowly up the hill into Bruisyard village and stopped her pony at the gate of the mill house. Mrs. Pearman came down the path to meet her, drying her hands on her apron and blinking impatiently at the genial April sunshine that streamed into her face.

' Why, Betsy,' she said, ' I've been expecting you this last half-hour and I'd got all forward with my work on purpose.'

' Yes, I'm all behind to-day, Mrs. Pearman,' said Betsy, ' like the cow's tail. That Mrs. Thresher of Rendham kept me talking I don't know how long. That woman have got a tongue, Mrs. Pearman.'

' Well, what have she got to say ? ' asked Mrs. Pearman.

' Nothing, Mrs. Pearman, nothing,' replied Betsy, shaking her head disgustedly. ' All about her husband's wheat and her setting of duck's eggs and her little boy's whooping cough : nothing of what you might call real conversation. And after all that she didn't ondly buy one card of buttons.'

' Ah, some women are like that,' said Mrs. Pearman sagely.

' That's the truth,' said Betsy. ' Too many on 'em.'

' Well, what have you got to tell me, Betsy ? ' asked Mrs. Pearman.

' Well, to tell you the truth, there ain't nothing worth telling,' replied Betsy apologetically. ' The Methody parson's wife at Kelsale have had a baby girl, both doing well, they say; and Bill Gurney's going out of the Trust farm at Swefling come Michaelmas ; and Mrs. Petticrew —she live opposite the church at Cransford, you know— she say her husband came home drunk again the other night and that'll land 'em all in the workhouse one of these days.'

' Ah, that that will,' said Mrs. Pearman. ' That ain't the first time.'

' Oh, and one other thing,' added Betsy. ' I met young Ern Geaiter going into Sax with the milk and he'd got young Miss Nancy with him in the back of the cart.'

' You mean Mrs. Geaiter, his step-mother, don't you ? ' Mrs. Pearman corrected sarcastically.

' Ah, that's it,' replied Betsy. ' Now she's mistress of the house and have got a woman up there to do the work, she go out just when she think she will and act the lady.'

' Mistress of the house indeed! ' snorted Mrs. Pearman. ' I suppose she think she can hold up her head among decent women now she've been married in that hole-and-corner fashion. Well, I don't call her married, Betsy. That ain't Christian wedlock.'

' No more that ain't,' rejoined Betsy. ' She's a rare hussy, she is, and no mistake, and I reckon she's now leading the old man a fine dance. That's what have made him go downhill ever since he married her. Have you noticed, Mrs. Pearman, right from the day he had that stroke, she began gadding about and going in to Sax in the milk-float : and him sitting at home helpless and blind and all, poor owd man.'

' Poor owd man! ' repeated Mrs. Pearman scornfully. ' That's a judgment on him: that have come late, but I knew that'd come—after the way he treated the vicar's wife and her a real lady, and me and my husband and Nancy and poor Mrs. Geaiter. I've got no pity for him.'

' Nor me neither,' said Betsy.

' Yes,' continued Mrs. Pearman with an air of conviction, ' it sarve him right to be neglected in his old age, and I doubt he is. Old men as marry young wives, and all those men in the house—you know what it is, Betsy.' Betsy pursed her lips and nodded. ' But her sin'll find her out too, Betsy, you mark my words, like it have found out the old man. We can be thankful, Betsy, that there's a just God above us.'

There was a rumble of wheels and a milk-float came into view round the corner. The two women looked up and stared. Nancy was sitting next to Ern on a plank at the back behind the empty churns, with her baby on her lap and a basket at her feet. As soon as she caught sight of Betsy, she turned her head and looked haughtily up the road in front of her.

' There,' said Betsy to Mrs. Pearman, loudly enough for Nancy to hear as she and Ern drove past, ' you see she can't look me in the face.'

' And no wonder,' replied Mrs. Pearman, ' carrying the proof of her shame along of her for all the world to see.'

' There's a nice pair for you,' said Ern with a harsh laugh as they left the mill behind them. ' When them two get together——'

Nancy nodded dejectedly and they drove on to the farm in silence. Ern unharnessed the cob and Nancy went off indoors with her purchases.

Benjamin was sitting crouched over the kitchen fire in his wooden elbow-chair with a pile of disordered cushions at his back. Betsy was right; he had gone a long way downhill in the two years that had passed since his marriage. Like his first wife, he had worked too hard all his life and though he had never felt the strain of it before nor even suffered a day's illness, old age descended upon him suddenly and he had no power to resist it. For some time he continued to potter about the farm, doing such work as was still within the compass of his failing strength and infuriated to find himself no longer the man that he had been. Both Nancy and his sons, perceiving his condition, did their best to restrain him, but he would not listen. ' I'm master in this house,' he would reply angrily, ' and I know what's good for me.' Then one day a year ago he had been seized with a stroke in the hayfield and brought back to the house unconscious. He recovered, nevertheless, after a month in bed, but the use of his right arm was gone and soon after his sight began to fail. Decrepitude seemed to have taken possession of him at one blow. His hair and beard were now quite white, his cheeks sunken and colourless; his bowed back and hunched shoulders gave the impression that the whole of his massive body was shrinking inwards and downwards, as if seeking its centre: his one good hand shook continually. He was no longer fit for anything but to sit by the fire, brooding and drowsing: he could not even look out of the window now with his pale, almost sightless eyes. Amid this general wreck of his faculties, however, the power of his tongue survived unimpaired: it had even gained in violence and bitterness and he used it unsparingly: the only relief from the misery of such an existence was to visit it upon those around him.

Nancy put her basket down on the table and rummaged in it: it was full of cotton stuffs and balls of wool for the baby's clothes; he was well over two years old now and growing fast. She pulled out a newspaper and went over to Benjamin.

' I've brought you the *Suffolk Mercury*, father,' she said, laying it on his knees.

' Well, what's the good of that ? ' he replied gruffly. ' You know I can't read it.'

' All right, father,' said Nancy gently. ' I'll read it to you after dinner. I must now go up and make the beds.'

' Would you mind filling my pipe, Nance ? ' he said in a softer voice. ' That's right burnt out and I couldn't find my baccy.'

Nancy picked up his pouch from the hearthrug and filled the pipe. The dairy door opened and the day-woman who had been scrubbing the floor came out with a pail in her hand. Since the time of Benjamin's stroke it had been impossible to do without outside help: the entire conduct of the farm was now in the hands of the brothers and they could no longer be expected to saddle themselves with half the housework. With much reluctance Benjamin had consented to have a woman in to help Nancy, but he insisted that she should not come from the village.

' Well, Mrs. Snaith,' said Nancy, ' is the fire lit under the bake-oven yet ? '

' That is,' replied the woman, ' and that'll soon be right hot.'

'Well, we'll get on with the bread directly after dinner,' said Nancy. 'I'm now going to make the beds.'

She gathered up Joseph, who had been playing on the hearthrug, and went upstairs, leaving Benjamin by the fire, puffing slowly at his pipe and grunting to himself.

An hour later she came down again and laid the table for dinner. Benjamin was fidgeting in his chair.

'Why, your cushions are all lop-sided, father,' she said. 'No wonder you're uncomfortable. Sit up a minute.'

She readjusted the cushions behind him and he lay back in his chair. Nancy picked up the newspaper and sat down opposite him.

'Mrs. Snaith,' she said, 'will you dish up now? I can hear the men in the yard. What would you like me to read, father?'

'If it have got a bit about last week's market at Sax,' replied Benjamin, 'do you read that.'

'Ah, here it is,' said Nancy, after scanning the sheets for a moment.

She began to read rather laboriously in a loud voice a long rigmarole of prices and names of buyers, Benjamin periodically interjecting a grunt of indignation or astonishment. She was half-way through when the brothers came clattering in and sat down at the table. Nancy stopped reading and got up from her chair. She took a plate of meat and vegetables from Mrs. Snaith, who was already at the head of the table carving, and having cut the meat up in small pieces, put it on a chair in front of Benjamin with a glass of beer beside it.

'There you are, father,' she said, putting the fork into his hand. 'There's your dinner.'

The brothers were already beginning their meal and hardly took any notice of her. This was an every-day occurrence.

'Thank you, Nance,' said Benjamin. 'You're the only one as ever do anything for me.'

Ben and Hiram looked at one another.

'Those good-for-nothing sons of mine,' pursued Benjamin, who seemed more cantankerous than usual this morning, ' they never do nothing for me like you, Nance. They never talk to me, they never tell me how the farm s getting on : you'd think it was their farm.'

' We work for you, father,' protested Ern, ' real hard.'

' Yes, I know,' sneered Benjamin, ' but I know why. You think it's your farm and you can do what you like with it. You're only waiting till you get it into your clutches. I know you.'

He gesticulated with his fork and his face went quite red with anger.

' Ssh, father,' said Nancy, who was busily engaged in feeding Joseph with a spoon. ' Don't go on like that.'

' I will speak if I want to,' cried Benjamin. ' I know you, you good-for-nothings. But I'll do you out of it. You thought you were going to get Nance and you didn't. She's worth a score of you. Just you wait, you swine.'

He sank back in his chair, exhausted, dropping his fork on the floor as he did so. Nancy went over and picked it up and as she returned to her seat, she became aware all at once of five pairs of eyes, all fixed upon her in a reproachful glare. The unselfish, solicitous regard of the brothers for her had come to an end long ago, quite suddenly, soon after her marriage with Benjamin ; she was not surprised at that ; but they had never looked at her like this before. She did not quail, however, but returned their gaze angrily, her cheeks flushing hotly with the sudden bitter resentment that swelled up within her. What right had they to stare at her so ? It was not her fault if Benjamin hated them : she did not want to curry favour with him, she had not asked to be his wife or bear his child : if they had not blamed her then, why should they blame her now for doing her duty as a virtuous wife ? How would they like to see their father comfortless and uncared for in his old age ? Angry words framed themselves on her lips, but she kept them back : their reproach had been silent after all. They slowly turned their heads away and went on with their meal.

When they had finished, they rose together as with a

common impulse, went out into the yard and gathered round Ben in the stable for a smoke ; they needed the comfort of one another's presence nowadays. For a few minutes they lolled against the walls and smoked in silence. Ern knocked out the ashes of his pipe against the door.

' It fare to me,' he said savagely, ' as if I could do some-one in.'

' Who, Ern ? ' said Ben.

' I don't know,' growled Ern, looking down at his feet, ' but I guess you know how I feel.'

' Yes, we all feel like that,' said Ben, nodding sympathetically.

' First father take Nance away from us,' pursued Ern angrily, ' and now Nance have took father : the next thing she'll take 'll be the farm, you see if she don't.'

' Ay, she want a thrashing, she do,' said Bob impulsively, caressing the lash of a horsewhip in the palm of his hand.

' Well, I don't know,' said Ben. ' I don't know as she can help it. She look after him well, she's a good wife. You wouldn't like to see father neglected now he can't do for himself, would you ? He's our father.'

' No, you're right,' admitted Bob, cooling down again, ' I wouldn't. Still that's hard all the same. Father've been pretty down on us, but he've never spoke out like that before. He mean to give her the farm, sure enough.'

' I'm wholly afraid he do,' said Ben. ' Yet what have we done to desarve it ? Why, we've made the farm what it is : and now it's us do all the work and no one to do us a hand's turn, winter or summer. It isn't as if we treated Nance cruel.'

' No,' said Ern, ' I sometimes feel it's father I'd like to do in.'

' Yes,' said Hiram sardonically, ' and turn us out of the farm all the sooner. He've made his will, you bet. Remember that lawyer bloke came here from Frannigan ? '

' What beat me,' said Harry, ' is that he ain't afraid of

us leaving the place before he die : he know that'd go to hell without us. He'd have to have a steward, and he couldn't see what he did.'

' Ah,' replied Ben with a bitter laugh, ' but he know too well that we don't want to go. He've got the whip hand of us and he can say what he like.'

' That's it,' cried Bob, thumping the stock of his whip on the bricks. ' He know we 'on't leave till we have to : so we can stop on to keep the farm in good heart till it come to Nance. It stand to reason she 'on't want us then. She'll sell out.'

' Ay, that's it,' said Ern, ' that's what she'll do. But what's to be done, Ben ? You're the eldest, you ought to know.'

' There ain't nothing to be done,' replied Ben hopelessly, ' and you know it, Ern. We can only sit down and wait for what's in store for us and you can guess what that is. We ain't done nothing to desarve it : that's our misfortune, that is.'

' Maybe,' grumbled Ern. ' That's all very fine and Nance may be a real good girl and all that, but that was a wholly bad day for us when she set foot inside our door. That's what I say.'

The other four shrugged their shoulders and said nothing : it was what they all felt. Ben put his pipe in his pocket and took down a horse-collar.

' Come along, boys,' he said.

XXIII

ONE bright Sunday morning in July little Joseph
looked up from his toys on the hearthrug and perceived that the kitchen door was open. His mother was
upstairs making beds, Mrs. Snaith had gone out into the
yard to throw some scraps to the chickens, Benjamin was
dozing in his chair. The open door fascinated him. At
two and a half, in the summer-time the world was full of
new and wonderful things for him to see and touch and
listen to ; he wanted to make their acquaintance ; he was
tired of the farm kitchen and his mother's apron-strings.
There were five big men who came in and sat down at the
table four times a day to eat and smoke ; they seldom
spoke to each other and never to him. He was a little
frightened of them, but not so frightened as he was of the
old man with the great white beard and one arm hanging
stiff from his shoulder, who always sat huddled by the
fireside and always seemed to be looking at him, but never
saw him ; at times he would roar and shake his fist at the
others and then Joseph would run to his mother's side and
clutch her hand tightly, trying hard not to cry. He
wanted to see the better world beyond and slipped
stealthily out of the kitchen door in search of it.

As he toddled across the farmyard, he caught sight of
Mrs. Snaith coming back with her empty dish and artfully
slipped behind the water-butt at the stable door. She
passed without noticing him and went straight into the
kitchen. As soon as the door was shut behind her, Joseph
darted out from behind the butt and made for the yard
gate as fast as he could go. He was in the rickyard now,
staring up at the mountains of hay and straw that
towered above him ; he wondered who could live in these
queer-shaped houses which had no doors or windows, but
smelt so sweet. A duck emerged from between two ricks
and quacked loudly at the sight of him—a new enemy
perhaps. Joseph gave chase : in and out of the ricks and

round behind the barn, but the duck was always ahead. Joseph suddenly found himself in front of the gate of the kitchen garden. Ern and Harry were leaning against it with their hands in their pockets and their pipes in their mouths. Joseph, recognising them, stopped: they looked different here in the outside world, less frightening: they might be induced to play with him. He sidled shyly up within a yard of them and then turned his head away in embarrassment. They stared down balefully at him.

'How have that brat got out?' said Harry. 'Nance generally keep him indoors.'

Joseph looked round and smiled coyly at them. Their faces remained unmoved. Joseph was not going to have his advances rebuffed in this fashion. He insisted on being recognised. He toddled up to Ern and slapped him familiarly on the knee.

'Be off with you,' said Ern roughly, with a jerk of his thumb. 'We don't want you here.'

Joseph looked wonderingly up at him with his mouth wide open.

'Yes, I mean it,' said Ern. 'Get you back home.'

Ern's face looked very stern and made Joseph want to cry. He scuttled off along the hedge of the kitchen garden out of his sight. A big gap in the hedge loomed up beside him and he stopped. The men could no longer see him. He looked through the gap: scarlet runner beans twining snakily up their sticks to thrice his own height, two smooth yellow marrows glistening on the manure heap and a whole row of purple pickling cabbages almost as big as himself—adventure. He plunged through.

'If it weren't for that brat,' said Ern, turning to Harry, 'we should be all right here, shouldn't we?'

'Yes,' replied Harry, 'and no mistake. He's the cause of all the trouble, he is. But for him, father'd never have married Nance.'

'No,' said Ern, 'and look you here, Harry, I reckon it's him we're a-working for and all now, him and Nance. That's what make you feel a bit mad sometimes, Harry.

A squalling kid—it wouldn't take much to finish him off.'

' Maybe,' said Harry, ' but what's the good ? Father've married Nance and the harm's done now, kid or no kid.'

' Ay, that's true,' admitted Ern gloomily.

He turned round and knocked out his pipe on the top bar of the gate.

' Why, look there, young Harry ! ' he exclaimed.

Harry, too, turned round. Down at the bottom of the garden, squatted between two rows of raspberry canes, was Joseph, ramming the raspberries into his mouth with both hands as fast as he could pick them.

' That 'on't do,' cried Harry. ' Hi, youngster ! come you out of that.'

Joseph looked up for a moment at them and then turned to his raspberries again. He could afford to reject their advances now : the outside world was very good.

' Well, if he 'on't come, we shall have to fetch him, 'said Ern. ' Do, we shan't get any more raspberry pies.'

He strode down the garden and hauled the child out from the canes by his blue overall.

' Out you come, you brat,' he growled. ' I'll larn you.'

' Better take him indoors,' said Harry, who had walked down after him.

Ern picked up the child and put him on his arm. It was the first time Joseph had ever been taken up by any of the brothers and Ern's face looked very grim : worse than that, he could see his luscious raspberries receding fast in the distance. It was too much for him : he set up a loud wail. A bedroom window overlooking the yard flew open with a bang and Nancy's head emerged. She just caught a glimpse of Joseph, struggling and screaming in Ern's arms as he came out of the gate of the kitchen garden. Without waiting to see more, she dashed downstairs and out of the kitchen door. Ern, finding it impossible to pacify Joseph, had put him down on a heap of straw in the rickyard, still kicking and sobbing, his cheeks scarlet with raspberry juice.

' What are you doing to my child ? ' cried Nancy, as she

came running up. She snatched Joseph to her breast and rocked him in her arms.

' He've been eating the raspberries,' replied Ern with a grin, ' and he didn't like being took away.'

' Oh,' retorted Nancy hotly. ' Well, he wouldn't have cried like that if you hadn't been rough with him. Don't you ever touch my child again.'

She ran off towards the house, clutching him tightly to her.

' There's a nice one for you, eh ? ' said Ern.

' Yes,' replied Harry. ' Next time he fall into the duck-pond, we'll leave him there.'

Nancy took the child upstairs and washed the juice off his face. She found a few scratches on his hands, too, from the thorns on the raspberry canes.

' You poor darling,' she whispered, kissing him again and again. ' Why shouldn't you have a few raspberries if you want to. My poor little Joey, I'll never let them touch you again.'

Through the window she saw Ern and Harry saunter down the garden and inspect the raspberry canes ; they plucked a few berries for themselves. A gust of rancorous feeling swept over her : she herself could put up with the mute hostility of their lowering glances well enough, although it was not her fault if Benjamin wanted to leave Crakenhill to her ; to live at peace among men with a place at someone's fireside was all that she had asked. But now her child was in danger, an immemorial, tigress-like ferocity kindled in her. She saw herself battling alone for them both against an unjust and suspicious world ; if it sought to crush her, she could hit back, if it had set its mark upon her, she would set her mark upon it. These five brothers—what had she not done for them ?—they had not saved her from Benjamin ; angry looks and churlishness, that was what she had got from them. Raking the past over in her mind, she suddenly awoke to the magnitude of her grievances. Well, she would show them. She was mistress of Crakenhill, she was Benjamin's wife and their step-mother ; they should feel the weight of her authority and know their place. She would protect her cub.

When Nancy sat down in her usual place at dinner that morning after preparing Benjamin's plate for him, there was a hard, determined look on her face. Joseph from his high chair at her side looked ruefully down the table at Ern, the big man with the rough voice, who had so heartlessly thwarted his new-born cravings. Nancy could see that he was still frightened and his timid glances whetted her indignation again. The five brothers went on eating steadily in stolid, unhappy silence. The oppressive gloom which had now settled down upon the household was no longer a thing to be dispelled by savoury roasts or flaky pie-crusts : there was too much suppressed feeling at its roots for that. At last the meal came to an end and they began to fill their pipes : they would soon be up and outside the house ; they were not anxious for Nancy's company now. She felt that it was time to assert herself and cleared her throat.

' Ern,' she said, in a strange, forced voice, ' I want you to pick those raspberries for me this afternoon. If you go on eating them, we shan't have any left soon and I want to make some jelly.'

The five men stared at her : it was unmistakably a command. There was a pause while Ern found his voice.

' Well,' he growled morosely, ' I can't. I've got something better to do this arternoon.'

' Well, I want 'em to-day,' replied Nancy emphatically. ' It may rain to-morrow and spoil 'em. If you don't pick 'em to-day, I shan't make you any jam this year.'

They stared harder at her : this was a deliberate threat. Benjamin, who a moment ago had been nodding with his elbow on the arm of his chair, suddenly came to life

' What's all this about, you dam great lout ? ' he bellowed. ' Becourse you'll pick them blasted berries if Nance says so. She's mistress here and I'm master, and you'll do what she tells you. What d'you think you're here for, eating my bread and wasting my money ? '

His voice had sunk to a dry, hoarse cackle and he took breath to go on again : but all at once the violence of his outburst overcame him and he dropped his chin on to his hand, muttering angrily to himself. No one spoke for a moment. Nancy pushed back her chair.

' We'll wash up, Mrs. Snaith,' she said.

She rose to her feet and took Joseph out of his chair. As she lowered him on to the floor, she was aware of Ben's eyes fixed strangely upon her. By now she was used enough to being stared at, but there was something in Ben's gaze that held her : there was no hatred, no anger in it, only his face seemed drawn and old as if all the sorrows of a lifetime had in that one moment been concentrated upon it. Did he think that she was in league with Benjamin against them ?   Nancy felt frightened, almost remorseful ; then, looking down at Joseph sprawling on the floor, she hardened her heart and began to gather up the plates.

XXIV

IT never looked as if Benjamin, with all his infirmities, could last much longer and yet he lingered stubbornly on, determined to exact from life its uttermost gleanings; at least, he would not now be done out of his allotted three score years and ten. He was entirely dependent upon Nancy, who fussed him and surrounded him with comforts, without affection, helplessly waiting for him to die; her fate was in his hands. Joseph was constantly at her side, a subdued, wistful child without playmates, half-bewildered, half-frightened by the unfathomable ways of the five big sombre men who lived in the same house, but never spoke to him. They kept themselves aloof and Nancy had no further occasion, or indeed desire, to assert her authority : but she would not trust the child out of her sight.

Meanwhile the capacious life of the farm went on with its myriad and inevitable cycle of tillage, sowing and harvest, extinction and regeneration, and the fields of Crakenhill were more than ever the pattern of good husbandry. Day in, day out, the five brothers laboured, with a passionate, fearful intensity, as if every furrow they ploughed, every sheaf they pitched, were the last. It was their only relief from the dark atmosphere of bitterness and distrust in which they were now condemned to live : but the farm could never wholly submerge them and their anxieties in its own consoling larger entity because it was the cause of all their suspense ; its own life was at stake.

Another harvest came round, the sixth since Benjamin's marriage ; he was almost seventy-two. The brothers had just come back to the kitchen for their dinner, hungry, tired and sweaty. It was an erratic season. The weather could not be foretold two days ahead, but the middle of August had brought a sudden burst of scorching brilliant sunshine and they were straining hard to finish the cutting while it held.

'Well,' said Ben, yawning and wiping his damp forehead with the back of his hand, 'is that oats all down yet, Hiram?'

He was just back from the blacksmith's at Bruisyard with a mare that had cast a shoe in the oatfield that morning. He had taken care that Benjamin should know nothing about it: there was no time to go to Badingham or Cransford.

'Yes, that's all down,' replied Hiram, 'and the reaper all jacked up ready to move in to the beans this arternoon.'

'That piece of beans,' mused Ben, scratching his bristly chin, 'I wonder if that's fit. The wheat next door ought to be wholly ripe. I didn't look this morning.'

'You don't want to cut beans too ripe,' put in Bob. 'Do, they shell out.'

'Ay, that's true,' Ben nodded. 'We mayn't have another chance. The wheat can wait.'

'What's this about beans?' croaked Benjamin from the fireside, pricking up his ears.

They seldom discussed the farm work in front of him now: so long as he heard nothing, he asked no awkward questions.

'Small piece of winter beans, father,' answered Ben, 'up on the hill where the copses used to be. That's fit to cut this arternoon, it fare to me.'

'H'm, you didn't sound very sure about it,' Benjamin grumbled. 'What's the good of that?'

'It don't matter if they're a bit on the green side,' said Ben, 'with a sun like this.'

'Don't it?' scolded Benjamin. 'I tell you that do. There's a right time and a wrong time to cut.'

'That's the truth,' Ben admitted, 'but when it's all shine to-day and all wet to-morrow, you've got to do the best you can.'

'All very fine,' said Benjamin impatiently, 'but I ain't a-going to have beans cut on my farm afore they're fit. Now, lookye here. I'm coming up along of you this arternoon to have a look myself and I'll tell you whether they're fit or not.'

' No, father, you mustn't,' said Nancy. ' On a day like this and all that way up the hill : that's silly.'

' See here, my gal,' replied Benjamin, catching hold of his beard and tugging excitely at it. ' This here farm is mine and I'm going to have the work done proper. You think I can't see. Well, p'r'aps I can't ; but I can still tell when a piece of beans is fit to cut.'

' But, father,' Nancy expostulated.

' Now that's enough, Nance,' said Benjamin abruptly cutting her short. ' I'm going. Someone get the cart ready to take me up. This farm have been going on too long without me. They never tell me nothing. I'm a-going to find out for myself.'

There was no more to be said and they all went on eating in silence. Nancy hoped that by the end of the meal he might have forgotten—he was sitting with his chin on his hand and his eyes closed—but as soon as the brothers rose from the table, he lifted his head.

' Hurry up with that cart,' he said. ' I want to get to them beans afore dark.'

' Oh, father——' Nancy protested.

' Look here, Nance,' he snapped. ' You're my wife and you've got to do what you're told : so be quiet.'

Nancy sighed and said no more : any further remonstrance would only have thrown him into a passion ; he was nervously moistening his lips and fingering the arm of his chair.

Five minutes later Ern and Harry brought the trap round to the kitchen door. They hoisted the big wooden elbow-chair, which Benjamin insisted on taking with him, into the back, and then helped him up into the seat. Nancy, too, climbed up and sat down beside him with Joseph on her lap : she could not let the old man go up there by himself. Ern took the cob's head and they set off. It was a laborious, uncomfortable journey over lumpy meadows and rutted cart-tracks. Benjamin, tightly clutching the back of his seat, with Nancy at his elbow doing her best to steady him, lurched this way and that, but he did not complain : it was all his own doing. When they arrived in the bean field at the top of the ridge which formed the boundary of Crakenhill, they found the others waiting for them by the hedge with the sail-reaper already harnessed up. Ben and Hiram came over and lifted Benjamin bodily out of the trap.

' Now then, where are them beans ? ' said Benjamin, stepping forward rather shakily and steadying himself with his stick. ' Someone give me a hand.'

Ben slipped his hand through his father's arm and walked him over to the headland.

' There you are, father,' he said. ' I reckon they're wholly fit to cut.'

' All right,' said Benjamin, ' do you wait. Let go of my arm. I can walk all right.'

He shuffled forward a few yards among the crackling stalks and then stopped. He groped for a pod and pulled it off ; opened it with his thumbnail, chewed a bean and spat it out. He bent down, broke a stalk in two and squeezed the juice out with trembling fingers.

' That's no good,' he shouted. ' That's green and full of milk. Let me have a look at the wheat.'

Ben took his arm again and led him through the gate into the adjoining field. He looked across at Hiram and shook his head in despair. Benjamin brushed in among the stalks once more, plucked an ear and rubbed it between his fingers until some of the grain shelled out. He blew the husks away and carefully felt the grain with his fingers, put it in his mouth, chewed it and spat it out. He picked two more ears and did the same. It was slow work with only one hand and the others watched him impatiently.

' Dead ripe,' he cried suddenly. ' This is the stuff to cut. Bring the machine in here and get on with it. I'm going to stay and listen. Get my chair down.'

Ben shrugged his shoulders and led him back through the gate into the bean field where his chair was standing ready for him by the trap. Ben took Hiram aside.

' That can wait a couple more days,' he whispered.
' How do he expect to tell by testing a few ears—when he
can't see the whole field? Them beans 'll shell out if we
wait another day, I can see now.'

' Well, let's cut the beans,' said Hiram. ' He 'on't know
the difference. He can't see.'

Ben hesitated.

' I don't like to do it,' he said, shaking his head. ' That's
deceit.'

' Pity to spoil them beans,' murmured Hiram.

' All right, then, do you get on with it,' said Ben
recklessly.

' D'you mean it? ' asked Hiram.

Ben nodded and walking over to Nancy, beckoned her
aside. He whispered in her ear; she looked dubiously at
him for a moment and then nodded. She went back to
Benjamin.

' Don't you think you'd better be getting back, father? '
she said. ' It's a long way and so hot; and you'll be tired.'

' Tired? ' growled Benjamin. ' Becourse not. I'm going
to stay and listen to 'em for a bit. They want gingering
up, they do. I can't think what I gave up farming for.'

' Oh, father, you shouldn't,' she expostulated. ' You're
not fit for it.'

' Hold your tongue, girl,' he exclaimed, ' and put my
chair where I can hear the reaper pass.'

Nancy took up the chair and, after a moment's hesitation, carried it a few yards along the same side of the
hedge to the shade of a tall, capacious elm tree where she
left it. She went back to Benjamin and led him to it.

' Where's the wheat? ' said Benjamin, as he sat down.

' In front of you, father,' she replied, pointing to the
beans. The next moment she had repented of the lie:
here she was, helping those five men who hated her to
deceive her own husband: but it was no use going back
on it now.

' Get me a glass of beer,' said Benjamin. ' I'm hot.'

Nancy walked over to Ben and briefly told him what

she had done. Ben nodded thoughtfully and gave her the stone jar of beer and the tumbler they had brought up with them.

'We'll risk it,' he said. 'But do you get him home as soon as you can, Nance.'

She went back to Benjamin and having poured him out some beer, sat down on the grass at his side with Joseph nestling close against her.

For half an hour Benjamin sat there, his head bent forward on his knees, listening intently to the thudding, whirling clatter of the sail-reaper as it passed and repassed in front of him. Every now and then he picked up his glass and took a gulp of beer. He stroked his beard. It was still good to be alive, to feel the harsh, prickly wheat ears in his hand and nip the tough little grains between his teeth, good to dig his feet into the crumbly soil among the rustling stalks : the air was strong and sweet, it smelt of harvest, it was heavy with sunshine ; how dazzling it must be out there in the field, if only he could see it, if only he could be sitting on the springy iron seat of the old sail-reaper behind a sturdy pair of chestnut punches : he was glad he had been a tiller of the soil ; but now he was blind : those sons of his had all the luck.

'Give me another glass of beer, Nance,' he said. 'I'm that hot.'

He drank it in two gulps and let the glass drop beside his chair. The heat grew fiercer and fiercer : it seemed to roll over him in great banks and clouds, it jolted his brain and made him feel sick. He put his hand to his face : it was all wet. He was no longer fit for this sort of thing, not even to sit and listen to it : he would soon have to be going. He rose painfully from his chair.

'Soon be tea-time, father,' suggested Nancy timidly.

'All right,' he murmured. 'I'm coming in a minute. I'm just going across to tie one shof before I go, one shof.'

One sheaf—not easy with a withered arm perhaps, but one sheaf before he went back to his seat in the shade on the hearthrug.

' No, father, you mustn't,' cried Nancy in consternation, seizing his arm. ' You'll hurt yourself, that's all rough.'

' Let me alone, girl,' he snarled. ' I know what I can do all right.'

He began to pick his way across the headland, tottering on his stick. Nancy kept close to his side with Joseph trailing behind her.

' The stubble's main hard to the feet,' he complained. ' Where's a shof, Nance ? '

' There isn't any here, father,' she said desperately.

' Well, we'll go on till you find one,' he replied grimly. ' Don't you try none of that on me, my gal.'

' Ah!' he growled triumphantly, as his foot caught in a heap of crackling stalks. He knelt down in the stubble and picked up a handful to make the band. He fumbled them curiously.

' Why, these are beans,' he shouted. ' Ain't they beans, Nance ? '

' Yes, father,' she faltered.

' Why are they beans ? ' he demanded, tossing them away from him.

' 'Cause they're cutting the beans,' she replied.

Benjamin clenched his fist ; his cheeks went purple and his sightless eyes rolled in their sockets. He opened his mouth, but for very rage words would not come. He feebly raised his fist in the air and shook it : then he fell forward on his face.

Nancy dropped down beside him and with difficulty turned him over on his back. His head sagged limply from the neck and hit the ground with a thud ; his mouth was twisted in an elfish grimace, the pale, sightless eyes set in a stare that made them look more pale, more sightless. She tore off his neckerchief and loosened his shirt collar. She felt his hands ; they were strangely cold. She put her ear to his heart ; it did not beat. She scrambled to her feet and shouted. Hiram stopped his horses, clambered off the seat of the reaper and came running across the stubble.

The others, who were tying sheaves a little further off, followed close upon his heels.

' What's the matter ? ' gasped Hiram, as they came up, panting.

' Father's dead,' replied Nancy almost inaudibly and mechanically began to cry.

The brothers stood round the body for a few moments, staring dully and helplessly. They had not expected it to come without warning like this, out in the open field. But there he lay, their father, lifeless, all his strength, his self-will, his violence, his curses extinguished with him. They were dazed rather than saddened by this sudden intervention of the unknown : it threw all their thinking out of gear and they hardly knew if they regretted it or not. Joseph hid his face in his mother's skirts and whimpered.

Ben was the first to recover himself. He bent down over the dead man and with clumsy gentleness closed his eyes.

' We'd better get him home,' he said.

Down in the valley the sun dipped slowly to its setting through a copper-blazoned sky : but a little dusky light still hovered over the hillside field, enough to reveal the five shadowy figures flitting busily across and across it in an ordered system of evolutions, alternately advancing and retiring upon one another with large black burdens in their arms, like grotesque creatures out of some demoniac ballet. The sun sank out of sight and they merged in the enveloping darkness ; a star came out and the moon, rising suddenly above the trees, seemed to create out of nothing the long lines of stark black bean shocks that streaked the field from end to end.

Below at the farm Benjamin lay stretched on his bed with a white sheet over him. The doctor had come from Framlingham and made his examination, Mrs. Dibber had been summoned to come next morning to lay out the corpse : there was nothing more to be done that day. The brothers could stay no longer in the house. They were not afraid of the dead, they were not overcome with grief, but something oppressive in the air, the mere dead weight of death, drove them forth. One by one they trickled into the stable, their common meeting-place. But there it was no better : they felt uneasy, idle and superfluous, they could not talk, they could not think. Ten minutes later they set off up the hill with a pair of horses. It was Hiram who had first voiced the idea ; but it was already in the minds of all of them. If their hands were occupied, their heads might clear and it seemed a shame to let those good beans spoil for want of a few hours' work - it was only a little field. But just to be there and working, with their hands on the soil of Crakenhill, perhaps for the last time, that was the deepest of their desires and it wrung them like the yearning of a lost child for its mother.

The last shock was in its place and they paused by the hedge to rest and light their pipes. It had been hard work even to men such as they, who could tie sheaves and shock them almost as fast as they could walk ; but they felt better for it : all the tautness had gone out of their minds and their tongues were loosened.

' Come to think of it,' said Hiram, throwing a water-proof sheet over the reaper and making it fast to the wheel, ' it was in this here field that mother went off— how long ago is it ? '

' Let me see,' said Ben, reckoning on his fingers. ' Nance have been here near seven year and when she came, mother had been dead more'n eight year. That make fifteen year all told, yes, a good fifteen year.'

' And she went off sudden like, too,' added Ern. ' I can remember you a-crying, young Harry.'

' Well, I hope he's all right now,' said Ben, ' wherever he is. That'll be funny without him. He used to curse and swear a tidy bit, but you got used to it somehow. It's a rum 'un how you do get used to things—till they sorterly belong to you. But you don't know nothing about it till they're gone and then you miss 'em '

' That's the truth,' said Hiram, turning round and leaning against the reaper. ' That kitchen 'on't be the same
place without father.'

' Maybe we shan't be there to see,' said Ern bitterly.

' Maybe not,' admitted Hiram in a low voice.

A despairing silence fell upon them : it was a hard thing
to contemplate. Harry looked up suddenly and peered
down the field.

' Who's that ? ' he said.

A dark figure splashed with white was approaching
them between two lines of shocks ; as it drew closer they
could see it was a woman in a white apron.

' Why, that's Nance,' exclaimed Ern. ' What do she
want up here at this time of night ? '

' Don't ask me,' said Bob. ' Anything might happen a
day like this.'

Nancy walked up to the group around the reaper. She
had a sheet of paper in her hand and her manner was
nervous and excited.

' I wondered what had become of you,' she said. ' I
looked all over the yard for you and then Mrs. Snaith told
me she seed Hiram go off up the hill with a pair of horses :
so I guessed where you were. I wanted to speak to
you.'

They stared at her.

' I've found father's will,' she added in a trembling
voice. ' It was in the desk in the locked drawer.'

' Oh,' said Ben. She had soon got to work, he thought.

There was a pause while the five men tried to brace
themselves for something that would hurt.

' What's in it ? ' said Ben at last, doing his best to keep
the tremor out of his voice. The sudden pallor of his
cheeks was manifest even in the moonlight.

' I can't see to read it here,' Nancy faltered, ' but, but
he've left a hundred pound to each of you——' She
dropped her head.

' And the farm ? ' said Ben.

' He've left it to me,' she said, looking up at him.

' With all its crops, stock, buildings and appurtenances,' she added, quoting parrot-wise from the document.

' I told you so,' Ern whispered savagely in Bob's ear.

The five men looked on the ground, they looked at one another, they looked at Nancy. It was what they had expected ; there was nothing to be said. An owl hooted from a hollow tree near by and they all started violently : everything about them, moon, earth and trees, seemed fantastic and unreal. Nancy took breath several times to speak, but her courage failed her and she could only stare helplessly at them.

' What are you going to do with it ? ' Ben mumbled at last, moistening his dry lips.

It was the opening Nancy had been waiting for and her words came tumbling out.

' I'm going to farm it till my boy's old enough to take it over,' she replied breathlessly, ' and I'd be wholly glad if you and the others 'd stay on and help me.'

Ben scratched his head, rubbed his cheek with the palm of his hand, shuffled his feet in the stubble and looked at them. The others came forward and clustered around him. Ben looked up again at Nancy ; his eyes were moist.

' Why, why,' he stammered, ' that's just what we'd like, Nance. You see, we were brought up here ; we seed it grow and we sorterly belong to the place.'

' Well, that suit us both,' said Nancy with an air of relief. ' And father 've been that good to me, I'd like you to be my steward and we'll raise the wages a shilling a week all round.'

' Thank you very much, Nance, I'm sure,' faltered Ben, thunderstruck by this unexpected generosity. ' That's handsome of you.'

' That is,' said Harry. ' Thank you, Nance.'

' Thank you, Nance,' came from the other three together.

Hiram awkwardly seized her hand and crushed it in his own rough, horny palm.

' Well, that's all right,' said Nancy, gently disengaging

herself from his grip. ' Now come along home and have some supper.'

They moved away down the hill among the shocks, Ben and Bob on Nancy's right hand, Harry and Ern on her left and Hiram jogging along behind with his team : it was very like a triumphal procession.

XXV

BREAKFAST was just over at Crakenhill. Bob, Hiram and Harry had already gone away to their work and Ern was just finishing his last slice of bread and jam, but Ben still lingered behind with his pipe in his mouth and his hands in his pockets, looking with affected unconcern out of the window as if he had nothing to do that day and were thinking of taking a holiday : every now and then he scraped the toe of his boot on the bricks and looked over his shoulder to see if Ern had finished. Nancy, who was already at the sink helping Mrs. Snaith with the breakfast-things, knew by these signs that Ben was waiting to make some announcement to her. He bought and sold and planned for her as he thought proper, without asking her advice and she would not have advised him : but from time to time he liked her to know what was happening on the farm ; she was mistress and he was steward. Nancy always listened with great attention. As soon as Ern had drained his cup and gone out into the yard, she went over to the window where Ben was standing.

' What is it, Ben ? ' she said.

He took his pipe out of his mouth and looked at her diffidently.

' Something I've been thinking about for some time, Nance,' he said, ' about young Joey. It fare to me, if he's going to farm Crakenhill for you some day, it's time he got to know something about it.'

' What do you mean, Ben ? ' Nancy asked.

' Why,' he replied, ' he ought to get out a bit with us chaps and see what it's like. You can't get used to the look of soil too early, nor to stock and horses neither.'

' But he's so young,' demurred Nancy, who was still reluctant to allow the child out of her sight. ' He's only six.'

' So much the better,' said Ben. ' He 'on't grow up afeared of horses and cows if he get to know 'em now. It's for the sake of the farm, I mean. Do you let him come along o' me this morning. I'll look after him and that'll do him good.'

' I wonder,' murmured Nancy, half to herself

She wanted to go into Saxmundham that morning : it would be so much easier if she could leave Joey behind in safe hands out of mischief. But a last remnant of her long-standing distrust of the brothers still made her hesitate.

' Don't you worry,' said Ben, half-guessing her thought. ' I'll look after him : he 'on't come to no harm.'

' All right,' Nancy assented reluctantly, ' but be very careful he don't hurt himself.'

' That I will,' said Ben. ' He'll be safe enough along o' me. I'm taking the horse-hoe through that piece of turnips by the spinney and I'm all by myself.'

' Joey,' called Nancy to the child, who was playing on the hearthrug. ' Come here and let me put your boots on. You're going up the field with Ben this morning.'

A little later Ben set out for the spinney, leading a single horse, with Joey at his heels. Every other minute the child broke into a trot so as not to fall behind and peered up timidly into Ben's face, quite unable to comprehend why his mother had put him in the hands of this strange burly man with whom he had never had any dealings before, although he knew all his personal mannerisms off by heart. He was far more frightened than his mother. When they reached the turnip field, he stared curiously while Ben hitched the horse on to the whipple-tree of the hoe. Why had he been brought here to watch that ?

' Now then, youngster,' said Ben briskly, turning to him. ' You'd better walk behind me between the rows. Then I shall know where you are.'

He clicked his tongue to the horse and the hoe slid off across the field at a rapid pace. He had no time to look behind him until he reached the headland and he stopped to turn. Five yards away was Joey, toiling manfully over the upturned weeds and stumbling in the loose soil. He came up panting and on the brink of tears.

' I can't keep up,' he whimpered. ' I'm that tired.'

Ben scratched his head. He could not leave him alone by the hedge : he had promised Nancy to take such care of him. Joey looked up at him with his head on one side ; if he had had any breath left, he would have run away.

' I know! ' exclaimed Ben, slapping his thigh. ' Come you here, youngster.'

Joey sidled up suspiciously. Ben picked him up bodily and set him astride the beam of the horse-hoe.

' Now then, Joey,' he said, ' do you lean back against the handles and off we go.'

The horse tugged, the chains tautened, the whipple-tree lifted with a sudden jerk, the knife bit the soil and the hoe went giddily lurching across the field. Joey did not know whether to laugh or cry. The earth beneath him seemed every moment on the point of falling away and precipitating him into some bottomless gulf ; the weeds at the horse's feet looked like a forest advancing to crush him : but somehow neither of these disasters overtook him. The wheel in front went rattling busily on, the knives rasped steadily in the soil, clinking against the pebbles : up hill and down dale they went, sliding, quivering, swaying from side to side. Joey, clinging to the beam with all his hands, could feel Ben's firm grip on the handles, guiding and tilting with watchful precision to balance his burden ; it was as much an adventure for him as for Joey. The long straight rows of turnips seemed as if they would never end : then suddenly the headland appeared in sight, the horse slowed up and the hoe stopped.

'Well,' said Ben, pausing to lean on the handles before he turned again, ' how d'you like it, young 'un ? '

Joey looked up at him : his eyes glistened and his flushed cheeks broke into a smile.

' That's fine and no mistake,' he said, beating his fists on the beam in front of him. ' Goo on, Blossom.'

Ben chuckled into his moustache : but it was a great relief to him.

' Hold tight, then ! ' he shouted, pulling on his line

' Woory, Blossom, woory now ! Goo on, gal ! ' They were off again.

Joey learnt a multitude of things that morning as soon as he became used to the vagaries of his heady career across the turnips. There was a patch of ground at one end of the field where the slope was so steep that time after time he was sure he would be tipped off and cut to pieces under the knives ; but it never happened and he soon discovered he liked that slope best of all ; it felt rather like sliding down the branches of the old willow that overhung the duck-pond. There was another spot where the turnips were shorter and scantier than else-where ; Ben said it was always like that down there ; it wanted draining. And then the weeds ; so many of them and so much prettier than the turnips ; it seemed a pity to tear them up so ruthlessly. Ben told him the names of some of them ; paigle, the stubborn creeping butter-cup, bellbind, the convolvulus whose roots had no end, mint that smelt so warm when you bruised it, watergrass that covered the ground like a mat ; blue-eyed speedwells and shy little wild pansies—surely they did no harm. One of Blossom's fetlocks had a white streak on it, she clicked her shoes every now and again ; but her great chestnut quarters went swinging on in front as if the weight of a little boy of six made not the least difference to her day's work. Thud ! the hoe drove heavily into a crafty thorn root, concealed beneath the surface. Up went the handles and before Ben could stop the horse, Joey was grovelling on his nose among the turnips. Ben ran over to him in alarm, but the child had already picked himself up and was laughing in his face.

' Do it again, Ben,' he cried. ' I like that, I do.'

' You young sweep,' growled Ben, smiling. ' Up you get then.'

Joseph now gave himself up to the contemplation of the hedges ; so many different shapes and shades of green and the may-buds bursting ; he wondered how long it would take them to reach that pink-white cloud of crab-apple bloom away on the right; if Blossom flicked her tail backwards, would it reach his eye? The hoe stopped with a jolt.

' Off you get,' said Ben. ' Time for beavers.'

They went and sat down in the sunshine by Ben's coat at the foot of an elm tree. Ben took out a bottle and a packet of bread and cheese wrapped up in a handkerchief. He cut off a hunk with his jack-knife and handed it to Joey who put both hands to it and worried it like a puppy with a bone; this was man's food, strong-flavoured and tough; he had never thought it could be so delicious. Ben watched him gnawing with approval. He uncorked his bottle and took a swig at it. Joey turned round and watched him, fascinated by the sight of the liquor slowly disappearing down his upstretched, gurgling throat.

' What've you got there, Ben? ' he asked.

' That's beer, my lad,' Ben replied. ' You'll drink it, too, when you grow up. You ain't old enough yet.'

Joey's face dropped and his ardour for bread and cheese all at once diminished; he was thirsty.

' I'll bring some milk along for you next time,' said Ben consolingly, rising to his feet. ' Now do you hurry up and finish that and I'll show you something.'

Joey crammed the last crust into his mouth and jumped up, wiping his hands on his corduroys.

Ben led the way to an oak tree a few yards further down the hedge. He took Joey by the shoulders and hoisted him up among the lower branches.

' In you go, lad,' he panted. ' Get your backside on my shoulder and push. See it? '

Joey's head forced its way through the stiff network of branches with a sudden snap. His hat fell off and he blinked. A little round nest took shape before his eyes, wedged close up against the trunk, smooth and round inside like a cup, with five speckled, sky-blue eggs reposing snugly on the bottom as if they had grown there. He had never before seen such a thing and he tasted pure delight at the beauty and adventure of it. He gazed

greedily at it, he felt the inside of the nest with his
fingers, he timidly stroked one of the eggs; it was still
warm and he thrilled at the touch of it.

' Finished ? ' shouted Ben from below.

' Just a minute,' cried Joey, unable to tear his eyes
away from the nest.

' Down you come,' shouted Ben. ' I must get to work.'
He took the boy by the waist and hauled him down
through the branches, which slithered over his head like
a collar. As soon as his feet touched the ground, Joey
put his hand to his face.

' What's the matter ? ' said Ben.

' That there twig,' murmured Joey, beginning to rub
his eye. ' That hurt, that do.'

There was a big red weal on his cheek where a sharp
twig had scored him and a drop of blood was gathering
at one end of it. Ben rubbed it as soothingly as he could
with his rough palm.

' Now you ain't a-going to cry over a little thing like
that, ' he said, ' are you, Joey, old man ? '

Joey gulped twice and gazed ruefully at him ; there was
a kind look in Ben's eyes.

' No, Ben,' he faltered. ' I ain't.'

' There's a good lad,' said Ben heartily, hoisting him up
on to his shoulder again. ' Come on and let's do another
bout.'

Five minutes later they were jolting their way between
the turnips again and cheek, pain and tears were all forgotten.

At twelve o'clock Ben stopped the hoe and unhitched
the horse.

' Hungry, lad ? ' he said, as he hooked the chains on to
the collar.

Joey nodded. Ben could not help smiling at him ; his
cheeks were so like little red apples. He picked him
up and setting him astride on Blossom's neck, jumped up
behind himself. Another adventure for Joey ; every step
that Blossom took made every bone in his body lurch

and whenever she dropped her head, he thought he would slide over her neck on to the ground. But the wooden hames on the collar in front of him stood firm and Ben was close behind him, warm and strong and solid, with his rich smell of corduroy. He would not fall; he was a man now, he was riding a horse, he was high up in the world.

.   .   .   .

' Well, Joey, and what have you been doing this morning?' said Nancy from behind the joint, when they were all seated at the kitchen table.

Joey paused a moment to swallow a piece of potato.

' I've been riding all the morning,' he said solemnly.

' Where? ' said Nancy.

' Why, on the hoss-hoe,' replied Joey importantly. ' We've done more'n an acre.'

Harry at the end of the table tittered.

' And when it go fast,' continued Joey, clutching his fork excitedly in his fist, ' that's lovely—just like falling in the duck-pond.'

Nancy stared at him : she had never seen him so gay before.

' Like falling in the duck-pond,' Ben repeated slowly. ' That's a good 'un, that is.'

He put his head on his hands and burst out laughing. The others looked curiously at him. Bob thumped his fist on the table.

' That is a good 'un and no mistake,' he cried. ' Like falling in the duck-pond! '

The next minute they were all dissolved in laughter.

' See here, Joey,' said Hiram, when they had recovered a little. ' Suppose you come along o' me and Bob this arternoon. We're going to have a bonfire.'

' No,' said Ben stoutly, ' he ain't. He's coming along o' me this arternoon, aren't you, Joey? '

' Yes,' replied Joey. ' I am, and we're going to do another acre, aren't we, Ben? '

' There you are, Hiram,' said Ben triumphantly. ' He know where he's well off, he do.'

' But I'll come with you to-morrow, Hiram,' said Joey with a grand air of benevolent condescension—these offers were too good to be refused.

' No, you come down and help me feed the sheep,' said Harry. ' That's much better than a bonfire. I've got one lamb all black.'

' Now do you be quiet, young Harry,' said Hiram. ' He's coming along of us. You said so, didn't you, Joey ? '

' Yes,' Joey nodded, ' but I'll go and help you feed the sheep the day after to-morrow, Harry.'

' No, you 'on't,' said Ern, wagging his finger at him. ' You're coming into Sax with me on the milk-float. Harry's the youngest—he can wait till the last.'

Joey, out of sheer exuberance, looked up at his mother and winked.

XXVI

Down in the valley the smoke from a score of Sunday dinners filtered slowly up through the limpid air. Church bells, summoning to matins, answered one another from distant parishes : the fitful crowing of a cock, the lowing of a cow, were the only other sounds that stirred the hush of that radiant July morning. All Crakenhill lay basking in its peacefulness : horses in the paddock stretched themselves out on the grass and lazily rolled to stretch their joints ; cows chewed placidly and drowsed ; the sun mounted.

Joey stood in the rickyard and looked round him. He was sorry it was Sunday morning : there was nothing exciting happening on the farm to-day and all the men were occupied about the buildings with little fiddling jobs as if they had not enough energy for seven days' real activity in the week. Joey himself was master of everything he could see. He had ridden every one of the horses there over the hedge ; he had driven the cows up to the farm for milking all alone ; he had been to the top of every hayrick, with Hiram behind him on the ladder—and those geese. For a month they had chased him ignominiously from the rickyard whenever he appeared there, until one day, hemmed in by them against the paddock gate, he had desperately let fly with his foot and caught the old gander squarely under the beak. From that time onwards he had chased the geese ; they went in fear of him and he gave them no rest.

A trio of young calves trotted out from behind one of the ricks and stood gazing at him with great wondering eyes : they must have been turned out there after break-fast to pick up what they could. Joey put his hands in his pockets and looked them up and down : he was not afraid of them ; like their impudence to come there staring at him in that fashion. He flung his arms in the air and ran at them. In and out of the ricks, round behind the chicken-house among the nettles, past the cart-shed, back among the ricks again—a glorious chase. He paused in front of the barn to take breath. The calves slunk off and began to crop the poor straggly grass, eyeing him surreptitiously from behind an upturned tumbril ; they were still curious and did not trouble to go right out of sight : it was like a challenge.

Just where Joey was resting, a section of the barn jutted out into the rickyard and in the angle formed by it stood two ricks, separated from each other and from the barn walls by a narrow passage—the very place to drive the calves into. Joey promptly gave chase again. They dragged him all round the yard again before he finally manœuvred them into position in front of the opening between the two ricks. They wavered a moment, fumbling the hay with their muzzles. Joey spread out his arms and shouted. They kicked up their heels, up-ended their tails and disappeared down the dark slit at a canter. All at once the idea came into Joey's head to make them turn round between the rick and the barn wall in mid-career ; that would teach them to be afraid of him. He slipped over to the barn wall and peered round the corner. There they were, coming full tilt at him. Just as they were three yards off, he darted out, waving his arms at them, but he was too late to stop them. Terror-stricken, they plunged for the light and freedom they saw before them, and before Joey could get out of their way, he was down on his back beneath their feet in the sodden paste of a half-dried water-hole. Almost before he knew what had happened, they were over him and gone. He slowly picked himself up. There was no harm done—a few bruises and a strange shivery feeling in his legs—nothing to cry about ; but he was soused in mud from head to foot. It oozed out of his boots, it trickled down his knees and into his stockings ; his white sailor collar and best brown velvet suit were scarcely recognisable. He looked at them in consternation. A handful of straw with which he tried to wipe himself clean, only stuck to the mud and made it look worse :

concealment was impossible. Tears were coursing down his cheeks when he presented himself to his mother at the kitchen door. He told a simple story, quite true as far as it went : the calves had knocked him down.

' Perhaps they did,' replied Nancy severely, ' but they wouldn't have done if you hadn't driv 'em. You'll go straight to bed, you will.'

Three hours later and Joseph was sitting on the kitchen hearthrug playing listlessly with a box of toy bricks and marvelling at the inscrutable ways of his elders. He did not so much mind being punished, although he felt it was unreasonable of his mother to penetrate so quickly to the weak spot of a plausible story ; but it seemed such a meaningless way of expiating his offence to spend half a morning in bed doing nothing, just a desolate waste of time and no one the better for it. He had been allowed to come down for dinner, but everyone had been very quiet, and when his mother did speak to him, it was in a sharp, scolding tone as if nothing he could do were right. But his punishment was not yet over. After dinner, when all the men went out of doors, he was left alone in the kitchen to play by himself, condemned to the house until tea-time. Life seemed a very poor affair indeed. He could see the deep blue sky and the waving elm-tops outside through the window ; he could hear the drowsy call of the yellow-hammers in the hedgerows ; and Harry, he knew, was going to take the ferret with him to hunt out some rabbits down by the gull. Inside the kitchen the clock ticked on interminably, the flies buzzed tunelessly on the window panes and a strong tangy smell of pork, cheese, vinegar and a score of other things floated out through the open larder door : everything in the room seemed cold and drab and lifeless, and tea-time was still hours away.

The kitchen door opened and Ern came in from the yard.

' I want my pipe,' he said. ' I must have left it on the desk.'

He searched the top of the old bureau, looked inside, went down on his knees and rummaged behind it.

' Funny thing,' he said. ' I suppose I've lost it. Oh, before I forget.'

He pulled a handful of scarlet cherries out of his coat pocket and put them on the corner of the table in front of Joey.

' P'r'aps they'll do you good,' he said with a grin.

He strode out of the room, inadvertently taking his pipe out of his other coat pocket as he went.

The cherries were a great relief to Joey : to look at their glistening skins, to touch them with his fingers, to feel their cool sweet flesh melting on his tongue, gave life a new colour. Regretfully he slipped the last one into his mouth, made a little pile of the stones on the table and looked out of the window again. The five men were still out in the yard, talking among themselves. Joey wondered why they had not yet set out for their afternoon walk ; it was already half-past two. They seemed to be discussing a matter of great importance to judge by the seriousness of their faces. At length Ben left them and came indoors. He smiled at Joey and passed through the kitchen into the parlour where Nancy was sitting alone with her needlework. Five minutes later he came back into the kitchen.

' It's all right, Joey, my lad,' he said. ' Mother say you can come along of us. Harry have got the ferret all ready.'

Joey clapped his hands and Ben, seizing him by the shoulders, swung him out of the door in front of him.

Nancy came into the kitchen just in time to see the five brothers disappear through the farmyard gate, headed by Ben with Joey perched high on his shoulder. They were all laughing loudly at something the boy had said. Nancy could not help smiling and her heart warmed with a feeling of mild affection for these five men who ever since Benjamin's death had worked so hard for her, although they had been sacrificed for her sake : she, at least, had never heard a word of complaint from them. And during the last two months they had become different men—she had not believed such a change possible. Joey had completely won their hearts. They took him everywhere with them, they played with him, they bought him sweets; they laughed and talked at meal-times. The kitchen had been completely transformed. Nancy felt proud to preside over so contented a household; she herself was the only element of discontent in it.

XXVII

MRS. PEARMAN stood under the apple tree in her front garden and blinked at the dazzling sunshine through her spectacles. She heaved a sigh. Her world seemed to grow blanker every day. Betsy Barnes, who had given up the peddling trade four years ago and spent all her savings, had recently been received into a distant almshouse and she saw her no more ; she herself was beginning to feel a little old too. But, worst of all, nothing ever seemed to happen now, nothing worth talking about, or at least, it never came to her ears. Even Crakenhill had failed to yield any incident of interest during the three years that had passed since Benjamin Geaiter's death. It still went on prospering with the old monotonous consistency : its inmates behaved uncommonly like other decent, respectable people and except that they still held themselves somewhat aloof from the rest of the parish, would soon be indistinguishable from them. Mrs. Pearman curled her lip : so long as there was breath in her body, it would not be her fault if anyone were deceived about them. The sound of approaching footsteps made her look down the road. A tall, lightly-built young man with a gun on his shoulder was sauntering into the village street. He was good-looking in a careless, insolent way, with brown skin, black eyes and dark curly hair, as if he might have had some gipsy blood in his veins. Mrs. Pearman walked to the gate as he came up.

' Well, Ted,' she said, ' and what are you doing all this way from Dennington on a day like this ? '

' Good arternoon, Mrs. Pearman,' he replied, laughing. ' There ain't much doing in our line just now. All the carts father patch up last too long, and no mistake. So I thought I'd take a holiday.'

' Not the first time by a long way, I'll warrant,' said Mrs. Pearman severely. ' How's your father and Mrs. Willett ? '

'Nicely now,' he replied, 'though mother was laid up with a quinsy.'

'Oh!' exclaimed Mrs. Pearman. 'Anything happening in Dennington?'

'Nothing as I know of,' he said, aimlessly rubbing the butt of his gun with the palm of his hand; he must get away from this tiresome old woman.

'Oh,' sniffed Mrs. Pearman contemptuously. 'Dennington allus was a dead and alive place.' This young man was no use to her.

There was a rattle of wheels and a high dog-cart bowled past them, driven by a tall young woman with a basket at her side. Willett turned round to look at her.

'Who's that?' he asked.

'Why, don't you know?' said Mrs. Pearman. 'That's our young widow Geaiter, Nancy Hambling that was.'

'What, her that married old Benjamin Geaiter?' exclaimed Willett.

'The very same,' replied Mrs. Pearman. 'He left all the farm and most of his money to her. She live up there in grand style now, and all the sons work for her.'

'H'm,' said Willett, 'she's a nice-looking gal and no mistake.'

'So she may be,' snorted Mrs. Pearman, 'but she's a shameless wench all the same. Living up there with all those men and putting on airs like she do in the village: and that little rascal of hers born out of wedlock.'

'Why don't she get married agin?' said Willett.

'Don't ask me,' replied Mrs. Pearman. 'Fare to me she think she's better off as she is. She like her freedom, she do.'

'Well, I don't blame her,' said Willett.

'Don't you?' said Mrs. Pearman haughtily. 'Well, look here, young Ted Willett. She may be having a fine time now, gadding about and frolicking and sinning before the Lord; but I tell you, some day the wrath of heaven'll descend upon her and she'll pay for all. You see if she 'on't.

Willett laughed.

'Well, we'll wait and see, Mrs. Pearman,' he said. 'I must now be going. Good arternoon.'

He shouldered his gun and strolled off through the village. At the cross-roads he paused a moment as if to make up his mind which direction to take, and then followed Nancy down the Framlingham road. At the bottom of Crakenhill drift he paused again as if uncertain whether to follow her any further. He leant over the gate and looked up the hill : Nancy must have already reached the farm some minutes ago. There was a hare squatting in the grass by the hedge about thirty yards away. Willett looked up and down the road : there was no one in sight. He raised his gun to his shoulder and fired : the hare tumbled over on its side. He climbed the gate and walked up to it : it was a fine, plump animal. Then, having strung its legs together and slung it over his gun barrel, he trudged on up the hill to the farm. He walked straight through the farmyard and boldly knocked at the kitchen door. Nancy opened to him.

'Good arternoon, miss,' he said. 'I thought p'r'aps you might like this hare for dinner to-morrow.'

Nancy felt the animal critically.

'How much d'you want for it ? ' she said at last.

'Oh, I don't like to ask nothing from you,' replied Willett in a lordly fashion. 'I really kill 'em for the sport of the thing.'

Nancy looked sharply up at him. He stood there swaggering in front of her with his hand on his hip and a friendly gleam in his dark eyes ; he had a natural way with him as if he were used to giving young hares away to strange farmers' wives every afternoon of his life. His smooth brown cheek shone in the sunlight. There could be no doubt of his genuineness.

'But you can't let it go for nothing,' she protested. 'That'll serve us right well for to-morrow's dinner.'

'Well, I'll take a shilling for it,' said Willett condescendingly, as if doing her a favour. 'I suppose your people'll be cutting to-day ? '

' That's right,' said Nancy. ' They're up on the hill there, just finishing a bit of wheat. That'll be all down soon after tea.'

' Any rabbits ? ' he queried.

' They said there'd be a tidy few,' she replied

' D'you think I could go up there with my gun,' said Willett, ' and give 'em a hand—just for the sport like ? I don't want none of the rabbits.'

' Why, yes,' said Nancy. ' Harry have took his gun up there, but I expect another'd come in right useful. I'm now packing up their tea to take up to the field. If you'd just step in for a minute while I finish, I could show you the way up, Mr. —— '

' My name's Willett,' he replied. ' Thank you very much, I'm sure.'

He entered the kitchen and sat down while Nancy went on filling her basket with thick slices of cake and bread and butter.

' Don't you get tired of this sort of thing ? ' asked Willett, as he sat there watching her and toying with his watch-chain.

' I don't know,' said Nancy with a laugh. ' I sometimes feel I should like a bit of a holiday.'

' I should think so too,' replied Willett feelingly.

Nancy glanced gratefully at him. Overt sympathy of this sort was a pleasure unknown to her.

' A gal like you ought to be enjoying herself a bit,' he added.

' P'r'haps I ought,' replied Nancy with a sigh. ' The basket's full now if you're ready, Mr. Willett.'

They set off up the hillside to the wheatfield side by side, Willett carrying the basket which Nancy after a brief show of resistance had relinquished to him. She was secretly rather pleased by the attentions of this attractive stranger. He was certainly a most handsome man ; his trim check breeches and black gaiters gave him an air of distinction, and he walked with a light, springy step—a change from the unkempt, lumbering men with whom she had lived for the past eight years. He seemed to understand her too, without her telling him anything.

When they reached the field, there was only a narrow strip of corn in the middle left standing and the rabbits were already beginning to bolt. Hiram was driving the sail-reaper, Harry and Ern were back at the farm milking : the other two brothers were tying sheaves. Nancy went up to Ben.

' I've brought Mr. Willett here to help shoot the rabbits,' she explained.

Ben swung round and looked suspiciously at Willett : he seemed to recognise him.

' All right,' he said. ' He'd better look sharp and get down the fur end. I'm going up here where Harry have left his gun. There's several rabbits there yet.'

Willett took up his position at the end of the strip of corn and Nancy, having set her basket down in the hedge, walked across the stubble and stood behind him. He held his gun ready. The next moment three rabbits bolted, two of them heading towards Willett and the third towards Ben. Willett raised his gun to his shoulder in a leisurely manner and fired ; the rabbit furthest from him rolled over kicking. He waited for a moment, keeping his gun upon the other without firing, letting it reach within an inch of safety, playing with it. Nancy held her breath : was he going to lose it? Willett suddenly fired and it, too, rolled over dead, at forty yards. Ben meanwhile had emptied both his barrels without hitting his rabbit, which was rapidly making for the hedge. Willett, perceiving it, darted across to it, loading his gun as he went, and succeeded in turning it back. He fired and killed it just as it was entering the corn again. He reloaded and coolly lighted a cigarette. Nancy watched him admiringly.

The strip of corn dwindled ; two more bouts and it would all be down. The rabbits began to run in all directions ; there seemed no end to them. Willett gave quite an astonishing exhibition of skill. For him it was only a question of reloading in time: whenever he fired, he hit, and two rabbits he knocked out with one shot. He danced about from side to side, heading them back to the corn, loading and firing as he went, at any speed, from any attitude. At last, when he had a dozen to his credit, his cartridges gave out and he laid his gun on a sheaf. Six rabbits had escaped into the hedge and a seventh that Ben had just missed, flashed past him. He dashed after it, yelling wildly. The poor animal, terrified by the noise, swerved in and out of the sheaves and suddenly made a right-angle turn. Willett saw his chance and spurted to cut it off. Their paths converged : the rabbit spurted too : he was too late by a yard. But before the rabbit could shoot past him, he had thrown himself full length on the stubble, pinning it to the ground with his body. He seized it by the legs, killed it with a blow behind the neck and walked slowly back to Nancy, nonchalantly swinging the limp body in his hand. He threw it down at her feet.

' I thought I'd lost him,' he said with a laugh, as he lit another cigarette ; he hardly seemed out of breath. Nancy smiled at him.

' Come and have a cup of tea with us, Mr. Willett,' she said. ' It fare to me you've earnt it properly.'

' Well, I 'on't say no,' he replied. ' This sort of thing make you right thirsty.'

He picked up the rabbit and carried it over to the hedge where Ben and Bob were already piling the rest. Nancy began to take the food and the cups out of the basket.

' How many did you shoot, Ben ? ' asked Nancy. It was an unhappy question.

' Three, I think,' growled Ben. ' You haven't got much of an eye left after a hard day's work.'

He seemed annoyed and Nancy said no more. Hiram, after tethering the horses to the gate, came over and joined them. He nodded to Willett and sat down.

' You must take some of these rabbits back with you, Mr. Willett,' said Nancy, handing him a cup of tea. ' We shall never get through all these ourselves.'

' We hardly touch a rabbit at ours,' replied Willett,

' thank you all the same. I only do it for the sport of the thing.'

' How's sport at Dennington? ' said Bob with a grin.

Willett's cheeks coloured up and his mouth hardened.

' Oh, middling,' he replied casually.

' The wheelwright business fare a bit slack, don't it? ' said Hiram sarcastically.

Willett did not reply, but went on drinking his tea with a scowl on his face. Nancy's cheeks glowed. Why should they all turn upon the new-comer just because he shot better than themselves? They all seemed to know him, but they evidently did not like him—she could tell that from the suspicious way they regarded him out of the corner of their eyes: and yet, what gawks they looked beside him! Their perversity exasperated her.

' Do you get on with your tea, Hiram,' she snapped, ' and don't talk so much. Another cup of tea, Mr. Willett? '

There was a strained silence for the rest of the meal: even Nancy had not the courage to make conversation with Willett. The three brothers munched away sullenly and hungrily at their bread and butter and cake: they needed their food after four hours' sweating in the sun and nothing could take their appetite away. As soon as they had all finished, Ben rolled his shirt-sleeves up another inch and rose to his feet.

' Come you along, Hiram,' he said. ' Let's get that tied up.'

' Don't you get tired of being lonely? ' asked Willett abruptly, as soon as he and Nancy were left alone.

' How did you know I was lonely? ' said Nancy archly.

' Oh, I just guessed,' replied Willett with a smile. ' You fare as if you was.'

' Well, I do feel a bit tired of it now and again,' said Nancy, as she collected the cups and put them into the basket, ' but I suppose I must put up with it.'

' Why should you? ' said Willett. ' You're young yet.'

' P'r'aps I am,' murmured Nancy, ' p'r'aps I am.'

He was young too, and the more she looked at him, the

more she liked him. When he smiled at her, his eyes seemed to stroke her with their softness : there was a little curve in the middle of his long nose that took her fancy and she longed to touch it with her fingers.

' Yes, that's a real shame,' added **Willett**. ' A nice pretty gal like you.'

' Get along with you,' she said, turning her head away and blushing. She picked up her basket and put it on her arm. ' I must now be gooing, Mr. Willett. I've got some work to do.'

' Let me carry that for you,' said Willett, jumping up and seizing the handle of the basket. ' That's far too heavy for you.'

She smilingly allowed him to slip the handle off her arm and they walked out of the field side by side. Willett turned his head as they passed through the gate, and noticed Ben, Bob and Hiram standing up in the middle of the field and staring grimly after them.

' Those men of yours don't fare to like me,' he said with a laugh.

' Oh, don't you mind them,' replied Nancy warmly. ' They often get a bee in their bonnets.'

They walked on in silence for a few minutes across a field where the corn had already been cut and shocked.

' You do shoot wonderful well, Mr. Willett,' said Nancy at last. ' That's a treat to watch you.'

' Oh, that's nothing,' said Willett, shrugging his shoulders. ' To tell you the truth, I like it, real like it. That's why I can do it. Look there! '

A rabbit darted out of a shock beside them and went scuttling off across the stubble. Willett had no cartridges, but he could not resist the temptation to put down the basket and give chase. The rabbit had a long start and the pursuit looked hopeless : another moment and it would be plunged deep in the safe obscurity of the hedge. But instead, whether seized by a sudden whim or frightened by Willett's shouts, it swerved suddenly and took refuge underneath one of the shocks that had been tumbled over by the wind. Willett waved his hand and shouted to Nancy. She left the basket and came running up.

'Do you help me to catch him,' he said. 'We'll make sure of him. He's under this end shof I know. Go you that side and I'll go this. When I say now, put your hands under and grab.'

They knelt down facing each other, one on each side of the sheaf.

'Now!' cried Willett.

They dug their hands hard beneath the sheaf and at the same moment the rabbit scooted away across the field from another sheaf two yards away. Nancy looked at Willett in bewilderment: they were holding each other's hands. Then all at once his eyes seemed to melt and her head fell forward on his shoulder.

XXVIII

THE faint October sun had vanished, leaving earth and sky to meet in a dark embrace ; the stars came out. Ben contentedly watched them pointing in the sky above him as he plodded up the drift to Crakenhill. Yet another harvest over, as good as any he could remember, with bumper crops and long days of scorching sunshine for cutting and carrying, so that work had seemed almost a game and the rickyard was full to overflowing. Already half the stubbles were ploughed for the winter corn ; up at the farm Bob and Hiram were busy dipping the seed wheat, and the broken coulter of the drill which he had just been down to the blacksmith's to fetch, was mended; everything would be ready for to-morrow's sowing. The farm was in good heart. Spring would come and then another harvest and so life went on, one season gliding smoothly into another in a stable dignified tenor that seemed to reflect the vastness and immutability of the stars : it did Ben good to look at them. After all, the legal ownership of Crakenhill was of no importance so long as he and his brothers were there to work it, and Nancy was almost one of themselves, hardly more noticeable as mistress than he himself as steward. A good girl, he reflected ; she had treated them well and he no longer repented her coming to Crakenhill ; but for that there would have been no Joey, and Joey was half the warmth of the household. A rare little chap, with the makings of a farmer in him ; Ben had some brandy balls in his pocket for him. The past had faded out of memory : there seemed no reason why the future should not continue the present without end. Ben sighed at the thought of such happiness.

A half-open gate jutted out across his path. Ben stopped suddenly and peered : there was someone sitting on it.

' Why, Ted Willett! ' he exclaimed. ' What are you doing here at this time of night ? '

' Mind your own business,' replied Willett sourly.

' But that is my business,' persisted Ben, ' at this time of night.'

' Well, if you want to know,' sneered Willett, ' I'm just out for a walk.'

' Oh, are you ? ' said Ben. ' And I suppose your gun's in the hedge waiting for the first pheasant you hear scutter. Yes, a very nice walk indeed. You fare to think just because you shot a few rabbits on our stubbles last harvest, you can go where you please on our land.'

' Well, so I can,' replied Willett insolently.

' We'll soon see about that,' said Ben.

' Who's a-going to stop me ? ' asked Willett.

' I am,' said Ben grimly. ' I've had enough of your lip. Now then, off that gate and hook it, sharp.'

' I'll see you damned first,' said Willett.

Ben grabbed him by the wrist and pulled him off the gate with a jerk. As he touched ground, his foot slipped on a soft hoof-mark and he toppled over backwards into a blackberry bush. He picked himself up and stood look-ing angrily at Ben with his fists clenched as if he were going to spar up to him, but he thought better of it ; Ben might try to bring the law on him.

' Ah, Ben Geaiter,' he snarled, ' you think just because you're steward of Crakenhill Hall, you can do what you bloody well please and play the high and mighty. You'll find out your mistake one day.'

' I shan't need a poacher to tell me, anyhow,' retorted Ben. ' If I see that blasted face of yourn on our land again —do you look out.'

' You go to hell,' muttered Willett.

He turned on his heel and swaggered off down the drift. Ben looked after him until he disappeared in the murk. He laughed ; he had certainly had the best of the en-counter, but Willett was a slippery fellow.

He walked on up the hill to the farm, crossed the yard and opened the kitchen door. The house was in darkness. He shut the door and went over to the barn where Bob and Hiram were at work dipping the wheat by the light of a hurricane lantern.

'Where's Joey?' said Ben as he entered. 'I've got some sweets for him.'

'Nance sent him to bed early,' answered Hiram. 'She went out about an hour after Mrs. Snaith left : said she'd got a letter to post and wanted to talk to Mrs. Eves.'

'She've been out several times of an evening lately,' observed Bob. 'Tired of being indoors, I suppose.'

'Well, she's young,' said Ben. 'I don't blame her.'

'No, nor me neither,' agreed Hiram.

Ben sat down on the edge of a bin and took out his pipe.

'I met that fox, Willett, on the way up,' he said, 'a-sitting on a gate. I told him to take himself off.'

'Good,' said Hiram. 'We don't want the likes of him prowling round here.'

'He was wholly saucy,' continued Ben, 'so I pulled him off and he fell into a bramble bush.'

'I hope it scratched his arse,' said Bob, with a high-pitched laugh.

'I doubt that did,' said Ben. 'I'll do more than scratch him next time. I thought he was going for me, but he cleared off all right. He'll be back again though to-night, sure enough, you see. I want you two to come down with me to the spinney in a minute. Ten to one he'll be round there after the pheasants.'

'I'm your man,' said Hiram eagerly.

'So'm I,' added Bob. 'Just you let us finish this sack and we'll be with you.'

Twenty minutes later the three brothers set off down the hill, all with thick sticks in their hands.

'We'll give him what for if we catch him !' cried Bob excitedly as they climbed over the first gate.

'Now do you hold your tongue, Bob,' said Hiram. 'We've got to do this job quietly.'

'You're right,' whispered Bob as he jumped down beside him.

'Shet up and come on,' muttered Ben. 'Did you hear that pheasant?'

The spinney loomed up in front of them, a long, narrow, triangular strip of woodland, planted with larches and oak trees They halted for a moment and listened. Thirty yards away on the side furthest from the drift a pheasant screamed and went soaring across into the open with noisily flapping wings

'Hark!' whispered Ben. 'Did you hear that stick crack? There's someone over there, sure's there's water in this ditch. Now do you follow me. Best keep together.'

'Yes,' whispered Bob, 'that's more companionable like, ain't it, Hiram?'

Hiram nodded.

They crept along in single file on the lip of the ditch which bounded the spinney. Ben, who was leading, stopped all at once. There was a faint murmur of voices in front of them. Ben turned round.

'He've got a mate,' he murmured. 'They're in that gap where the stile is, I'll warrant.'

Another stick cracked and another pheasant went soaring up into the air.

'Now look here,' said Ben. 'We've got to take 'em unawares like. We'll creep up within a yard of that gap and then we'll rush 'em. And mind you don't trip over that stile, Bob.'

'Trust me,' said Bob. 'We'll give 'em a dusting.'

'Do you give the word, Ben,' said Hiram, 'and we'll follow you to the death.'

They clutched their sticks tightly and crept on. A yard or so from the gap they paused to gather themselves for the attack. They heard another murmur of voices: it seemed to come directly from the stile itself, but they could see nothing through the bushes.

'My! ain't this grass wet?' said Bob in a loud whisper.

Ben turned round and shook his fist at him.

'Come on,' he hissed.

They rose and rushed for the stile; but on the very

brink of the ditch they stopped short. There in front of them on the top bar of the stile sat two lovers, clasped tightly in each other's arms. Bob lost his balance and tumbled sideways into the water with a splash. The woman hastily unlocked herself from the man's embrace.

' 'Struth!' exclaimed Hiram. ' It's Nance!'

' Nance,' repeated Bob, clambering out on to the bank. ' Nance and Ted Willett!'

For fully a minute the two parties gaped at one another across the ditch with open mouths, both equally dumbfounded. Nancy was the first to find words.

' Well, what do you want to come here spying on me for?' she said angrily.

' We ain't spying,' stammered Ben.

' Well, what are you doing out here at this time of night then,' she said, ' with those great sticks?'

' We thought there was someone out after the pheasants,' Ben explained, ' but fare to me it was different game he was after. We didn't mean to disturb you, Nance, and that's the truth.'

' Oh, I see,' she replied, a little incredulously. ' Well, I don't think Bob'll catch many poachers. He've splashed me all over.'

' Sorry, Nance,' said Bob, who was trying to wring the water out of his coat, ' but I'm wholly wet.'

Willett continued sitting by Nancy's side in uneasy silence, biting his lip and drumming his fingers on the top bar of the stile.

' Well, now you're here,' said Nancy a little nervously, ' I might as well tell you '—she paused—' Ted and I are going to be married next month.'

The three brothers stared at her without replying and then dropped their eyes to the ground.

' Well,' she said, ' aren't you going to congratulate me?'

' We don't know whether to or not,' faltered Ben, without looking at her.

' Oh, it's like that, is it?' she replied indignantly.

She slipped down off the stile and turning her back on

them, fled away along the path which led back to the drift. Willett remained on the stile facing the brothers: they all stared at him without speaking. At last Willett could endure it no longer and swinging himself across the stile, he too disappeared among the trees. None of them attempted to stop him.

'Well I'm blamed,' gasped Hiram, gazing at the deserted stile.

Ben turned round and began to walk up the hill along the side of the spinney. He did not speak. Bob and Hiram silently followed him. When they reached the farm, they found Ern and Harry alone in the kitchen.

'Where's Nance?' asked Ben.

'She came in five minutes ago,' said Harry, 'and went straight upstairs. She fared all of a flurry.'

Without a word Ben left the kitchen and tramped up the hollow wooden stairs to Nancy's room. He tapped on the door.

'Yes?' came a faint voice.

Ben entered. She was sitting on the edge of the bed with her chin on her hands: she looked as if she had been crying.

'See here, Nance,' said Ben. 'I want to speak to you.'

'Yes?' she replied.

Ben leant back against the doorpost and folded his arms.

'We didn't mean no harm, my gal,' he said, 'but we wondered if you knowed anything about Ted Willett?'

'I ought to by now,' she replied scornfully. 'He love me.'

'That's as may be,' continued Ben, 'but he's the worst drunkard for miles round Bruisyard. P'r'aps you didn't know it: but you've only got to go to Sax any sale-day to see. He swill like a fish, and he's a poacher. If he've been up before the beak once for it, he've been half a dozen times.'

'Yes, that's what people say,' she returned hotly, 'but how do you know it's true? Look how they talked about us down in the village. You folk are all the same. You'll say anything about anybody.'

' Now look here, Nance,' he protested. ' You know that ain't true.'

' I know what you say isn't true,' Nancy burst out. ' He may have a bit more spirit than you and the rest: but he love me and I love him. I don't care if he is poor. I can afford to marry for love and I'm going to.'

' That's all very fine, my gal,' said Ben, ' but a man who do no work, but live on his parents and what he can pick up by poaching, can afford to marry you for what you've got. It fare to me he ain't good enough for you.'

' How dare you say such things about my Ted ? ' she cried. ' It's wholly shameful of you. As if he'd marry me for what I've got! If he do have a few little faults, I'll cure him of 'em ; if he do take a glass too much now and again, he 'on't when we're married. He love me, I tell you, and I love him. I 'on't have you say such things about my poor Ted.'

' Well, all I can say is, you're wholly hopeful,' replied Ben.

' Besides,' continued Nancy, ignoring the remark, ' I didn't ought to be alone in the house with all you men. Look what happened once before.'

' What, are you afraid of us ? ' gasped Ben.

' Well, not exactly that,' she replied, repenting a little of her harshness, ' but I think I ought to get married.'

' Get married, my gal, and good luck to you,' said Ben, ' but not to Ted Willett.'

' I shall marry who I please,' said Nancy tartly, ' and I don't want to hear no more about it from you.'

Ben shook his head and left her crestfallen.

XXIX

WHEN next month Nancy and Willett were married, the ceremony took place in Dennington church. which was reasonable enough, seeing that the vicar of Bruisyard had not been on speaking terms with the Geaiter family since old Benjamin showed his wife the door over eight years ago. People in the village told a different tale.

' I don't wonder,' said Mrs. Pearman to Mrs. Spatchard, when she heard of it. ' I dare say she's only marrying him to save her face and she'll go to Dennington to hide her shame from us. She needn't have been afraid : I shouldn't have gone.'

Mrs. Pearman secretly resented being deprived of the opportunity of absenting herself publicly from the wedding.

' Anyhow, she's going to the altar this time,' said Mrs. Spatchard.

' Yes, with Ted Willett,' sneered Mrs. Pearman. ' That show the sort she is. All I can say is, they desarve each other, them two.'

So their tongues wagged : but Nancy was far too happy to care if they wagged at all. She was properly wedded now to the man she loved, with God's blessing on them both and a fine farm to live on. Only one anxiety remained to trouble her—the brothers. She was annoyed with them for not liking Willett ; they had even refused to come to her wedding, pleading work in excuse. It seemed unaccountable to her ; she never seemed to be able to do anything to please them. On the other hand, she was well aware how vital they were to the prosperity of Crakenhill. They would have to put up with Willett, but Willett, too, would have to put up with them : she could not have him meddling with the business of the farm ; he was her husband.

Constraint descended upon the household once more as was inevitable ; no one could be lighthearted in the presence of so much tacit hostility. But there was no actual friction. The brothers, as soon as they perceived that Nancy was prepared to leave the farm in their hands, prepared to tolerate Willett as they had tolerated other unpleasant things before: and Joey had not deserted them. The farm and Joey—together they made up the bigger half of life; they would have gone through far more for their sake.

It was in Willett's interest, too, to keep the peace, as he very soon realised. He had a comfortable house to live in and an abundance of good food such as he had never known before; he had an affectionate wife and five strong men to work for them both: if only he could swallow his enmity, he was made for life. For the first week after his marriage he pottered about on the farm with his gun, getting to know the lie of the land: there was good shooting to be had and he enjoyed it thoroughly. But it was not quite so easy as he had thought to eat his wife's bread without working for it. Not that Nancy pressed him to work: so long as he was about the place to talk to her and make love to her when she wanted him, she did not care what he did. But when he passed any of the brothers at work together in the fields, he saw them look up and grin and he could guess what they were saying. Already he had overheard them call him Squire behind his back and it infuriated him: he was as good a man as they, he would beat them on their own ground and make them respect him: it was well, too, that he should, for though Nancy was now mistress of the farm, some day he would be master.

One morning after breakfast, when the brothers rose from the table, he followed Ben out into the yard.

' Say, Ben,' he said in a lofty manner, ' I want to give you a hand this morning. Have you got a job for me ? '

Ben did not jump at the offer. He grunted.

' You can't plough, can you ? ' he said slowly. ' Well, we're carting muck to-day. You'd best go along of Ern in the bullock yard and help him fill the carts.'

It was a dirty job at the best of times and Willett, being but a clumsy hand with a fork, bedaubed himself up to the elbows in muck, but however much he sweated and puffed and swore, he could only pitch one forkful to Ern's two.

'You'll soon get the knack,' said Ern with a grin. 'It ain't strength. Look here.'

He took up a heavy lump on the end of his fork and with a jerk of his elbow sent it hurtling over the barn thatch.

'There you are, Ted,' he cried. 'Now do you try and put one over the ne'thouse.'

Willett swore under his breath and heaved another lump into the tumbril. Ern laughed.

For two days Willett delved in the stench and the filth of the bullock-yard until his arms ached and his back burned. That was enough, he decided. The next day he asked for another job. Ben twitched his lip.

'Well,' he said, 'there's a hedge down by the gull want flashing. You might try your hand at it. Bob'll show you where it lay.'

When dinner-time came, Bob and Hiram took care to bring their horses back by way of the gull.

'Must see how the Squire's getting on,' piped Bob.

'Where is he?' said Hiram. 'I don't see him nowheres. He've gone home early to dinner.'

'Look there!' cried Bob. "See what he've done. I'll lay you a crown that ain't half a rod.'

'Nor it is,' said Hiram, stopping his horses by the hedge. 'And here's his rub lying in the grass and the hook too. My! it's that blunt you could ride to Romford on it. Do you feel, Bob.'

'Ay, that is,' said Bob, running his finger along the edge of the hook. 'But what did he want to leave it in the hedge like that for? He must have gone off right early.'

A shot rang out in the next field.

' Hark!' said Hiram. ' Now you know, Bob. Rabbit for dinner agin to-morrow. That's him right enough. Squire've got tired of farming.'

Willett was tired of farming. For him it was hard work and dull work: there was nobody to talk to, the thorns tore his hands, the hook grew blunt and his wrists ached: he was tired of the farm, tired of Nancy even; he wanted some life, some excitement. After dinner that day he did not go back to work, but put the young cob into the trap and drove off down the drift. He did not return until late that night, but he was in high spirits: he had a dealer's and hawker's licence in his pocket. It was a clever move. However little he earned, he was now no longer without an occupation: and at least, the humiliation he had envisaged, of asking Nancy for pocket-money, would be avoided. The life, doing a deal and getting the better of the other man, driving about from one village, one market-town to another and seeing the world—it was what he had always hankered after, though he had never had enough money to buy a horse and trap for himself; it was a lucky thing there were two driving horses on the farm now, one for Ern, to take the milk in, and one for him. He would have his freedom now: he could revisit his old haunts and his old cronies, drink a glass and lift a pheasant as the whim took him; and come back to Nancy's embraces when he wanted them. She would not know what he did in Debenham or Halesworth or Wickham Market; and even if she did, it was of no great consequence, for he already perceived that she was quite infatuated with him. He was in love with life that night.

.   .   .   .

Three months passed and the winter drew to its close It was just before supper-time at Crakenhill. All the brothers were seated round the room and Joey, about to be taken up to bed, was going round to each in turn to say good-night, while his mother waited for him at the foot of the staircase. The latch of the door rattled and

Willett strode in. He closed the door and stared at them for a moment. Then, with a curt nod to Nancy, he walked rather unsteadily across the room and propped himself up against the dresser, exhaling a strong odour of whisky.

Joey kissed the bristly cheeks of the brothers one by one.

' Ben, you'll let me ride Duke down to the blacksmith's to-morrow, 'on't you ? ' he said.

' Ay, don't you fret, boy,' replied Ben. ' Good-night, Joey.'

The child kissed him and was running over to his mother when Willett called to him.

' Aren't you going to say good-night to me, youngster ? ' he said, rather thickly.

' Go and say good-night to Daddy,' said Nancy encouragingly.

Joey pattered slowly back to the dresser and, a little reluctant, held up his cheek. Willett bent over him, but instead of kissing him, he picked him up by the collar and held him out at arm's length.

' Steady on, Ted,' shouted Ben from the other side of the room.

Willett set Joey on his feet again, but the child began to whimper, more from fright than pain.

' Here, stop that row,' said Willett.

Joey did not stop and Willett promptly boxed his ears. Joey began to cry in earnest now. Willett was raising his hand to clout him again when Hiram, who had slipped across the room, seized his arm and twisted it behind his back. The other four brothers had all risen from their chairs.

' We don't want any of that game here,' said Hiram, forcing him back against the dresser.

As Willett struggled to free himself, Nancy, her eyes glowing and her face as white as a sheet, came rushing to them.

' You leave my husband alone!' she cried, shaking her fist.

Hiram promptly dropped Willett's arm and stepped back a few paces. They stood glaring at each other.

' Well,' said Hiram at last, very slowly, ' do you tell him to leave our brother alone.'

' Ay,' murmured the other four in chorus.

Willett seemed quite oblivious of what was going on around him and turned once more to the child who was sobbing in front of him.

' Hold your noise, you little bastard!' he shouted.

He raised his arm once more to strike, but before the blow could fall, Ern, who had been watching him closely, darted in and catching him fairly between the eyes with his fist, stretched him full length and unconscious on the brick floor. Nancy, with a wail of horror, dropped down on her knees beside him and began loosening his collar. Ben, seizing the opportunity, snatched up Joey in his arms and carried him off to bed. Twenty minutes later Willett, having regained consciousness, staggered upstairs on Nancy's arm. The brothers ate their supper alone that night.

The following morning Willett did not appear at breakfast and Nancy herself came down late. Her face was very pale and she only sipped a cup of tea without touching any food. The brothers watched her with strained, uneasy glances ; they felt that something was impending. Not until she saw Ben move to leave the table did she speak.

' I want to tell you something,' she said in a faint, trembling voice. ' We shan't want any of you after this week.'

They stared at her.

' D'you mean—you want us—to go ? ' stammered Ben.

' Yes,' she replied, ' and here's a week's wages.'

She threw an envelope down on the table and hurried out of the room.

XXX

THE landlord of The Cart and Horses in Bruisyard Street, as the lower part of the village, a mile away from the church, was called, left the chattering Sunday morning crowd in the tap-room and went into the little bar-parlour at the back of the inn, carrying a pile of plates with him. It was a pleasant room with a brick floor and high-backed wooden settles ranged round a worn old elm table, scored with shove-ha'-penny lines : three highly-coloured advertisements for different brands of whisky hung upon the walls and in one corner a wired wooden target, stuck with a handful of darts ; a case of stuffed birds decorated the mantelpiece ; add half a dozen blackleaded spittoons and the furniture of the room was complete. It was little different from the tap-room except that it was less used, and there was a faint musty smell in the air such as hangs about stillrooms, wine-cellars, village churches and similar enclosed spaces that are left to themselves for long periods at a stretch, an odour of gentle decay. The landlord set five plates of bread and cheese on the table, each with a large Spanish onion beside it : he went out and returned a few minutes after with five pint mugs of beer which he also put on the table. A wheezy little fox-terrier bitch trotted in and curled up by the empty fireplace.

' Ah, Tip,' said the landlord, ' you know the time, you do.'

The tap-room clock struck twelve with a noise like a rapid succession of pistol shots, as if it were in a hurry to press on to the next hour. The innkeeper strolled to the door and looked out on the road. Five men were converging upon the inn, two from the direction of Rendham and a group of three from the Framlingham road.

' Ah, there they are,' the innkeeper murmured. ' That's all right then.'

It was a ritual this, which he had solemnly observed

now for the five months and more since the Geaiter brothers had been turned out of Crakenhill and he treated it with all the ceremonious respect due to a ritual. It gave him a feeling of importance and made his house seem something more than a mere drinking-shop although the five men never ate more than their portion of bread and cheese and an onion. But they came there regularly, the room was bespoke, as he proudly informed any traveller on a Sunday morning who asked if he might sit in there : and they had once been people of substance. Altogether they did not spend as much on the whole meal as some of his other customers on drink alone, but he esteemed them more than any : they conferred upon his house the dignity of an institution.

To the five brothers the ritual was a thing of even greater importance, being their principal substitute for all that they had lost, and in leaving Crakenhill they had lost almost everything. Ben, who was just forty, had lived and worked there twenty-four years and the others could hardly remember any other home. Their reputation in the district as farmers was wide-spread and they had no difficulty in finding work. Ben and Hiram went as chief horsemen on a big farm near Dennington and lived together in that village ; but Bob, Ern and Harry, scattered among the villages of Badingham, Cransford and Rendham, were compelled to live alone. Everything in the new surroundings was strange, the horses, the cows, the buildings, the implements, the fields : it all seemed wrong ; they were no longer working for their own family, they had to do what they were told. They were like trees torn up by their roots and for a long time their home-sickness was sheer pain to them. Coming home to lodgings after the day's work was a far different affair from coming home to Crakenhill and separated from one another for the first time, they realised for the first time how much they were attached to one another : they clung desperately together. Ben and Hiram of an evening would exchange visits with Bob between Dennington and Badingham ; Ern and Harry at Cransford and Rendham did the same. But the one day of the week when the cloud really lifted was Sunday. 'That boy have got a hid on him,' Ben had whispered to Hiram when Harry first propounded the idea. They all embraced it eagerly. Every Sunday at mid-day, as regular as the clock, they could be seen making for the inn door from their respective directions. They ate their bread, cheese and onions slowly and, for the most part, silently, leaving the discussion of the week's news until they had lighted their pipes and ordered another pint of beer all round; then their tongues loosened. At two o'clock they issued from the inn door again and made their way by devious paths up to the hill-top fields of Crakenhill, where they waited for Joey to come and join them. This was another scheme of Harry's; he had met the boy one morning on his way to school and arranged it all as a surprise for the rest. Joey could not afford to be so punctual as the others: the affair had to be kept secret from his mother and it required a good deal of artifice to slip away from the farm unobserved. His arrival was the brightest moment of the day. For ten minutes they laughed and played with him, swinging him about from shoulder to shoulder and filling his pockets with a medley of tasty and curious things, apples, toffee, birds' eggs, feathers, nuts, coloured pebbles and anything else which they thought might please him. Then all together they perambulated the fields of Crakenhill as they had done in the old days, as close up to the farmhouse as they dared go, criticising the crops and poking their heads into every hedge to find birds' nests for Joey. At four o'clock Joey left them and they scattered by other devious ways to their respective villages, to live upon their recollections until Sunday came round again.

Thus the weeks had passed by until it was nearly harvest-time. The brothers were anxious to take one more look at the corn before the cutting began and estimate the yield. They left the inn somewhat earlier and made their usual circuit up the hillside.

'There's a nice piece of oats,' said Hiram, pausing to pluck an ear. ' You couldn't want a better. There's ten or eleven coomb to the acre there, I'll lay a dollar.'

' Becourse there is,' said Ben, ' and do you know why, Hiram ? 'Cause me and you ploughed it up last October, and Bob helped us to drill it. All the winter corn on this farm's all right : we put it in.'

' Ay, that's the truth,' agreed Bob.

' Now do you look here, Hiram,' said Ben.

He led them over to a gap in the hedge through which they could see the next field. It had originally been planted with barley, but now it was half-covered with thistles which completely overtopped the barley—a wretched crop, thin and straggly, with pale, starved ears.

' There you are,' said Ben. ' There's a crop for you. That's what hired men do, that is.'

' I'm not so sure,' put in Harry. ' A few hired men'd soon have those thistles up. It's them as do the managing that's to blame.'

' You're right, young Harry,' replied Ben. ' They didn't ought to have planted barley here at all; it had barley last year. On a farm you want a man as know how to farm.'

' Why don't Nance have a steward ? ' said Ern as they walked on.

' Less money to enjoy 'emselves,' said Bob with a bitter laugh. ' Besides, Squire think he know all about it. That's why.'

' Yes, that's it,' said Ben, ' but that's cruel hard on the farm. By God! boys, look at this summerland! Never in all my days have I seen such a piece. By rights that should have had five ploughings and I'll lay there ain't a ploughshare have touched it since Bob and Hiram broke it up last year. Look at that rubbish! That's a wilderness, that is.'

' Yes, I know,' replied Hiram. ' He 'on't plough that now : he'll let it go and say he put it down to grass.'

' Ay,' Bob nodded, ' and then it 'on't even grow good rubbish. That break your heart to see.'

All the way up to the farm it was the same—miserable crops, half-strangled by triumphant weeds, the fruits of ill-judged and neglected cultivation; the cattle too were out of condition. The brothers had watched the steady decline week by week; a farm can go a long way downhill in five months.

'I thought our Nance had more sense,' said Ern gloomily, 'than to let the Squire farm the place. She was a wonderful sensible gal.'

'Why, Ern,' sighed Ben, 'she's in love, don't you see. That explain everything, don't it?'

'Yes, I suppose that do,' admitted Ern. 'That fare to shet people's eyes right up and no mistake. I don't know what'll come of it all.'

'Nor do I,' muttered Ben.

They walked on in silence to the little thicket at the top of the hill where they were accustomed to wait for Joey. He was late that afternoon and looked a little rueful when at last he did arrive with his hands thrust deep in the pockets of his Sunday coat.

'Well, Joey, what's the matter?' cried Bob. 'Your face is as long as the barn door.'

'Mother say I wasn't to go abroad this arternoon,' said Joey, coming to a stop in front of them. 'So she shet me up in the kitchen and locked the door.'

'How'd you get here then?' asked Ben.

'Out of the dairy window,' replied Joey.

Bob and Hiram grinned at each other; they remembered that dairy window well. The others laughed.

'What hev you been doing then,' said Harry, 'that made mother lock you in?'

Joey rubbed the side of his nose with his forefinger.

'Come, lad, out with it,' said Hiram. 'You must have been doing something.'

'Well,' faltered Joey, 'last night she made me kiss daddy good-night and I didn't want to and when he kissed me, I wiped it off.'

'Oh!' said Hiram. The brothers looked at one another.

' And I 'on't kiss him,' added Joey emphatically. ' I don't like him and he don't like me and he ain't my proper daddy, is he ? '

No one answered him.

' What'll your mother say,' asked Ben, ' when she come to the kitchen and find you gone ? '

' I don't care,' said Joey, putting his hands in his pockets and squaring his shoulders defiantly. ' I wanted to see you.'

' There's a brave lad,' said Ern, gripping his arm. ' Don't you worry. She'll forget all about it by next Sunday. You get your teeth into this gingerbread. That come all the way from Frannigan.'

' Cheer up, Joey,' cried Bob. ' How'd that top go that I gave you last week ? '

' That go fine,' said Joey, ' and I can pick it up in my hand now, when its going, Bob.'

' Well done, lad,' said Ben, ' and how's your mother ? '

' She's all right,' replied Joey. ' But she haven't been in to give me my supper for the last week. She've been out abroad every night with daddy.'

' Oh! ' said Ben. ' Where ? '

' I don't know,' said Joey. ' She've been dancing twice, I know.'

' Oho! ' said Harry to Ern. ' So that's how the land lay.'

' And the other night,' continued Joey, ' she came in to say good-night after she came back and she smelt ever so funny, like daddy do sometimes.'

Ben raised his eyebrows and looked significantly at Hiram.

' Going the pace a bit, eh ? ' he said in an undertone.

' Well, don't you worry, old man,' said Hiram. ' That 'on't hurt you.'

' I know,' said Joey. ' Oh, and mother say I might be having a little brother or sister, she didn't know which.'

' Oh ? ' said Ben. ' Did she say when ? '

' No,' replied Joey. ' She only said some day soon.'

' Which do you want, Joey ? ' said Bob.

' I don't want neither,' laughed Joey. ' I've got five big brothers already. That's enough.'

' You young rascal! ' cried Hiram, seizing him by the waist and hoisting him on to his shoulder. ' I'll larn you to cheek your big brothers.'

Joey giggled and tweaked Hiram's ear.

' Now then, off we go,' said Hiram, giving his shoulder a jerk and bouncing Joey up into the air. ' We want to see how you've been farming this week.'

They moved off in procession along the hedge with Joey and Hiram at their head.

' Drinking and dancing,' muttered Ben to Ern, ' that don't look well for a new baby, do it ? '

' That don't,' replied Ern. ' Just the way to get a weakly calf, that.'

As Hiram passed beneath a bowed old elm tree, Joey seized hold of one of the overhanging branches and swinging himself off Hiram's shoulder, swarmed up against the trunk.

' You young jackanapes ! ' cried Hiram.

' Ah, Hiram! ' Joey mocked, pelting him with pieces of twig. He ceased suddenly and gazed into the distance. ' Oh, I say ! ' he exclaimed.

' What's the matter, boy ? ' said Ben.

' Why there's mother coming across the stile there,' said Joey in a trembling voice, ' and she've seen me already.'

The brothers swung round and looked at the stile ; there was Nancy, sure enough. She clambered over and advanced rapidly towards them. They watched her helplessly : it was no use running away or pretending to ignore her with Joey there among them : all they could do was to wait for her. She came up with her cheeks flushed and an angry gleam in her eye.

' What are you men doing on my land ? ' she demanded.

' We're just out for a walk,' said Ben.

' Oh, are you ? ' she replied sarcastically. ' Well, I'll trouble you to keep off. You don't belong here and you know it. Come you down at once, Joey.'

Joey slithered down a branch and dropped to the ground with a thud. He looked shamefacedly at his mother.

'Now I know where it is he goes off to on a Sunday afternoon,' continued Nancy indignantly. 'I suspected something last week, when he brought that new top home and said he found it in the road. So this afternoon when he got out of the kitchen, I thought I'd come and see. A nice lot you are, teaching a boy to tell lies and break out of the house when he's told to stay in.'

'You know that ain't true, Nance,' protested Ben. 'We wouldn't harm him for anything in the world.'

'Oh, wouldn't you?' retorted Nancy sharply 'Yes, I know you, you good, kind men. What about that night you all went for my Ted. You didn't do him any harm, did you?'

'Well, he was hurting Joey,' said Ern. 'What do you think——'

'He wasn't doing anything to hurt,' interrupted Nancy, 'or even if he was, he didn't mean it. That's only your excuse. You're jealous of him, that's what it is, and you'd do anything to spite him. Yes, I know all about you. A good thing I got rid of you. I wish I'd done it before.'

'Nance, do listen,' pleaded Hiram.

'Yes, I know,' she railed, ignoring him, 'and now you're trying to set the child against his father. Now I know why he 'on't kiss him when he go to bed. A low, mean trick, I call it.'

'Look here, Nance,' said Harry, 'be quiet a minute and listen to me.'

'Who are you?' said Nance, more enraged than ever. 'Who are you to tell me to be quiet on my own land? I 'on't be spoke to like that by a common farm-labourer. Now listen here. Don't you let me catch you here again, any of you, or I'll have the law on you. Ted say the partridges are scarce this year and I don't wonder. And you needn't think you'll find Joey here any more, 'cause you 'on't. It's high time he went to Sunday school. Come here, Joey.'

Joey edged timidly up to her, rubbing his eyes with his knuckles. Nancy seized him roughly by the hand.

' Now then,' she said, ' I'm going to see you men off my land.'

' Your land! ' retorted Ern. ' You've only got to look at it to see it ain't ourn.'

' Shet up, Ern,' said Ben, taking him by the arm and drawing him away. ' Do you leave her alone and come on.'

They filed silently along the hedge to the little thicket from which they had started. Ern looked back over his shoulder as they stepped across the ditch : Nancy was still gazing fiercely after them with Joey sobbing at her side. Out of her sight among the trees, they halted and looked at one another.

' God! ' Ern burst out. ' There's a proper bitch for you : and Joey all alone in that house, poor kid! '

' Fare to me she's going a bit jim,' said Bob, ' like father did.'

' No,' replied Ben, ' she ain't old enough for that.'

' Who'd have thought our Nance'd ever turn out like that ? ' said Hiram. ' She was a real good gal, she was.'

' I doubt she still is,' said Harry. ' She can't see straight, that's what's the matter with her : and when she've got a thing in her head, there ain't no shifting it.'

Ern savagely tore a twig off an ash tree and broke it in pieces.

' Well,' he grunted, ' it ain't much loss to be turned off the farm. That'll soon make your eyes sore to look at it, I'll warrant.'

' Ay, that's wholly true,' said Harry, ' but we can still catch Joey sometimes on his way to Sunday school.'

' No,' interposed Ben, ' that 'on't do. That'd only get the poor kid in a row. He've had enough trouble already. Best leave him alone.'

' Ay, that's right,' Hiram nodded.

' Well, what is there left ? ' said Ern bitterly. ' She've took everything from us now. What can we do ? '

Why we must put up with it,' said Ben despondently. ' That's what we must do.'

' Fare to me,' rejoined Ern, ' we're allus putting up with things.'

' Well,' said Ben, ' can you think of anything else to do ? '

' No,' said Ern in a low voice. ' I can't, Ben.'

' I'm getting hungry, boys,' piped Bob. ' Let's get home to tea and thank God we can still eat.'

' Ay,' said Hiram, ' thank God for that.'

They brushed their way out of the thicket and trudged moodily down the hill : even a good appetite was scarcely consolation enough on such a day.

XXXI

NANCY kissed her baby gently on the forehead and tiptoed across to the window. A puff of wind rippled over a field of red-gold wheat and spent itself with a faint hiss in the elm-tops by the drift, blurring for a moment their feathery outlines and leaving behind it a stillness more profound than that which it had broken. Another day ended, another week and harvest would be upon them. It was pleasant to sit there gazing at the chequer-work of green and gold that covered the whole hillside; the trees and hedges looked so clumpy at this time of year, as if they were trying to keep the rising sea of corn from overflowing its banks. Pleasanter still, she thought, to be out there with the warm air curling round her cheeks, smelling the smells of summer, courting again. She sighed and looked back at the cot with a smile. She had no regrets: Susan had made up for all the liberty she had lost and more. Joey, sturdy little rogue, was down in the yard, whittling at a stick with his pocket-knife; she was fond of him too. But Susan was different; she was the child of the man she loved, part of them both and shared by them both. To feel such a child at her breast was a new and marvellous happiness to her, almost as great as the joy of being loved, and of Willett's love she was sure, in spite of his careless, harum-scarum ways; they only made her love him the more. From the day the brothers left the farm, he had changed the whole aspect of life for her: he had given up his dealing and stayed at home with her to manage the farm: whenever he went out, he took her with him, as if he were proud to show her off, to dances, to fairs, to parties, on visits to his friends; he had such innumerable friends and he was the life and soul of every party. Sometimes he would take the trap and just drive from village to village, stopping at an inn here and there by the way: a little gaiety, a drink or two, it made all the difference. The farm, it was true, was not running so

well as it might and this harvest would be no better than
the last, even worse, perhaps: but Ted, after all, was still
learning his trade and in a year or two, when he had gained
a little more experience, things would be better than they
had ever been before, and when Susan was a little older,
she herself would be able to help him. Anyhow, a few
bushels of corn, a few gallons of milk the less, it was not a
heavy price to pay to be rid of the Geaiters, those men, how
she hated them : there was no knowing what they might
have done to her husband if she had not stood up for him :
and now, at least, there was a little cheerfulness in the
house. The shadows deepened around the barn : Ted
would be home soon. Nancy sighed again, but it was a sigh
of contentment.

There was a jingle of harness on the drift and Willett's
trap came into view. Nancy hurried downstairs and began
to get the supper ready. Five minutes later Willett strode
jauntily into the kitchen : he seemed in a good humour.

' Well, Nance, my gal,' he said, rubbing his hands,
' we've done well over them two pigs. They both weighed
a couple of score more'n I thought. That make a tidy
little sum. Fatting pigs pay and no mistake.'

' Well done,' said Nancy, ' and now I expect you're
tired, dear.'

' Oh, not so bad,' replied Willett hastily, ' but look here,
Nance, I've got something to tell you.'

' Oh ? ' she said, putting her hands on her hips and
laughing in his face. ' What is it ? You fare in proper
high spirits.'

Willett laid a finger on her shoulder.

' Have you got a couple of hundred pound or so handy,
Nance ? ' he said in a low voice.

Nancy slowly shook her head and opened her eyes wide.

' That I haven't,' she replied. ' What d'you want it
for ? '

' It's like this,' said Willett. ' After I'd left them pigs
at the butcher's, I went into The Feathers to wet my
whistle and there was a bloke there from Ipswich, come

down for a company. He say they've just discovered a new way of growing rubber, cheaper and better'n any of the other ways: and they've bought a piece of land in Africa where they're going to grow it, and in a year or two's time they'll undersell all the other companies, he say, and capture the world market.'

'Oh?' said Nancy, without any show of interest. 'What about it?'

'Well,' continued Willett, 'they haven't got enough by 'em yet to get all the land they want and set up the business; so they've come round to see if any of us folk'd put some money into it. He say that's as good as a gold mine and as safe as Frannigan church tower, and if you buy shares in it, you'll soon be getting all your money back every year.'

'Ah,' said Nancy incredulously, 'I've heard of that sort of thing before. How d'you know what he say is true?'

'Why,' exclaimed Willett, 'he've got it all there in black and white, with pictures of the place and no end of a rigmarole about how they're going to grow it, all signed by blokes with strings of letters after their names. If only we had a few hundred pound to put in it, that'd make us rich for the rest of our lives, that would.'

'Well, you know I haven't got the money,' said Nancy, 'so there's an end of it.'

She went to the dresser and took down some plates.

'Listen, Nance,' said Willett. 'I've got an idea.'

Nancy turned round and faced him with the plates in her hand.

'It fare to me this farm's too big for us,' he went on. 'The house and barn and stables weren't built for two hundred acres and that extra hundred is poor owd land. It cost us in labour and don't bring nothing in. Now I happen to know that Mr. Snowland who've bought a couple of farms over the hill there'd like to get hold of it: he want a bit more shooting. Suppose we sold it to him and kept the rest. We should only have a hundred acres left to work, that'd be main easier and we should do better,

I'll warrant ; and there'd be two men less to pay each week. Then we could put half the money into that there company and keep the rest to carry on the farm.'

Nancy shook her head.

' That couldn't be done, Ted,' she said. ' That hundred acres have belonged to the place ever since I've lived here. I can't break the farm up.'

' Now look here, Nance, 'said Willett, tapping his finger on her shoulder again. ' It's no use talking like that. If that's worth it, that ought to be done, break up or no. And we shall need the money right bad : there's a mighty great bill from the miller's to pay come Michaelmas. And I tell you what, Nance. In a year or two we shall get so much back from that rubber farm that we can buy back the land we've sold and more if you like. Think of it, Nance : suppose we put five hundred pound into it and got five hundred pound back each year for it. You wouldn't have to do no more work and you could live like a lady. We could have a new trap and a servant to live in the house and port wine at dinner.'

' No,' said Nancy, shaking her head again. ' That sound all right, Ted dear, but you don't know whether that'll come true ; and I'm not going to throw away our money on a chance thing like that. If we go on working hard, the farm'll come round all right and give us a good living.'

' But listen, Nance,' he persisted. ' Ain't it worth while risking a bit for all that ? Think what it'd be like being a lady, with no work to do, no beds to make, no washing up to do and all the clothes you like to buy ; you could go a-frolicking every night. And there's the children to think of too.'

' Now, Ted dear,' said Nancy very firmly, ' there's enough. Crakenhill came to me with two hundred acres and with two hundred acres it's going to stay. So there's an end of it.'

She went over to the table and began arranging the plates on the cloth. Willett shrugged his shoulders and throwing himself down on the sofa, sullenly hid himself behind the sheets of the *East Anglian Daily Times*. The door opened and Joey crept in, stealthily and mouse-like. He sat down on a chair by the window and swung his legs to and fro, furtively watching his step-father. There was no one to talk to now when he came in of an evening and ever since tea he had been playing alone in the farmyard and the orchard. His mother did not like him far away from the house : he might meet the Geaiters. Joey sighed : the kitchen seemed empty.

'Come on, Joey,' said Nancy. 'Come and eat this pasty. Here's a glass of milk for you.'

Joey sat down at the table and slowly devoured the pasty while Willett continued to sulk behind his newspaper. Nancy went into the larder and cut some slices off a cold leg of mutton : she came back and put the meat on the table.

'Supper's ready, Ted,' she said.

Willett did not move. There was a lifeless gloom over the table which oppressed Joey. It reminded him of chill summer days when the sun vanished suddenly behind the clouds, draining the landscape of all its colour and plunging it in a strange, uneasy solitude. His mother's voice, the rustle of Willett's newspaper, the ticking of the clock, were all uncouth sounds which jarred upon the silence. He emptied his glass, got up from his chair and walked over to the door.

'Where are you off to?' his mother demanded.

'I'm now going into the orchard to look for glow-worms,' he replied.

'That you aren't,' said Nancy sharply. 'It's time you were in bed. Go and say good-night to daddy.'

Joey hesitated for a moment with his hand still on the latch.

'Off you go,' said Nancy.

He edged slowly up to the back of the sofa and stood looking over Willett's shoulder.

'Good-night, daddy,' he said, half-heartedly, holding up his cheek.

Willett rustled the sheets of his newspaper impatiently.

' Be off with you,' he growled.

Joey crept thankfully away from him, kissed his mother and disappeared up the stairs, gingerly closing the door behind him.

' Why wouldn't you say good-night to Joey ? ' asked Nancy. She felt rather disquieted. Her husband had never been like this before ; he went his own way when he liked, but he was always cheerful in the house.

Willett said nothing and noisily rustled his paper again.

' What's the matter with you, Ted ? ' she said in an anxious voice.

He muttered something inaudible.

' Aren't you coming to have your supper, dear ? ' she said.

' I don't want none,' he grunted.

Nancy walked round the table and slipped down beside him on the sofa.

' What is the matter, Ted ? ' she repeated.

' Plenty the matter,' replied Willett, turning away from her.

' What, Ted dear ? ' she persisted, putting her hand on his shoulder.

He folded up his newspaper and tossed it on the floor.

' You're wholly selfish, you are,' he complained. ' You never listen to anything I say, do you ? You never do anything I want, do you ? I've given up my dealing and stayed at home here, all for the sake of your farm, and you treat me as if I knowed nothing about it. I don't believe you love me at all.'

' Oh, Ted,' she cried, throwing her arms around his neck, ' you know I do. I've never loved anyone else in my life. I'd do anything for you.'

' No, you wouldn't,' he replied, roughly loosening her arms and thrusting her away from him.

' Oh, Ted,' she cried, ' you are cruel. What have I done now ? '

' I believe you think more of your damned owd farm

than you do of me,' he rejoined. ' You want me to go on working like a slave on it for the rest of my life, it fare to me. I'm sick to death of it.'

He folded his arms and turned his head away with an aggrieved air.

Nancy put her arms round his neck again and kissed him on the cheek.

' My poor darling Ted,' she whispered. ' I know it's hard on you. I wish I could do something to help you.'

' Well, you can,' he said, without turning his head, ' if you like.'

' What, sell the farm?' she said. ' Never, Ted. I couldn't do that.'

' Now look here, Nance,' he said, facing round and loosening her arms from his neck once more. ' I know what I'm talking about and I can tell a good thing when I see one. Say we got a thousand pound for that bit of land: we could put five hundred into the rubber company and that'd make our fortune in a few years. The other half I'd put into pigs while we waited for the money to come in. It's not corn that pay, but pigs, and they ain't the trouble sheep are. Look what that couple fetched to-day. We'll have some new styes built over behind the orchard and get a score of pedigree sows. Two farrows a year and say, taking the good with the bad, six in a farrow: then sell 'em at a month or six weeks or fat 'em up for the butcher—that's the way to make money, like wild-fire.'

' Oh, Ted,' cried Nancy despairingly, ' don't ask me to sell the farm.'

' I ain't asking you to sell the farm,' he rejoined, ' only a bit of it. What do a few acres of poor owd land matter if we make our fortunes? I used to think you were a courageous sort of gal, but now I see you're just like all the rest.'

' I'm not afraid of anybody,' replied Nancy, 'and if only I had the money by n.e, I'd let you have it right away : but you can't tell how it frighten me to think of breaking up the farm. It have gone so well all together up till now.'

' Oh, well,' said Willett, shrugging his shoulders, ' I think I shall clear out. I can see I'm not wanted here. I ain't a-going on slaving away for nothing.'

' Oh, Ted,' cried Nancy tearfully, embracing him a third time, ' you mustn't talk like that. You know I love you and want you here. You mustn't say such things. Ted, Ted darling, kiss me.'

He turned his head and kissed her lightly on the cheek. She pressed him close to her. Five minutes later his arms were around her and he was stroking her hair. He whispered in her ear.

' Yes, Ted,' she murmured, with half-closed eyes. ' I'll do anything you like so long as you'll go on loving me.'

XXXII

IT was more than eighteen months since Ben had last climbed up the drift to Crakenhill and he walked slowly, stopping every now and then to take stock of the fields on either side of him. There had been good feed in the meadow on his left when he was on the farm, good sweet, short grass, thick at the root: it had taken many years to make that pasture. But in the last six months a couple of sows with their litters had been let loose to forage there and the turf was all scored and pitted with the holes they had routed: half a dozen skinny bullocks were cropping the scanty, faded grass that remained. The thorn hedge which had been due for cutting when he and his brothers left the farm, soared still uncut above his head in a disorderly tangle and, more serious, the ditch below was choked with brambles. Through the gaps between the branches he caught sight from time to time of this year's summerland, as yet untouched by the plough, with the remains of last year's stubble still rotting on it, rapidly going down to useless self-sown grass and weeds. A little further up the hedge lay a pile of hurdles, gradually falling to pieces where they had been thrown when the last fold had been unstaked: there were no longer any sheep on the farm. Ben shook his head dejectedly and walked on with his eyes fixed steadfastly on the rutty track before him to save himself further harrowing. There was enough on his mind already this evening.

' Hullo, Ben! Fancy you here! '

A child's voice made him stop and look up. There, fifty yards from the farmyard gate, stood Joey in front of him with his hands in his pockets, his little brown face one huge grin of astonished delight.

' Why, Joey! '

Ben stooped down and hugged him. Then, suddenly at a loss for words suitable to the occasion, they stood and smiled at each other.

' Did you have a good harvest ? ' said Ben awkwardly at last.

' Daddy didn't fare very pleased,' replied Joey, ' but mother say that couldn't be helped.'

' I didn't mean that,' said Ben. ' What sort of harvest did you have ? Did you enjoy yourself ? '

' I don't know,' said Joey dubiously. ' I rode the horses a few times and called hold-tight for 'em when they were a-carting wheat. But they wouldn't take me up on the waggon : they're a rough lot, them new chaps, especially Bill Sayers. I did some work, Ben, this year. I learnt to tie shoves and shock and use a fork : but whenever Bill seed me doing anything, he used to laugh and say, " What do he think he's a-doing of ? "   And I was doing my best to help and I'm ten now.' He drew himself up and proudly expanded his chest.

' I know the sort,' snorted Ben indignantly. ' I wish I'd been there. But don't you worry yourself about the likes of them. You'll have the laugh of 'em one day.'

' I didn't,' replied Joey. ' I just left 'em to go on by 'emselves without me and went off and set snares for rabbits.'

' Well done ! ' said Ben. ' And how's your mother ? '

' She fare all right,' said Joey, ' but she spend all her time with the baby now. She forget all about me now, except when she want me to fetch an errand for her.'

' What a shame ! ' said Ben sympathetically. ' And how do your daddy treat you ? '

' Well, yesterday he gave me a penny,' said Joey thoughtfully, ' and he say we shall soon be rich : and the day before he clouted my head for snaring rabbits up on the hill-top ; he say it ain't ourn any longer.'

' Oh, do he ? ' grunted Ben. ' There's more up there than rabbits to lose, I doubt.'

' I wish you'd come back to the farm, Ben,' said Joey, looking pensively at a distant hedge, ' you and Hiram and the rest. It haven't been the same place since you went.'

' So do I,' said Ben. ' Here's a tanner for you, lad. That's a long time since I seed you last.'

'Thanks, Ben.' Joey gravely pocketed the coin, pulled a blade of grass and chewed it.

'Hi, Joey! Come you here!' A voice from the farm-yard gate made them turn round with a start.

'That's daddy a-calling me,' said Joey. 'I must now be going.'

'All right,' said Ben. 'I'll go along with you. I want to see your mother.'

They walked on side by side to the gate where Willett was lolling with his arms over the top bar. He affected to take no notice of Ben, but pushed the gate ajar a foot to admit Joey.

'Come here, boy,' he said roughly, as soon as Joey was inside. 'Give me that money, d'you hear?'

'What money?' faltered Joey.

'The money he now gave you,' replied Willett. 'I had my eye on you.'

Joey reluctantly pulled out his sixpence and handed it over.

'Now listen here,' said Willett, as he took it from him. 'I ain't a-going to have you taking money from them Geaiters. I 'on't have it. You're not to speak to 'em, d'you hear?'

Joey stared at him in rebellious silence. Willett tossed the coin over the gate at Ben's feet.

'Do you find something better to do with your money,' he sneered. 'We ain't so poor as all that. What do you want up here? Nance told you to keep off.'

'I want to see her for a minute,' replied Ben, without troubling to pick up the sixpence.

''On't I do?' inquired Willett.

'No, you 'on't,' replied Ben. 'What I want to say's for her. That's important.'

'Oh, I see,' said Willett sullenly, 'but I ain't so sure she want to see you.'

At that moment Nancy came out of the kitchen door with her baby on her arm, followed by Joey, who had just slipped in to tell her that Ben had come to see her. She walked slowly up to the gate.

'Well, what is it, Ben?' she asked coldly, slowly rocking her baby from side to side.

'I wanted a word with you, Nance,' replied Ben.

'Well, here I am,' she said.

'I meant private like,' said Ben.

'Well, if you've got anything to say,' she replied, 'you can say it in front of my husband. What's my business is his too.'

'Oh!' Ben paused and looked at his feet, trying to collect words.

'Well?' said Willett impatiently. 'We can't wait here all night for you; it'll soon be supper-time.'

'It's like this,' Ben began. 'I've just heard master say this arternoon that you were going to sell them upper fields to Snowland there over the hill.'

'Well, what of it, Ben?' said Nancy.

Ben hesitated, and fidgeted with his toe among some straws by the gatepost.

'There's still a few days to go afore Michaelmas,' he said, looking up. 'I wondered if it was too late.'

'Too late for what?' said Nancy.

'Too late to change your mind,' he explained.

'Why should I?' retorted Nancy. 'That's not your affair either.'

'Maybe not,' said Ben, 'but in some ways that is. You see, Nance, when father took over them fields twenty year ago, they were in a terrible state, I know; but then we brought 'em round and they sarved us well. They're wonderful stubborn, but they pay for working. That's a real pity to let 'em go.'

'Still, they are going,' said Willett, 'whatever you say. That's dirty owd land and by rights it don't belong to Crakenhill at all. When we've got that out of the way, we can do justice by what's left. It's no use hanging on to land that's no good just because you've got it.'

'No,' admitted Ben, 'you're right there. But that ain't bad land. That only want farming properly.'

Willett flushed angrily.

'When we want your advice,' he snapped, 'we'll ask for it.'

'Yes, but listen to me, Nance,' Ben continued. 'I don't like to see the farm broke up like this. You know, Nance, you said you were going to keep it for Joey to farm when he was old enough. There'll only be half of it then; and those two halves hold together like; Crakenhill was more than twice the farm with both of 'em.'

'Now look here, Ben,' said Nancy, 'do you be quiet. The deal's done and the land's sold and already paid for. Besides, we know what we're doing. It ain't your farm, do you remember that. It's like your impudence: is that all you came up for?'

She gazed fiercely at him over the top of the gate. He seemed such a shambling, insignificant creature to her now: she could not think why she had ever taken him seriously before, much less been afraid of him. Here she was, mistress of Crakenhill, being told her business by a common ploughman who worked for hire: her blood warmed at the idea.

'Oh, Nance, Nance,' Ben blurted out, casting off all discretion, 'you know what that mean to all of us: those fields up there and all the work we put into 'em, all gone out of the family—the farm 'on't look the same without 'em. If you're a bit short of cash, why, I might be able to lend you a bit and I dare say the other boys down there'd be ready to give a hand to keep things going. Do think it over, Nance, even if he'—he indicated Willett with a jerk of his head—'have persuaded you to sell it. And don't you forget Joey.'

'I've got other things besides Joey to think of now,' replied Nancy indignantly, tossing her head and stroking her baby's cheek. 'Going out of the family indeed! D'you think I belong to your family? I hope I think a little better of myself than that.' She laughed scornfully. 'And you may well talk of lending us money when you know the land's already sold. You know it's no use offering it then. Yes, I know what you're made of.' She laughed

again. ' That's only an excuse for coming up here, that
is—as if the place belonged to you. I've turned you off
this farm once before. Don't you let me catch you up here
again. I've had enough of you and your brothers.'

' Yes,' added Willett warmly, ' if I catch you up here at
the yard again, I'll set that dog on you, I will.' He pointed
to a large half-bred retriever growling on its chain in a
corner of the yard. ' And he bite, he do.'

Ben opened his mouth to speak and shut it again.

' Go on, take yourself off,' cried Willett, shaking his fist.
' We've had enough of you here.'

' Well, I'll go,' said Ben, ' but not for anything you say,
Ted. I'm not afraid of you or your blasted dog; but I
don't want to come where I'm not wanted.'

There was a queer, strained look about his eyes as if he
were struggling with some violent physical pain: it was
the only sign of emotion that he gave. He turned round
and walked slowly away down the drift with his hands
behind his back and his head a little bowed. He climbed
the gate at the end of the first field without turning his
head.

' Good riddance!' sneered Willett as he watched him
disappear. ' He know how to put it on, he do. Coming up
here like that.'

' Yes,' said Nancy, ' you'd think the place belonged to
him. I've had enough of those Geaiters. Say good-night
to Susan, Ted. I'm going up to put her to bed.'

Willett bent down and kissed the baby's cheek. Nancy
pulled him towards her and playfully kissed him on the
forehead.

' Now don't be late, will you, dear?' she said. ' I've
hardly seen you all day. '

' All right, Nance,' he replied. ' I'll do my best. But I
must get those styes ready by then the sows come.'

Nancy went off indoors with the baby and Willett sat
down in the yard on a wooden pig-trough that he had just
knocked together. He heaved a sigh and yawned wearily.
A score of sows were coming in two days' time and quarters

must be found for them : new pig-styes would have to be built sooner or later. He was tired out : marrying Nancy had meant far more work than he had bargained for, far more work than he had ever been accustomed to ; he had passed a whole fortnight now without once going out for a jaunt in the trap.

The dog in the corner of the yard leaped on his chain and barked. Willett looked up. Someone had just opened the yard gate. Willett put his hand to his eyes and peered through the failing light. It was a man of the same height and build as Ben, carrying in his hand a roughly-trimmed elm bough, fresh-cut from the hedge as if he had been driving cattle. Surely it could not be Ben come back again.

' Who is it ? ' shouted Willett.

' It's only me,' the man called back. ' I want to see Nance a minute.'

Willett, recognising Ern's voice, rose to his feet.

' If you've got anything to say,' he said curtly, ' you'd best say it to me. She's indoors.'

' What I've got to say's private,' said Ern in a gruff voice. ' I want to see Nance.'

' Well, Ern Geaiter, I tell you, you can't,' retorted Willett. ' She's putting the baby to bed. I reckon I'm good enough to hear anything you've got to say.'

' Well, you ain't,' rejoined Ern emphatically, advancing to the middle of the yard and regarding Willett scornfully with his stick planted between his feet. ' I want Nance.'

' Well, you can't see her,' said Willett, ' that's flat. I've just sent Ben about his business. He came up after the same thing.'

' All right,' said Ern, shrugging his shoulders. ' I shall wait here till I do see her. You ain't a-going to stop me, Ted Willett, and you know it.'

' Look here, Ern,' threatened Willett, ' if you ain't on the other side of that gate inside a minute I'll set that dog on you. He's savage and he's hungry, I can tell you.'

' I'm a-going to stay here till Nance come,' replied Ern stubbornly, ' and I don't care a snap for your bloody dog.'

The dog continued to bark, straining madly on its chain and working itself into a fury.

' All right,' shouted Willett, walking over to the kennel, ' don't you say I didn't warn you. Go for him, Darkie! '

The dog, loosed from the chain, rushed upon Ern with teeth bared and growling savagely, Willett urging it on from behind. Ern took up his stick and waited calmly. It did not stop to choose its ground or take him in the rear, but sprang on him at once, viciously snapping its jaws. Ern, watching his opportunity, suddenly dashed his stick down with both hands hard between its jaws and before the enraged animal could disengage itself, he had dropped the stick and caught it by the collar. In a trice he had it down, with his knee on its side and both his hands on its throat. Then with one hand forcing its muzzle back and straining the neck taut, with the other he took a complete turn, twisting a loop in the heavy brass-studded collar. The dog heaved and struggled in vain. It could not move under Ern's weight and his grip on its throat was like iron—Ern had always had strong hands, as the recruiting sergeant had observed a good many years ago. It gasped and frothed at the mouth, its eyes bulged. Ern rose to his feet and held it up by the collar, its legs kicking convulsively.

' There, Ted Willett,' he cried. ' Do you go indoors and call Nance or I'll do your bloody dog in, I swear I will.'

' All right,' shouted Willett, ' let the poor brute go. I'll fetch her.'

Ern took the half-choked animal in both hands and threw it contemptuously over the pig-trough. It alighted on its feet and limped wretchedly off to the kennel with its tail between its legs, nor daring to look behind it. Ern picked up his stick, looked at the teeth-marks on it and then walked up to the kitchen door where Nancy was standing, pale and frightened, with a pair of baby's socks in her hand.

' Well, what is it, Ern ? ' she said a little shakily. ' I'm busy.'

'You might tell your man to keep a hand on his dog another time,' replied Ern gruffly. 'I don't want to have to kill it. That's a dangerous brute to have about the place.'

'You didn't come to tell me that,' said Nancy sharply, recovering her composure once more.

'No, I didn't, Nance,' said Ern in a softer voice. 'But I had something to tell you.'

'Well, hurry up and get it out,' she replied. 'I can't stay.'

'I heard this morning,' said Ern, 'that you were going to buy a score of sows of Steve Bracebridge over at Great Glemham.'

'It's a marvel to me,' replied Nancy, 'how your business do get about the place till every Tom, Dick and Harry know it. We are going to buy some sows, but that's not your affair.'

'You can keep your high words till I've finished, young woman,' rejoined Ern, 'but I've got something to tell you about them pigs. I know a thing or two about that Bracebridge. He ain't straight: and he've had a boar up there on his farm that have got something wrong with him. Every sow that he've sarved slip half its farrow and the pigs that do come are poor little owd things only fit to knock on the head. My master was bitten once over 'em. I don't know if he've still got the boar, but I know he want to get rid of the sows. That stand to reason he do. I don't say they're all wrong, but you 'on't know what you're getting.'

'But they're pedigree pigs,' protested Nancy.

'That don't matter,' replied Ern. 'If the boar's wrong, they might just as well be any owd mongrels.'

'What's all this about Steve Bracebridge?' interrupted Willett. 'He's as straight as they make 'em. I know him well and he's letting me have them sows at a fair price.'

'Ay,' sneered Ern, 'you know him well enough across the bar-parlour table of The Feathers, I doubt; but you haven't never bought a pig of him: he'll do you down as soon as look at you. He can afford to let you have 'em cheap. He want to get rid on 'em.'

' Don't you talk such nonsense, Ern,' said Nancy hotly. ' He's a friend of my husband's, and Ted understand what he's talking about. You think you know all about pigs, you do.'

' Maybe I do and maybe I don't,' replied Ern, thumping his stick on the doorstep for emphasis. ' That don't signify. But I can tell a crooked feller when I see him, and I tell you Bracebridge is crooked.'

' Well, it's no use telling us that now,' said Nancy. ' They're already as good as paid for : they'll be here to-morrow or the day after.'

' Well, don't blame me, young woman,' said Ern, ' if you don't get what you expect. You can't say I didn't tell you, anyhow. And look here, I've got another bit of advice for you.' Nancy stamped her foot impatiently. ' Yes, young woman, you may stamp your foot, but you can wait to hear this. I 'on't keep you long. If I were you, I wouldn't go buying sows just now.'

' Why not ? ' said Willett. ' We're going to make this a pig farm. Pigs pay. We've got a bit of enterprise, we have. We don't allus go on in the same silly old way like you chaps did. Pigs pay, I tell you : they sell like hot cakes.'

' Ay, so they do—to-year,' replied Ern. ' But do you wait. Everybody's going in for pigs now and next year there'll be a slump, do you see. You 'on't be able to give 'em away. My master told me so : he do a wonderful lot of dealing, he do, and what he don't know about the pig trade ain't worth knowing.'

' You go and tell that to your grandmother,' mocked Willett. ' I know when I've got good money.'

' Yes, no wonder he don't want us to go in for pigs,' sneered Nancy. ' His master's in the pig trade. P'r'aps he want those twenty sows we've ordered for himself.'

' P'r'aps he don't,' replied Ern with a sour grimace. ' But I've given you good warning, anyhow. Besides, if

I was you, I wouldn't put all my eggs in one basket. That ain't worth it, I tell you. You want sheep and cows and corn and fowls on a farm as well as pigs. When one of 'em's down, the others'll keep you going. You never know what's a-going to happen.'

'Maybe,' said Willett, 'but that's worth the risk, that is.'

'All right,' replied Ern, 'I've given you my advice. What you do's your own look-out.'

'Thank you for nothing,' said Nancy tartly. 'It's time you took yourself off.'

'How's Joey?' said Ern, ignoring the remark.

'You needn't think you're going to see him,' snapped Nancy, ''cause you aren't. That's what you came up for, I know. You'd teach him all manner of mischief if you had the chance; you'd put all sorts of wicked ideas into his head and set him against us. I've had about enough of you Geaiters. I'll have the police on your track if I see any more of you up here.'

'Next time I catch you in this yard,' added Willett from behind Nancy's shoulder, 'I'll fetch a gun to you.'

'You stick to rabbits, Ted Willett,' Ern growled. 'I ain't afraid of you and your pop-gun; and you wouldn't have the guts to use it on me, neither. But don't you fret, Nance. You 'on't see me up here agin in a hurry. I like to see a farm that look like a farm and not like a rubbish heap. Well, farewell, young woman, and I hope you get rich quick. You'll soon need it, fare to me.'

He strode firmly away through the farmyard gate and vanished among the shadows.

'The swine!' muttered Willett, as he closed the kitchen door. 'I'll larn 'em to come up here, I will.'

'Well, let's hope that's the last of them,' said Nancy. 'You can't tell how those men worry me. I don't know what I should do if it wasn't for you, Ted dear.'

She put her arms round his neck and kissed him.

'All right, Nance,' he said, patting her consolingly on the shoulder, 'don't you fret; we'll soon be rich. Let's go and have supper.'

XXXIII

THE tide of returning traffic from Saxmundham market was rapidly spreading over the surrounding country-side. People could not afford to linger in the town after the serious work of the market was done, with everywhere the hay cut and the weather looking uncertain; there was still time to get home for an early tea and make the most of the long June evening, cocking or carrying the hay.

Nancy sat on the drift gate with Susan on her arm, watching the carts go by along the Framlingham road. It was not often that she had time to go so far since the halving of the farm last Michaelmas, when they could no longer afford to keep Mrs. Snaith with them. After four years of comparative liberty it was a little hard to take up the whole burden of the housework again with Susan on her hands; for although now she no longer had so many in the house to look after, she now had no one to help her; Willett was always busy on the farm or at market and Joey slipped out of the house whenever he could: she never seemed to have time to rest. But she did not grumble, it was no use: everything that had happened to her seemed inevitable and she accepted the change in her manner of life with her accustomed resignation. But this fine afternoon had stirred a sudden mild feeling of rebellion in her, not against her husband or anyone else, but something vague and impersonal, the wilfulness of mere circumstance that had made such a shuttlecock of her life. Just to be out in the sun, to feel the yielding turf under her feet, to look at the sleepy rankness of the June hedgerows, simple, common things, yet they seemed most desirable to her. She had worked enough for to-day; the house was in order everywhere, the table laid for tea, the kettle on the hob, ready to boil: the pile of mending on the kitchen sofa could well afford to wait a day. Her husband had said he would be back from market for tea: nothing should stop her from going down to meet him.

A dealer's cart rattled by, full of iron bins and troughs, picked up among the dead stock in the market as a speculation : it was followed by a family party in a high dog-cart with a lumbering young cart-horse between the shafts and a lean-ribbed pony trotting behind on a halter. Five minutes later another dog-cart came into view with a tall man lolling over the reins : he pulled his horse in as he drew near the gate. Nancy looked up expectantly : it was not her husband after all. He stopped in front of her.

' Good afternoon, ma'am,' he said. ' Is this the way to Crakenhill Hall ? '

' Yes, that is,' replied Nancy. ' What is it ? My husband's not back from market yet.'

' I know,' answered the man. ' I saw him in Sax this afternoon and he asked me to call in and look at a couple of sick sows if I had time.'

' Ah, yes,' said Nancy, ' I remember he said he wanted the vet to come, before he went away this morning. Do you go straight on up the drift. You'll find the pig-man in the yard. I can't come up with you : I'm waiting for my husband.'

She climbed down from the gate and opened it to let him pass.

' Did you see my husband on the road ? ' she enquired, as she shut the gate after him.

' No,' he replied, ' he hadn't started when I left Sax. I expect he'd met some friends. You may have to wait a bit. You know what Ted is.' He winked at her and ambled off up the drift.

Nancy turned to the road again with an indignant frown. It always angered her to hear men talk like that of her husband : they did not seem to comprehend the change which had come over him since his marriage. However wild he might have been once, he was running straight now : he hardly ever left the farm except to go to market and he never came home drunk, he worked early and late with the pigs : and he had done it all for her, because he loved her : in the eyes of these callous, cynical men she made no difference at all. Poor Ted, she thought, how hard he worked for her, and yet they did not seem any the richer for it. There was something wrong with those sows of Bracebridge's; in every litter there were still-born pigs and the survivors were weakly and bad doers: the market too was growing poorer every day. This justification of Ern's warnings was infuriating; just another prank of circumstance to annoy them, to put them out of countenance: but she refused to repent of the step they had taken; she would show these brothers that she could do without them, she and Ted would weather the bad time. Her Ted, of course he would be home for tea: he had said so. The crisp tap of hoofs on the road roused her from her reflection. A high dog-cart with a pig-net over the back was bowling towards her at a smart pace, the driver savagely lashing it on as if it could not go fast enough for him: some pigs in the back of the cart were squealing vociferously. Nancy recognised her husband. He pulled up short at the gate and stared at her.

' What, you, Nance? ' he said. ' I didn't expect you.'

' I thought you'd like me to come down to meet you, dear,' she said, opening the gate for him.

Willett smiled at her as he drove through: she shut the gate and clambering up beside him with the baby, kissed his cheek affectionately. He smelt strongly of whisky, but Nancy said nothing: he seemed sober enough, and after a hard day in the market, who could grudge him a drink?

' What made you go so fast, dear? ' she said, pointing to the pony's streaming sides.

' Oh, I wanted to get back in time for tea,' he said, shaking the reins and giving the pony its head up the hill. It was the best excuse he could think of for his furious driving; he was in a bad temper and he had drunk a good deal.

Nancy smiled gratefully at him: then, turning round, she looked anxiously at the pigs behind the seat.

' What, have you brought 'em back again, Ted? ' she exclaimed. ' That's the third time.'

'I know,' he replied sulkily. 'That's the butchers and the pig-ring and all. I ain't a-going to let 'em go for less than they're worth.'

'I should think not,' replied Nancy indignantly.

'No, we'll keep 'em at home and fat 'em up,' he continued. 'I'll do them fellows down yet. I 'on't give them pigs away.'

'That's a shame,' said Nancy sympathetically, 'when you work so hard.'

'Still, my gal,' said Willett, squeezing her arm in a sudden access of affection, 'we'll pull through all right, don't you fret. If we can last out till next year, there'll be a boom in pigs: there allus is after a poor year. Then we shall reap the benefit. We ain't like little people with only a couple of sows.'

'That's right,' said Nancy, a little half-heartedly, as she thought of the feed bills that were mounting higher each day.

'There's a letter come for you this morning, Ted,' she said after a pause. 'Oh, and the vet came along here five minutes ago and I told him to go up into the yard. He said you'd asked him to come.'

'Good,' said Willett. 'I want to find out what's wrong with them two sows off their feed. It ain't much, but I like to know. I'm hungry, my gal.'

'Well, I've only got to make the tea, Ted,' she replied, smiling fondly up at him, 'and I've kept you some meat-patties from dinner.'

'You're a good gal, Nance,' said Willett, as he drove into the yard. 'Ah, there's the vet's trap. I must now go and see what he've got to say. I 'on't be long, Nance.'

He got down from his seat and leaving the pony and trap where they were, hurried away to the pig-styes.

Nancy went off indoors with the baby and began to make the tea. She felt distinctly better for her walk: the world was still as good as it always had been, and her man had been glad to see her: he was tired and hungry, he needed mothering. She looked up at the clock: the tea was beginning to spoil and he had said he would not be long. He was in the yard now, talking to the vet; they seemed to have a great deal to say. Ten minutes passed and they were still talking: those pigs! or had he forgotten her and her meat-patties and were they just gossiping? At last they had finished. The vet drove off and Willett took his pony out of the trap.

' I thought you were never going to stop,' said Nancy ruefully, as he came in. ' I shall have to make a fresh pot of tea.'

Willett collapsed into his chair without answering. His face was very pale. Nancy ran over to him with a cry of alarm.

' What's the matter, Ted dear?' she cried.

' Oh, that's all right,' he muttered, stiffening himself in a visible effort to regain control. ' I'll be all right in a minute.'

He moistened his lips and passed his hand over his forehead.

' Listen, Nance,' he said, sitting up in his chair. ' The vet say it's swine fever and they'll both have to be killed. But that ain't all. We shall have to kill all the rest before they catch it, to save what we can of 'em. The vet have now gone to tell the police on his way back.'

' Oh, Ted,' wailed Nancy, wringing her hands. ' What shall we do, what shall we do? And all that great bill to pay the miller! If only you'd kept those sheep, Ted! We'd have had something to fall back on then.'

' Well, don't blame me,' said Willett morosely. ' I've done my best. It's just our ill-luck, that's all.'

' I know you've done your best, Ted,' said Nancy tenderly, ' and I'm not blaming you, but oh, Ted, what shall we do?'

' Well, the pork may fetch something,' he replied, ' if we get rid of it afore the others start killing. That may pay some of the bills and then we shall have to make out as best we can with what's left. There's still the milk: we might get another few cows.'

' You do have bad luck, Ted,' said Nancy consolingly.
' That's a real shame when you work so hard. Let's have
tea now : and don't be down about it, Ted. I'll stand by
you.'

She pressed his cheek in the palm of her hand and kissed
his forehead. Willett thrust her roughly away from him :
her caresses were no use to him now. Nancy sighed and
went over to the fireplace to fill the teapot.

' Oh, I forgot,' she said. ' There's that thing came for
you this morning.'

She took a letter from the mantelpiece and handed it
to him. He tore it open listlessly without looking at it,
as if he were making some mental calculation. When at
last he looked down at the sheet he had taken out of the
envelope, his whole demeanour changed : his eyes brightened and he gripped the paper in both hands.

' Nance! ' he cried.

' Yes? ' she replied dully from the fireplace, still
nursing her rebuff. ' What is it ? '

' Here's a letter from that rubber company,' he said.
' They say everything's going fine, and here's the first
half-year's dividend with it, Nance—a cheque for twenty
pound. There's luck for you! They say that'll be double
next time.'

' Oh? ' said Nance without enthusiasm : she was not
to be jockeyed out of her grievance so easily.

' That's fine,' said Willett, thrusting the cheque in his
pocket and getting up from his chair. ' That come in
just handy.'

He went over to the fireplace and put his arm round her
waist.

' Didn't I tell you, Nance,' he coaxed. ' I was right
after all. You'll soon be a lady now. Don't you worry over
a few pigs.'

' Yes, Ted,' she murmured, pressing his hand and
smiling up at him, ' you were right. I am so glad.'

' Well, let's have tea now, gal,' he said, sitting down at
the table once more and rubbing his hands. ' I must get

to work and help Bill Sayers kill some of them pigs to-night —he said he'd stay.'

A quarter of an hour later, when they had almost finished, Joey crept into the kitchen and slid silently into his chair.

'Late for tea again, Joey,' scolded his mother. 'I'll have to whip you, I can see.'

Joey mumbled something into his tea-cup : he had no excuse worth offering : but he did everything now to avoid his step-father's company.

'Oh, leave the lad alone, Nance,' cried Willett heartily. 'Our ship's coming home, Joey. Here's a tanner for you.'

He jerked a coin down the table to the boy's plate. Joey picked it up and after eyeing it suspiciously, put it in his pocket. Willett, getting up from the table, walked out of the kitchen with a jaunty air, humming a tune : he stopped on his way to bend down and kiss Nancy on the cheek.

'What's the matter with daddy ? ' queried Joey, when his steps had died away across the yard. 'What do he want to give me money for ? '

'Oh, nothing,' replied Nancy, smiling. 'He've had some good news and he feel happy. You can give me the sixpence back if you don't want it.'

Joey suddenly dived into his pocket and throwing the sixpence down on the table in front of his mother, raced out of the room. Nancy stared at the coin in amazement.

'The little monkey!' she gasped at length. 'I'll give him what for.'

She began to clear the tea-things away.

At eight o'clock, as she was laying the cloth for supper, Willett came into the kitchen, spattered in blood to the elbows.

'Draw me half a gallon of beer, Nance,' he said, going to the sink and beginning to wash his hands. 'Bill and Tom both stayed to help me and we're all mortal thirsty.'

Nancy took a jug into the larder and put it under the

tap of the beer-barrel. A minute or two later Willett followed her in, drying his hands.

' Now you 'on't be late, will you, dear?' she said. ' Supper's almost ready.'

' No, I 'on't,' he replied. He reached up to the top shelf of the pantry and took down a full bottle of whisky that had caught his eye. ' I think we might have a little drop of short as well,' he added.

' Oh no, Ted, don't,' pleaded Nancy, seized with sudden alarm. ' You don't want that to-night. Come in and have supper.'

' Don't you worry, dear,' he answered. ' I shan't be long. We've been hard at work killing and dressing ever since tea-time and we're that thirsty : besides we don't have news like this every day of the week.'

He picked up the jug of beer and carried it off along with the whisky bottle and three tumblers which he took from the kitchen dresser. Nancy looked after him and sighed.

After she had finished laying the supper, she sat down on the sofa to wait. He could not be long, she thought ; he had come home to tea that day as he had promised : he would come in to supper in the same way ; there was nothing to be afraid of. Nevertheless, she felt disquieted : what could he want with all that drink ? he had seemed strangely hilarious already to-day. An hour passed : she went to the door and looked out into the yard. Dusk was falling, but there was no sign of him. For a moment she thought of going over to the barn and telling him to come, but only to dismiss the idea : that would be to humiliate him in front of the men. Joey came in for his supper and went to bed : she had not the heart to scold him for his behaviour at tea-time or even for being late.

Another hour passed and ten o'clock struck : something must be wrong. Throwing a shawl around her shoulders, she went out and picked her way across the yard to the barn. The door was ajar and a faint light shone through the opening. She listened : there was no sound of voices. Gently pushing the door open, she entered on tip-toe. For a moment she blinked, adjusting herself to the faint glimmer of the hurricane lantern, and then shuddered at the sight which met her eyes. The whole floor of the near end of the barn was smeared with blood, it lay about in pools and trickles everywhere, the air stank of it. In front of the door on a piece of sacking were stretched three carcasses, ready singed and dressed for the butcher, gaunt and horrible, a heap of gory offal over against them. Right in the corner, against the wall, their feet in a pool of blood, lay the inert figures of two men, sprawled out full length on the floor and breathing heavily: beside them stood the whisky bottle and the beer jug, both empty. Nancy stepped over to them and bent down. They were Bill Sayers and her husband. The other man had apparently found his way home.

' Ted! ' she called. He did not answer. She shook him by the shoulder, but he did not move : she lifted his head and pinched his cheek, but he only grunted and breathed more heavily than ever. She looked at him in consternation : he could not be left there all night in that morass of blood. Without further hesitation she stooped down and, picking him up by the shoulders, began to drag him out of the barn. Although he was thin, he was a dead weight and it was all she could do to get him to the door without dropping his head. Outside she paused to rest : at least he was clear of all that blood now. Having regained her breath, she set to work to haul him foot by foot across the farmyard to the house. It seemed an endless way. Every other second the heels of his boots lodged on a stone or in a rut and pulled her up : a stray piece of barbed wire caught his breeches and ripped them up. She was almost exhausted when she reached the kitchen doorstep, her heart beating wildly and her breath coming in great painful gasps : but after another short rest, she had enough strength left to drag him through the door and hoist him on to the sofa. Then, after throwing her shawl over his still limp body and propping his head on a cushion, she knelt down by his side and burst into tears.

XXXIV

THE harvest waggon, swaying and creaking over the stubble behind Bruisyard mill, came to a stop by the last oat shock. It was heaved over with a thrust of the fork and its sheaves borne up aloft with rapid swings by two pairs of sinewy brown arms. The last sheaf was up, the shock was no longer there, the field was empty. The loader, having extricated himself from the sheaves which imprisoned him waist-high, and filled up the hole in which he had been standing, caught the rope slung up to him from below and held it while the two pitchers made it fast to the side of the waggon : one of them dug his fork into the side of the load and the man above, putting his hand on the haft, slid to the ground with a thump. All three repaired to the back of the waggon where their coats were hanging and took a long swig at their bottles. The horses, their patient heads wreathed in elm boughs, stamped their feet and whisked their tails to keep off the flies : then at a shout from one of the men who had put their bottles back and shouldered their forks, they plunged forward and the waggon went jolting after them across stetch and water-furrow.

Mrs. Pearman gazed wistfully at it through the little leaded window at the foot of her bed as it disappeared from sight. It had been passing and repassing in front of her eyes all that morning and half the previous day until she was quite familiar with the step of the horses and the characteristic motions of the pitchers' forks : but now it was gone and would come back no more. All that remained for her eyes to rest upon was a dreary patch of unpopulated stubble. Harvest—sooner or later all those sheaves would bring grist to her husband's mill as crop after crop on that field had done for more years than she cared to remember. Jim Pearman was seventy-two now, two years younger than herself, but although his nephew did all the hard work, he still kept an eye on the mill. A little deaf and short-sighted perhaps, and fond of his chair by the fire, but he had his health and strength, he could potter about, watching the sacks fill, the mill-stones whirl round : he could still have a word with a passing neighbour and drive a hard bargain with a farmer for his corn. The ordinary business of life—now that Mrs. Pearman had been obliged to take to her bed, she understood how much, without her knowing, it had meant to her. Just doing the everyday work of the house, sweeping, washing, cooking, mending and talking trivialities with the woman across the street—they were the things which made life worth living : deprived of them, she found it tasteless, even burdensome. Yet, she reflected, to be alive and conscious was something, just to possess her faculties, even if there was no chance of using them. George Grebe and the churchyard could well afford to wait. She shuddered involuntarily and then sighed. It was so wearisome lying there all alone with no one to talk to, nothing to see : other people were concerned with their own doings and forgot : she no longer counted for anything in their world. It must soon be time for Edith, her nephew's wife, to bring up her mid-morning glass of milk—soon ; why was the gal so long in coming ? Her eyes closed, her cheek drooped slowly on to the pillow and she fell into a doze.

The door opened and someone came softly into the room. Mrs. Pearman opened her eyes and blinked at the ceiling.

' Is that my milk ? ' she murmured drowsily.

' Yes,' came the reply. ' I thought you were asleep.'

Mrs. Pearman turned her head sharply on the pillow : it was not the voice she had expected.

' Why, Mrs. Spatchard ! ' she exclaimed. ' Who'd have thought of seeing you at this time in the morning ? '

' Oh, I thought I'd look in,' replied Mrs. Spatchard, putting the glass of milk down on a table and pulling a chair up to the bedside. ' My husband's gone to a sale to-day to pick up a few things and I haven't got much to do : I don't want to cook for myself alone.'

' No, that's right,' agreed Mrs. Pearman. ' You don't feel to want it, do you ? '

' Well, how are you ? ' asked Mrs. Spatchard.

' Oh well, you know,' replied Mrs. Pearman, ' I feel a bit poorly like, but better'n yesterday. The doctor, he say I've got to stay in bed and keep quiet. He say I mustn't get excited! do, that'll goo to my heart : as if I was one to get excited! Have you ever seen me excited, Mrs. Spatchard ? '

She looked indignantly at her, plucking nervously at the fringe of her black woollen shawl.

' No, that I haven't,' said Mrs. Spatchard warmly. ' These doctor folk fare to think they can say what they like to us 'cause we don't know any better : they don't know how we live. Get excited, indeed! I don't believe in these doctors, Mrs. Pearman.'

' No, nor me neither,' replied Mrs. Pearman vigorously. ' Still, Mrs. Spatchard, I have been wholly poorly all the same, you know. I've allus suffered from my heart, ever since I was a gal ; my mother did, too, and her mother before her : and they both lived good, quiet lives, like I have, Mrs. Spatchard. Well, well, I don't know. It's allus like that. The rackety ones never seem to have nothing wrong with 'em : but they pay in the end, Mrs. Spatchard.'

' Yes, that's the truth, Mrs. Pearman, that is,' said Mrs. Spatchard, nodding gravely.

' Is there anything new in Bruisyard ? ' asked Mrs. Pearman, taking a sip at her milk.

' Well,' replied Mrs. Spatchard, ' nothing as you might call new in Bruisyard, but—well, there is something else. That's what I really came to tell you.'

' Ah, I thought there was something,' said Mrs. Pearman knowingly. ' You wouldn't have come so early else.'

She turned over on her side and settled down where she could watch Mrs. Spatchard's face. Mrs. Spatchard drew her chair a little closer to the bed and folded her hands on her lap.

' Do you remember, Mrs. Pearman,' she began, ' there was a man come to Frannigan two years ago to try to get people to buy shares in a rubber company or something like that ? '

' Yes, yes, I remember,' said Mrs. Pearman.

' Well, you know he said that was a grand thing,' continued Mrs. Spatchard, ' and them shares'd bring in pounds and pounds after a little while and they'd all be as rich as rich. A lot of people, poor folk and all, managed to put a few pounds together and buy a few shares. They thought they'd get rich quick.'

' Yes, yes, I remember,' interjected Mrs. Pearman impatiently. ' What about it ? '

' Why,' said Mrs. Spatchard, holding up her hands before her, ' it fare that was all a fraud. They sent all the people a pound or two after the first six months just to keep 'em quiet for a bit : but there wasn't no land in Africa, there wasn't no rubber nor no new way of making it. They forged the names of a lot of nobs and swells to put down on the paper like and make it look smart and take people in. And now the manager or head one or whatever they call him, have run off with all the money.'

' Well, there! ' ejaculated Mrs. Pearman, staring at her with her mouth open.

' Think of all them poor people,' said Mrs. Spatchard tragically, ' with all their savings gone and nothing left for their old age. A shame, I call it. It oughtn't to be allowed. If I caught that man, I know what I'd do to him.'

' Still, you know,' objected Mrs. Pearman, screwing up her mouth censoriously, ' people didn't ought to be such fools. It ain't no use thinking you can get rich quick without working for it. That's tempting the Lord, I say, and if they've lost their money, it's a judgment on 'em.'

' Yes, maybe you're right,' said Mrs. Spatchard, thoughtfully nodding her head.

' I know I am,' replied Mrs. Pearman emphatically. ' But was there anybody from Bruisyard that put money into it as you know of, Mrs. Spatchard ? '

' That's just what I was a-going to tell you about,' said Mrs. Spatchard, bending forward confidentially over the bed. ' Do you drink up your milk and I'll tell you.'

Mrs. Pearman hastily drained her glass and lay back on the pillow with her eyes fixed eagerly on Mrs. Spatchard.

' Now then, Mrs. Spatchard,' she said, ' don't keep me on tenterhooks.'

' Well now,' began Mrs. Spatchard, holding up a finger, ' you call to mind last Michaelmas that Ted Willett and his wife sold half of Crakenhill to Mr. Snowland on the other side of the hill ? '

' Yes,' added Mrs. Pearman, ' and bought all them pigs that they lost with the swine fever. I remember.'

' Well,' resumed Mrs. Spatchard, ' it appear that the rest of the money they got for the farm, they put into this here rubber mine or whatever it is—a wonderful lot of money that must have been.'

Mrs. Pearman gasped, opening her eyes wider than ever.

' And that ain't all,' continued Mrs. Spatchard. ' You know how that Willett have carried on since they lost them pigs ? '

' I should think I do,' said Mrs. Pearman. ' Drinking and gambling and fighting—something dreadful.'

' Well,' said Mrs. Spatchard, ' they're up to their eyes in debt, with all the money they put into them pigs and the pig-food.'

' Ah, I know,' interrupted Mrs. Pearman. ' I'm wholly glad my husband wouldn't have no dealings with 'em, nor that Geaiter family neither.'

' And Ted Willett,' pursued Mrs. Spatchard, ' he fare to have borrowed money to drink with and Miss Nancy have been running up bills with the grocer and the butcher and I don't know what : all 'cause they thought they were going to get rich quick and live like the gentry.'

' I know the sort,' said Mrs. Pearman. ' Money burn holes in their pockets.'

' And it ain't ondly that,' continued Mrs. Spatchard, determined now to finish her story. ' All them they owe money to have closed on 'em and they've got to sell up.'

' And much use that'll be to them,' said Mrs. Pearman sardonically. ' That land's in such a pickle now, it'll be a wonder if they find anyone to buy it of 'em. And what sort of valeration will they get? If they've got a cart-load of muck and a half a dozen rows of dwingy turnips, that's all.'

' Just so,' said Mrs. Spatchard. ' My husband say that Mr. Eves, the postmaster, told him last night that when they've sold the farm and paid all their debts, he reckon they 'on't have more than a few pounds left to 'emselves. That's what he say. They've got through all she had the same way as her father, Josiah, did before her : and her with that little baby girl and all. There now, Mrs. Pearman, you know as much as I do.'

' I'm wholly thankful, I'm sure,' replied Mrs. Pearman. ' It was real good of you to come in like that to tell me. But didn't I tell you, Mrs. Spatchard ? Those two desarve each other, I say. I've got no pity for 'em.'

' You did, Mrs. Pearman,' said Mrs. Spatchard. ' That's the truth. Let me give you another pillow.'

Mrs. Pearman was sitting up in bed now with her black shawl around her shoulders : her eyes were strangely bright and there were two little red spots on her pale, sunken cheeks.

' Ah, thank you,' she said, as Mrs. Spatchard tucked another pillow in behind her back. ' Yes, it was bound to come to that, Mrs. Spatchard. That's a judgment on them, too. Look how all of 'em in that house have got the punishment their sins cried out for. First that wicked old Benjamin Geaiter, wife-beater, murderer and I don't know what else, he go blind and paralytic and then he die. Then his sons are done out of their farm and then driv off it to earn their living as hired men. And now Mistress Nancy who done 'em out of it, she let this scamp of a Willett ruin her and she go too. One after another, Mrs. Spatchard,' she chanted solemnly, holding up her hand. ' Don't you see the hand of God in all this ? '

' Yes, indeed I do,' replied Mrs. Spatchard, quite rapt with awe at Mrs. Pearman's utterance.

' Didn't I say now,' cried Mrs. Pearman in a trembling voice, ' didn't I say the day'd come when they'd pay the penalty, every one of 'em? The wrath of God, Mrs. Spatchard, it may be slow in coming, but it do come in the end and it have fallen upon that there family, sure enough. You can depend upon it, Mrs. Spatchard, that was why they were brought to that there farm. No good ever came out of Crakenhill yet. That farm was created for the punishment of sinners before the Lord.'

Mrs. Spatchard raised her eyebrows and nodded assent, not daring to interrupt.

' And,' continued Mrs. Pearman, shaking her fist at the window, ' let that be a warning to all other men who commit murders, who beat their wives and lead young women astray : let it be a warning to all young women who go astray and flaunt their sin before the world and exalt themselves in pride above their neighbours. The Lord give and the Lord take away, and He punish in His own good time.'

' Mrs. Pearman,' whispered Mrs. Spatchard admiringly, ' your words do me real good and that's the truth.'

But Mrs. Pearman had not finished. She clasped her wrinkled hands together and gazed at the ceiling : her eyes burnt more brightly than ever.

' Yes, Mrs. Spatchard,' she cried in a voice shaking with emotion, ' I was once afraid of death, but now, if ever I doubted it, Mrs. Spatchard, now I know there's a just God in heaven. If He punish the wicked on earth for their sins, Mrs. Spatchard, then you can be sure that He'll give the righteous their reward in heaven. Now I know that I haven't lived the life I have lived in vain. There's a crown a-waiting for me beyond the heavenly gates : I can die happy.'

Her voice sank to a hollow whisper. Mrs. Spatchard gently laid a hand upon her arm.

' Don't tire yourself, Mrs. Pearman,' she said. ' You aren't strong, you know.'

Mrs. Pearman made no answer. Mrs. Spatchard peered closely at her : she was still gazing fixedly at the ceiling and a smile of ineffable beatitude played over her face, quite transfiguring the aged features. Mrs. Spatchard was not used to transports of this kind : she shook her arm.

' Lie down, dear, now,' she whispered.

The body suddenly collapsed under her hand and toppled back upon the bed : the mouth sagged open and the eyes rolled. Mrs. Spatchard ran out of the room screaming.

XXXV

It was a quieter day than usual in the quiet little town of
Framlingham. The people who generally came in from
the neighbouring villages to do their shopping had preferred to wait until the weather changed and the roads
had recovered from the effects of the recent January
storms : all the tradespeople were within doors, eating
their dinners or warming themselves in front of their fires,
well out of the chill, raw drizzle that was falling in the
narrow, winding streets. The little cobbled yard in front
of The Feathers was quite empty of vehicles and no one
protested when Ben with much stamping of horses' feet
and rumbling of wheels backed a large farm waggon,
heavily loaded with mangold, into it. He threw a couple
of sacks over each horse's back and having strapped on
their nose-bags, he strode into the tap-room, shaking the
water out of his clothes. Trade was poor that morning and
the landlord frowned when Ben said he was waiting for his
brother and sat down on a bench by the window without
ordering anything.

That morning it happened that he was carting roots
from his master's farm at Dennington to another farm
just wide of Framlingham, while Hiram had gone to Earl
Soham with a bullock-cart to fetch a couple of heifers.
Hiram's journey was much the longer and he was bound
to have his mid-day meal on the road. Ben, on the other
hand, had already carted two loads of roots to their
destination and returned to Dennington for more : he
could easily have gone across to the cottage in the village
where he lodged for a hot dinner in a comfortable room.
Every other day of the week he had had his dinner with
Hiram, he had been at plough with him in the same field
the day before, they would be together for tea that night ;
a meal apart was of little importance : yet, rather than
miss an hour of Hiram's company, he preferred to take a
packet of bread and cheese with him and eat it at a bare

table in a cheerless tap-room. More than their own misfortunes, it was the final ruin of Crakenhill which had drawn them thus close together. For all of them it had been agony enough to stand by, helplessly watching all their dismal prognostications fulfilled, one by one : but now that their last link with the farm was gone, the very pith seemed to have dropped out of existence, leaving it hollow and purposeless. It was as if the whole of their previous lives had never been and all the labour they had bestowed upon those fields were some vast illusion, as if the name of Geaiter had never meant anything to Crakenhill. They no longer had any centre even in thought, on which to group their daily acts, their own persons, the continued process of living : the world appeared to them with very much the same blankness and lack of meaning as it might do to a man who had lost his memory : they were adrift, bewildered, isolated : all that they had left to them now was each other, and seeing there the one fixed point in their chaos, they cleaved together more desperately than ever. There was nothing more for them to do now than they had done before ever since they had left the farm. They still met each Sunday at The Cart and Horses in Bruisyard for their dinner and their afternoon walk, they still exchanged visits between their respective cottages : only now both visits and meetings were longer and treasured more. It was not unnatural that Ben and Hiram, more fortunate than the rest in working on the same farm and living in the same house, should have formed so strong an attachment, far stronger than the easy companionship which had formerly united Bob and Hiram. There was nothing demonstrative in this attachment : so long as they could just be together, working, smoking or eating, they were content and so far as circumstances permitted, they were hardly ever apart.

Ben looked at his watch and then out of the window at the steaming backs of his horses, resignedly chewing their oats in the pitiless drizzle. Hiram had said he would be there by half past one and it was already a quarter to two.

Ben wondered what could have kept him. He was about to pick up a newspaper from the chair beside him when the grate of wheels on the cobbles outside made him look up again. The bullock-cart was drawing into the yard.

'Two pints!' he called to the landlord, and began unwrapping his packet of bread and cheese.

Hiram, having seen to his horses, walked into the tap-room and shut the door with a bang. He stumbled over to the table and dropped into a chair, staring wildly at Ben and nervously fingering his moustache—somewhat darker and bushier now—as he always did when he was agitated.

'Why, what's the matter, man?' said Ben.

'Matter?' gasped Hiram. He moistened his lips. 'Do you listen, Ben. As I was a-driving into Frannigan twenty minutes ago, who should come running out on the road but our young Joey—you know Nancy's cotterage is there. But, Ben, you never seed such a thing in your life. His coat all out at elbows and the seat half out of his trousers and his boots all wore up: and that dirty and puggy, you'd never believe.'

'What did he say?' asked Ben.

'Say?' repeated Hiram. 'What did he do? Why, as soon as he seed me coming, he pulled his little owd coat around him and ran and hid in the cotterage with his face all red—for shame, Ben, for shame. That sent me all of a dither and I took the wrong turning and had to come all round the back of the town to get here.'

Hiram dropped his head on his hands and cried like a child.

'Oh dear, dear!' said Ben, shaking his head in consternation. 'What ever have Nance been a-doing of to let him get in that state? She was allus such a clean gal, she was. And to think Joey have lost his self-respect—all dirty and puggy! Oh, Hiram!'

'Yes, that's real terrible,' muttered Hiram in a husky voice. 'That wholly make your heart bleed.'

His face was quite puckered with grief. Ben scratched his cheek and looked thoughtfully out of the window.

'Hiram,' he said, fixing his eyes on his brother again, ' we must do something.'

' What ? ' replied Hiram dully.

' Why, it fare to me,' said Ben, ' that young Joey's as much our brother as he's Nance's son. Look here, Hiram, there's room enough where we sleep for another bed, ain't there ? '

' Sure, there is,' replied Hiram. ' What about it ? '

' Why,' said Ben, ' if we could get Joey to come and live along of us—that wouldn't cost much and Mrs. Spinner's fond of children, ain't she ? '

' Ay,' said Hiram enthusiastically, ' that'd be grand to have him back again—if Nance'd let us take him, but d'you think she would, Ben ? '

' I don't know,' replied Ben pensively. ' I don't know what she think of us now nor of Joey neither.'

' She might put us to the door,' said Hiram pensively.

' Or she might be glad to let him go,' added Ben. ' You can't tell. Lookye here, Hiram, let's go and see her now and find out.'

' Ay, that we will,' replied Hiram, pounding his fist on the table, ' we can but ax her.'

' Well, do you hurry up with your bread and cheese, Hiram,' said Ben, ' and we'll go at once.'

Ten minutes later they emerged from the tap-room door and trudged away down the street, leaving their horses and carts in the inn yard.

Nancy's cottage stood by itself in the corner of a field of cabbages, just beyond the other end of the town. Its front was so narrow that it looked more like the surviving slice of a house that had been partly destroyed by lightning than a complete building in itself. The shell of white plaster with which the walls had been covered, was everywhere scaling off and exposing the bricks beneath, which gave the whole house a pock-marked appearance: the thatch was half tumbling off the eaves and patched all over with dirty green moss. The little plot of ground that surrounded it was an unkempt waste, overgrown with weeds and littered with rubbish : no spade could have touched it for a twelvemonth. At one side of the house stood an open shelter built of rough poles and bundles of dry gorse, which served to house Willett's pony and trap when he was not on the road : beside it stood a tall, narrow shed of tarred boards, with a peaked roof surmounted by a few clumsily cemented ridge-tiles : it was here that Willett cured the herrings and haddocks which he fetched from the coast at Dunwich and Sizewell and hawked about the vicinity of Framlingham for a living. There was nothing to relieve the atmosphere of ugliness and desolation which hung over the whole place.

'There's a hole for you!' said Hiram, as they entered through the rickety gate. 'That ain't fit for pigs, that ain't.'

Ben rapped his knuckles on the door and after a pause they heard the sound of feet shuffling across the floor. The door opened and Nancy stood before them, a mere shadow of the Nancy they had known in their good days. There was no pink in her gaunt cheeks now : her hazel eyes were lustreless and ringed ; her hair straggled in untidy coils from under the blue woollen cap she was wearing ; her dress was old and worn—and dirty, it was impossible to conceal it. She started back at the sight of the two familiar stolid countenances before her, Hiram's much the same as it had always been, Ben's a little thinned and furrowed, so that beneath the mask of stolidity the capacity for suffering was manifest. She stared at them in wonder across the doorstep.

'You ?' she gasped at length.

'Yes, us,' replied Ben. 'We wanted to see you.'

'Come in then, out of the rain,' she said, stepping back from the door.

They entered the room and instinctively looked round them to take stock of it. There was not much to see : a table and three chairs, a dresser and a few scattered pieces of odd crockery, most of it dirty. There were scraps of food lying about on the dresser on plates, on the table a half-eaten slice of bread and butter, an empty tea-cup and a two-penny novelette in a pink paper cover lying open beside it. A baby of two years or so was squatting on the floor underneath the table, playing with a pair of dirty, down-at-heel women's boots which must have belonged to Nancy. A pane was missing from one of the windows and the rain was driving in : a piece of damp wood smoked and sizzled in the grate without giving out any heat. The floor and the walls were undeniably dirty, as if they had not seen a broom for a week.

'Yes, I know it's dirty,' said Nancy, observing their critical gaze, 'I know, but I haven't the heart to clean it. Well, what have you come for ? '

Ben hesitated. At least she had not shown them the door : but words were difficult to find.

'We came about Joey,' he said rather nervously.

'Joey ? ' repeated Nancy.

'Yes,' he replied. 'You see, Nance, we don't know how you're placed now ; but with a baby and all, we thought you might have more than you can manage with Joey on your hands.'

'That's the truth,' said Nancy. 'I can't manage him, he's that mischievous, and I can't keep him in clothes. But what did you want to know for ? '

'Why,' said Ben cautiously, 'we thought p'r'aps you might let him come to live along of us at Dennington. That ain't far and there's plenty of room in our cotterage and Mrs. Spinner's a good body : she'd look after him all right. That'd make things main easier for you and me and Hiram'd be glad to keep him.'

'Yes, that'd be a load off my shoulders,' replied Nancy nonchalantly, ' that would. He hate his father and as it was you made him do it, you'd better take him all to yourselves.'

'Do you mean that, Nance ? ' exclaimed Ben, looking hard at her.

'Yes, I suppose so,' she answered, shrugging her shoulders. 'When do you want him ? '

' Can we take him along now ? ' Ben ventured.

' When you like,' she said, aimlessly scratching the back of her hand with a splinter of firewood, ' when you like : the sooner the better. He's up there in the bedroom, playing by himself.'

She crossed the room and called up the stairs. Joey came clumping down and stood in a corner of the room, hanging his head ; he could not face Ben's eyes.

' Hey, boy,' said Ben, ' you're coming along of us.'

' Where ? ' Joey's eye brightened and he looked up, forgetting his confusion.

' Why to Dennington, this very arternoon,' said Ben, walking over to him and hugging the boy's head against his coat.

Joey looked up in Ben's face and smiled : then he began to cry quietly.

' He'd better go and get himself ready,' said Hiram. ' We must now be going.'

' He haven't got nothing to get ready,' replied Nancy, ' but what he stand up in. That's all.'

She made the statement without excuse, as if it meant nothing to her. It distressed Ben profoundly.

' Nance,' he faltered, ' do you still hate us like you used ? '

' No, Ben,' she replied, a little less nonchalantly, stirred out of herself by the question. ' You were right about the farm and those pigs : that was real kind of you. But you shouldn't have hit my Ted. Still I suppose you couldn't help it after all. People can't help anything. It don't matter; nothing matter.' She shrugged her shoulders.

' But that do matter,' Ben protested.

Nancy shook her head with an air of finality : it was no use arguing with her. Nothing could shake her indifference : she seemed to have closed up everything that was herself, her intelligence, her emotions, her senses.

' Don't you find this a bit hard, Nance ? ' said Hiram, indicating the bare room with a sweep of his hand. ' It ain't wholly comfortable.'

Nancy laughed mirthlessly and shrugged her shoulders again : it seemed her favourite gesture.

' That's not like Crakenhill,' she replied, looking critically round the room as if she had noticed its squalor for the first time, ' but we can't help it and so we must just put up with it. Ted's out all day and not back till late and he don't bring back much money from the fish with him.'

' From the pub, she mean,' murmured Hiram to Ben under his breath.

' He work right hard,' Nancy went on, ' but it ain't much of a trade. If only he brought home a bit more, that'd be different ; but we're poor and that's no use worrying. That's our luck, that is.'

' Do he drink now, Nance ? ' asked Ben warily.

' Oh, sometimes he come home a bit merry,' replied Nancy with a sigh, ' but I don't blame him : it's such a hard life out in the weather all day long. That's hard for both of us : but that don't matter.'

' Look here, Nance, that do matter,' Ben objected. ' Why don't you leave him ? If you'd come along and keep house for us, me and Hiram'd take a cotterage to ourselves. Ted ain't no use to you, he never have been : he've ruined you and ruined us, he's a real bad 'un, he is. You'd be better off without him. Do you come along of us and have a bit of comfort and let Ted go to hell his own way by himself. You'd be wholly welcome.'

Nancy listened dully as if at first his words had not penetrated her consciousness. Then suddenly all her apathy and listlessness dropped from her ; her whole body stiffened and her eyes flared up in the old way.

' What's this you're saying about my Ted ? ' she cried. ' Don't you let me hear another word, Ben. As if I'd think of leaving him ! Look how he've stood by me through good and bad. D'you think I'd desert him now ? I love him, I tell you ; you don't understand that I know, but I love him. He may take a drop too much now and again, poor Ted, but you don't know how hard he've tried to run straight ever since we married. Why, do you know, he's now saving up what little money he can spare so as we can go to Canada some day and try our luck. We might get rich there, you never know.'

' He'll have to wait a good while afore he gets to Canada,' grunted Ben, ' at the rate he's going now.'

' Be quiet, Ben,' cried Nancy, flushing angrily. ' I 'on't let you say such things of my Ted. It's no use us talking about him. You've got your knife into him and you 'on't hear no good of him. So if we're to stop friends, be quiet.'

' All right, Nance,' said Ben sorrowfully, ' I will. All I can say is, I hope your luck'll turn and you'll get to Canada and make your fortune. But if you go, will you leave Joey behind with us ? We'd be wholly glad to have him. He's our brother, you know, and we'd send him to school and teach him to be a farmer '

' If you take him,' said Nancy, lapsing into her former nonchalance, ' you'd better keep him. That's all the same to me.'

Ben stared wonderingly at her expressionless face for a moment and then, taking a sack from under his arm, he threw it round Joey's shoulders : he had brought it on purpose to protect the boy from the rain.

' Come on, lad,' he said. ' Hullo, what's this ? '

He went over to the table and picked up the pink-covered novelette.

' Oh, that's just a story I'm reading,' replied Nancy. ' I read a lot nowadays. There's nothing else to do during the day.'

' I see,' said Ben, putting it down on the table again and furtively slipping a half-sovereign beneath it. ' Well, come on, Hiram ; we must get back to work now. Good-bye, Nance, and good luck ! '

' Good-bye,' said Nancy half-heartedly, as she closed the door on them.

She had not even thought of giving Joey a kiss and he had not troubled to ask for one.

' My ! ' said Hiram, as they tramped away through the

rain with Joey silent between them. 'There's cool for you. She didn't even say good-bye to the lad : she don't fare to mind if she never see him again.'

'It's Ted've done it,' replied Ben. 'That's something wonderful, that is. And they say that when poverty come in at the door, love fly out of the window I don't know '

'If you ask me,' rejoined Hiram, 'she've gone a bit wrong in the head like Bob said. She've had more ups and downs than she can well stand.'

Ben grunted and they walked on silently through the rain : they were all three too excited to speak.

When they reached The Feathers again, they found a horse and trap standing out in the yard behind the bullock-cart.

'H'm, that's our master's trap,' said Hiram, taking the nose-bag off his own horse.

'So that is,' replied Ben. 'I wonder what he want up here on a day like this.'

The door opened and a burly figure in overcoat and leggings came striding out.

'What the hell do all this mean ? ' he cried, standing on the step and looking Ben up and down. 'My two horse-men go and leave their horses all alone for nearly an hour in the middle of Frannigan with a load of beet and two heifers belonging to me. So that's what I pay you wages for.'

Ben took out his watch and looked at it.

'Now listen here, master,' he said 'For one thing, we told the hostler to keep an eye on them carts—so that isn't as if they were all alone : and what's more, this is our dinner-hour although it's late, and only a quarter of an hour of your time have we wasted. How many times have I stayed on an extra half-hour at plough to finish a field for you and haven't asked no more for it ?

'That's your own look-out,' shouted the farmer. 'I pay you to work for me proper hours and if I want beet carted from one till five of an afternoon, it's a-going to be carted then.'

'Well, master, I'm sorry,' said Ben, 'but we had business to do to-day that couldn't wait. We don't have business every day'

'I don't care a damn about your business,' their master shouted. 'I want my work done.'

'Well, it ain't no use shouting at us,' replied Ben imperturbably. 'We don't care over-much who we work for ; we can allus find a job when we want one.'

The threat took effect and their master's choler subsided with quite astonishing suddenness.

'Oh, well,' he grumbled, 'I suppose it's all right. But you might tell me when you're going to have business.'

'We don't allus know, master,' replied Ben. 'You see we've just found our young brother to-day and we're taking him along home with us. I don't think we shall hev any more business in Frannigan now.'

'Ah,' said the farmer quite jovially, 'so that's your young brother, is it ? Well, if he's anything like you chaps —I shall be wanting a boy on my farm soon.'

'Thank you, I'm sure,' said Ben. 'He's a good 'un, I can tell you.'

'That's capital,' said his master. 'Come you in and have a drink. There isn't any hurry for those heifers.'

XXXVI

Harry slammed the door of his cottage behind him and sauntered out on to the Bruisyard road, shading his eyes with his hand and gazing after a brightly painted dog-cart that was rounding the bend a hundred yards further up the road. He walked slowly on with his hands in his pockets, his eyes wandering listlessly from one hedgerow to another. All his beasts up at the farm where he worked were fed and the neathouse cleaned out ; he himself had changed into his Sunday clothes and nothing now remained to do until milking time in the afternoon, a welcome respite after the first week of harvest. It wanted yet an hour to mid-day, but already the whole earth seemed asleep. Above the Alde in its narrow strip of dark green water-meadows tall willows and poplars dreamed unstirred with kissing branches, as if enchanted by the crowding haze which enmeshed them, while from the banks the loosestrife dipped its purple blooms in the lazy waters with hardly a ripple : the birds were not silent, but their voices sounded hushed and remote through the sultry air. The whole day invited mind and body to a similar reposefulness : but Harry could not yield himself to its influence. It was no particular anxiety which troubled him : only a vague malaise, a sudden unquiet urge to thought which had descended on him at the sight of that gay dog-cart with Jessie, her husband and her two boys in it. Not that it hurt him to see her : he had seen her many times in the fourteen years that had passed since he parted from her and other sorrows had come to obliterate the wound in his heart. But to-day her face brought back so many things to him. She had done well for herself. Her husband was a small farmer near Peasenhall where she had gone into service for a short while ten years ago. They had had a hard struggle at first to make ends meet, but now at last the farm was beginning to do well, she had her own house and a growing family : and six months ago a distant relative had quite unexpectedly left her a legacy of a thousand pounds. Gossip went that she and her husband quarrelled a good deal, but they had bought a new trap: that was what had first caught Harry's eye this morning from his cottage window. Jessie and he might have shared that money if he had acted differently: how happy they could have been, even without it. He could have had Nancy too for the asking: it was just three months now since she had gone off to Canada with Willett and her baby, more witless and apathetic than ever, without even coming to say good-bye to Joey: he might have been happy with her, too, she loved him. Both these women he had given up for the sake of Crakenhill—it seemed so ironical that in spite of all these sacrifices he should lose Crakenhill after all, and to one of the women he had given up for it. Yet, when his mind went back to his sheep—that flock, all gone now, without a trace left of it—he could not conceive himself doing otherwise; knowing all he did now, he could but do the same again to-morrow: and if he had not left Crakenhill, who knows, he might never have discovered what men his four brothers were. It was something to have them still and Joey too: life had begun again when Ben and Hiram brought him back from Frannigan and the following Sunday took him along to The Cart and Horses to see the rest.

'Me and Hiram can manage all right,' Ben had explained, ' but if so be as you chaps'd like to help——'

'By God! yes,' Ern had shouted.

It seemed only yesterday to Harry and yet eighteen months had passed and Joey was shooting up fast: he had already left school and was learning his trade at Ben's side on the farm at Dennington. This very day he was coming over to Rendham along with Ern to have tea in Harry's cottage after the usual afternoon walk. It was indeed something to have Joey and watch him grow. But at this moment such compensations did not make the inevitableness of all that had happened any less bitter to contemplate.

When he reached the cross-roads by The Cart and Horses at Bruisyard Street, there was still more than half an hour to go before mid-day. Any other morning he would have walked down the Cransford road to meet Ern : but to-day he was in a solitary mood and a sudden, overpowering desire took possession of him to go and look at Crakenhill, not in any spirit of tender, sentimental regret, but to glut himself with savage melancholy at the depressing sight : he and his brothers rarely passed that way, knowing well what it would be like. Harry took the back road on the other side of the river so as to avoid Ben and Hiram who would be already on the road from Dennington that led past Bruisyard church. The chimneypots of the old house came gradually into sight and the crow-stepped gable with them : even at that distance he could see the gap where three tiles were missing near the top of it : so the house was going the same way as the fields. A bill affixed to the gatepost at the bottom of the drift attracted his attention : some fair or village fête, he thought ; it was too early for harvest festival. But as he drew nearer, all doubt concerning the nature of the bill vanished. It was a sale notice drawn up in the familiar red, white and black characters of the Saxmundham auctioneer. Arrived at the gate, Harry paused to read the headlines.

' Bruisyard,' it ran, ' Crakenhill Hall, The Capital Live and Dead Stock, comprising——' He dropped his eyes to the bottom of the bill. ' For Mr. Tom Gale, who is leaving the district.'

Harry pushed back his hat off his brow, scratched his head and read the notice through in detail, nodding thoughtfully. It had taken only two years then to finish off the last tenant and no wonder, after three years of Willett : Crakenhill was already in a fair way to recover its former reputation as the most ruinous farm in the parish. What better proof was needed that the Geaiters were the only men in Suffolk fit to farm it ? Harry was so engrossed with the sale bill that for two or three minutes he did not observe another notice at the side, printed in tar

on a rough wooden slat and nailed to a sapling in the hedge.
' To Let or for Sale. Apply Mytton, Framlingham.' That
was all it said. Harry burst out laughing as soon as he
saw it. The slightest hint that a tenant was leaving was
generally enough to bring applicants swarming to the
landlord's door : but Mytton, the Framlingham butcher,
who had bought the farm from Nancy, evidently had no
illusions about its worth. It was the old story all over
again, that, too well-known to find a tenant in the neighbourhood, it must angle for a fool from some district
where its reputation had not yet reached : that was what
that little notice meant. Harry laughed again as he
turned away and hurried back along the road to Bruisyard
Street. He would have something to tell his brothers at
the inn if they had not already seen the bill ; but it would
be like telling them of the decline of an old, loved friend.

The other four brothers were already seated before their
bread and cheese and onions in the bar-parlour of the inn
when Harry arrived : Joey was not allowed to deprive
himself of his Sunday dinner and walked over from Dennington an hour or so later, when he had finished.

' Where've you been, Harry ? ' said Ern. ' I walked
half-way down the Rendham road to meet you.'

' Any of you been up the drift lately ? ' replied Harry
enigmatically, as he sat down in front of his beer.

They all shook their heads.

' Why ? ' said Hiram.

' I don't know,' continued Harry, ignoring the question,
' what you chaps have done with the money father left us.
I haven't touched mine yet.'

' We haven't got no cause to spend it,' said Ern, ' not
at our time of life.'

' So it fared to me,' said Harry, nodding mysteriously.

' Look here, young Harry,' cried Ben impatiently,
' what's all this rigmarole about. If you've got something
to say, out with it and don't go beating about the bush.'

' All right, Ben, do you wait a minute,' replied Harry
tantalizingly. ' What I meant was that it fare to me us

five chaps are the only ones as can make a do of Craken-hill.'

'Too true,' said Hiram, 'do you tell us something we don't know, young Harry'

'Get on with your beer,' growled Ben, 'and don't talk so much.'

'Well, look here, Ben,' said Harry, leaning forward over the table to him, 'Crakenhill have only got a hundred acres now and it fare to me we've got enough by us to take that there farm ourselves. That's empty at Michaelmas.'

'What ? ' cried Ben.

'Lor! ' exclaimed Hiram.

'Yes,' replied Harry, 'Gale's having a sale and Mytton's put up a little owd piece of wood by the gate with "To Let or For Sale" on it. That show you, don't it ? Fare to me that'd just do for us.'

'Yes, but what do we want with a farm now ? ' protested Bob discouragingly : it was always his way at first with a new idea. 'We're getting too old for that sort of game now. 'Tisn't as if we were married folks.'

'I wasn't thinking of us, Bob,' replied Harry, 'but of the boy. That'd be something to give Joey a start.'

''Struth, young Harry! ' cried Ben, bringing his mug down on the table with a thump, 'you've fair hit the nail. That'd be just the thing for Joey, that would. And by rights the farm should have come to him.'

'Becourse that would,' cried Bob excitedly, thumping his own mug on the table and going quite red in the face. 'You've got a proper little hid on you, young Harry, and no mistake.'

'Ay, that he have,' agreed Hiram, 'but,' he added cautiously, 'do you think we can stand it ? Are our backs broad enough ? '

Harry took a pull at his beer and put his mug down on the table.

'Well, see here,' he said, leaning forward again. 'You know what a condicament that there land is in : Mytton know, too ; do, he wouldn't have put up that little owd notice.'

' Ay, them fields down by the gull——' began Bob at his fastest pace.

' Well,' said Harry, raising his voice and striking the table with his fist to silence the interruption, ' nobody but a fool or us chaps'd take that there place on and it fare to me that if Mytton knowed we thought of going there, he'd take any rent we offered.'

' That's as true as I sit here,' said Ben. ' I knew young Gale wouldn't make a do of it : but that come in fine for us. That's in a rare pickle, that is, but it's not so bad as it was when me and father first set to work on it and that's the truth. If we can't bring that round, no one can't. Well, what do you say, boys ? We've each got our hundred pound and we've all saved a bit extra, I doubt.'

' Becourse, Ben,' said Ern. ' You can take all I've got. Do you go into Frannigan to-morrow and see Mytton right away.'

' Ay, that's it,' added Hiram, ' and do you look out he don't play you a trick. I know them butchers.'

' Boys, boys,' cried Bob, gleefully rubbing his hands, ' there's some luck for you. Hey, Charley, fetch us a drop more beer ! '

' We shall have to go careful, Bob,' said Ben thoughtfully, when the landlord had filled up their mugs. ' There'll be several things to buy : a couple of teams and a drill and ploughs and a reaper ; and we haven't got no furniture.'

' And cows,' added Ern. ' No good trying to farm without cows. They bring in money while you're waiting for the corn to grow.'

' That's true,' said Hiram. ' And then we shall want someone to come and do for us. I ain't a-going to do no more cooking.'

' Ah, well,' said Ern, ' Mrs. Snaith'd be right glad to come and do for us. She've just lost her husband. I live next door, so I know.'

' A lot of money that'll cost,' ruminated Ben, ' a lot of money.'

' Still, that's only a hundred acres,' said Bob. ' We ought to be able to stand that. I reckon Mytton'll be that thankful to have us back, he'll almost pay our rent for us.'

'Ay, that's only a hundred acres,' admitted Ben, ' and what's more, Bob, that 'on't take all five on us. If the boy go too, there 'on't be room for more'n three on us.'

The other four looked blankly at one another : someone would have to be sacrificed and it would be very hard to bear.

' Becourse,' said Ben, ' as soon as we've got going and there's a bit of money to spare, we'll try and get a bit more land so's we can all come back. Mr. Snowland'd probably let us have some of those fields on the hill that he bought of Nance : he only keep 'em for the shooting.'

The faces of the other four brightened again.

' Well, we'd better settle now,' said Bob somewhat nervously, ' who's to go up and who's to stay behind.'

' Ay,' replied Ben, rubbing his moustache and looking sternly into the depths of his beer for counsel. ' We shall want two horsemen, anyhow, for the ploughing.'

' Well, that's you and Hiram,' put in Bob hastily.

' Becourse Ben must go, but I don't know about me,' protested Hiram. ' Bob's just as good as me with a plough.'

' Still, you and Ben have had Joey all this time,' replied Bob, ' and he's working with you now. That's only right you should go up together. I can wait.'

' All right,' said Hiram with a sigh of relief, ' have it your own way then, Bob. P'r'aps you're right.'

' And then,' continued Ben, ' we shall want someone to see after the cows.'

' Well, it fare to me,' said Ern, solemnly wagging his forefinger, ' that young Harry ought to go up and see after 'em. That was all his idea, that was, and he desarve it : he's a reg'lar fine little feller, he is.'

' Now, listen here, Ern,' replied Harry, swallowing a mouthful of bread and cheese. ' If I hadn't thought of that, somebody else would. I should right like to go : but

you know, Ben, that where it's cows, Ern's your man :
cows and pigs. Ern could allus milk me to bed any night
and if he go up there, the sooner me and Bob'll be able to
come back. Now, ain't that right, Ben ? '

He took a big bite out of his onion.

' Yes, Harry, that is,' said Ben gratefully ; they had
taken a delicate problem out of his hands and solved it for
themselves. ' I think Ern ought to come.'

' Yes, now when you can afford a pen or two of sheep,'
said Harry, licking his lips, ' then I'm your man. I shall
have to find you a billet on my farm at Rendham, Bob,'
he added, laughing, ' so as you can come and live along o'
me.'

' That's right,' said Bob, ' and then we can go up o'
Sundays and give a hand sometimes.'

' Becourse, Bob,' said Ben, ' and we'll do our best not to
keep you waiting long. My, 'on't that be grand for Joey?'

' That'll be like going home for him,' said Hiram, ' and
for us too.'

Bob winced, but checked himself before Hiram could
notice.

' Look here, Hiram,' he began, at the top of the scale,
' what'll you do to clean them fields down by the gull?
Fare to me it want a crab-harrow, don't it, or one of them
steam-engine ploughs p'r'aps? '

' Here, let that be now, Bob,' cried Ern, clapping him
on the shoulder as the door opened. ' Here's Joey.'

XXXVII

THE ensuing Michaelmas saw Ben with Hiram, Ern and Joey effectively installed at Crakenhill. Mytton had been only too glad to let them have the farm at a reduced rent and Mrs. Snaith, when they asked her to come and keep house for them, jumped at the offer : it was all they could have wished. Without delay they set to work to bring the farm into heart once more. For Ben it was like a return to his own young days when he and his father had wrestled alone with that stubborn piece of land, and his former experience came in useful although, thanks to twenty years of their own cultivation, the farm had not yet quite sunk back to the same miserable condition in which they first had found it, and he had more strong hands to help him now than Benjamin had commanded then. For the first two years the plough was hardly ever idle : the fields that had been let go, were turned up again and again, torn to pieces with harrows, crushed to dust with rollers ; they had no peace until they were clean and Ben and Hiram, knowing from of old just where the extra rolling, the deeper drilling, the richer manuring, were required, humoured the land like a sick man until perforce it began to recover strength and virtue. Then at last the crops came and the rickyard filled. Meanwhile Ern laboured hard among the few pigs and cows with which they had started, planning and contriving incessantly to bring in enough money to feed the family until the land began to yield and at the same time to build up a good milking herd. Every Sunday Bob and Harry would come up to see how things were getting on and solemnly puffing at their pipes, accompanied by the other three and Joey, they duly visited every field, poked all the fat beasts in the ribs with their walking sticks and said their say in the discussion of plans for the coming week. It was a most precious ritual for these men cut off from the rest of the family, and beside it all their week's work for their masters

seemed meaningless and futile. But knowing that their
time, too, would come, they did not grumble.

At the end of five years Crakenhill was again enjoying
a prosperity worthy of its best days. Each year the margin
had increased and at last Ben felt justified in taking over
the other hundred acres which Snowland, who had bought
them from Nancy for the shooting, was quite willing to
let to them. Bob and Harry came back to Crakenhill : the
farm and the family were complete. The five brothers had
never been happier—the more so because their sufferings
had somehow mellowed them and rendered them more
sensitive to the light and shade of experience ; even the
Geaiter features had lost something of their old stolidity
and expressionlessness : and for once they had all they
desired ; they were back at Crakenhill if they did not own
it, they were farming well and above all, they had Joey
with them, growing up into a tall, sturdy lad and learning
his trade under their eyes as he could have done nowhere
else. They watched over him with fatherly care, correcting
him and guiding his hands, each telling him all that he
knew. With so much solicitude for his welfare, Joey might
have been completely spoilt and developed into an idle,
presumptuous and conceited young man, if it had not been
for the work which he shared with his brothers from the
day they returned to Crakenhill : that at least they did not
spare him. As it was, before he had reached manhood, he
could plough as clean a furrow and mow as clean a swath
as any of them. They had a reaper on the farm, of course,
and everywhere self-binders were coming into fashion ;
but it was part of the Crakenhill tradition that no man
could be a farmer who did not know how to use a scythe—
Benjamin himself had been above all things a mower ; and
so, although the scythe was needed little more than once
a year, at harvest-time to cut a way for the reaper around
the corn, Joey was taught to mow. They were all as proud
of him as if he had been their own son.

To Joey, who had only spent two years of his life away
from Crakenhill and hardly knew of any other trade, it all

seemed the most natural thing in the world. His companionship of play with the brothers had become a companionship of work, he ate his food with an appetite and stretched his growing muscles exultantly: for the first few years he was as happy as the rest and asked no more than to be lustily alive. But when he reached his twentieth year, he began to look about him and wonder if that was all that life had to offer: there was a world outside the farm with new sights, new faces and amusements untasted. That summer he went down into Bruisyard more and made a few friends, drank a glass or two at the inn and kissed a girl at the village fête. But even this little burst of gaiety was not enough to still the restlessness which had begun to creep over him. He could not complain of the way his brothers treated him; they paid and fed him well, they did not work him excessively hard: they were good fellows. But for the first time it struck him that the youngest of them was more than twenty years older than himself. Shut up with those five men on a remote farm—he wondered if he was wasting his life: he had had enough of the land, he wanted youth and excitement, he wanted to see the world. He had inherited in full measure his father Benjamin's abounding energy and it needed some outlet or other. During the winter he bought an old riding-saddle among the dead stock at Saxmundham market and began breaking the colt which they had bred from the pony mare Ern drove in with the milk each morning. It was a fiery little beast with a strain of the thoroughbred in it on its father's side and it kept him busy for some months. It bit and kicked him, it threw him in every possible manner; then one day he quite unexpectedly found himself its master and all his interest in it died: he began to chafe again. It was all natural enough.

The year drew on, the grasses swelled and haysel approached. Joey was at work with Ern at the bottom of the drift, clearing the ditch and braiding the hedge. He felt more discontented and out of humour than usual this morning. There seemed no end to this work: when one branch was lopped off, there was another behind, waiting its turn, and even when the whole hedge was down, it only grew again. Already his cheek was bleeding with a tear from a blackthorn switch—malicious, cunning stuff that bounced up in your face when you struck it—and his fingers were full of thorns : senseless work, it seemed to him. He paused to breathe for a moment and gazed down at the Framlingham road, tenderly rubbing his smarting cheek. A large procession of caravans wound slowly into view, followed by a drove of horses of every colour and a large number of waggons packed with closed cages and stacks of garishly painted boards and canvas. They halted by the drift gate and a man, getting down from the first caravan, waved his arm to Joey and shouted. Joey dropped his hook and ran down to the gate.

The stranger was a shrewd-faced little man in a shabby suit of town clothes.

' Is this the way to Frannigan ? ' he called sharply. ' We lost our way coming from Saxmundham.'

' Ay, straight on,' replied Joey, ' though you've come out of your way a bit to get there.'

' Well, we shall have to hurry then,' said the man. ' We're only stopping one night in Frannigan and then on to Debenham. Stout's circus we are. That's a good show. Come and see us to-night. I must be off now. 'Morning.'

He climbed back into his caravan and the line of vehicles trailed on. Joey, having watched them out of sight, walked back to Ern.

' What's that ? ' said Ern.

' A circus,' replied Joey. ' That's stopping the night at Frannigan. I've never seen a circus. Come with me to-night, Ern.'

Ern shook his head.

' Can't Joey,' he said. ' I've got a sow farrowing to-night I must sit up with.'

' But that'll farrow all right without you,' grumbled Joey, ' just for once.'

' Maybe,' replied Ern, starting to whet his hook on the

rub, ' but I allus like to see 'em through it and I like to see the young 'uns. But do you go all the same.'

Joey shrugged his shoulders and began hewing savagely at the hedge again. He could not understand Ern : the man must have sat up with scores of farrowing sows in his life and yet he still seemed to look forward to it as if it were a new experience : he preferred it to a circus. He himself did not mind if he never cut another hedge : he was sick of doing the same things.

That night every one of his brothers was tired or had something else to do and Joey went in to Framlingham to the circus alone. It was not a very grand affair, but it was the first circus that Joey had ever seen and his unaccustomed eyes were quite fascinated by the glitter of it. The little man who had spoken to him in the morning was there in the middle of the ring, magnificent in evening dress, with a scintillating false diamond in his shirt-front, incessantly cracking an enormous whip as if to call attention to his own importance. Clowns tumbled and turned cartwheels around his feet, but he went on cracking his whip without taking any notice of them. Joey wondered how he could refrain from laughing at their jokes : he had never heard such wit in his life. Then a whistle blew, the band struck up and the show began.

First a group of four black horses came on and pranced and wheeled in time to the music until the ring-master halted them with a crack of his whip ; they each raised a fore-leg in the air and trotted off. They were followed by a troupe of performing dogs who were put through their paces by a little woman dressed as a Dresden shepherdess, complete with white curls and a crook adorned with a black silk bow. The dogs walked on their hind legs, jumped through hoops and climbed ladders, but Joey paid no attention to them, quite captivated by the shepherdess and jealously watching every movement she made : he could scarcely bring himself to believe in the real existence of such a dainty creature and when the turn was over, he went on clapping long after the rest had finished, much to the general amusement. The next turn was a gymnastic display by two twin sisters, infant prodigies, as the bill proclaimed. They minced on to the stage, muffled up to the eyes in cloaks and accompanied by their mother, a massive matron of determined aspect who would obviously allow no nonsense with her two daughters—who, however, looked quite old enough to take care of themselves, when, after a low bow to the audience, they swept off their cloaks with a queenly gesture and revealed their powdered cheeks and plump contours encased in flesh-pink tights. Joey's heart seemed to jump into his mouth : the girls of Bruisyard could not hold a candle to them. He hardly knew what they did for gazing at them and when, amid roars of applause, they bowed themselves off, he was sure that one of them winked at him : dozens of young men in the audience thought the same. Five minutes later the mother of the two buxom prodigies came round among the seats with photographs of her daughters in different poses and Joey eagerly bought three of them. The air in the marquee warmed, the music throbbed, the conversation buzzed and the crowd grew lively. Joey himself, infected with the general gaiety, felt his cheeks glow and clenched and unclenched his fists with excitement : he had certainly never lived before this.

Turn followed turn in quick succession, performing bears, a dwarf elephant, acrobats, but the greatest thrill of the evening for Joey came when the two demon riders trotted into the ring, a man in gold silk jockey's cap and blouse, and a woman in white leather riding-boots and scarlet breeches. They cantered round the ring in every possible position, standing, sitting, kneeling in their saddles ; they tied their feet in the stirrups and hanging down over their horses' flanks, picked up handkerchiefs with their teeth ; they vaulted into their saddles and stepped clean on to them at the canter. Joey's eyes bulged with amazement and envy. What a life theirs must be. To wear such dazzling costumes and career round the ring in that daring manner before the admiring eyes of such vast crowds: always delighting and always applauded! Some people had all the luck.

The man suddenly reappeared in the ring, dressed as a cow-boy in a red shirt and leather trousers and mounted on a fresh horse.

' The Bucking Wonder!' announced the ring-master with a crack of his whip.

The horse ambled quietly into the middle of the ring: then all at once, putting its ears back, it began to do its worst. It reared, it bucked, it lashed out with its heels: but through it all the rider remained on its back undisturbed, and when at length the horse, tired out, ceased its antics, he took off his hat and bowed to the cheering audience. Then, jumping off, he gave the bridle a tug and the horse, sinking down on its knees, slowly stretched itself out full length on the floor of the ring. The applause redoubled.

' Five shillings for anybody in the audience who can sit this horse for two minutes!' cried the Bucking Wonder, striking a heroic attitude with one foot on the horse's flank.

A hush fell upon the crowd and a little man stepped awkwardly forward into the ring: it was the hostler from The Feathers. The Bucking Wonder snapped his fingers and the horse scrambled to its feet. The hostler mounted and in two seconds he was grovelling in the sand, off at the first buck. He limped away, painfully rubbing his shoulder, having fallen badly and bruised himself.

' Who else?' cried the man in the ring. ' Come along, boys. There's five bob waiting for you.'

There was silence again: no one cared to take the risk with a horse that knew its tricks so well: the hostler was reputed a good horseman. The Bucking Wonder shrugged his shoulders and seizing the bridle, was about to leave the ring when someone shouted to him to stop. Joey, very red in the face, was clambering laboriously down from the back row.

' Come along, lad!' cried the Bucking Wonder. ' Come and give us a bit of entertainment: you'll soon be off.'

Joey stumbled sheepishly over to the horse and took the bridle from him. He vaulted into the saddle without a pause and letting the stirrups go loose, locked his feet under the horse's belly : it was fortunate that he had long legs. The horse bucked once, twice, three times, but Joey's toes held fast. It reared high in the air on its hind-legs, but Joey, without letting the bridle go, slipped both his arms round its neck and hung on, contriving at the same time to dig it hard in the flank with his heel. It dropped on all-fours again and set off at a canter round the ring with its head down and bucking every few yards. But Joey, though shaken to the marrow, remained immovable in the saddle : so long as his feet were lodged beneath its belly, it could not shift him : his practice with the colt at Crakenhill last winter had taught him a thing or two. The horse, acknowledging its master at length, trotted quietly into the middle of the ring and came to a halt. The crowd cheered uproariously as Joey dismounted and the Bucking Wonder clapped him on the shoulder. The ring-master came forward and pressed a crown piece into his hand.

' Come round behind when it's over, my lad,' he whispered in Joey's ear. ' I'd like a word with you.'

Joey, more red and confused than ever, but quivering with pride, hurried out of the ring, clutching his crown piece tightly in his pocket and trying to avoid the slaps on the back with which his admirers in the audience greeted him. The band struck up ' God Save the King.'

Five minutes later Joey, who had lingered behind after the crowd, presented himself at the ring-door.

' Ah,' said the little ring-master, impatiently tapping the butt of his whip on the ground, ' here you are at last. You're a real good 'un with a horse. How'd you like to come along of us? We need another young chap to help the Bucking Wonder. I like the look of you.'

Joey gasped. Here was fortune seeking him out. Life among men like these, men with real style about them, a whole world above his slow, stupid, ridiculous brothers, it was just the thing he had been praying for ; the ring-master must have read his thoughts that evening : this was true kindness.

' That I should,' he replied eagerly.

' Very well,' said the ring-master, ' but we can't wait for you. We start for Debenham in the morning.'

' All right,' said Joey, ' I'll join you to-night. I'm that thankful to get away from the farmyard.' It was no use returning home : his brothers would never let him go.

' Good for you, youngster,' said the ring-master. ' We get up early in the morning. We've got to pack up. The Bucking Wonder 'll find you a bed somewhere.'

Half an hour later Joey, wrapped up in a couple of dirty blankets, sank gratefully to sleep on a straw-stuffed tick in one of the caravans and dreamed all night of the infant prodigies.

XXXVIII

THE next morning, well before it was light, the whole company was hard at work dismantling the marquee and stacking it on to the waggons with all its appurtenances. Joey was awakened even earlier by the Bucking Wonder, who took him off to feed and water the horses.

' I'll put you through your paces, young feller,' he said, ' when we get set up at Debenham. It ain't all roses, this life, I can tell you. You'll have to shake down with the other blokes and do your whack with them till you know your job like me. We can't all be gentlemen here.'

He slapped his chest with a consequential air, satisfied that he at least was one of the gentlemen of the company.

Joey was used enough to baiting horses in the fresh, stinging air before dawn, but there was a vast difference between the bare canvas enclosure where the circus horses were tethered and the warm interior of the stable at Crakenhill with its familiar smells of hay and hartshorn. The horses stamped and snorted, the men swore: all last night's finery—paint, streamers and tassels—in the half-light looked tawdry and bedraggled. Joey caught himself hankering regretfully after the farmyard that he had so light-heartedly renounced the night before : but the next moment he bit his lip and pulled himself together. This was not the way to begin the gay, vagabond life that he had so longed for : of course, it was not all roses : but he would show these fellows that he could stand a little hardship and was worth his salt. One of the infant prodigies descended the steps of her caravan with a frying-pan in her hand. Dressed in an old black and white check frock with a brown woollen shawl over her shoulders, she did not look quite so ravishing as she had done the night before in her flesh-pink tights, but still, who could be home-sick in the vicinity of such a charmer? Joey glanced up at her over a truss of hay and smiled, but she passed coldly on. Just her tantalizing way, thought Joey : better luck next time.

He was in a thoroughly good humour now ; he swore manfully at his horses and cracked jokes with the other men. One of them, feeling that this young rustic who had just joined them, was giving himself too many airs, tripped him up with the handle of a pitchfork just as he was returning to the enclosure with a pail of water, and straightway took to his heels. Joey scrambled to his feet and chased the man round the paddock until he caught him ; then, amid the cheers of the whole company, he picked him up like a sheaf of corn and ducked his head in what was left of his pail of water. He was in a better humour than ever after that : they respected him now. An hour later, after a breakfast of bread and salt bacon and a souse in the same pail, he felt fit for anything the vagabond life might bring with it.

At nine o'clock they were on the road once more. Joey sat on a pile of sacks at the back of one of the waggons, his legs dangling over the tail-board. Two other hands at his side were discussing the girls they had met the last time they were in Ipswich. Joey, a little sleepy now after his brief night's rest, listened with contented admiration to the gallant reminiscences of these two men of the world : there were untold joys in store for him, he could see. The waggon jogged on and Joey fell asleep.

When he woke up again, they were passing a little white-washed farmhouse standing right on the road. The kitchen door was flung back and the first thing that Joey saw when he opened his eyes, was the interior of the room. The table was laid for dinner ; four men and a lad were seated round it with their eyes fixed intently on a grey-headed woman who was serving stew from a large steaming dish ; she handed a plate to the lad. The waggon rolled past and the scene vanished from his sight. He passed his hand across his brow to make sure that he was not dream-ing. Those men might have been his own brothers : that was just how they sat down to dinner at Crakenhill, just how they watched Mrs. Snaith when she served the stew or carved the joint. His five brothers—every minute he was moving further away from them, as likely as not he would never sit down to dinner with them again, might never even see them again. They were good chaps too, in spite of their old-fashioned ways : they had brought him up and taught him all he knew. He searched his memory to call their faces back : Ben's with the grizzled side-whiskers he had latterly grown—how they had laughed over them—and his slow blue eyes. Joey squirmed with shame to think that last night he had inwardly denounced him as stupid and ridiculous. He had no smart talk, he did not run after girls, he would never cut a dash in the world : but he was uncommonly kind ; Joey's throat swelled as he remembered Ben's kindness. Then he stiffened himself, suddenly spurning his own thoughts. It was no use going on like this ; such severances had to be faced by an adventurer : he was going to see the world and there would be a host of new things to make up for what he had left behind and more than make up for it ; he would forget his brothers. And yet—they would be wondering now where he had got to.

He set his teeth and tried to listen to his two companions again, but somehow they no longer interested him. He turned his head and looked at the fields which slowly unfolded beside him as the long train crept on. Everywhere the grass was tall and lush : they would soon have to cut. One man was already at work in his clover with the scythe, his shoulders bowed like a sapling before the wind and his eyes fixed unwaveringly on his blade, as if rapt by the rhythmical swing of his own tense arms out of all consciousness of the world about him. As soon as Joey saw the steel flash and heard its soft hiss among the falling stalks, a hand seemed to clutch at his heart. He, too, had used a scythe many times before, but not until now had he comprehended the wonder of it : every detail came up vividly before his mind, the crisp grate of the blade against the stalk, the rank smell of the green juice, the exhilarating pulse of the timed sweep. He knew now why it was that Ern could sit up night after night to watch over his farrowing sows and not tire of it : what if he himself should never hold a scythe again ? He had not thought of that last night : just the thought, the simplest memory of it would have saved him from making this prodigious mistake. Beyond doubt it was a mistake : he had severed himself from all that was nearest his heart : he did not want to be a circus rider and a vagabond, he did not want to see the world : it was not worth seeing. His head throbbed, he caught his breath and looked desperately from side to side of him like a fugitive seeking refuge from his pursuers. At all costs he must escape.

' What's the matter, youngster ? ' said the elder of his companions. Joey made no answer, but continued staring wildly at the dwindling figure of the solitary mower.

' He's cracked, he is,' said the other. They both laughed.

The circus drew slowly into Earl Soham. A few men slipped across to the inn for a quick drink and then ran back to their waggons or caravans. Joey, too, slid down from his waggon as it came level with the inn.

' Thirsty,' he said. ' Must have a drink.'

He entered the tap-room and paid for a glass of beer. He took it into the bar-parlour and put it on the table ; opened the back door and walked into the garden : there was no one there. He walked to the bottom and climbing the fence, found himself in a field of turnips. He began to run, skirting the hedge ; he ran as if he had the devil behind him.

. . . . .

It was nearly tea-time when Joey reached Crakenhill. Ern and Harry were in the neathouse milking ; Ben, Hiram and Bob stood by the farmyard gate, looking disconsolately down the drift. But Joey had not the courage to approach the farm by so direct a way. Half a mile from the drift gate he had taken to the fields and he stole guiltily into the farmyard from the kitchen garden. He walked softly up behind Ben and Hiram. They turned round with a start.

' Why, Joey ? ' exclaimed Ben, looking amazedly at him. ' Where hev you been, lad ? '

Joey hung his head and blushed fierily.

' What is it, lad ? ' said Ben gently. ' Don't you be afraid. We're that glad to see you back.'

' Well, you see, Ben,' said Joey, looking up shame-facedly, ' it's like this. I went to the circus last night and —and——'

' Had a drop too much ? ' suggested Bob helpfully.

' No,' replied Joey, ' I won a crown for riding one of their show hosses and the bloke with the whip asked me if so be as I'd like to go along of 'em and I did.'

' What did you want to do that for, you jim ? ' asked Hiram.

' I wanted to see the world,' answered Joey ruefully.

' But you came back after all,' said Ben in relieved tones. ' I'm not surprised at that.'

Something seemed to tickle him. He winked at Hiram and began to laugh softly to himself. Hiram and Bob looked a little embarrassed : they knew what he was laughing at.

' Look here, Joey boy,' he said a moment after, ' I'm that glad you've come back, you don't know, but don't you go making a fool of yourself agin. You've got a good life here and that'd be a pity to leave it. You live hard : but you live clean and you sleep sound. And it fare to me you couldn't leave Crakenhill even if you wanted to. You sorterly growed up out of the earth here like all the rest on us.'

Joey nodded penitently : he understood all that now. Bob and Hiram nodded too.

' And look here, boy,' added Ben, ' if you must see the world, I know of something as'll satisfy your craving like. Ern was saying only to-day that he was tired of driving the milk into Sax every morning. Well, I don't see why you shouldn't do it instead. That'd be something fresh,

that would, and if you go into Sax and back once a day,
you'll see all of the world you're likely to want, it fare to
me.'

'Thanks, Ben,' muttered Joey, quite affected by the
gentleness of his reception. 'I'd real like it and that's the
truth.'

'Well, boy,' said Ben, clapping him on the shoulder,
'do you go in and have your tea. You're hungry, I
reckon. We shall all be there in a minute.'

Joey turned round and walked away across the yard
to the stable. He hesitated for a moment by the door and
then disappeared inside. Five minutes passed and he did
not come out.

'Now what's he a-doing of there?' said Bob. 'Stand
to reason he's hungry and yet he want to go messing about
in that there stable.'

'P'r'aps he want to make sure it's still there,' grinned
Hiram. 'He thought he'd lost it for good.'

'Well, he ought to know by now,' said Ben. 'I'm going
to have a look.'

He walked quietly over to the stable door and peeped
cautiously in. A moment after he came back to the gate,
holding his hand over his mouth to stifle his laughter.

'What d'you think he's a-doing of?' he gasped. 'He's
a-sharping his scythe.'

XXXIX

THE milk-float crawled slowly up the long hill which led from Saxmundham station out on to the Rendham road, with Joey trudging pensively by its side. The milk churns from Crakenhill were already on their way to London along with scores of other churns from the same district. Joey had watched them trundled into the train and had wondered what they could want with all that milk up there; London must be a big place indeed : but it held no glamour for him. Every day for nearly three years now he had driven the milk-float into Saxmundham and every day he was glad when he turned his back on the little town. Having lived almost the whole of his life on a hillside farm, little less than a mile from any other habitation, he always felt penned up even among the few rows of houses that Saxmundham could boast of. There must be even more houses in London, more traffic, more smells, more shopkeepers living by cheating their neighbours, more pale faces ; and everyone watching everyone else's comings and goings. He marvelled at the folly of people who preferred to live cooped up in a town nearly a hundred miles from the cows that gave them milk, when there was such a goodly countryside close at hand ; more so than ever on such a morning as this. He was at the top of the hill now, looking across at Carlton woods shimmering green and gold with the May sunlight among their bursting oak-buds and hawthorn shoots. He could not help smiling as he savoured the strong, sweet-scented air in his nostrils, with the sheer delight of being alive and young and the whole landscape seemed to smile back at him. He wondered why it was that every spring he felt this obscure, joyful tingling in his blood : his brothers never showed any sign of it ; they went on their solid way at their own solid pace, taking everything for granted : perhaps in twenty years' time he, too, would be like that, perhaps that was the difference between youth and age.   He jumped into the float and the pony set off at a trot.

A little further on, as they rounded a bend in the road, the pony pulled up with a start and shied. There was a heap of stones beside the hedge and a girl of about twenty sitting on it, a large cardboard box bound with leather straps beside her.   Joey got out of the float and going to the pony's head, tried to lead it past, but it would not budge.

' I say, miss,' he said, turning to the girl, ' it's you he's afraid of. He 'on't move until he know what you're made of, he's that tetchy. So if you'd be so kind——'

Without speaking she rose to her feet and picked up her box. She was wearing a smart navy blue costume, a large black hat with a large black feather and high-heeled patent leather shoes. She moved slowly to the other side of the heap of stones and Joey, as he led the nervous pony past her, noticed that she was limping as if her feet hurt her.

' Thank you, miss,' he said, jumping in again.

The pony rattled off at a sharp trot. Twenty yards further on Joey turned his head and looked back furtively at her : she had seemed a pretty girl in that brief glimpse. She, too, was looking wistfully after him with her box still in her hand. Joey's heart smote him as he remembered how she had limped : he promptly turned the float round and drove back to her.

' I don't know if you're going my way, miss,' he said, stopping level with her, ' but if you'd like a ride—that box fare heavy.'

' Thank you,' she replied in a faint voice. ' I'm going to Bruisyard Street.'

' Well, that's right lucky,' said Joey. ' I can take you the whole way. Do you give me that box.'

He took the package from her and deposited it among the empty churns as she climbed up and sat down beside him on the plank at the back of the float. He turned the pony again and they drove off. She sat very still, looking straight in front of her without saying anything while

Joey stealthily scanned her pink cheek out of the corner of his eye : it was very smooth and round, he had never seen anything quite so dainty before ; indeed, she was so very smart altogether, she might be a real lady. He turned his eyes away and began to go red in the face : he was not used to such people. He grew redder and hotter and a mist came up before his eyes. He blinked hard, but failed to notice how sharply the pony was taking the curve at Rendham cross-roads until with a jolt the near wheel of the float mounted the bank at the side of the road and hurled his passenger violently against him. She snatched his arm tightly with both hands. In another second the wheel found the road again and Joey pulled the pony to a standstill. The girl was still clinging to his arm with a frightened look in her eyes.

' Sorry, miss,' he said reassuringly. ' That's all right now. Pony's a bit fresh this morning.'

' He won't do it again, will he ? ' she asked timidly, as she disengaged herself from his arm.

' No, miss,' replied Joey, clicking his tongue to the pony. ' I'll see to that. That was my fault, really.'

Then he went red again, remembering how she had fallen against him. Her cheek had just grazed his and he had caught a breath of perfume from her skin, sweeter than anything he had ever smelt : her white silk blouse too had brushed his hand : it was wonderfully soft and delicate, like everything else about her.

' Oh, that's all right,' she said with a smile. ' Only I want to get there safe.'

She looked even prettier when she smiled, and Joey blushed redder than ever.

' Were you a-going to walk all the way from Sax to Bruisyard in those shoes ? ' he faltered at last, determined to keep the conversation going somehow : it relieved the tension. ' That's a good four mile, that is.'

' Well, there wasn't anyone to meet me at the station,' she replied, ' and a cab cost a lot of money and I didn't think my box was all that heavy.'

' A good thing my pony shied,' said Joey with a laugh.

' Yes, I don't know what I should have done else,' she confessed. ' I couldn't go another step. Another minute and I should have cried.'

She dabbed her little nose significantly with her handkerchief. Joey looked discreetly away.

' Are you going to stay in Bruisyard ? ' he queried after a pause, to prevent the conversation from languishing again.

' Yes,' she replied. ' Do you know Mr. Chilvers, the shoemaker ? '

' I should think I do,' said Joey. ' He mend all our boots.'

' Well, he's my father,' she said.

Joey heaved a sigh of relief : she was not so far above him as he had imagined ; she talked like a country girl too.

' But I've lived in Bruisyard all my life,' he said, ' and I don't call you to mind.'

' Ah, well, you wouldn't,' she replied condescendingly. ' You see, I've been in Ipswich the last eight years, living with my aunt. I'm in a milliner's shop,' she added importantly.

' What, do you sell oats and middlings ? ' exclaimed Joey in astonishment : he could not picture so exquisite a creature in such crude surroundings.

' I said milliner's, not miller's,' she corrected haughtily.

' Oh, I see,' replied Joey respectfully : he had no idea what a milliner was.

They drove on in silence for a few minutes.

' So you're down here on a visit ? ' he ventured at length.

' More than a visit,' said Miss Chilvers, carefully readjusting the tilt of her hat. ' You see, my mother've been ill and the doctor say she must have someone to help with the house for a bit, she's that weak. So I've got leave from my shop for three months.'

' I expect you'll be glad to get back to Bruisyard,' said Joey : it seemed the most natural thing to say.

' Indeed I shan't,' she replied indignantly. ' I'm much better off in Ipswich. A slow place like Bruisyard with nothing but fields and cows and trees and no society, that you might call society, that won't suit me : I like a bit of life, I do. I only came here because I had to, I can tell you.'

Joey gazed wonderingly at her. It passed his comprehension how she could so despise all the things which, for him, made up life : but, he supposed, such an elegant, self-possessed young person must have good reasons for thinking so : perhaps he was wrong after all.

They passed through Rendham village and drove on, silent again. Miss Chilvers kept her eyes disconsolately fixed on the bottom of the float as if she were still contemplating the hardships she would have to suffer for the next three months, cut off from the pleasures of Ipswich society. Every now and then Joey stole a sidelong glance at her and his fingers tingled at the memory of the touch of her silk blouse. His cheeks burned : it was exciting to be sitting so close to so much delicacy even if she did despise him and all he stood for. They had left Rendham well behind them now and were threading along beside the Alde : another half-mile and they would be in Bruisyard Street. Joey determined to make the most of it. He tightened his rein and made the pony slacken his pace.

' So you'll be in Bruisyard three months,' he said thoughtfully. ' P'r'aps you'll like it better after a week or two : and then you 'on't want to go away.'

' Indeed I shall,' replied Miss Chilvers, bridling.

' I'm sorry if I've offended you,' said Joey gallantly : it was such a long time since she had smiled.

' You haven't offended me,' she replied, staring coldly at the pony's ears.

Joey hesitated.

' I live in Bruisyard too,' he said, ' or leastways, not far out.

' Oh, do you ? ' said Miss Chilvers, tossing her head, as if that were of no consequence to her.

' Do you know Crakenhill,' pursued Joey, ' out on the Frannigan road ? '

' I've heard tell of it,' said Miss Chilvers casually, buttoning one of her gloves that had come undone.

' That's where I live,' said Joey. ' My name's Geaiter, Joe Geaiter.'

' Indeed ? ' Miss Chilvers glanced round at him with a startled expression : she had heard a good many tales of that family. Still, in spite of them all, Joey looked harmless enough.

' I live with my five brothers,' added Joey, not without a little thrill of pride, ' and we farm two hundred acres.'

' Oh, do you ? ' replied Miss Chilvers in a dull voice, turning her eyes away again : they might have been two hundred band-boxes for all she cared.

' Yes,' continued Joey, undaunted by her nonchalance, ' and I drive the milk in every day to Sax. I pass through Bruisyard Street every morning at half past eight.'

' Yes ? ' said Miss Chilvers wearily, stopping a yawn and wondering what could be the point of all this rigmarole : but country people were like that, she remembered.

Joey cleared his throat and blushed once more.

' So if you want to go into Sax to do some shopping,' he went on, nervously fingering his reins, ' you can allus have a lift.'

' Oh, thank you,' she replied guardedly, in a non-committal tone.

' You will want to go in to Sax, I expect,' persisted Joey desperately.

' Shall I ? ' she queried airily.

' I hope so,' said Joey, quite reckless now.

She turned and looked at him. There was none of the Geaiter about Joey's face : he had all his mother's features, her fresh colour and bright hazel eyes : his lips were parted in a half-shy, half-roguish smile. Miss Chilvers became suddenly aware that he was good-looking : she thought of the arm she had clutched less than half an hour ago, how strong and firm it was, and unable to maintain her dignity any longer, she too smiled.

' So do I,' she whispered with a flutter of her eye-lids—she hardly knew what she was saying. The next moment she had recovered herself.

' Oh, Mr. Geaiter,' she said, ' do put me down now, please. We're almost in Bruisyard Street and it wouldn't look nice, you know, if they saw me driving in with you—in a milk-cart.'

' That's the truth,' said Joey, pulling the pony up and helping her out of the float. ' But you 'on't forget, will you,' he added, as he handed her the box, ' when you want to go in to Sax ? '

' We'll see about that,' she replied with tantalizing demureness, looking severely at his brown, collarless neck. ' You're very forward, you know. Thank you very much for the ride, Mr. Geaiter. Good-morning.'

' Good morning, miss.'

Reluctantly Joey shook his reins and drove off, leaving her standing in the hedge beside her box. As he rounded the corner at Bruisyard Street, he turned his head and looked back over his shoulder at her. She was still standing there beside her box, looking after him. Joey's heart beat hard. The next moment he was out of sight and Miss Chilvers, picking up her box, limped painfully on into the village : she had not wanted him to see how much it hurt her to walk.

XL

MISS DAISY CHILVERS picked up her skirts and sat down carefully on the rail of the little wooden footbridge over the Alde, beyond Bruisyard church. Taking a tiny pocket-mirror out of her handbag, she scrutinised herself minutely, gave her hat a touch or two to set it straight, tucked a stray wisp of hair out of sight and removed an imaginary speck of dust from the tip of her nose with the corner of her handkerchief; then, having gently smoothed down the front of her pink silk blouse and shaken a few flecks of grass-pollen from the hem of her skirt, she put the mirror back into the bag and turned round to gaze at her faint and blurred reflection in the shadowy water that talked quietly to itself beneath the bridge, satisfied that her appearance was now beyond reproach.

She looked at her watch: ten minutes yet to go before the time Joey had arranged to meet her: there was no sign of him. She pouted: the young men who waited on her pleasure in Ipswich—and they were not a few—always took care to arrive before her for their assignations and they were lucky if she did not keep them hanging about an extra quarter of an hour. Altogether her graciousness to this undeserving youth was beyond her own comprehension. Already she had allowed him to drive her three times into Saxmundham in the milk-float for her shopping and to take her for two walks in the evening. The first evening he had met her just outside Bruisyard Street and walked dutifully at her side as far as Rendham and back, gravely listening while she descanted on the mysteries of the millinery business and the amenities of life in Ipswich, to which he had responded with a rather involved forecast of the coming harvest at Crakenhill: he behaved very properly, but he had no conversation, she decided. The second evening they walked to Rendham again and Joey, his tongue loosened, related with gusto how he had ridden the buck-jumper at Frannigan circus three years ago (carefully omitting the sequel, however). She did not show much outward interest in his story, but secretly she felt a little thrilled by his intrepidity and when on the way back in the gathering dusk he discreetly and respectfully slipped his arm through hers, she suffered him. And now to-night she was going out with him for the third time ; she had even offered of her own free will to come more than half-way to Crakenhill to meet him at the bridge, because Ern had shingles and Joey, who was helping Harry with the stock, could not get away so early as usual. When she reflected, it seemed ridiculous that a person of her quality and refinement should lavish so much consideration on an ill-dressed, unsophisticated young farm-labourer of rather questionable antecedents : if her smart friends at Ipswich knew, she would never hear the last of it : she could not make out what it was that made her do it. To-night, moreover, she had a presentiment that he would take further liberties : it was the natural consequence of walking arm-in-arm. She drew herself up stiffly and gripped the rail of the bridge with both her hands. The affair must be stopped now, once for all : it was not only ridiculous, it was not proper, to be kissed in a dark lane by a ploughman without a collar. Joey must be put in his place ; perhaps it was a good thing she had come after all. And yet, she meditated, breaking off a little piece of twig from an overhanging branch and flicking it into the water, there was something about him that made the hours she had passed with him at least not unpleasant : he was shy, but he was not awkward, and when he smiled, she could not stop looking at him. There was no one for her to talk to in this dull, remote village after the day's work in her father's cottage was done : it was natural that she should look forward to these meetings with Joey—and she had looked forward to them : he was better than no one at all. It was already nearly the end of July and although her mother was now regaining strength, she would have to stay at least another month in Bruisyard—she sighed at the thought. Perhaps it might be worth while keeping Joey on ; he might do something to enliven her evenings; but he certainly must not kiss her.

A soft touch on her neck made her turn round with a start. Joey was standing behind her with a blade of feathery grass in his hand, grinning broadly at her.

' You're very cheeky,' she scolded, attempting to be severe, but smiling in spite of herself. ' How did you get up here so quiet ? '

' Ah, I saw you thinking so hard,' said Joey, tossing his blade of grass into the stream, ' I didn't like to disturb you ; so I came up like a mouse on the grass in the hedge.'

' Oh, did you ? ' she replied. ' Well, you mustn't do it again. You frightened me properly.'

' No, I 'on't,' said Joey hastily. ' but I've got something for you here.'

He fumbled nervously in his pocket and after a good deal of effort succeeded in extracting a small packet wrapped up in white paper. He handed it to her with trembling fingers.

' I thought you might like this,' he explained.

' What is it ? ' said Daisy, looking critically at the packet.

' They're only chocolates,' Joey replied, ' but they're the sort the grand folks like, so the man in the shop at Sax say : anyhow, that's what I asked for.'

Daisy's cheeks coloured and a little tremor of delight ran through her that he should have been at such pains to please her : it made her feel that she belonged to the grand folks herself.

' Oh yes, I love this kind,' she said, as she undid the packet and disclosed the wrapper of a well-known brand. ' Thank you, Joey. That was real kind of you. I wonder how you knew I liked them.'

' Oh, I sorterly guessed,' said Joey, his eyes shining with pleasure. ' Where shall we go ? '

Daisy hesitated for a moment.

' Let's go across the fields somewhere,' she said, opening the box and offering it to him. ' I'm tired of the road.'

' Yes, there'll be less people there,' said Joey, taking a chocolate.

' Oh, I wasn't thinking of that,' she replied hastily, looking very hard at the chocolates while she made her choice. ' You can take me where you like.'

They walked on in silence for some minutes, munching the chocolates and trying to think of something to say.

' What a pretty blouse that is you've got,' said Joey at length. ' That's such a lovely colour and that feel so soft.' He slipped his hand under her arm on the pretext of feeling it. ' That must have cost a wonderful lot of money.'

' No, that didn't,' replied Daisy, pressing his hand to her side. ' I made it myself. I'm glad you like it.' Once again his good taste made her quiver with pleasure.

' I've never seen anyone like you before,' added Joey : he blushed.

' Haven't you ? ' said Daisy, blushing too.

They were silent again.

' What lovely honeysuckle that is ! ' she said all at once, pointing to a great whorl of flowers jutting out from the trunk of an oak tree some ten feet above them.

' Would you like some ? ' said Joey eagerly.

' You'd never reach them,' faltered Daisy.

' That I will ! ' cried Joey, dropping her arm.

He caught hold of the lower branches and hauled himself into the fork of the tree. Two minutes later he slid down again with a great bunch of honeysuckle in his arm. He handed it to Daisy and she snuffed it delicately.

' They're lovely and sweet,' she said, raising her head. ' Why, what's the matter with your finger, Joey ? '

' Oh, nothing,' replied Joey, taking his finger out of his mouth. ' I must have caught a thorn sliding down. There was a bramble there among the branches.'

' Let me get it out for you,' said Daisy sympathetically, throwing down the bunch of honeysuckle. ' I'm good at that.'

Joey willingly relinquished his hand to her and tucking

it under her arm, she began working at the sore spot with her finger-nails to squeeze the thorn out.

'You mustn't mind if I hurt you,' she said. 'That's in deep and I shall have to press hard.'

Joey smiled : her soft, white fingers could make little impression on his toughened skin. He prayed for the thorn to resist to the uttermost.

'That's coming,' cried Daisy excitedly, 'that's coming, that's half out now. It's enormous.'

'Is it?' said Joey half-heartedly.

'Now isn't that annoying?' she said. 'That won't come any farther. Wait a minute,' she added in a trembling voice. 'I know.'

She bent down over his hand and sought the thorn with her teeth, her cheeks blushing scarlet. But somehow it seemed to elude her and the next moment Joey felt her lips descend burning and quivering on the palm of his hand. Half-bewildered by the rapture of this unexpected caress, he timidly bowed his head and drew her to him. Her arms stole slowly around his neck and she laid her head on his rough, warm coat, pressing close against him.

'Oh, Joey,' she whispered, 'you don't know how I love you.'

'Do you mean that, Daisy?' he muttered.

She nodded her head against his coat in answer.

'And I love you too, Daisy,' he said, 'I can't say how much : and I want to marry you and never leave you.' She clutched him tighter. 'Will you marry me, Daisy?'

She raised her head suddenly and, holding him away from her, looked him in the face almost sternly, as if she were trying to recall herself to a sense of the proprieties.

'Listen, Joey,' she said, 'I will if you'll do one thing.'

'What?' said Joey.

'I want you to leave this place and come to Ipswich,' she replied.

'What should I do in Ipswich?' exclaimed Joey, opening his mouth wide in astonishment.

'Why, you'd be sure to find some sort of work, Joey,'

she said, ' on the railway or in a shop or in the police or
something : there's plenty to do.'

' But why can't we stop here ? ' he asked. ' That'd be so
much easier.'

' Because, Joey,' she replied, ' if I lived a year in
Bruisyard, I should go mad, I know I should : that'd kill
me. You've never lived in a town, so you don't know any
different. But if only you knew—why, the shops where
you can get things you never see here, and all the people
and the trams, the dances and the picture theatres, and
no muddy roads or oil lamps or water to fetch from the
pump. If once you'd lived there, you'd never want to go
back to the country. You'd just miss the life.'

' Daisy, sweetheart,' said Joey, putting his arms round
her again, ' there's nothing in the world I wouldn't do for
you if you asked me. I love you.'

Her point was gained, the proprieties no longer served
any purpose and she abandoned them incontinently.

' Joey darling,' she whispered, holding her face up to
him, ' please—please kiss me.'

XLI

A wet spring followed by a dry, scorching summer brought harvest early that year. For two months hardly a cloud appeared in the sky to stem the sun's fierce blaze and away on the light lands near the coast, parched to the consistency of sand by the heat, farmers wrung their hands over withered and stunted corn that would not pay for the cutting. But at Crakenhill the heavy land from its hidden stores of moisture, laid up months ago in the wet season, sent up mighty crops of wheat and oats with loaded ears and straw shoulder-high ; the wheat was all carted without shocking as soon as the sheaves were tied, so dry was it, and by the Saturday evening of the third week in August the last field had been cleared and the last rick topped up. On Monday Hiram would set to work thatching the ricks and Ben, Bob and Joey would be at plough on the stubbles, breaking up the land for the winter corn. For the intervening Sunday, with so much time on hand, they could well afford to leave the odd jobs to look after themselves and take their ease : they were glad of it. After breakfast they gravitated one by one to the rickyard until by ten o'clock all the brothers except Joey, who had not yet returned from Saxmundham with the empty milk churns, were lolling round the iron horse-rake with their pipes in their mouths, gazing in placid content at the close-packed ricks around them.

' I reckon there's a good twelve coomb to the acre in that,' said Hiram, pointing to a big tawny-coloured rick in front of him with the stem of his pipe.

' Ay, there's all that in it,' replied Ben, nodding his head reflectively, ' and we ought to get a tidy bit for the straw too : that stood up like soldiers.'

' There ain't nothing like this heavy owd land,' said Bob. ' That's not easy to work, but that pay double when you treat it proper. I don't call to mind a better harvest nor this.'

He clenched his pipe at a defiant angle between his teeth, as if there was no more to be said about it, and settled himself more firmly against the tines of the rake.

'There was that year our Nance got married,' said Ern. 'That summer was near as good as this; but we didn't have the corn we've got this year, and we didn't get done so early.'

'That's true, Ern,' rejoined Ben, rubbing his back against the iron wheel of the rake with a satisfied grunt, 'but you mustn't forget that we had one pair of hands the less in those days: we hadn't got Joey to help us then.'

'Ay, and he make a lot of difference,' said Bob. 'There ain't nothing he can't do. He's a rare hand with a fork and when he's on top of a load you can't pitch too fast for him; and when he plough, that look like a copy-book. I can't better him.'

'And he know how to milk too,' added Harry from the shaft of the rake. 'With a little more practice, he'd soon be as fast as you, Ern.'

'Ay, he would,' agreed Ern, 'and what's more, he don't give himself no airs with it all. He work like a horse and he never grumble. He's a real nice little chap.'

'Come to think of it, Ern,' said Harry, 'he's full as old as you were when Nance first came here, and yet he still fare a youngster like, don't he?'

'Why, yes,' said Ben, turning round to Harry. 'D'you remember, Harry, that time I gave him a ride on the horse-hoe—he said it was like falling in the pond.'

'Ay, that I do,' replied Harry.

'Well, I shouldn't be surprised to hear him say that agin to-morrow,' said Ben, 'he fare that young. And yet I suppose he's a-growing up.'

'That he is,' said Ern. 'He's taller than any on us.'

'And when I was down at the blacksmith's yesterday,' said Bob, 'old Mrs. Spatchard say he've got a gal in the village.'

'Who?' asked Ben jealously.

'Old Chilvers's daughter,' replied Bob, 'her that've

come home from Ipswich. I've only seen her once: she look a hoity-toity sort of baggage.'

' H'm,' grunted Ben, ' he'll soon get over that, I doubt.'

' Besides,' added Bob, ' she've only come down to do for her father while her mother get well. She's going back to Ipswich next week, Mrs. Spatchard say.'

' Well, that's all right,' said Ben sagely. ' He'll settle down all the better for it. They allus get a bit flighty at his age: that's only natural. Look how he ran off with that circus: but he came back right enough.'

Harry rubbed his chin thoughtfully: they had not taken such an indulgent view of his courtship with Jessie, twenty-five years ago.

There was a pause in the conversation: they smoked in silence for a few minutes and ruminated.

' Fare to me,' said Hiram, suddenly breaking the silence, ' we've done real well for ourselves coming back to Crakenhill: we've never been better off in our lives.'

' Ay, that's the truth,' added Ben. ' We've got a lot to thank young Harry for and no mistake.'

' Oh, that ain't nothing,' muttered Harry, going rather red and looking hard at the rickyard gate. ' Why, here come Joey.'

' Why, so that is! ' cried Bob. ' Don't he look glum this morning ? '

Joey slouched across the rickyard towards them with his hands in his pockets and his eyes fixed on the ground.

' Well, Joey,' said Bob, gripping him by the arm, ' cheer up, lad. You haven't upset the milk, have you ? '

' No,' replied Joey in a husky, almost inaudible voice, looking from one to another, ' but I'm afraid I shall have to be leaving you chaps soon.'

' What ever for ? ' exclaimed Ben.

' 'Cause I want to get married,' replied Joey ; he hung his head and blushed.

Ben licked his lips and cleared his throat. The others all turned to him expectantly.

' Well, why can't you bring your wife to live along of us ? ' he said.

' Yes, why not ? ' echoed Hiram.

' The trouble is,' said Joey, putting his hands on his hips and nervously shifting his feet, ' she don't like the country and she want me to go to Ipswich to find work there.'

' That's all nonsense! ' cried Bob impetuously.

' That ain't nonsense, Bob,' answered Joey, sadly shaking his head.

' What d'you want to marry a gal like that for ? ' burst out Ern in disgust.

' Ah, Ern,' said Joey tragically. ' You don't know what it is to be in love.'

' What's that ? ' said Hiram sharply.

The words smote their ears like a challenge : he had not known the days when they and Nancy were younger.

' I tell you, I'm in love with her, Hiram,' said Joey desperately, ' and I'll follow her wherever she go. I'm wholly sorry to leave you chaps, but I reckon I shall have to think about going next week.'

' Now look here, Joey,' coaxed Ben. ' Do you listen to reason a minute. You were brought up at Crakenhill and you've lived all your life there : you ain't made for living in a town. What d'you think you're going to do there ? What's the good of making a fool of yourself ? '

' It ain't no use talking like that, Ben,' said Joey shortly. ' I tell you I've made up my mind. I've got a strong pair of arms and if I can't find work in Ipswich, I ain't fit to marry anybody. And there ain't another girl like Daisy in the whole of Suffolk. It 'on't do no good talking about it, but I thought I'd tell you in good time.'

He turned round and walked out of the rickyard, as disconsolately as he had entered it.

' Well, there's a rum 'un for you! ' said Bob, his eye-brow twitching violently.

' That is,' agreed Hiram, scratching his moustache in consternation. ' What'd Crakenhill be without Joey, boys ? '

' That wouldn't be Crakenhill, that's all,' said Ern savagely. ' We might just as well go back to our cotterages and work for a master. I should like to get hold of that pernickety young bitch, I should. I'd larn her.'

' Well, we must stop him going then,' said Harry. ' That ain't fair to him. What'd he do in a town ? He'd go all mopy like.'

' Who is a-going to stop him ? ' demanded Ben with despair in his voice. ' You know, young Harry, Joey's like his mother : when he set his mind on a thing, there ain't no stopping him. He's in love all right and you remember what our Nance was like when she was in love : she wouldn't stop at nothing. He mean what he say all right.'

' P'r'aps we could get round him somehow,' suggested Bob.

' Do you try it yourself, Bob,' growled Ern. ' Can't you think of something, young Harry ? '

Harry shook his head.

' Well, what's to be done, Ben ? ' said Hiram helplessly.

' That's more'n I can tell, Hiram,' replied Ben. ' It fare to me what Ern say, we might as well shut up Crakenhill and go back to our cotterages. I want to go away and think it over. I'll see you chaps at dinner-time.'

He picked himself up from the rake and walked slowly away to the paddock gate : the others stared distractedly after him.

' I never knowed him go off like that afore,' said Hiram.

' Nor me,' said Bob. ' Why, did you notice, when young Joey said he was a-going to Ipswich, Ben looked an old man, he did, real old, and him not fifty-five yet.'

' I don't wonder,' muttered Ern between his teeth. ' I'm going to look at the pigs.'

Five minutes later the rickyard was empty.

When twelve o'clock came and they all trooped in to dinner, Ben's face wore a less troubled expression as if his deliberations in solitude had brought him comfort, and he sat down with a slightly mysterious air. From time to time the other four cast curious, wistful glances up the table at him : evidently something was brewing in his mind and all their hopes rested on him. Joey sat through the whole meal with his eyes fixed sullenly on his plate. Ern and Harry carried on a desultory conversation with Mrs. Snaith at the end of the table, but no one else spoke. At last when all had finished and Mrs. Snaith had gone to the sink to wash up, Ben raised his head and significantly cleared his throat. The others looked up anxiously at him.

' I say, Joey,' he began, ' I expect you'll be seeing your young woman this arternoon.'

Joey nodded.

' Well, do you bring her along to tea with us,' Ben went on. ' Mrs. Snaith is going out this arternoon, but I doubt we can make out all right without her.'

' I don't know if she'd come,' faltered Joey, a little puzzled by this apparent collapse of opposition.

' Do you ax her then, lad,' said Ben. ' We should like to make the acquaintance of your intended—if so be as she 'on't mind us rough chaps.'

' All right then, I will,' said Joey. The cloud had passed much more easily than he had ever hoped : it was worth while humouring them. ' I must go up and put on my Sunday clothes.'

He got up from the table and disappeared upstairs.

' Now, boys,' said Ben, as soon as he was out of hearing, ' I've got something to say to you. Come you over to the barn with me.'

They all rose from their chairs with one accord and followed him out of the room.

An hour later they re-entered the house and hurried upstairs to change into their Sunday clothes, an operation which to-day took three times as long as usual. Long-forgotten collars and ties had to be unearthed from obscure drawers and adjusted by fingers which for years had been used to nothing more complicated than a neck-cloth ; coats required a special brushing and boots an extra polish. When all was done, they descended to the kitchen, strongly smelling of moth-ball, and Ben solemnly passed them in review, picking off the stray hairs and ends of cotton that still clung to their coats and pulling their ties straight; he sent Bob upstairs again to put some oil on a refractory tuft of hair. The inspection over, although it was still quite early in the afternoon, Harry went out and took up a position behind the hedge of the drift from which he could signal to Ern, who was stationed at the kitchen window, when their visitors had reached the last gate but one, a quarter of a mile away from the farmyard, while the other three proceeded to lay the table for tea and put the kettle on the fire. Bob, in his excitement, dropped two cups on the floor and would have broken the teapot as well if Ern had not managed to catch it as it fell from his hand. Hiram, in his anxiety to cut thin bread and butter, gashed his finger so badly with the bread-knife that Ben had to take the task out of his hands and, less ambitious, cut a plateful of slices nearly half an inch thick and buttered to match: they had at least the virtue of consistency, which was more than could be said for Hiram's attempt at dainty slices. Between them they brought out every cake and jam-dish they could find in the pantry until there was hardly a bare space of cloth left upon the table. Then they sat down to wait.

It was half past three when Harry, having signalled the approach of the enemy, fell back from his outpost and slipped unobserved into the kitchen. Five minutes later footsteps were heard in the yard, the door opened and Joey entered, followed by Daisy Chilvers arrayed in the same navy blue costume, black feathered hat and high-heeled patent leather shoes in which he had first met her. In addition she carried a pink silk sunshade which she had had specially forwarded to her from Ipswich as soon as the hot weather began. There was an awkward pause while she looked timidly round the room and the five men stared owlishly at her, their hearts sinking within them. Then Ben recovered himself and stepped forward.

'Ben, this is Miss Daisy Chilvers,' said Joey, coughing nervously.

Ben shook hands gravely and said he was pleased to meet her. The other brothers were presented in turn and duly shook hands, but they were so overwhelmed by Daisy's grand appearance that they dared not open their mouths. Hiram smiled affably, but forgot to let go her hand until she removed it herself. Bob hardly touched it with his own trembling fingers before he snatched them away and, very red in the face, retired stiffly as if his legs were in splints. Ern crushed it in his own iron grasp until she winced, looking her sternly in the eyes. Harry, who was trying to fasten his collar which had come undone during his look-out in the hedge, plunging wildly, seized her by one finger and having squeezed it, edged away behind Ern.

The ceremony over, Ben came forward again with an air of taking command of the situation, the others marvelling at his composure and readiness of tongue : they did not know that he had been practising these speeches ever since the morning.

' It's a bit early for tea, miss,' he explained, ' and I'd like to show you the house. It fare to me we might start with the kitchen now we're here. It have got two windows, you see, miss, one on the garden and one on the yard ; the floor's bricks. It have got a dresser and a good stove with an oven : that's a bake-oven next to it for the bread. We used to have different furniture, but this is what we got when we came in again nine years ago, and we were in a bit of a hurry, so that ain't much. That door lead into the larder and that other into the dairy : there's all the room you need in both of 'em. Now, if you wouldn't mind, we'll step into the parlour.'

Ben led the way, with Daisy just behind him, followed by Joey and the other four in a long line.

' This passage,' continued Ben, pausing on the threshold of the parlour, ' lead to the front door ; but nobody come to the front door, so that ain't used. The parlour here ain't used either and so the furniture ain't much, but with a few knick-knacks that'd make a nice room for a lady. Our

Nance used to sit there a good deal. That's a good strong door, ain't it ? '

' Yes, that is,' stammered Daisy, quite bewildered by the whole proceeding and hardly knowing what to reply to this vast stream of information.

' Now we'll go upstairs, if you don't mind,' said Ben, turning back to the kitchen. He paused again at the bottom of the staircase. ' Now you see,' he went on, ' the house is wholly old and it fare to me the man that built it was a bit jim, 'cause when he'd done all the rest, he found he'd forgotten to put the stairs in, and so he had to tuck 'em into the corner of the kitchen like this and they're as steep as a ladder, I warn you. Once when Joey was a nipper he slipped at the top and slid down 'em on his seat and when he got to the bottom, he broke the latch off the door, he hit it so hard. Here's the mark where his feet hit the door. So be careful when you go up.'

He led the way up the hollow wooden stairs and the procession trailed slowly after him.

' What's all this for ? ' whispered Daisy in Joey's ear, as they reached the top stair.

' That's more'n I can tell,' Joey answered. ' Fare to me Ben's a bit cracked.'

On the bottom stair Ern turned round and squeezed Harry's arm.

' She's a wholly smart young filly, ain't she ? ' he muttered. ' Did you see her leg on the stair ? I don't wonder Joey run after her.'

' Ay,' Harry whispered back, ' and that pink umbrella and all.'

Ben turned round on the landing and waited until the rest had ascended before moving on himself, like a guide conducting a party of tourists over a historic building.

' Now this passage,' he began, fixing his eyes on Daisy, ' run the whole length of this wing and the other wing, and there's more rooms up here than downstairs 'cause the kitchen and the larder and the dairy's so large. Now this is my bedroom.' He opened the door and motioned Daisy

inside. ' The furniture ain't much : as I said before, that
was bought in a hurry. But there's a good big cupboard
there in the corner and there's a fireplace too : the flue
run into the kitchen chimney under that there great
funnel-topped chimney-pot you can see outside.'

' My! ' whispered Hiram in an awestruck voice to Bob.
' Ben talk like a book, don't he ? '

' Now this is where Bob and Hiram sleep,' continued
Ben, moving out and opening the next door. ' Same sort
of room with the same-sized cupboard. That'd hold a
wonderful lot of clothes, wouldn't it ? '

He looked inquiringly at Daisy, who put her head in
and dutifully nodded.

' And this next one,' said Ben, opening the last door in
the back wing, ' is where Ern and Harry sleep. We've all
slept in the same rooms since we were lads. That's just
like the rest. Another good big cupboard, you see.'

Daisy nodded again and Ben, having shut the door,
conducted her back to the landing, the others making
room for them to pass and closing up once more on them
in single file.

' Now this is the other wing,' said Ben, with his hand on
the knob of another door. ' It stand over the parlour and
there ain't only two rooms. This one is where Joey sleep :
it was where he was born too, and mother and father allus
used to sleep there ; but no one have ever died there, leastways, not in our family—mother and father both died out
in the fields. There now, ain't that a fine big room ? Two
great cupboards and a fireplace. Becourse that fare a bit
empty now : it want a good big double bed to make it
look proper. But look at the view from the window. You
can see the tower of Bruisyard church if you like that kind
of thing.'

' Why, so you can,' said Daisy to Joey for the sake of
saying something. ' Don't that look tiny ? '

' Now,' said Ben, shepherding her out of the room into
the passage again, ' this little room next door is where
Mrs. Snaith sleep. It ain't very large, but then she's a

little woman and that sarve for her.' He opened the door.
' You see, that have got a good big cupboard; that'd
hold a lot of clothes, too.'

' Yes, I see,' said Daisy mechanically, peeping in.

' Oh, I forgot,' said Ben, as he shut the door, ' there's one
other little room there at the end. They allus called it the
stillroom and we keep the apples there.   You've seen
that zig-zaggy bit of roof on the outside of the house, I
expect ? '

' I don't quite remember,' replied Daisy.

' Well, it's under that,' said Ben. ' It haven't only got
one tiny little owd window and you go up that ladder to
get to it. Mother allus kept the ladder downstairs when
we were nippers so's we shouldn't steal the apples. Come
you up and have a look at it.'

He slowly mounted the ladder, which groaned under
his weight, and opened the door. Daisy looked timidly
after him and then at her own high heels.

' I don't think I can go up there,' she said.

' Do you give her a hand, Joey,' said Ben from inside.
' She ought to see the stillroom.'

With Joey and Hiram at her elbows, Daisy painfully
and reluctantly scrambled half-way up the ladder and,
leaning on the threshold, peeped cautiously inside.

' What a smell! ' she exclaimed disgustedly.

' Yes, miss,' replied Ben, ' that's the apples, and the
door and window's allus shut. It ain't much of a room, but
if we wanted another bedroom, it wouldn't be hard to
knock another window in the wall. Yes, well, there ain't
any more to see upstairs.'

Daisy slowly descended the ladder and wiped the dust
from the stillroom threshold off her fingers with an
embroidered handkerchief.

' She ain't much good on a ladder,' whispered Bob contemptuously to Hiram behind his hand.

' What d'you expect with heels like that ? ' Hiram
hissed back.

Ben led them down the precipitous wooden staircase

again into the kitchen and Daisy sighed with relief as she set foot once more on the solid brick floor ; but the visitation was not yet over. Ben beckoned her across the kitchen.

' I forgot to show you the dairy just now,' he said, opening the door. ' That's a fine big room. All whitewashed, you see, and three rows of shelves ; but we generally manage to fill all them milk-pans every day. Joey used to get out of that window where the wire-gauze is when his mother locked him up in the kitchen. But we've nailed it up tight now.'

Daisy tittered, but Ben's face was quite serious : it was a historical fact. Hiram scratched his moustache : that window still had memories for him too.

' And this is the larder,' said Ben, opening the adjoining door, ' and a good big larder too. You see we manage to keep it pretty full.'

Daisy gazed admiringly at the imposing array of neatly-stacked jam-pots and pickle-jars that lined the shelves. Side by side in one corner stood the remains of an enormous apple pie and the limbless carcasses of two fat ducks, left over from dinner that day : they still fed well at Crakenhill although Nancy was no longer there to cook for them.

' There now,' said Ben, walking out behind her and shutting the door, ' I think that's all and we might as well sit down.'

The other men disposed themselves around the laden table, leaving two places for Daisy and Joey at Ben's right hand. The fire was almost out and the kettle cold, but no one heeded them now. All eyes were fixed on Ben.

' Well now,' he said, planting his hands on his knees and turning to Daisy, ' how do you like the house, miss ? '

' I think it's very nice,' she replied nervously.

' Good,' said Ben. ' Now listen here, you two young folks. We've done pretty well out of the farm the nine years we've been here. To-morrow me and Hiram are going into Frannigan to see Mr. Mytton, our landlord, and we're a-going to buy Crakenhill—the old Crakenhill with the house and buildings and the hundred acres; I reckon we shall, 'cause I know he want to get rid on it. And if you, Joey, and you, miss, 'll come here and live along of us, that's yours, lock, stock and barrel.'

' Ay, that's it,' said Hiram.

The other three nodded vigorous assent.

' I didn't want you to buy a pig in a poke,' Ben pursued, laying his finger on the table, ' and so I thought I'd show you the house afore I axed you. We're rough, common chaps; but we wouldn't give you no trouble and if you'll come and be mistress of Crakenhill, you'll be wholly welcome and that's the truth.'

Joey, quite overcome by this unforeseen generosity, rose to his feet and seized Ben's hand; but Ben waved him gently aside.

' You know all about it, Joey lad,' he said. ' That's for your young woman to choose.'

Daisy stared hard at the kitchen hearthrug. In some ways it was a forbidding old house and the furniture was rather ramshackle; but the thought of becoming mistress of so much bricks and mortar made her heart beat fast. Here were none of the excitements, the modern conveniences, the society and bustle, which had been so dear to her in Ipswich; but all these things appeared suddenly hollow and insignificant beside the spacious vision of life just opened up to her by the vast, low-ceilinged kitchen, the amply-stored dairy and larder, even by the peaceful view from Joey's bedroom window of Bruisyard's humble little round-towered church, nestling among the trees in the valley. Not every milliner has the chance of becoming a well-to-do farmer's wife. She raised her eyes and looked ruefully at her pink sunshade: it made all the urban amenities grow to significance again: they were the quality of life not lightly to be exchanged for mere quantity. Then she thought of Joey. She got up from her chair.

' I'd like to go out and talk to Joey for a minute,' she said in a trembling voice, ' if you don't mind.'

' Certainly, my gal,' said Ben, getting up and opening the door for her. ' Take your time.'

Joey followed Daisy out into the yard and the door closed on them. The brothers remained sitting round the table, eyeing one another furtively, but none daring to speak. They scratched the tablecloth, shuffled their feet and fidgeted with their collars to relieve the suspense as the minutes dragged by : the whole of life was at stake. A quarter of an hour passed and the door with a clatter flew open. Ben heaved a tremendous sigh.

Daisy entered with Joey behind her : her face was flushed, but her eyes shone. She walked up to Ben.

' Yes, Mr. Geaiter,' she said, flushing more deeply than ever, ' I'd like to come and live here and thank you very much.'

With one impulse the brothers leaped to their feet and crowded round to shake her hand. They shook hands with Joey too, and slapped him on the back.

' And now,' cried Bob at the top of his voice, ' I reckon young Joey ought to give our Daisy a kiss.'

' Ay, that's it,' said Ern. ' Come on, Joey.'

Joey made a dive for the door, but Ern and Harry seized him by the arms and brought him back.

' Come along, lad,' said Ben. ' She's a-waiting for you.'

Daisy was standing quite still by the table with her head hanging shyly down and the suspicion of a tear on her eyelash. Joey, seeing that resistance was useless, stepped up to her side, hesitated for a moment and then kissed her lightly on her crimson cheek, while the brothers cheered them till the ornaments on the mantelpiece rattled.

' And now,' said Ben, picking up the kettle from the hob, ' we'll have tea.'

XLII

IT had rained all through February, March had come and it was still raining. The whole countryside was steeped in a chill, leaden gloom through which all shape and all colour were obliterated ; the only sounds to be heard were the hissing patter of raindrops and the muffled swirl of brimming ditches : everywhere life seemed extinct. Down in the valley at Bruisyard the Alde had overflowed its banks, flooding the water-meadows and making the little ford by the church well-nigh impassable : even on the hillside at Crakenhill the water lay about in pools, unable to find an outlet through the stiff and sodden clay in which the horses' feet would have sunk fetlock-deep. Work in the fields was out of the question and now all the indoor jobs had come to an end. There was enough chaff cut and linseed cake ground up to last the cattle for a month ; all the broken hurdles and harness were mended, the farm machinery cleaned and greased : a new floor had been laid down in the stable. Finally, for want of something better to do, the men had wrapped themselves up in anything they could find to keep them dry and had gone out to cut the hedges in the rain.

Daisy pulled herself up from the kitchen floor where she had been kneeling with scrubbing-brush and pail, and looked out at the rain driving savagely against the blurred window-panes. The bricks were clean now, but half an hour later, when the men came into dinner, they would want scrubbing once more : the yard outside was a paste of liquid mud and no amount of sacks on the doorstep could prevent it from finding its way in on somebody's feet. She was tired of scrubbing bricks and drying wet clothes and now that Mrs. Snaith had caught a chill and taken to her bed, the whole of the housework had fallen on her shoulders. She turned round and looked hopelessly at the clothes-horse in front of the fire, weighted with piles of linen that would have to be ironed some time during the afternoon: there were a dozen milk-pans in the dairy, waiting to be scalded, and a basketful of socks on the sofa that wanted darning : it would soon be time to dish up the dinner. She looked down at her red chapped hands and broken finger-nails. That was what marriage meant and being mistress of Crakenhill : it was more than she had bargained for when she married Joey.

Even so, she reflected, all this toil might have been supportable if only she could have some occasional respite from it, some change of scene, some petty diversion to relax her nerves. But during the five months since her marriage, the best that Joey could think of to amuse her had been to take her to the October fair at Frannigan and drive her in to Saxmundham now and again to do the shopping : and for the past month, what with the rain and Mrs. Snaith's illness, she had hardly set foot outside the house at all. To-morrow night there was to be a dance in the parish hall at Bruisyard, but she knew that it was no use even asking Joey to take her : he could not dance. She bit her lip and pettishly stamped her foot. Joey's love for her seemed a very sorry thing if it meant the sacrifice of all that made life worth living for her : it was impossible to love such a man : it would be far better to run away and save the remnant of her life from total wreck while there was still time—if only there had been somewhere to run to.

A rap at the door brought her back to reality again : she looked out of the window and saw that it was the postman.

' A letter for you, Mrs. Geaiter,' he said, as she opened the door to him.

' You're wholly late,' said Daisy irritably, taking it from him.

' And no wonder,' he replied. ' That took me nearly half an hour to get up your drift. You shouldn't live so far away.'

' Ah, that's the truth,' said Daisy bitterly. ' Good morning.'

She shut the door with a bang and looked at the letter: it bore an Ipswich postmark. She was about to tear it open when a sputter of steam from behind the clothes-horse made her thrust it in her apron pocket and run to the stove. A saucepan of chicken broth was boiling over. She took it off the stove, poured it into a bowl and carried it straight upstairs to Mrs. Snaith, who in spite of her weakness was still garrulous and tried to inveigle her into a conversation. But Daisy was not to be detained and hurried out at once to her own bedroom. She sat down at the little table in front of the window and tore open her letter. It was from her former employer in the millinery shop at Ipswich. She had done so well, she said, that she was opening a branch establishment in a new suburb of the town: she did not know if Daisy had buried herself for good on her out-of-the-way farm at Bruisyard: but would she care to come back as manageress of the new branch?

Daisy caught her breath and nervously drummed her fingers on the table. There danced before her eyes an enticing vision of herself, in a warm, dry shop, full of the latest Paris hats, severely laying down the law to her underlings and waiting with decorous courtesy upon a crowd of smartly-dressed, refined customers: that would be life indeed. She looked down at her coarse print apron and clenched her fist. Her chance had come and nothing should stop her now from leaving this humiliating drudgery and these six uncouth yokels behind her. Even as her resolve took shape, her brain was busy with a plan to carry it out. To-morrow she would insist on being taken into Sax with the milk to do some shopping long overdue: she would give Joey the slip in the town and catch the first train to Ipswich. She would leave a letter in her bedroom explaining all. It was easy enough. She looked down once more at her apron: her mind was made up.

The rain had abated a little and Daisy, as she rose to her feet, seized the opportunity of opening the casement which had been too long shut, and giving the stuffy room

some air. Ben and Joey, who had just come out of the
stable with sacks flung over their shoulders and sacks tied
round their legs with string, splashed their way across the
farmyard to the kitchen door. Ben suddenly stopped short
under Daisy's window and fixed Joey with his eye. Daisy
paused to watch.

' Joey lad,' he said, ' that gal of ours is moping a bit.'

' Fare to me she is,' replied Joey. ' I don't know what
to do.'

' I tell you what,' said Ben, gripping him by the
shoulder. ' Do you take her into Ipswich one day and
have a thorough good frolic.'

' Why, that's just the thing of it! ' exclaimed Joey
excitedly. ' We'll go to-morrow.'

They moved on into the kitchen.

Daisy sat down on her chair again and picking up her
letter from the table, slowly tore it in little pieces. She
stuffed them in her apron pocket and went downstairs
into the kitchen. At the bottom of the stairs she paused
and looked down the long, low room at the familiar kettle
singing on the hob : a lump came in her throat at the
thought of deserting it : there was country blood in her
veins. Then, walking over to the sink and raising herself
on tiptoe, she kissed Ben's stubbly cheek.

' Why, gal,' he gasped, somewhat taken aback, ' what
was that for ? '

Daisy giggled.

' Oh, I don't know, Ben—'cause I like you.'

THE END

THE GREEN HAT

Michael Arlen

The Green Hat is the quintessence of the 'twenties: gay, stylish, mannered and bitter-sweet, a brilliant mixture of cynicism and sentiment. When it first appeared in 1924, it was (as Margaret Bellasis said in *The Dictionary of National Biography*) 'acclaimed, attacked, parodied and read, to the most fabulous degree of best-sellerdom ...' The character of the heroine, Iris Storm, that wanton of quality, "shameless, shameful lady", gallantly crashing to her death in her great yellow Hispano-Suiza – "for Purity" – set a new fashion in fatal charmers: and the pictures of London cafè society were exact as glossy photographs.' Michael Arlen was Armenian by birth, but he was educated in England and was thus entirely at home in English society and yet distanced enough from it to write about it accurately and mockingly, with that brilliance and wit which the English are always supposed to permit to foreigners but to decry in their fellow countrymen. *The Green Hat* is above all a witty tragi-comedy of manners that captures the spirit of the glittering, colourful, yet slightly unreal world of London after the First World War.

Michael Arlen was born in 1895 in Bulgaria. He changed his name from Dikram Kouyoumdjian in 1922 when he became a naturalised British citizen, having already published novels and short stories under his new name. Following the success of *The Green Hat* he wrote a number of further novels, the last of which appeared in 1939. He died in New York in 1956.

244pp, 192 x 129mm, ISBN 0 85115 210 4

THE HOLE IN THE WALL

Arthur Morrison

The Hole in the Wall is one of the most gripping adventure stories ever written. From its unforgetable opening – 'My grandfather was a publican and a sinner, as you will see. His public house was the Hole in the Wall, on the river's edge at Wapping; and his sins – all of them that I know of – are recorded in these pages' – it is a book that you genuinely cannot put down. Stephen Kemp goes to live with his mysterious grandfather after his mother's death, and is gradually drawn into the seedy world which Captain Nat Kemp inhabits, but of which he is determined Stephen shall not become part. Morrison brilliantly conveys the child's sharp observation of all that goes on around him, and builds up a portrait of the East End he himself may have known as a boy; and against this background of dockside life, he unfolds his story in masterly fashion.

179pp, 216 x 135mm, ISBN 0 85115 205 8

LIGHT FREIGHTS

W.W. Jacobs

'Every moment [in *Light Freights*], from the nonchalant opening to the gentle click of the closing door, is deliberately planned and faultlessly controlled. . . . His economy of language, his perpetual understatement, his refusal himself to be the joker but the suggestion in a rapid exchange of conversation by his characters of the ludicrous catastrophes which have overtaken them or are about to overtake them – these are qualities in a writer granted only to a master of his craft.' Michael Sadler in *Dictionary of National Biography*.

'*A forgotten master of the humorous sketch.*' Miles Kington.

160pp, 216 x 135mm, ISBN 0 85115 202 3

A CHILD OF THE JAGO

Arthur Morrison

Of all the dark corners of London in the 1890s, the Old Nichol, lying off Bethnal Green Road, was the murkiest. In 1895, Arthur Morrison, a successful journalist and writer of short stories, was invited to visit it by the Rector of Shoreditch, who had read and admired Morrison's stories about the East End, but felt that they reflected only part of East End life. Even Morrison, born in the East End and familiar with its ways, was horrified by what he saw. Within a year he had shaped his experiences into his first full-length novel, lightly disguising the Nichol as 'the Jago'. *A Child of the Jago* is the story of Dicky Perrott, born and bred in this area; but it is also a brilliant portrait of a community where crime and violence are the only way of life, and from which there is no escape for the inhabitants. Only the characters themselves are fictional: Morrison's descriptions of the fearful physical conditions are based directly on what he saw. He conjures up an extraordinarily vivid picture of a world which, even as he wrote, was about to vanish in one of the first of the slum clearance schemes. Although Morrison, as an excellent teller of tales, disliked the label 'realist', this is indeed one of the great realist novels in English literature, the equivalent in fiction of Hogarth's fierce artistic observation of the London slums.

Arthur Morrison was born in the East End in 1863; little is known of his early life, but he became a journalist in 1890, after working for the idealistic 'People's Palace' in the East End. He wrote short stories and detective fiction as a sideline, *Tale of Mean Streets* (1894) being his first success. After *A Child of the Jago* he wrote two historical novels, *Cunning Murrell* (available in hardback from Boydell Press) and *The Hole in the Wall*, the latter being his best-known book. He became an expert on oriental art (partly through buying Japanese prints in the East End), and after 1913 made his career in this field. He died in 1945.

208pp, 216 x 135mm, ISBN 0 85115 203 1

THE STORY OF MY LIFE

Ellen Terry

Ellen Terry (1847–1928) was the most magical figure of the
Victorian stage, and her enchanting memoirs were described
by Ian McKellen recently on Radio 3 as 'the best theatrical
autobiography I've ever read.' She wrote these memoirs in
1908, at the end of her main stage career, though her last stage
appearance was in 1925. She tells her story very simply and
unaffectedly, beginning with her childhood as a travelling
player (she first appeared on stage at the age of nine), her
ill-fated marriage to the painter G.F. Watts when she was
sixteen, her return to the stage and to a series of triumphant
successes in London and New York, particularly during her
time at the Lyceum with Henry Irving. Her wry and humorous
self-portrait is matched by vivid sketches of the great actors
and actresses she worked with, and her character study of
Irving himself, spendthrift and prodigious in all he did, is in
itself enough to ensure the book's place among the classics of
the theatre.

240pp, 216 x 135mm, ISBN 0 85115 204 X

THE MONKEY'S PAW

W.W. Jacobs

W.W. Jacobs was at the height of his powers when this volume was first published in 1902, under the title *The Lady of the Barge*. It shows to perfection his skills in thumbnail characterisation and his flawless timing. He could turn these skills to widely differing ends, from the broad comedy of his tales of life aboard Thames barges or in the rural peace of Claybury, to the spine-chilling tragedy of *The Monkey's Paw*. This story, together with *The Well*, has that gothic atmosphere of horror familiar to readers of M.R. James. But where other stories of the supernatural rely on elaborate trappings, Jacobs is economical and direct; a dozen pages are sufficient for him to create the atmosphere, set the plot in motion and bring it to its eerie conclusion. A writer who in one volume can range from a masterly ghost story such as *The Monkey's Paw* to sketches worthy of P.G. Wodehouse – who once described himself as a disciple of W.W. Jacobs – deserves a place on any reader's bookshelf.

W.W. Jacobs (1870–1943) was one of the leading popular writers of the 1890s, the golden age of the short story. Of *Light Freights* (also available in Bookmasters 0 85115 202 3) Michael Sadlier wrote 'His economy of language, his perpetual understatement, his refusal himself to be the joker but the suggestion in a rapid exchange of conversation of the ludicrous catastrophes which have overtaken them – these are qualities in a writer granted only to a master of his craft.'

160pp, 216 x 135mm, ISBN 0 85115 216 3

BRIEF LIVES

John Aubrey

John Aubrey's *Brief Lives*, those racy portraits of the great figures of 17th-century England, stand alongside Pepys's diary as a vivid evocation of the period; in recent years they have been brought memorably to life on television and in the theatre by Roy Dotrice. Yet Aubrey never actually completed his project, nor did he ever manage to put even a single life into logical order. All we have are the raw materials, his jumbled, confused notebooks. Added to this, his language and spelling are often obscure for the reader of today, and it is therefore surprising that there has never been a 'complete' edition in modern spelling. Richard Barber provides just this, reproducing as closely as possible what Aubrey wrote, modernising the spelling and paraphrasing obsolete words, in a version that will allow many new readers to enjoy this vivid and eccentric masterpiece.

John Aubrey was born in 1626, the son of a Wiltshire squire. He never completed his education at Oxford or at the Middle Temple, and when he inherited the family estate at the age of 26 he fought a losing struggle with his father's debts. He finally went bankrupt in the 1670s, and led a sociable, rootless existence at the houses of friends, pursuing the antiquarian studies which had always obsessed him. He published only one book in his lifetime, suitable entitled *Miscellanies*, and died in 1697, leaving a mass of notes and manuscripts, among them the material for *Brief Lives*.

332pp, 216 x 135mm, ISBN 0 85115 206 6